Christmas at Silverberry Hall

Also by Lucy Coleman

Christmas at Silverberry Hall

LUCY COLEMAN

First published in Great Britain in 2024 by

Bonnier Books UK Limited
4th Floor, Victoria House, Bloomsbury Square, London, WC1B 4DA
Owned by Bonnier Books
Sveavägen 56, Stockholm, Sweden

A CIP catalogue record for this book is available from the British Library.

ISBN: 9781471417009

This book is typeset using Atomik ePublisher.

Embla Books is an imprint of Bonnier Books UK.
www.bonnierbooks.co.uk

In memory of James: a true romantic at heart

Darlingham village, in the Cotswolds

Wednesday, 4th October

Sienna Sanderson

1

Planning an Old-Fashioned Christmas

Watching my maternal grandma, Charlotte, chattering away with her best friend – and my employer, Elizabeth Blakesley – you'd think they were young girls rather than a year away from celebrating their seventy-fifth birthdays. They never fail to amaze me and I head off to get some refreshments to give them a little time to themselves. Today they're in full-on planning mode and there's a buzz in the air.

What began as a Christmas Eve bash for the lively bunch of ladies who live in Darlingham village has, over the years, turned into the biggest party of the festive season for miles around. It's hosted here at Elizabeth's home, the stately Silverberry Hall, in the beautifully renovated barn that stands in the lavish, manicured grounds.

The estate borders the delightful River Severn as it travels inland. Nestled in the heart of a quintessential English village, the Hall's beautiful honey-coloured stone buildings, extensive cottage gardens and vast woodlands are a rare jewel.

To the front of what was at one time an amply proportioned vicarage, the main building is set within an attractive walled area lined with copious trees and shrubs. Off to one side is a sweeping drive abutting generous parking facilities. The main building is believed to date back to the eighteenth century and with its slate roofs, dormer windows and stately chimney stacks, it's a handsome property.

Elizabeth has caterers in to put on a sumptuous buffet and the guest list continues to grow year on year. We've had everything from a string quartet and inspiring harpists to heart-stopping a cappella performances, in addition to the opportunity to dance the night away at a truly sparkling event.

There is a tinge of sadness to it this year, though, as it's also a tribute to Elizabeth's late husband, Frederic.

As Elizabeth's personal assistant, I sometimes get invited to the regular lunches with the ladies and it's always an experience to remember. They plan charitable events and fund-raisers, but inevitably they also share all the latest *news*. The usual things . . . who has upset whom, complaints about walkers straying off public footpaths and the latest hot topic – speculation over the love interests of the locum veterinary surgeon. Following a retirement, he's providing cover until a permanent replacement can be found. Xavier Martinez is in his early forties, part Spanish and with enough of an accent to make a woman go weak at the knees; he's also single and drop-dead gorgeous. If he so much as accepts a cup of coffee in someone's house it's cause for speculation – sick animal to tend to, or not.

When I carry the tea tray into the sitting room, Elizabeth looks up, giving me a knowing smile.

'Where would I be without your wonderful granddaughter, Charlotte?' Elizabeth lowers her voice, reaching out to touch Grandma's arm. 'Georgina has been my housekeeper now for eighteen months and she still doesn't know how to brew a proper pot of tea. It's never strong enough, so it's a treat when Sienna steps in.'

Grandma winks at me and Elizabeth laughs.

'Georgina thinks it's bad for you,' I repeat, for the umpteenth time. 'I did look it up online and maybe she's right. These days with soil contamination and heavy metals affecting the plants, it's all about everything in moderation.'

They both happily drink three cups in one sitting and

while Georgina means well, it's a lost cause. It's not so much the amount of tea per se, but the number of biscuits they consume with it.

I can't argue that healthy smoothies full of vitamins and minerals are a good tonic at any age. However, I will admit the green ones do taste a little too earthy. I'm pretty sure that Georgina only makes those for me though, to balance out the ready meals I often end up grabbing. Well, at the end of a busy day who has time to head home and cook for one?

They both stare back at me, shaking their heads. 'Everyone has to die of something,' Elizabeth points out. 'And we've lasted this long on copious cups of tea.'

I try not to roll my eyes. And a generous gin and tonic as soon as the clock chimes four in the afternoon. Go figure! But these two stalwarts of the community have a fair number of years left in them yet.

It's true that six months on, Elizabeth is still battling to come to terms with losing her soul mate Freddie, but anyone who was close to him feels that loss too. He was a kind man, with a larger-than-life personality and a big heart. So far as I'm concerned, my boss can have as many cups of tea as she wants. You can only live life one day at a time and, as Freddie would have expected, she's putting a brave face on working through the painful grieving process.

'Right, ladies, I'm ready to take notes.' I settle myself down into the armchair opposite them, opening my iPad and connecting the keyboard. 'What have you decided?'

They shuffle pieces of paper around the coffee table in the rather grand orangery, with its proliferation of plants creating a wonderfully relaxing ambience. The large Victorian addition to the rear of the property is my favourite room in Silverberry Hall. With its dwarf stone walls, low-pitched lantern roof and large glass panelled picture windows, it's the perfect setting in which to sit and unwind.

I wait patiently while there's a bit of back-and-forth chatter between them. I can't wait to hear what they'll come up with this time around. It's just as well that Christmas is my favourite time of the year and I'm sure I'll be up to the challenge, whatever ideas they throw at me.

My mind wanders as they continue to natter away. They're two very strong personalities and they don't always agree. However, they're only on their first cup of tea so this could take a while.

When Freddie and Elizabeth offered me a position as their personal assistant, the truth is that they rescued me. It wasn't just as a favour to Grandma because the two women had known each other since they were children, and I was able to quite quickly take over some of the mundane jobs to lessen their load.

After having dropped out at the end of the first year of a BSc course in marketing at the University of Bristol, Mum and Grandma tried hard to hide their concern for my state of mind. They both did their best to reassure me that I was still discovering who I was and what I wanted to do with my life. They were confident that if I took a year off, I'd return to university refreshed.

But after working my way through a quick succession of temporary jobs, it was Freddie who persuaded me that both he and Elizabeth needed some assistance. It was mainly general admin associated with the various committees they were heavily involved in at the time, as well as tasks related to running such a large property. 'Who better than you?' he'd insisted. Being someone they regarded almost as family, I could be relied upon to be discreet, and they felt comfortable having me around.

However, I'm guessing the real reason I initially got the job was the pity factor; in hindsight it's obvious that Freddie had no intention of letting me waste my life. The upside was that once I was on board my role expanded way beyond anyone's expectations and that's how I paid them back for their kindness.

After a distinguished career in London as a consultant

neurologist, Freddie retired almost fifteen years ago. For Elizabeth, returning to the village in which she grew up was like coming home after a lifetime away. Being within an hour's drive of her two brothers was also a bonus. With my grandma Charlotte living close by, Freddie knew his wife would be happy. Elizabeth had long admired Silverberry Hall and the moment they both walked up the curving path to the front door, Freddie was sold on it too.

He was gifted when it came to that old-fashioned bedside manner, relaxing his patients whether the news was good, or bad. And he recognised in me that something wasn't right. I was a twenty-year-old at a crossroads and I could so easily have gone off the rails.

So, for the last seven years I've been an integral part of this busy household. When Freddie fell, breaking his hip and his left arm, we all thought he'd battle through it. But a month later, in April of this year, he contracted pneumonia and went downhill so fast it took us all by surprise.

'I think we're agreed that the dress code is *an old-fashioned Christmas* this year. Freddie would approve and I so wish we'd thought of it last year,' Elizabeth replies, sadly.

Grandma nods her head in agreement, heaving a gentle sigh.

'I'll get to work drafting the invitations for your approval,' I reply. There's always a colour or theme to inspire what is regarded as quite a glamorous affair, with cocktail dresses and suits. Last year it was tartan and there were sashes, ties, jackets and shawls, but no one was brave enough to wear a kilt. In all honesty, being on the banks of the River Severn, the winds here can be bitingly cold. And we get a lot of black ice and snow, so people tend to wrap up warmly.

'Bygone days,' Grandma mutters. 'It was less commercial and a lot more fun.'

Elizabeth gives a wistful smile. 'Freddie would want everyone's spirits to be high and what better way to do that than to turn back the clock and indulge in a little nostalgia?'

They both look at me expectantly as I mull it over.

'We could get the caterers to set up a hog roast in the courtyard, you know, under the old brick shelter if we clean it up. Perhaps we can have a small group of carollers wandering around and a station with hot toddies and hot chocolate . . .'

The two women look at each other, grinning.

'How about a cart with roasted chestnuts?' Grandma suggests. 'Imagine the smell!'

Elizabeth's eyes light up. 'Oh, that would be delightful. I love the idea of both indoor and outdoor entertainment this year.'

'The carollers can't sing throughout the entire evening,' Grandma points out.

'You're right, Charlotte. We'll have our usual music man come along, so people can dance after the buffet. We could ask the carollers to dress up in Victorian costumes to add to the atmosphere.'

'How about reaching out to an amateur dramatics club to get a handful of performers in to enact a scene, or two, from a Christmas play?' I suggest, boldly.

Both Elizabeth and Grandma draw in a sharp breath. 'Perfect!' they reply, in unison.

By the end of our brainstorming session, I have a lengthy list of ideas to flesh out and Operation Christmas is about to begin. The main thing is that Elizabeth and Grandma Charlotte are both happy; turning the party into a nostalgic and heartwarming spectacle might be just what's needed to get everyone through it with a smile on their faces. Freddie loved entertaining people and was the joker at every party, so we can't let him down.

It's time to set the wheels in motion and start reaching out to people. I do love turning a list into a master plan and this year's event is dear to my heart. As a teenager, I was consistently inconsistent; how ironic that a decade later, I'm regarded as a skilled organiser. If you're looking down on us, Freddie, I've got this. And I know that thought will put a huge smile on your face.

* * *

It's Saturday night and I shouldn't be working, but I have a major problem with the main highlight that will kick off the evening celebrations. I press the phone icon and let it ring five times, then disconnect; it's a secret code whenever I need help. My best friend, Daniela, will be putting my godchildren to bed, but as soon as she's free she'll call me back.

While I sit and wait, I pore over the spreadsheet on the screen. The lengthy to-do list is beginning to shape up nicely for the party, but having spent three days reaching out to a list of amateur dramatic clubs within an increasingly wide radius, naturally, they're all busy rehearsing for the upcoming season. With only just over eleven weeks until the big day is here I know it's a tall order, but unless I can get something tied up quickly it's going to leave me with a major gap in the programme.

Finally, my phone lights up. 'Sorry I missed your call. William took ages to settle down. He's teething. And then Clara wanted two stories and, as you know, she always picks the long ones.' Poor Daniela sounds exhausted.

'I thought Nigel was due back yesterday?'

'Hmph. So did I, until he phoned late last night to say they've hit a problem. Something to do with one of the signatories on a contract not being available, which is delaying funds being sent to Italy. Building work has stopped on the development and he's flying out tomorrow to get it sorted. Anyway, what's going on with you? Why aren't you out with the girls sipping cocktails and enjoying your freedom?'

It's a struggle not to roll my eyes at her. Since Liam arrived in my life, the number of times I joined in with the girls' nights out I could probably count on one hand. That thought makes me chuckle. 'The group has shrunk considerably and you can't talk! How often do you go along?' We started out as a group of about a dozen or so, but half have since moved away from the area and three are now married with children, rarely putting in an appearance.

Aside from Daniela, the only two schoolmates that I'm still close with are Ruby from our local pub and Lottie, who works at the vet's surgery, mainly because our paths cross quite frequently. Neither of them have ever been in a serious, long-term relationship, which means they still know how to party! As for me, letting my hair down means something totally different these days.

Daniela shrugs her shoulders. 'I know . . . but I'm not single, am I?' she points out and I get it but I'm just not ready. 'You're not missing Liam . . . are you?' She mutters a soft groan. 'Sorry, I spoke before I had a chance to engage my brain.'

Since I broke off our engagement at the start of the summer, it's only recently that Liam has given up sending me texts at odd hours of the day and night. Naturally, he's sorry that he took me for granted but I'm even sorrier I fell for his charm in the first place.

'No. He had his chance, and he blew it when he cheated on me. But my head isn't in the right place and I don't want to be the one sitting in the corner nursing a drink and wondering what I'm doing, Daniela.'

An empathetic 'oh' echoes down the line. 'Sorry, I didn't mean to put you on a downer. So, what's the emergency?'

'I'm hoping that you can do me a huge favour. I sort of promised something before checking it was doable.'

There's a little groan. 'Is this work? Don't you have anything better to do on a Saturday night?'

I glance around the cosy sitting room in my bijou cottage and I'm grateful. It's one of the estate's former farm-workers' cottages that used to be rented out. Oakleigh is now my home, at least for the foreseeable future. Elizabeth had the decorators in to give it a fresh lick of paint and it's infinitely better than the house I shared with Liam for nearly two years. It's in the heart of the village and rent-free, which is a boost to my savings. My aim is to get a substantial deposit together so that one day soon I'll be able to afford to buy a place of my own.

'It's cold and it's raining; I love sitting in front of the log fire relaxing and . . . thinking.'

'Hmm. You mean tapping away on the keyboard. It sounds more like hibernating to me when you should be out there, socialising. Anyway, normally you use the word "little" when you want something, so "huge" is worrying.'

'It's for a good cause,' I assure her. 'Elizabeth has expanded this year's guest list to include some of Freddie's old friends, who live further afield. Plus, she'll have a full house of family members to cope with in addition to the party, which is going to be bigger than last year's spectacle.'

'I know how much the Christmas party means to the village, but everyone would understand if she didn't feel up for it this year. She's still coming to terms with life without Freddie there beside her.'

A sigh escapes my lips. 'She's determined to honour him in this way and Elizabeth prides herself on being the ultimate host. In her words, it'll stop her "wallowing". I told her that I thought she was being hard on herself. With two brothers, her nieces and nephews and their offspring to rally around her, she was never going to be alone this Christmas but she's a woman on a mission.'

'Elizabeth is one determined lady, for sure.'

'She wants everyone to remember Freddie in a happy way. Unlike the celebration of his life after the funeral.' I grimace to myself. Yes, people shed tears, but sobbing out loud when the widow herself is trying to be stoic is out of order. And there were two of them, distant relatives of Freddie's, who made a spectacle of themselves.

'Oh, Sienna. Elizabeth is like a social butterfly, isn't she? She flits from person to person, ensuring her guests have everything they need and making introductions. It was Freddie who was the real conversationalist, wasn't it? He'd happily talk about every subject under the sun, but he had the knack of making people smile even when their opinions differed. Her eyes were always on him, no matter what else she was doing, or how far apart they were in a room. It's going to test her to the limit. So, this favour is to do with the party?'

'Yes. I rashly suggested it would be a marvellous idea to enact a couple of scenes from a play. Something suitably festive, naturally.'

There's a loud splutter. 'Are you mad? You do know that at this time of the year all of the amateur dramatic clubs are in rehearsal. Many of them go straight from a pre-Christmas farce into pantomime season.'

Inwardly, I'm groaning and I'm glad she can't see the look of despair on my face. 'Well . . . I didn't really think it through, but Elizabeth and Grandma Charlotte are already telling everyone we have something extra special planned.'

'Oh, so just because I have contacts, you think I can whip up a troupe to stage a *little* play? That's in between chasing William around to stop him putting everything he can find in his mouth, and making sure Clara isn't up to mischief in my makeup drawer?'

We both burst out laughing. Last Saturday I spent the day with the three of them. When Daniela's husband, Nigel, is away for more than a couple of days, she struggles. So, I babysit while she takes an afternoon off to pamper herself. She was having a leisurely bubble bath and enjoying one of those relaxing cucumber face masks, when I realised Clara was nowhere to be seen.

I'd been fussing over Pixie, the cutest caramel-coloured Yorkshire terrier in the world, who had run off with one of little William's toys. It's not easy placating an eighteen-month-old and when he burst into tears it took a minute or two to distract him. Then I noticed that Clara had disappeared. Hoisting the lad up onto my hip and getting him to stay there while we went in search of his sister, rather than Pixie, wasn't easy. I was hot and bothered, and worried about the noise as he began to sob his heart out. Ugh, it was a bit of a nightmare.

'I took my eyes off Clara for two minutes,' I admit. When I found her, she simply smiled at me – her face was a picture. It was a rainbow of colours, and it wasn't easy getting all of that makeup off.

'Two minutes in which she discovered a treasure trove and now I've had to get a carpenter in to put a lock on my bedroom door.'

'No!' I breathe out sharply, feeling guilty.

'Yes. She paid another little trip there the day before yesterday and I've had to chuck virtually the whole lot out. And waterproof mascara on carpet isn't a good mix. I've ordered a rug to cover it up.'

'I'm so, so sorry and I didn't mean to laugh. She just looked so happy and so . . .'

'Colourful,' Daniela giggles. 'I'll forgive you. You do need eyes in the back of your head. She got into the fridge the other day and decided she was going to make an omelette in her play saucepan. Why do you think I'm so exhausted all the time?'

'I understand. When's Nigel due back?'

'Wednesday, fingers crossed. I've already warned him he might need to get his mother over to lend a hand as I'm going to take a couple of days off.'

I'm trying really hard to suppress a chuckle. Out of the two of us, I was the one who dreamt of having a family, Daniela was unashamedly in search of a man who could keep her in the lifestyle to which she wanted to become accustomed; I don't think she'd thought any further ahead than that. Now she has a big country house on the edge of Darlingham, but having two children in such quick succession is more to do with Nigel being such a charmer and so dashingly handsome. I mean, what woman could resist?

The problem is that when you fall in love with someone,

you find yourself doing the daftest of things. For Daniela, she admitted it was coming off birth control before she fully appreciated what she was letting herself in for. For me, it was getting engaged and moving in with Liam, even though something didn't feel quite right. It was a shock to discover that he has a roving eye and thinks a one-night stand doesn't count. I should listen to my gut instincts more often.

'You're not judging me, are you?' Daniela checks.

'Goodness, no. Children are a handful. I only had them for three hours and look how I messed up!'

She lets out a sigh of satisfaction. 'But they do put a big smile on our faces, don't they? Sometimes I think I don't deserve them; they run circles around me, and I'm supposed to be the one in charge.'

'Aww . . . I'm sure a lot of mums feel that way,' I empathise. 'You gave up a lot to have them and it will get easier. Won't it?'

'That's what some of the other mums at the nursery say. I live in hope. As for your problem, I'm not making any promises, but I'll see what I can do. It could be a nice distraction for me, actually. We all miss Freddie; he was one of the good ones and if Elizabeth wants the party of all parties, then I'll make a few calls to see if it's doable.'

'Thanks, Daniela – and Freddie was one in million.' I stop short of adding that I don't know where I'd be now if it weren't for him.

2

From Planning . . . to Plotting

I walk through the door to see Grandma sitting at her kitchen table in some sort of daze. She doesn't even look up to acknowledge me. Invariably, when I pop in at this time on a Sunday morning, she's on her third cup of tea and sitting here reading a book.

I draw to a halt and finally she glances up as I slip off my coat and hurry over to sit down next to her.

'Whatever's wrong?' My heart begins to thud in my chest. Is she feeling unwell? I wonder.

'It's Elizabeth. She rang about half an hour ago. She had some tragic news yesterday and she's rather distraught. When I suggested I go straight round to keep her company, she said she'd been up most of the night and was just about to go and lie down for a while.'

Oh no . . . that's a bad sign indeed. The two of them have supported each other through thick and thin, and she always turns to Grandma. 'Has someone died?'

'Yes, I'm afraid so. Would you like some tea? This has gone cold.' Grandma begins to ease herself up off the seat, but I give her shoulder a reassuring squeeze.

'I'll make it.'

Gosh, I sincerely hope it isn't one of Elizabeth's close family, not so soon after losing Freddie.

Grandma remains silent, which is unusual for her as she's a chatterbox by nature. When I return to the table with the tray, I sit patiently for a few minutes to let the tea brew before pouring it.

'Is there anything I can do . . . should I call in and check on her?'

'Veronica's there and she'll keep an eye out. She'll ring me if there's a problem. Elizabeth was insistent that all she needed was a little time to process what's happened.'

Georgina is the live-in housekeeper at the Hall from Monday to Friday. First thing on a Saturday morning her daughter picks her up for the weekend and pops her back early at the start of the working week. Veronica lives locally and covers at weekends, but she's never stayed overnight. I doubt Elizabeth would ask her to, given that she has three school-age children at home and a husband who works on a farm and is up with the lark on Saturday mornings.

'I don't think she has family staying this weekend. Is it wise for her to be there all alone tonight?' I question.

Grandma sighs. 'Maybe I'll give Elizabeth a call a bit later. She might change her mind after a short nap and appreciate some company.'

I place a fresh cup of tea in front of Grandma, and I can see she's conflicted.

'Anything you share with me I'll keep to myself; you know that. I've always been loyal to Elizabeth and Freddie.'

It's hard to see her so agitated and I watch as she wrings her hands. 'Oh, Sienna. It's awful, truly awful.'

What can be more awful than losing Freddie? I ask myself.

'It's . . . it's her son, Peter. He was only fifty-four!' There's a note of disbelief in her voice.

I gasp. 'She has a son?'

'You can't mention this to anyone, Sienna, including your mum. No one in Freddie and Elizabeth's family ever talk about Peter, as he cut all contact with them many years ago. Long before they moved to Darlingham, and in that respect, it made life easier for them here.'

My eyes widen as her words sinks in. 'What on earth

could Freddie and Elizabeth have done to cause their only son to cut all contact with them? They are two of the most caring people I know,' I declare.

Grandma gives me a winsome smile. 'It's hard to comprehend, isn't it? I think you ended up becoming a bit of a substitute for what was missing in their lives, Sienna. For whatever reason they couldn't rescue Peter, but they both knew that all you needed was a chance to . . . blossom at a time when you were finding life a little overwhelming. And look at you now!'

'Yes, but . . . to have no contact at all, that's unimaginable . . .' I tail off.

'I know. My last memory of Peter was the summer they all came to visit Elizabeth's brothers. It was before you were born. Pops and I joined them for a picnic, but Freddie and his son had a huge row. It spoiled the day out for everyone. It was their last holiday together as a family.'

Curiosity gets the better of me. 'What on earth is so unforgivable that it ends up turning their lives upside down forever?'

Grandma shrugs her shoulders, sadly. 'The answer to that is bad enough, apparently, that there was no recovering from it.'

I push the teacup and saucer closer, encouraging her to take a sip.

'I don't know the full story, Sienna. It all happened while they were living in London. It's not something I feel comfortable talking about so this conversation is . . . just between us, right?'

'Of course. Now drink your tea and, when you're ready, give Elizabeth another call. If she's ready for company, I'll drop you round there.'

It's a relatively short walk from Grandma's cottage to Silverberry Hall, but there's a light drizzle in the air again today. There's nothing worse than being wet and miserable.

An hour later and I can rest a little easier, having dropped

Grandma and her overnight bag at the Hall. I know from experience that in times of great distress, talking helps. But I'm struggling to understand; you don't turn your back on family because of a row. In the heat of the moment we're all capable of blurting out things we regret. However I can't even begin to imagine what happened that was so serious it tore their family apart. This goes much deeper and what I find particularly disturbing, is that neither Freddie nor Elizabeth are the sort of people who hold grudges. So this was all down to their son, and that too, is puzzling.

When I arrive at the Hall on Monday morning, I make my way to the kitchen. Georgina is busy scrambling some eggs, but she looks a tad flustered.

'Morning, Georgina. Is everything all right?' I ask, trying to sound bright and breezy.

She beckons me over. 'Elizabeth and your grandma are in the orangery. Something's not right. I'm taking them in a light breakfast, so I suggest you leave them to it.'

'Thanks for the heads-up. If anyone asks, I'll be in the study working on the Christmas party itinerary.'

'You don't know what's going on, then?'

I shrug my shoulders. 'I'll just grab a coffee and make myself scarce. Some days are better than others, at the moment, aren't they?'

I have a lot of respect for Georgina. As both the cook and the housekeeper, she's in charge of two part-time helpers. Silverberry Hall is a large property and a lot to take on but she fitted in from day one. Freddie was a stickler for using local, organic produce. He also appreciated her attempts to wean him and his wife off high sugar desserts and replace them with healthier ones.

She's in her mid-forties and has been a widow for quite a few years. Her daughter lives in the delightful village of Bromsberrow, in the Forest of Dean. Georgina has two grandchildren, but that's all I know about her. However, even though her heart is in the right place, my lips are sealed because of the promise I made to Grandma.

'Oh well, if I can get them to eat something, at least it might lift their spirits.'

The tray on the table has a plate heaped high with a selection of chopped fresh fruit and a bowl of yoghurt. Along with some toast and a pot of home-made jam, I think they might be tempted.

As I head into the study I, too, am feeling concerned. How much grief can a person handle at one time? I ponder. I can't even begin to imagine what it must feel like losing a son under normal circumstances. Having lost contact so many years ago, this will have raked up all manner of emotions for Elizabeth. The fact that Freddie isn't with her to share the sorrow, and the inevitable pain, is heart-rending. I'm glad Grandma is here, because often it's easier to open up to a close and trusted friend, than it is to a family member. Especially as it's a such a painful subject to broach.

Yesterday the mood at the Hall was somewhat sombre. It's clear that Elizabeth is battling to come to terms with what has happened. Thankfully, those around her not in the know simply assume it's due to the natural ups and downs of the grieving process after losing Freddie. This morning, Georgina told me that she was late down to breakfast and we've yet to cross paths.

It's almost eleven o'clock when my phone begins to buzz, and I see that it's a call from Daniela.

'I have a cast!' she exclaims, the moment I put the phone to my ear.

'Uh . . .' I sit back in my chair, trying to clear my head. It's full of figures from costing out the different elements of the party. 'A cast?'

'You wanted a little Christmas entertainment. I've talked some old friends into doing a repeat performance of a short play we did together back in our uni days.'

'You have? That's awesome news and very welcome at the moment.'

'You sound a little down this morning. Are you OK?'

'Yeah,' I bluster, 'I'm fine. I . . . uh . . . didn't sleep well last night, that's all. My head was buzzing. You know me, until I have everything tied up, I'm on edge. But I'm getting there and now I can tick another item off the list!'

'The thing is . . . it's a Christmas sketch I wrote, and as time isn't on our side, it's the easiest option.'

After I quit my studies at Bristol University, Daniela went on to gain a BA in Theatre and English.

'You did? You kept that incredibly quiet.'

'It was a one-night performance in aid of charity and there were several performances. It was when you were . . . when you returned to Darlingham.'

We both know she's talking about the year I quit the shared house that five of us rented in Bristol. Leaving them in the lurch to find a replacement wasn't my proudest moment but the pressure was too much. I did what most people would do in that situation, I headed home to my mum.

It would have been nerve-wracking for Daniela actually writing something her little crowd performed, and I missed it. Now I feel badly for being so wrapped up in myself at the time.

'It solves a big problem,' she continues. 'No licences, or permissions required. We rehearsed like crazy as if it were a gala performance. Everyone has agreed to perform their old role, except one. I'm not giving up on him, as he's a Mr Darcy lookalike. Well, he was seven years ago,' she laughs.

'Why won't he join in?'

'Oliver lives and works in London these days. He designs sets for videos and occasionally for plays. The bonus is that he can also roll up his sleeves and get hands on when necessary. His parents have a small farm, but he says he's allergic to the countryside. They go to visit him, not the other way around.'

'Allergies, really? Poor chap.' I'm thinking maybe when

the pollen count is high but what's his excuse in the winter months? Maybe it's the country smells he turns his nose up at after the delights of exhaust fumes. 'I bet his parents enjoy a trip to the big city, though.'

'I think the truth might be that he's nervous about performing again,' she continues. 'Even so, I'm sure I can talk him into it. Even though I penned the script, it went down so well I think it'll be perfect for Elizabeth's special party this year. It's thirty-five minutes long, so short enough to be entertaining, but not long enough to bore people.'

'Aww . . . thank you, Daniela. You have no idea what a boost it'll give Elizabeth when I tell her. I'm just about to finalise the design for the invitations. What's the play called?'

'*One Magical Christmas*. It's about a young woman looking out and watching a man having fun in the snow with his children.'

'Oh, that instantly conjures up some pictures in my head.' I imagine a shop with a snow-covered window and someone gazing out in wonder. 'It sounds perfect! Honestly, I owe you big time for this!'

'I know you do. Anyway, aside from talking Oliver into doing a repeat performance, I will need to sort out some overnight accommodation. Two of the cast live a short drive away but the other three would probably appreciate an overnight stay, especially if the weather is bad. I only have two spare bedrooms, so they'll have to toss a coin for them.'

'Leave sorting out the other room to me. One of the estate's cottages might be empty at the time, you never know.'

'Then we're all set. We will need to work out what props are required to make it work; that's why I'm determined to talk Oliver into getting involved. Let me know if there are any restrictions gaining access to the barn.'

The door opens and it's a relief to see Elizabeth walk into the room with a folder in her hands, ready to start the working day. It seems she's finally rallying a little after this recent setback and I smile at her as she takes a seat.

'I'm pretty sure we don't have any upcoming events, Daniela, but I'll check and get back to you. Thanks, and I mean that! We'll speak soon.'

Elizabeth returns my smile as I put down the phone, but there's a general air of weariness reflected in her demeanour.

'Good morning, Sienna. Was that good news?' Elizabeth looks worryingly pale, but her voice is steady.

'Yes.' I watch as her face brightens. 'We have a performance lined up for the party. They will need to come on site though, to do a bit of rehearsing and design some props for the stage.'

'That's fine by me. You have free rein as usual.'

However, it's as if a light has gone out inside of her. No wonder Grandma has been keeping a close eye; she's been spending more time here than she has in her own home. It's tough seeing her dearest friend looking so forlorn and lost. But the fact that Grandma isn't here this morning, bodes well.

As for me, it's hard to know what to say when I'm supposed to know nothing. But I owe this proud woman so much; she's like family to me now, and it feels wrong not acknowledging her loss.

'Elizabeth, if there's anything at all I can do, you only have to say.'

'Oh, Sienna. I have nowhere to turn and what I need is information, but it's such a delicate matter.'

There's a look of desperation reflected in her eyes that is troubling to see.

'I'm all about the detail and you know that I would never share your personal business with anyone.'

She straightens her back and draws in a deep breath. 'Your grandma told me she confided in you about my estranged son, Peter. No one else in my circle, other than the two of you, are aware of what's happened. It's a lot to take in, obviously.'

Elizabeth turns her head to stare out the window for the briefest of moments, as I sit quietly watching her.

'Old friends and family know that Peter cut us off completely and his name is never mentioned. I think it's best it stays that way. As for the new friends we've made since we moved here following Freddie's retirement, well . . . people assumed we didn't have any children and it was something we never alluded to. However, Peter left a part of his estate to his son.'

I gaze at her blankly. 'You have a grandson?'

'Yes, and that was totally unexpected. His name is James, apparently. Peter's widow is the executor of the estate. According to the letter I received from her solicitors, she isn't James's mother, and she wasn't even aware of his existence. Or that Peter had made provision for him in his will until it was read. Argh!' Elizabeth chokes back a bitter sob. 'What a mess and the bitter irony of it is too overwhelming to comprehend. Freddie and Peter . . . two stubborn men, neither of them really listening to what the other one was saying and look where that led.' The sigh she emits is harrowing to hear.

I shake my head sadly, because words fail me.

Elizabeth gazes down at the folder in her hands, her expression frozen for a few seconds, before she hands it across the desk to me. 'There isn't a single day since Peter disappeared from our lives that Freddie, or I, haven't thought about him . . . hoping that he'd reach out to us. Knowing that a part of Peter lives on in his son means so much, so very much, even though we're total strangers,' she says, shakily.

'Oh, Elizabeth, it's heartbreaking.'

The look I see reflected in her eyes is hard to witness: turmoil, confusion and a depth of sadness that strikes me to the core.

She draws in a deep breath, steeling herself. 'It turns out that Peter had been living in Italy all this time. He died several months ago, and it's only since the reading of the will that this *development* has come to light. The solicitors dealing with his estate on behalf of his wife, Mrs Isabella Blakesley, hired a specialist agency to track James down. They haven't been able to find him, although they did trace his birth mother, Briony—' Her voice wavers and she pauses for a moment to compose herself. 'There was a letter in his personal effects from her to Peter, telling him she was pregnant and that she was sorry they'd argued. It was dated shortly after he disappeared from our lives, so I assume they were still seeing each other at that point. However, there was nothing to confirm they had any further contact and, if they did, he chose not to keep a record of it. I find it almost impossible, and distressing, to believe that my son would simply turn his back on them until now; sadly, that seems to be the case.'

I sit quietly until Elizabeth is ready to continue, her emotions in free fall.

'What the investigators can confirm is that Briony had a son six months later, but the father's name was missing from the birth certificate. The thing is . . . I remember her! Peter brought a young lady to tea once at the old house in London just before the big row. He was involved in some sort of project and was working in Gloucester at the time, although he was based in Oxford.

'Even though it was frosty between Freddie and Peter that day, Briony was such a pleasant young lady and easy to talk to. She told us that her family live in Gloucestershire and when she mentioned her surname, Stuart-Adams, Freddie was delighted. He told her that he'd played golf with her grandfather once. We had high hopes the relationship might go somewhere, and Peter would consider settling down.'

'You said *was*?'

'According to the report in this folder, she died a while back. Briony's family refused to answer any questions about her, or her son, saying she lost touch with them when she moved away. When exactly that was, isn't clear. The investigator believes that James changed his name by deed poll, because there's no trace of him under his mother's family name. Anyway, the full report is in there. They're reaching out to see if we can supply any information that might help further their enquiries.'

No wonder Elizabeth is reeling. The unexpected death of her son and the news that she has a grandson she knows nothing about is shock enough; but to discover that from a solicitor's letter is almost beyond belief.

'Why didn't Peter's widow contact you directly?'

'Isabella speaks hardly any English. Discovering that her husband has close family members alive in the UK, came as a total surprise to her . . .' She draws to a halt, staring into space. 'Somewhere out there is a man in his early thirties, who probably believes he was abandoned not only by his father, but by just about every other family member he has.' Her voice is almost hoarse.

'What can I do to help?'

Elizabeth sighs, and as our eyes meet, that haunted look makes my stomach begin to churn. 'I can't change the past, but my conscience won't allow me to sit back and do nothing when he's made a bequest to his son.'

I understand Elizabeth can't let this go, but the reality is – given what she's told me – that she's as much in the dark as everyone else. However, a cold chill suddenly sends a shiver down my spine. Normally, Elizabeth is very open with me and yet it's what she's not telling me that is concerning. Family members row all the time and it might be a coincidence, of course, but fleeing to Italy is a rather dramatic turn of events. Alarm bells are starting to ring in my head. As I sit here trying to dovetail this information with what Grandma told me, Elizabeth begins speaking again.

'The investigator did manage to talk to a friend of the family, but they simply confirmed that Briony cut all ties with her past. Naturally, that resonates with me only too well. I never dreamt it would happen to Freddie and me, but it did.

'I can't imagine how hard it was for Briony not to bring Peter's name into it when she discovered that she was pregnant. Her parents must have been shocked to think of her bringing up her son without any support from the father. And for a well-known and respected family, it would have been something that attracted a lot of speculation at the time. I'm assuming that's why she never reached out to us. If only she had . . . we could at least have been there for her . . . for them both.'

I have no doubt at all that Freddie and Elizabeth would have treasured their grandson and supported Briony in whatever way she needed.

'Was Peter already in Italy when Briony got in touch with him?' I question. If they hadn't been seeing each for very long, I can see how the timing would have worked against them, let alone the fact that he was in a different country.

Elizabeth pauses, closing her eyes for a second or two. 'Unfortunately, I think that might have been the case, but no one knows for sure. I like to think that Peter didn't just disappear from her life too, without so much as a call. If that were the case, I doubt she would have been able to track him down. Freddie and I weren't able to do that and goodness knows, we tried!'

Did Briony hide the truth from her family because Peter wasn't willing to step up when she reached out to him?

'It breaks my heart!' Elizabeth stifles a sob. 'He wasn't a bad man, just young and a tad naive at times. He must have felt so desperate to do what he did.'

The look on her face is soulful and I'm at a loss for words. It's like trying to piece together a jigsaw puzzle when someone has thrown the box away and you have no idea what the final picture looks like.

'What if James had a close friend, someone he kept in touch with after he and his mother moved away?' Elizabeth blurts out, but I think she's grasping at straws.

'Given the circumstances do you think that's likely? I mean, he wouldn't have wanted to upset his mother, Briony, as it was her decision to start a new life.'

'Who knows, Sienna, but I have to try. Your grandma is going to reach out to a mutual friend of your late granddad's.'

Now I'm confused. 'A friend of Pop's. Why?'

'I told Charlotte about Freddie playing golf with Briony's grandfather. Even after we moved to London, whenever we came back to visit family, Freddie and your grandfather would always head off for a round of golf.'

'The club near Cirencester?' I remember Pops taking me there on several occasions when I was in my early teens, but he soon gave up on me as I kept missing the ball and creating divots on the green.

'Yes. It's a tenuous link, but I owe it to my son to do whatever I can to find James. I know it's a lot to ask, but if we can get a name of a friend, or relative of James's who is willing to talk off the record, would you call them as my representative?'

'Me? Wouldn't it be better to use a professional? Someone who knows what questions to ask.'

Elizabeth points to the file. 'Your grandma and I came to the conclusion it was the best way forward. Not only is it more discreet than pulling in a total stranger, but I can also rely upon you to handle this sensitively. It's a case of getting some contact details so that Isabella's solicitors can get in touch with James direct.'

'And if he's curious, the chance to find out more about his father's family?' I enquire, softly.

She pauses momentarily, her hand sweeping over her glistening eyes. 'That would be entirely up to him. He's been through a lot, and I have no right to assume he'd be open to having some form of contact. If he was curious, I'm sure he would have sought us out long ago. No mother would hide the truth from her son, would she?'

Goodness, that's not the Elizabeth I know, a woman who goes the extra mile for everyone she comes into contact with, and this is her grandson we're talking about! I just get this horribly unsettling feeling that there's more to what happened with Peter, something that she can't bring herself to admit. Is it possible that if it came out, it could affect James – even now – in a negative way? Maybe it's simply my imagination going into overdrive but when it comes to the proverbial skeleton in the closet, this is a huge one. Anyway, the upshot is how can I refuse her request? 'If that's what you want, then of course I'll do whatever I can.' But in truth, it's with a hint of trepidation.

'Be guided by your grandma, Sienna. I found it too upsetting to read the file word for word, but she read every single page in its entirety. It's the best we can do. I . . . at the time I interfered in the dispute between Freddie and Peter, and fear I ended up making it even worse. This could be a chance to at least do something right. Peter obviously wanted to make amends in the only way he could. But he chose not to involve his family directly, so discretion is the order of the day.'

The lump that has risen in my throat is hard to swallow. Elizabeth must long to know more about her grandson and it's troubling that she's doing everything she can to remain at arm's length.

'Everything hinges on Grandma coming up with a lead, then.' A part of me hopes she doesn't. If James can be found, all of this will suddenly become very real indeed. Whatever happened in the past, how much heartbreak can one woman endure?

Life is so horribly unfair at times because Elizabeth is one of the kindest and most generous people I know. She's also the last person in the world who would spring to mind when it comes to hiding a secret of this nature. It's beyond belief.

3

Rumours of Christmas Jumpers Abound

A week later and the plans for the Christmas Eve party have been the talk of the village.

'What's all this nonsense about the party and Christmas jumpers?' Georgina asks the moment I walk into the kitchen on a typically windy, autumnal Tuesday morning. With the invitations due to go out at any time, no doubt it's already a hot topic of conversation and some speculation in the village.

'The theme is an old-fashioned Christmas,' I reply. 'I hardly think they'll all turn up in jumpers with snowflakes and Santa's face on them.'

She laughs. 'I thought they'd got the wrong end of the stick. I hear that Mrs Jessop, at the post office up by the green, was gossiping about it.'

It didn't take long for the rumours to start, I muse. I bet Georgina got that from Harry. He loves to pull people's legs and joke around but sometimes it backfires. Harry works over at Brentwood Farm and will have been here bright and early this morning with a delivery of milk, eggs, fresh vegetables and time to share a little gossip.

'It's a tribute to Freddie because it was his favourite time of the year. The emphasis is on bygone years and it's going to be rather nostalgic.'

'It won't be the same without him,' she replies, sadly. 'Am I ordering in mince pies by the crate as usual?'

'Yes, late afternoon the parish choir will be singing on the green and I'll arrange for some volunteers to hand out hot drinks as well.' Like the party, it's a tradition Freddie and Elizabeth started when they moved here, and this year is no exception.

Georgina stops chopping vegetables to glance in my direction, as I grab a mug from the kitchen cupboard. 'I'm worried about Elizabeth, Sienna. She's barely eating.'

'I know, but all things pass with time. It's a case of giving her some space and, with luck, her spirits will rise a little as we get closer to the party. At the moment she's telling everyone she's fine when she isn't, but once she's ready to let people back in again she'll perk up.'

Georgina wrinkles her forehead. 'I hope so, I really do. Elizabeth seemed to be rallying a little, but now she's become distant again. Do you think it's worth encouraging her to consider having a little afternoon tea party for the ladies who lunch? I think the company might boost her spirits.'

'That's a great idea! I'll mention it to her and let you know what she says.'

Talk about treading on eggshells. No one, apart from Grandma and me, know what Elizabeth is really dealing with. The fewer people who know about it, the better. Sympathy won't heal this wound, but gossip could rip it open again and cause untold damage.

'And did you hear that our handsome vet was seen coming out of Ashburn House yesterday evening?'

'Oh . . . I hope Pixie is all right. I'll have to give Daniela a ring.' I suppose sometimes word on the village grapevine does come in handy but seriously . . . Xavier's flamboyant style is a tad much for me, albeit he is rather swoon-worthy. As for Daniela, she only has eyes for Nigel. However, I do wonder whether our locum veterinary surgeon is even aware that he only has to smile at someone in passing to create a stir. That thought makes me chuckle. Poor chap. If that's the case, it could put him off village life forever.

* * *

'What's this I hear about you having an unexpected visitor last night?' I ask, the moment Daniela picks up.

'How did you know?' She sounds amused.

'Obviously, there was nothing interesting going on in Darlingham yesterday, for you to be the hot topic of conversation first thing this morning. Is Pixie OK?'

'She is now, thanks to Xavier. I was just about to put the kids to bed when Clara dropped her glass of milk. Pixie was straight there and, I swear, I almost fainted because all of a sudden there was blood everywhere!'

Ooh, she does sound a tad traumatised. 'Poor you!'

'Honestly, it was bedlam trying to do everything one-handed as I daren't put William down and Clara was screaming her head off. Xavier was on call, and he was here in no time at all.'

'Where was Nigel?'

'Neither of us felt like cooking and he headed off to collect takeaway from our favourite restaurant.'

'Takeaway?' The nearest one I can think of is at least a twenty-five-minute drive from here.

'I know . . . but I reheat it in the air fryer. It was supposed to kick off a relaxing evening once I got the kids to bed. When Nigel got back it took an hour to clear everything up but at least Pixie's paw was bandaged. She's housebound now until it heals as it was a pretty bad cut, which required stitches.'

'Well, if you need any help just give me a call.'

'The good news is that Nigel now realises I'm struggling, and he's agreed that I need some help.'

My eyes widen. 'Really?'

'Well, I did totally lose it; it felt like the final straw and I think my over-the-top reaction scared him. We agreed to employ a nanny to look after the children on Tuesdays and Thursdays to begin with. I already have someone in mind. And Nigel promised me that he'll do his best to make sure he's at home every weekend. Unless there's an emergency at work that he can't delegate, of course.' She sighs, and it's harrowing to hear. 'I've lost all sense of . . . me. I told Nigel that I want to start writing again whenever I can grab a few hours of undisturbed time. I need something just for me and I know that sounds selfish, but I do.'

'Aww, Daniela, that's understandable. Most of the time you're exhausted just from the lack of sleep, but the children won't be little forever.'

'What with Pixie being a minx at times, and the house to run, I get moments when it feels like I'm sinking. I also told Nigel about this little performance for Elizabeth's party and he thinks it'll do me the world of good to have something different to occupy my mind.'

'He's such a sweetheart, Daniela. He'd do anything for you but you have to tell him what's going on inside that head of yours.' She's been putting on a brave face, pretending everything's fine when it isn't.

'I know and I should have said something to him well before now. Mum does what she can, but she feels guilty she can't do more. However, it's not easy getting someone to cover for her. Running a newsagent's and a convenience store is a full-time job all year round. My parents make a living from it but, given the hours they work, I wish they could afford to retire early and have a less demanding lifestyle. Still, it is what it is; it makes me really appreciate how hard Nigel works. He's a good husband and father, and he's focusing on securing our future. Once the kids are both in school, I hope to go back to work – part-time at first, obviously.'

Now that's a surprise. 'I didn't realise you felt so—'

'Cut off from the world?'

Gosh, how did I miss this? I thought she was simply an anxious parent of two young children, as I'd no doubt be if I were in her position.

'It's just that I stress about every little thing and the incident with Pixie shouldn't have turned me into a blubbering mess. When Xavier arrived, both me and the kids were all in tears.

The poor man wasn't prepared for what he walked into. Anyway—' she exhales sharply '—I'm glad you rang because I have some good news. It's a *yes* from Oliver.'

In the background I hear my name being called.

'That's awesome. Sorry, but I must go. Elizabeth is looking for me. Take care and I hope Pixie's paw heals quickly.'

'Me, too,' Daniela groans. 'She's such a little rocket, it's hard to keep her still. Bye for now.'

I walk out of the storeroom where the Christmas decorations are kept, and almost collide with Elizabeth.

'Oh, there you are!' She lowers her voice. 'Your grandma is here, and she has some news!'

We head off to the orangery and I walk straight over to give Grandma a hug.

'How is the Christmas programme coming together?' she enquires, as she settles herself back down.

'Everything is slotting quite nicely into place. It's going to be a Christmas Eve to remember, that's for sure.'

Grandma and Elizabeth glance at each other, excitedly. It's the highlight of their year and now they're both widows, it takes a lot of courage not to dwell on the past and focus firmly on ensuring there's laughter and gaiety.

I really miss Dad, Pops, and Freddie. Three bright lights have been extinguished but life goes on; death is a natural part of the cycle, but that sense of loss never really goes away.

I prefer to believe that they're here with us in spirit, rather than dwell on how much I miss them. However, it's a sharp reminder that each day is precious and it's important to grab on to the positive and push the negative away. We can't turn back the clock, but memories last a lifetime. They can continue to put a smile on our faces and gratitude in our hearts, if that's where we put our focus.

'Right, we have about half an hour before Georgina announces lunch. I've told her there will be three of us. She's insistent that I need building up, so you can expect something substantial,' Elizabeth apologises.

In truth, she has needed that encouragement, and she isn't nearly so peaky, or drawn, as she was following the loss of Freddie. I feared the setback with Peter would see her withdraw, and she has been noticeably quiet, but now she's getting into Christmas mode it's a blessing in disguise.

'Well, when you hear my good news, it might give us all a hearty appetite,' Grandma declares, proudly. 'An old friend of Ivor's is close to the Stuart-Adams family, enough to tell me that Briony's cousin, Richard, lives less than a mile from her parents. I managed to persuade him to get me Richard's telephone number.'

Elizabeth's hands fly up to her face. It's strange to hear Grandma refer to my late granddad by his Christian name. He was always just Pops to me.

'You did? Well done, Charlotte.' Elizabeth is clearly delighted.

Grandma's cheeks begin to colour up. 'Stroud isn't that different to Darlingham. It might be a town, but in the outlying villages some families go back generations. The only other option is an aunt who moved to Norfolk with her family in the late nineties. That seemed like a bit of a long shot to me.'

Grandma places a piece of paper down on the coffee table in front of us and I stare at it, before turning to look at Elizabeth. 'I hope I don't mess this up. Perhaps Grandma should make the call.'

Elizabeth reaches out to touch my arm to give it a reassuring squeeze. 'I'd rather this enquiry was at arm's length. You can assure whomsoever you talk to . . .' she pauses, making direct eye contract '. . . that you will simply pass on any information you obtain directly to the solicitors handling Peter's estate. I won't interfere in any way.'

'You don't want to know where James is, if it's possible to locate him?'

She sighs, shaking her head. 'In my heart, of course I do,

but to use that information to get in touch with him wouldn't be fair, would it?'

'Fair?' I query, feeling puzzled.

When I glance at Elizabeth I'm shocked to see a momentary look of panic reflected in her eyes.

'I . . . um . . . I have no idea what sort of life he's had.' The words come out in a rush but she looks agitated. 'Hopefully, a happy one. But I'd understand if he doesn't want anything at all to do with . . . Oh!' Her voice wavers as her breath catches in her throat. 'Peter chose not to tell Freddie and me about our grandson. In doing that, he not only robbed us of the chance to get to know his son, but he robbed James of that contact, too. What must he think of us? Cold and uncaring, probably.

'I simply want to ensure my son's wishes are honoured, if at all possible, without any interference from me in case it causes even more distress – to James, or Briony's family. If my grandson chooses to seek me out then, naturally, I will welcome him with open arms, but that decision isn't mine.'

It's just a phone call, I tell myself. Maybe two, if this Richard Stuart-Adams is in direct contact with James. As Elizabeth said, if he doesn't want to be found then that's his prerogative.

'OK. Leave it with me.'

The look of relief on Elizabeth's face is humbling.

The door opens and Georgina's head appears around the side of it.

'Five minutes, ladies?'

'Perfect timing.' Elizabeth smiles back at her.

'I hope you're ravenous,' Georgina replies, leaving the door ajar as she hurries away.

Elizabeth chuckles to herself. 'I think I am. And after lunch perhaps we could start going through the Christmas trimmings to decide what colour scheme we're having this year? What do you think?'

Grandma and I murmur our agreement as we stand and make our way through to the dining room.

'Of course,' Grandma adds, lightening the mood. 'Old-fashioned means going multicoloured.'

'Hmm . . .' Elizabeth sounds a tad dubious. 'We might need a trial run to test that out first.'

I walk along behind them, chuckling to myself. It could be a long afternoon. Grandma loves colour but Elizabeth favours a more coordinated approach. They have this little tussle every year and it's the differences between them that makes their friendship so lively.

'Hi, Mum. How're you doing?'

'Fine. How about you, my darling daughter?'

'It's all good here. Elizabeth says your invite to the party is on the way and she's looking forward to catching up with you and Greg *properly*.'

'Bless her! We hardly spoke more than a couple of words at the funeral, and the do back at the house afterwards wasn't quite the celebration of Freddie's life that she'd hoped it would be, was it?' That note of sadness in Mum's voice says more than words can convey.

My shoulders sag. 'It was a bit of a disaster. We could all have cheerfully sobbed our hearts out, but you don't do that out of respect. That's why the Christmas Eve party is so important to Elizabeth. She fully intends it to be the celebration that Freddie deserves. How's Greg?'

When my mum, Helen, and her best friend rented a holiday cottage in Cornwall two years ago, little did she know that it would lead to her eventually moving there. After literally bumping into a guy in a restaurant, causing him to spill his drink all over himself, they struck up a conversation. After several trips back over a period of eighteen months, an easy friendship turned into a full-blown relationship.

Greg owns a boat repair yard and when Mum moved in with him, earlier this year, she took over the admin side of his business. It was a huge upheaval, but both Grandma and I wanted her to find happiness a second time around. He'll never be a dad to me as I hardly know him still. However, Mum seems content and I guess that's the true test.

'Over-worked and underpaid, according to him,' Mum laughs. 'He moans that I keep a tight rein on the finances but he's finally turning a healthy profit, rather than simply making ends meet.'

I know she misses us all but sometimes you have to let go of the past and grab whatever chances come your way to build a new life. I was saddened by the change in Mum after we lost Dad. She floundered for a while. As the years passed, she came to terms with it by throwing herself into village life, but she was lonely and missed her soul mate. Now, together with Greg, she's building a new future. Finally, she has a real sense of purpose again. We all need that, without it what's the point in getting out of bed each day?

'Your grandma has suggested that we stay for two nights over the festive period. Greg said it's only fair, given that last year we spent Christmas afternoon and evening with his family. He's looking forward to a return trip to Darlingham.'

After Freddie and Elizabeth's party, the following morning Greg had set off for the drive back to Cornwall with Mum beside him. It was tough waving her off; it was the first time since Dad passed that Grandma, Mum and I weren't together around the Christmas table to enjoy a festive roast turkey dinner. But it was also the first time Mum was able to meet Greg's entire family, ahead of her moving down there permanently in April of this year.

Grandma and I ended up going to Elizabeth's and it was fun, albeit noisy. Liam ducked out and went to his parents, which says a lot about our relationship at the time. The writing was on the wall even back then. I was just too blinkered to see it.

'I am, too, Mum.'

'I appreciate that it's been a tough year and every time you've planned a visit you've had to cancel, but we're a ten-minute stroll away from a beautiful cove. When you do get a chance to come and see us, you'll love it.'

'I know and I promise that as soon as I can get away, I'll make the trip. Even if it's just for one night.'

'One night will do,' Mum muses. 'I miss you . . . and I miss your grandma, although she's always on the phone keeping me up to date on what's happening.'

I freeze. Has Grandma talked to Mum about Elizabeth's situation? I wonder. Or was it a hint that Mum rings me more often than I call her? 'She does?'

'Oh, I get all the gossip. And I can confirm that we won't be packing Christmas jumpers,' she chuckles. 'We're going to hire some costumes. Greg is totally up for it!'

I breathe a gentle sigh of relief, as for one moment I thought Grandma might have unwittingly let something slip about Peter, or James. 'I'm coming as an elf.'

Mum starts laughing. 'You make people smile, just like Freddie did. You'll do him proud, my darling and this year it's going to be more important than ever to keep everyone's spirits up.'

As we say goodbye and the line disconnects, I realise that I've never thought about it like that. It actually makes me feel a little tearful. Oh well, onwards and upwards.

4

A Not So Cosy Lunch . . .

By Wednesday, I'm looking forward to a leisurely lunchtime meeting with Daniela at Darlingham's local inn – The Sailor's Retreat – to talk about the play. Four years ago, the inn was teetering on the edge of extinction; it was badly in need of a huge cash injection to bring both the building and the interior up to date. But who buys a public house a stone's throw away from an estuary, on a narrow road going nowhere other than through some tiny hamlets? The answer to that is a cooperative of local people. They all have a vested interest in keeping alive what is one of the main meeting places, at the last stop before you hit the banks of the river.

When I step inside, there's a cluster of people around the bar. Most are ramblers, with backpacks, and they're standing two-deep, which is good to see at any time of the year. I tilt my head and spot Daniela sitting at a table next to the roaring log fire. She's deep in conversation with a man whose back is towards me, and I hurry over to them.

'Hi! I'm so sorry I'm running late.'

She stands and we hug, then she turns to the attractive-looking man sitting opposite her.

'Better late than never, Sienna. Look who was able to join us! This is Oliver Townsend.'

Interesting. It sounds like she wasn't sure he was actually going to turn up. He stands and comes a little closer. I thrust out my hand and we shake. 'Oh . . . right. It's nice to meet you, Oliver.'

'It's my pleasure entirely, Sienna. I've heard a lot about you.' Those deep brown eyes sweep over my face with interest. 'And if I'd known there was a great pub with draught beers on tap, Daniela would have had an easier job of tempting me down here.'

As I slip off my coat and sit down next to her, Daniela flashes me a momentary apologetic look, before her eyes travel back to gaze at her old friend.

'Really? So, you won't want to stay at my place on Christmas Eve then?'

He rewards her with an engaging little smile. 'I'll let you know when I've tasted the food but judging by this glass of Old Spot, I'm tempted to book a room here now.'

The eye contact between them is playful and a tad awkward to witness. It feels . . . flirtatious and I'm rather taken aback.

'It hails from Uley Brewery,' I inform him, sounding a little lame but it's all I can come up with. 'They're a local—'

'I know,' he stops me short. 'They're a traditional tower brewery built on top of a natural Cotswold spring. It's been a long while since I've been down this way, and I'd forgotten just how good their ales are. I have family in the area.'

Is he being dismissive? I'm only trying to make polite conversation; the gentlemanly thing to do would have been to hear me out and pretend it was news to him. Feeling a tad irked, I glance at Daniela. 'I had a little drama going on with my kitchen tap and it's going to need a plumber. I've left several messages with the estate's management company, but no one got back to me. I ended up turning the water off at the stopcock.'

She grimaces. 'I hope it can wait until Monday. Getting a plumber out on a weekend is like finding the pot of gold at the end of the rainbow.'

'Yeah, I thought the same thing. I'll have to pop around to Grandma's to get a shower this evening.'

The expression on Oliver's face is priceless. I guess I'm not making the best first impression but I have this unsettling feeling that two is company and three is a crowd. Maybe in her desire to simply get him here, Daniela chose not to mention the fact that I'd be joining them.

Daniela pushes back on her chair. 'What would you like to drink, Sienna? They're really busy so I'll grab some menus, or we'll be here all afternoon. I'm eager for you to show Oliver around the barn.'

'Oh, thanks . . . I'll have half a pint of Old Spot, please.'

She saunters off to the bar, leaving us to it. While I'm still casting around for something suitable to say, Oliver starts talking.

'Sorry. I cut you off just now. It was rude of me,' he apologises, his face a tad flushed. 'This is a great old inn and what a discovery. When I was in my teens, my father and I often came to watch the cricket matches on the green at Frampton on Severn, but we never ventured any further. How far back does this place date?'

His smile is genuine, as he sits there nervously fiddling with the coaster beneath his drink. Neither of us are feeling at ease. I'm sure he'd have preferred a quiet lunch with Daniela so they could catch up, and that's understandable, so I make a concerted effort to shirk off my annoyance.

'The late seventeen hundreds,' I state, softening the tone of my voice. 'When the tide was low, ships travelling along the Severn from Bristol to Gloucester would stop at Darlingham. The sailors would walk up to the village for an evening of revelry.'

I tilt my head to catch sight of Daniela, but she's still queuing at the bar.

'I bet beer and sea shanties made for a boisterous night out,' Oliver comments, catching my eye.

He's beginning to relax a little, maybe we just got off on the wrong foot. 'Yes. I bet it did. So, you live in London now?'

Oliver's mouth twitches as he looks down at his drink.

'I think I was born a city boy; I just didn't know it until I escaped.'

Ooh . . . *escaped*. That doesn't sound good. 'My family are from this village, and I've always regarded it as home, even when I lived in Bristol for a while.'

'You made it as far as Bristol?' Oliver's eyes widen and I give him a look of disdain.

'I was at university there. I have been further afield.'

'Well, that's good to hear.'

Is he being sarcastic? 'It sounds like you've travelled extensively.'

Oliver takes a sip of his beer, then wipes his mouth with a napkin. 'You could say that. I've also spent time working on projects in France, Italy and Germany.'

If he thinks that impresses me, it doesn't. Each to their own, as Grandma says. When I make no attempt to pick the conversation back up, he can sense I'm a little riled.

'It's a big wide world out there and it's a good job we're all different,' he adds.

Now he's patronising me!

Fortunately, Daniela reappears, a glass in one hand and some menus in the other.

'Here you go, Sienna. Ben apologises for the delay; Ruby will be with us shortly to take our orders. What have I missed?'

I'm about to open my mouth when Oliver beats me to it. 'Sienna was telling me a little bit about the history of the inn. I can't believe this was on my doorstep and I didn't get to discover it for myself.'

She flashes me an amused smile. 'Wonderful! Right, let's decide what we're eating, and hope Ruby gets to us before that lot at the bar filter through to their table.'

I already know what I'm ordering, so I surreptitiously watch Oliver as he studies the menu. His dark hair is curly on top and shaved around the back and sides; with those mysterious dark-brown eyes he certainly turns heads. I'd say he's what Freddie would have referred to as a man's man. Oliver comes across as the sort of guy who is happier going to the pub for a pint with his mates, rather than on a couples' night out. I vaguely remember Daniela describing him as a Mr Darcy lookalike, and she wasn't far wrong there. He definitely has that slightly offhand, almost edgy side to the character off to a T.

I also find myself noticing that he isn't wearing a ring, but not all married men do. He exudes that smart country casual style, but he doesn't look comfortable in it. He's even wearing hiking boots, although they look virtually brand new.

'Hey, guys.' Ruby rushes over to us. 'Sorry about the wait. I was helping prep the starters for the ramblers club luncheon. What can I get you?' As she's talking, I can't help but notice that she can't take her eyes off Oliver.

Tall, dark and handsome he might be, but I'm reserving my judgement for now. I'm beginning to wonder whether telling Daniela he was *allergic* to the countryside was a bit of a put-down and not merely a joke, or a polite way to decline her offer.

From what I've seen so far, Oliver seems a bit full of himself. He keeps glancing up at Ruby, giving her that ever so cool smile of his while Daniela and I place our orders. It's clear that it's making her a little flustered.

After the meal, we're off to inspect the barn. I can't wait to hear what he makes of that as a venue. Too rustic maybe, when it comes to hosting a play? Hmm . . . I might find myself having to hold my tongue.

We walk along the single-track lane that leads to the entrance to Silverberry Hall and I feel as if I'm eavesdropping. Oliver and Daniela catch up on what they've been doing since they last met up, which sounds like it was well before the children came along.

It's interesting, actually. Oliver reels off some of the projects he's been involved in, and it is impressive, I'll give him that.

But when it comes to Daniela's turn, I can't help but think that she's downplaying her role as a wife and a mother. Nigel is free to work all the hours he wants, only because Daniela successfully juggles family life to accommodate his absences. It's no mean feat.

'You're about to get back into playwriting, though,' I point out, from the rear.

She turns her head to grin at me. 'Well, have a stab at it again, at least.'

'This little performance might be just what you need to spur you on,' Oliver replies, enthusiastically. 'Is it much further? I could have driven the car down to the pub to save us the walk.'

Surely, he's kidding. It's no more than a ten-minute saunter from Daniela's house to The Sailor's Retreat, and less than fifteen minutes along a lovely, country lane to the Hall. On a wonderful day like this, with a gloriously blue sky, it's invigorating.

'It's hardly worth firing up the engine,' I muse. 'Besides, this is how you get to explore the countryside. See that rusty old gate over there, partially hidden among the brambles?' I incline my head as we draw to a halt.

Oliver gazes at it, clearly unimpressed.

'It's a path leading to an old pigsty. It's within the boundary of Silverberry Hall and the grounds stretch from here across to the banks of the River Severn in that direction.' I point and he at least has the courtesy to turn his head. 'It extends another two miles in that direction and beyond what you see here, is a vast swathe of woodland.'

'Oh, right.'

It's obvious that he's not that interested in taking in the scenery, even when we spot a sparrow hawk hovering over one of the fields.

When we walk up the drive to the main house I notice a navy-blue Range Rover parked up; it belongs to the eldest of Elizabeth's two younger brothers, Stephen. I suggest we head straight to the barn and introduce Oliver later.

'I love this place,' Daniela enthuses, as I lead them around the side of the original part of the house and under a covered walkway. 'This is the house of my dreams!'

It's a standing joke between the two of us because she's serious and we both start giggling. When we were growing up, our imaginations knew no bounds, but Daniela was in another league altogether. Her Georgian-style home is stunning and sizeable, but her vision was of a sprawling country property with original limestone floors and acres of land. However, you need very deep pockets indeed to run a place like this.

She used to laugh at me with my dream of owning a cute little country cottage with wisteria hanging down either side of the front door. Daniela would tease me and say that I needed to set my sights higher because . . . why not? But she was always the ambitious, outgoing one whereas I was shy and nervous. However, I never underestimated how much easier my childhood was, having such a bubbly friend encouraging me to wander outside my comfort zone from time to time. I'll always love her for that.

I do a bit of a running commentary as we continue walking towards the first of the outbuildings. 'The stables aren't used anymore, but as you can see, they're in good condition if you need to store anything. And the next building on our left is the main barn.'

The old sliding doors were replaced many years ago and inset with two huge oak panelled doors. They're very heavy and set into one of them is a normal-sized, working door. I pull the key from my pocket and unlock it.

'After you.' I motion for Oliver and Daniela to step inside.

'Wow. It's a lot bigger than I was expecting,' he comments. Finally, something in this little village in the middle of nowhere, aside from the beer that is, impresses him.

He walks around aimlessly, getting a feel for the space.

'There will be at least one hundred and thirty people here milling around on the night. To our right, that end will be taken up entirely with the buffet tables. A local DJ will set up in this corner behind us, ready for the dancing later in the evening.'

Oliver walks in parallel with the line of gas heaters, to the far end. He's wearing a frown.

'It's a pity it's not a little wider,' he remarks, seemingly to himself.

Daniela strides forward to catch up with him but I stay where I am.

'What're you thinking?' she asks.

'Well, first time around the staging worked well in the centre of the room.'

She nods her head. 'I know but given the size of the crowd they aren't going to be able to wander around, anyway. It has to be end-on against that far wall, but will what's there be too small for the performance?'

'It'll totally spoil the effect; you do appreciate that?'

I wish I knew what they were talking about. I mean, it's just a play and most audiences sit in rows facing the stage. Is he looking for problems because he'd rather not get involved, but couldn't bring himself to admit that to an old friend? I wonder.

Daniela reaches out to touch his arm. 'If anyone can pull this off, it's you, Oliver.'

Oh my! The way to get a man to do a job he doesn't want to do is to pander to his ego. In that instant, Oliver's expression changes. 'I have an idea that might work but it'll take a while to construct it. That uh . . . stage, is just an oblong box. I'll need some wood to extend it at one end to accommodate the main prop. And I think we'll need a bit of a backdrop to set the scene. That'll need painting. With a bit of luck, I can call in a favour and borrow some stage lighting from a mate of mine.'

'That sounds great! Just work out what you need and let me have a list. I can help with the painting and I'm sure Sienna will lend a hand.'

So much for leaving them to it. I wander over to join Daniela, as Oliver jumps up onto what we refer to as the podium. He's right, it's not a full-blown stage and I watch as he takes a rough measurement of the area in strides.

'I think it can be done. It'll be different to the first time around, obviously, but with a bit of manipulation I reckon it'll still be a showstopper.'

Daniela's smile grows exponentially. 'It was quite a small audience last time, wasn't it?' she muses.

He jumps down and saunters over to us. 'It was, but one's peers are the fiercest of judges. All credit to you, I think we'll succeed in wowing the guests on the night.'

'How many actors are involved?' I ask, curious to know more.

'Six adults and we had two young children playing in the background. As they're non-speaking parts, I'm hoping to enlist a couple of local volunteers,' Daniela explains. 'And with that, I think we're done.'

Well, almost. Oliver speaks up. 'How about the rehearsals?'

'We'll do that via video calls just to make sure we're all in synch and we should be able to get away with a couple of rehearsals prior to the day.'

I raise my eyebrows. 'We? Are you performing, too?'

Oliver gives a hearty laugh. 'Daniela is centre stage. You can reassure Elizabeth . . . I got the name right, didn't I?' His eyes meet mine and I nod my head. 'Good. Let her know that we'll make sure her guests are in for a real treat.'

'If I hand you the key, I'll leave you to wander around and have a little chat while I see if Elizabeth's free and you can tell her that for yourself. Come up to the Hall when you're ready and I'll meet you around the back in the orangery for a cup of tea.'

'Make that coffee for me, please,' Oliver adds. 'Tea isn't my thing.'

I chuckle to myself as I hurry away to alert Elizabeth. Oliver is definitely not the tiny cakes and cucumber sandwiches type of man, either. But he knows what he's doing and if he could relax a little, he'd probably be fun to be around.

I can't help but wonder whether he and Daniela ever had a bit of a fling, back in the day. We didn't mix in the same circles at university and I'm sure I'd remember if I'd crossed paths with him before. The fact I didn't probably means the answer to my question is no, and thank goodness for that. Daniela has a busy life and while she might need Oliver's help, she doesn't need any other complications thrown into the mix.

Oliver is quite a charmer when he wants to be, and Elizabeth is captivated when he talks about some of the projects he's been involved with. She's always been into the arts and the conversation is animated.

I switch off and dispense the tea, and coffee, making several trips back and forth to the kitchen. Veronica is covering for Georgina, who is taking a day's holiday, and she's in a bit of a tizzy. Elizabeth has company for dinner this evening but as far as I'm aware it's just three family members. Georgina has left detailed instructions for reheating the ready-prepared dishes and they'll serve themselves.

When Veronica ends up dropping a serving dish and it hits the floor, it's time for me to step in. 'Relax, take a deep breath. I'll clear that up.'

'Oh, Sienna! I just want everything to go smoothly.'

'I know you do, but it's not a posh dinner party, so don't stress over it.'

I grab a dustpan and brush while she takes a moment to calm herself. 'I know it's silly and all I have to do is assemble the starter, reheat the main course and serve the dessert, but I don't want to let anyone down.' Normally, Elizabeth gets in the caterers when Georgina isn't here, so it's understandable that Veronica is a little on edge. 'I thought I'd get the table all set up ready, as that's one thing off the list.'

'You can handle this. If you need an extra pair of hands a bit later, just give me a call. I'd better get back to the orangery, but don't forget – I'm close by if you need anything.'

She gives me a weak smile. Georgina makes it all look so easy but then she's worked in larger houses than this one in the past.

When I rejoin them, carrying a fresh pot of tea, I'm surprised to see that Elizabeth and Oliver are alone.

'Daniela had to rush home to look after the children; her mother has to get back to the shop,' Elizabeth informs me.

'Ah, that's a pity.'

'Come and sit down. I'll pour the tea. Would you like another coffee, Oliver?'

'I'd love one, Elizabeth, if I'm not taking up too much of your time. Daniela mentioned that you have family here today.'

'Yes. My sister-in-law is relaxing in the hot tub and my brother is playing pool with his eldest son in the games room. They see enough of me as it is!'

Gosh, that's a girlish laugh if ever I heard one.

Oliver smiles. 'Point me in the direction of the kitchen and I'll make the coffee myself.'

To say I'm shocked when Elizabeth does just that, is an understatement. He's a guest at the Hall and that's literally unheard of.

As soon as the door shuts behind him, I busy myself adding a dash of milk to my tea. 'Oliver is going to build something to extend the width of the stage at one end. Are you OK with that?'

'Oh, yes! He already talked me through it; the addition will come in useful when we hold auctions, too. I'm rather excited, actually. I gather they'll be performing a short play that Daniela wrote, imagine that! While we're on our own, did you manage to follow up on that *call* yet?'

'I left another message first thing yesterday morning. If Richard doesn't get back to me within a few days, I think we ought to assume he's not willing to talk.'

'Oh dear, what a pity. Well, all you can do is try and let's give it until the end of next week before we rethink the strategy.'

I sip my tea, a little disappointed to hear that she isn't giving up that easily.

'Oliver is a bit of a surprise, isn't he?' Elizabeth comments. It's good to hear her sounding a little perkier today but I don't know quite how to answer that.

'Um . . .' Luckily the door opens and the man himself hurries over to join us.

'Oliver, are you heading home after this?'

'No. I'm staying overnight with Daniela and Nigel. The plan was that after dinner we'd meet up with some of the other performers in Stroud, just to plan our online rehearsal sessions.'

'It's lucky that Nigel is home. His work can be quite stressful at times,' Elizabeth explains. 'He's involved in projects all around the world, and it doesn't matter what time of the day, or night, whenever there's a problem, he's expected to drop everything and go. It must be so frustrating for Daniela. Children are demanding when they're young and having two so close together is an even bigger challenge.'

Oliver shrugs his shoulders. 'I bet. If he does get called away I'm sure everyone will be fine if we end up changing our plans. I'll be back and forth while I build the structure, as and when I can, so we could always reschedule the troupe meet-up.'

Elizabeth beams at Oliver. 'You're free to come and go here as you please. Just liaise with Sienna. She's in charge and I couldn't cope without her. Isn't that right, my dear?'

Inwardly I groan. I was hoping to give Daniela a key to the barn and leave her to deal with Oliver.

'I'll give you my number,' I reply, trying to sound more enthusiastic than I feel.

'Perfect. A couple of weekends and the odd few days here and there, and I'll have it sorted, I'm sure.'

It seems that everyone is happy, then. I'm sure Daniela will be eager to give Oliver a hand and the new nanny will be a timely addition to the household.

5

Surprises All Round

After a weekend away visiting an old friend from my uni days, I'm still munching on my toast, enjoying a leisurely Monday morning breakfast before I head off to Silverberry Hall. When my phone rings I press speakerphone, then realise I have a blob of jam on my finger.

'Hello?' As I swipe it with a napkin, I only succeed in smearing the sweet stickiness over the screen.

'Is that Sienna Sanderson?'

'Yes.'

'It's Richard Stuart-Adams. You left a message for me to give you a call?'

That focuses my attention. I draw in a deep breath before I speak, plastering on a smile to lift my voice, even though I'm nervous. 'Hello, Richard, and thank you so much for getting back to me. I'm trying to make contact with your cousin Briony's son, um . . . James. Before I go any further, I'm contacting you in response to a solicitor's letter my employer received recently.'

'Oh, I see. I tend not to respond to numbers I don't recognise. I had a niggling feeling that it wasn't a spam call but your second message confirmed that.'

Well, he hasn't put the phone down on me yet, so that bodes well.

'My employer's late husband, and my late grandfather,

were both members of the same golf club as Briony's grandfather back in the day and—'

'Let me stop you there, as you aren't the first to ask; to my knowledge, James doesn't have any contact with the family at *all*. I think my aunt and uncle made that quite clear when someone called round to see them a while back.'

I had no idea it was done in person. 'What a shock that must have been for them, coming out of the blue like that,' I reply, sympathetically.

'It was.'

Goodness, I need to tread warily here. He doesn't sound angry, but he's edgy and naturally so. This is awkward as I have to be very careful what I say. I'm in two minds about which direction to go in and then I realise it's best to keep it simple.

'All I know is that it appears James was left some money in a will. I'm hoping to speak to him, or at least find some way of passing on the contact details so that he can get in touch with the Italian solicitors direct.'

There's a moment's silence. 'Italian? And he's been left some money, you say?'

'Yes.'

'As far as I'm aware, the person who came to see my aunt and uncle didn't mention anything about that, although it wouldn't have made any difference. The answer is that no one knows where he is.'

'I'm afraid I have no knowledge at all about how investigators work when they're trying to track down beneficiaries.'

I can't get myself in too deep for fear I'll unwittingly let something slip, but before I can make sense of my muddled thoughts, Richard begins to apologise.

'Sorry if I was a little abrupt. I guess they're reaching out to anyone who might have had any contact at all with my cousin.' He sighs. 'Our family was pulled apart over this, so it's difficult to discuss, you know . . . it feels disloyal. Briony never disclosed the name of James's father and that was her choice entirely. She was a very independent young woman and determined to make a good life for herself and her son as a single parent. I mean, this was thirty years ago, and my aunt and uncle felt strongly that James's biological father should be held accountable financially.'

My palms are literally sweating. This is much harder than I thought it would be, but I can't stop now. 'Please believe me when I say that I'm simply a third party who doesn't know the family at all. I think that by law the executors of the will have to make every effort to establish contact with beneficiaries.'

He sighs. 'It's ironic that something like this only surfaces after someone dies, isn't it? I guess there's no escaping one's conscience when you're facing your maker.'

'It seems so.'

'I was close to my cousin Briony right up until she moved away. After that I never heard from her again. It was her decision to cut all ties in the first place and I can't blame her. There was a lot of unpleasantness that never really went away. Things were said that couldn't be taken back and my uncle felt the gossip and speculation damaged not just Briony's reputation but his standing, too.'

His tone implies that's an end to it.

'Yes, and I can fully understand that.' I stop short of saying *but . . .*

There's a short pause and then, to my surprise, he continues.

'As a youngster growing up, James was obviously curious. At one of our family gatherings he asked me once what sort of man abandons a woman carrying his child and when I didn't answer him, he said, "A man who can't face up to his responsibilities, that's who," and I felt for him. He was still a boy, a mere eleven years old at the time but in some ways he'd had to grow up fast. It was always awkward when we all got together for Christmas, birthdays and anniversaries because my uncle felt Briony had shamed the family. James was growing increasingly protective of his mother and beginning to notice the disdain with which she was often treated. Briony was always on edge because she was there out of duty and feared that one day it would all erupt. She left before that happened.'

Thank goodness I haven't let Elizabeth's name slip. None of this is her fault and she's only trying to do the right thing, out of respect for her late son and James, not reopen old wounds.

'I'm not saying that money will change anything,' I reply, cringing as I say the words, 'but the fact that James is a beneficiary means he wasn't entirely forgotten.'

'Hmm, well the whole family suspects that Briony was eventually paid for her silence,' he replies, rather caustically. 'But it was the way she was treated that angered them.'

'Really?' I've read the solicitor's letter and the investigator's report. There's no mention of that at all.

'Briony suddenly came into some money. Sadly, it's the only logical explanation. How else could she afford to go from renting a flat, to being able to achieve her dream of buying a place in Cornwall?'

If that's true, no one else seems to be aware of it.

'Do you know where in Cornwall they settled? And how long ago are we talking about?'

There's an exasperated sigh. 'Umm . . . twenty-something years. At the time, James was in his first year at senior school. Briony told me that her son was the only person around her who made her smile, and she was determined that was all going to change.'

'Was that the last time you spoke to her?'

'Yes. They'd had a week's holiday, and on their return, she broke the news that they were moving. My dad told me that she'd had a big argument with my aunt and uncle, and I dropped by to see Briony at her flat to check that she was OK. The boxes were already packed. James was excited, and when she was out of earshot, he mentioned a harbour with tall ships, and he kept going on about the sea view from their new home. Oh, and that place with the domes.'

'The Eden Project?'

'I assume that's the one; I've never been there myself. It was just about to open its doors and he was looking forward to going there.'

'Did he say anything about the property itself?'

'No, it was Briony who mentioned that it was a small B&B hotel on a headland overlooking the sea. It sounded a bit isolated to me. But that's as much as I know.'

Just as I'm about to thank him for his time, Richard makes a parting comment.

'Look, I haven't repeated this to anyone. But maybe . . . I dunno, I believe in fate and perhaps I'm meant to share it just the once. Who knows? The money might come in handy for James if you can find him.'

I'm holding my breath, fearful of making any sound that might distract him for even a moment.

'It was just over ten, maybe eleven, years ago; James was in his early twenties back then. He rang me one day wanting to know if his grandparents were still alive. Whether it was guilt, or he knew at that time his mum wasn't well, I don't know. He didn't say much. I did keep his number but when I tried to call him a while later, it was no longer in use.'

And breathe. Anything is better than nothing. 'I really appreciate you sharing that with me, Richard.'

He gives a little laugh. 'It's not much, so good luck if you manage to get anywhere!'

I only have one question left to ask. 'I don't suppose you have any idea whether Briony and James changed their names?'

'If either of them had still been using her original surname, the investigator would probably have found them. My aunt and uncle received an unsigned letter telling them that Briony had died; they assumed it was from James, but there was no return address.'

It's hard not to feel deflated. 'Well, thank you for sharing that with me and for your honesty. If he doesn't want to be found, then that's his right. I really appreciate your call and I'm sorry to have troubled you.'

As I'm about to disconnect he blurts out, 'The day James got in touch, I heard someone in the background shout out "Ash", but I can't say for sure they were calling for him. Sorry.' And with that the line goes dead.

I stare at the phone feeling dejected. Instead of real clues what I have is a conundrum. I was hoping Richard could get a message to James and simply give him my number, or email address. It will take one heck of a lot of research to try to pinpoint where they might have settled and there are no guarantees James hasn't moved on since his mother's death.

Elizabeth will be disappointed, so I jump online and look for B&Bs and small hotels in Cornwall in an isolated location with a sea view. This could take a while, but I want to demonstrate that I gave it my best shot.

By mid-morning, I've managed to firm-up the arrangement with the parish choir for the pre-party festivities, and when I asked the Christmas carollers who will be performing in the barn if they could come in costume, they were delighted.

After letting Elizabeth down gently when I told her about my conversation with Richard, I sowed the seed that finding James isn't going to be easy. So, any good news I can pass on today has been more than welcome. It's important to keep her spirits up until it dawns on her that I'm unlikely to succeed in tracking down her grandson.

However, I can't take any credit for the lift having Oliver around has given her. He arrived late Saturday afternoon and he's staying with Daniela until tomorrow afternoon, so he's been constantly back and forth. Elizabeth mentioned that yesterday the two of them were busy working in the barn and she invited them to take afternoon tea with her. That put a smile on my face because it means that Nigel was home to look after the children and Daniela would have appreciated that.

Feeling rather pleased with myself as I'm just about to put another tick in a box on the spreadsheet, I glance up at the clock on the wall in front of me to see that I'm late for an important appointment with Elizabeth and Grandma Charlotte. Grabbing my coat off the back of the study door, I hurry over to the stable block.

'Hi, ladies. Sorry I'm running a little late, but I have more good news. How're you both getting on?'

In advance of setting up the real Christmas trees in the house, the main barn and the grounds in the run-up to the party, Elizabeth and Grandma are busy dressing two fake trees to decide on this year's style. I moved all of the boxes of decorations in here, so they have virtually every colour imaginable at their fingertips. After all, this is a major decision. They still haven't found a compromise between a rainbow effect, or a colour-coordinated look, hence today's little session.

Elizabeth straightens, standing back to survey the two trees. Grandma's is reminiscent of my childhood Christmases, whereas hers is a soft pale blue and silver. They both look at me expectantly, as if I'm the judge and the jury.

'What do you think?' Elizabeth encourages me to give an answer and my heart sinks in my chest.

'Well . . . I think they're both amazing!' I exclaim, which makes the two ladies turn to look at each other and start laughing.

'Really?' Grandma cajoles.

'The vibrant, multi-colours will be perfect for the courtyard. And I love the soft blue and the white theme for the barn, it has that timeless look. Don't we have some white Christmas roses with feathers?'

Their eyes widen. 'Oh, Elizabeth,' Grandma exclaims, 'Sienna is right!'

'Do you remember, Charlotte? I think it was about four years ago. The theme was snowflakes and feathers.'

'Who could forget?' Grandma gushes. 'The ladies were very inventive when it came to their costumes, and it was like something out of a film.'

I shake my head at them, laughing. The men struggled and I had call, after call, asking for inspiration. So, I came up with the idea of them dressing in formal suits, to show off their partners more elegant costumes, and wearing top hats adorned with feathers. That year, in the run-up to the festive season, I don't think there was a single second-hand top hat for sale online that wasn't snapped up by one of our partygoers.

'Which means,' Elizabeth sighs, 'we need to open all of the boxes, Charlotte.'

'I can help,' I offer.

Elizabeth gives me an apologetic glance. 'I was rather hoping you could give Oliver a hand. Daniela has the children today and he's all on his own. I'm sure he'd really appreciate a little help if you don't mind. And what's the good news you mentioned?'

'I've managed to talk Harry, from Brentwood Farm, into lending a hand to run the hot chestnut stall. We're going to get together to figure out what we'll need. He thinks there are some old carts in their hayloft no one wants, and he has a grill. I'll be heading up to the farm sometime soon to check them out.'

Elizabeth gives me a beaming smile. 'Oh, fingers crossed they'll do the trick! You know, Freddie would have dearly loved to have included the children given that we're turning back the clock.'

Grandma is standing behind her, and she pulls a face.

'Um . . . it goes on until very late and little ones get grouchy when they're tired,' I point out.

Elizabeth frowns because she knows I'm right; however, I can see Grandma's expression and we can both feel her sense of disappointment.

'What if we bring the pre-party carolling on the green into

the courtyard this year? Most of the local families bring their children along and we can have mince pies and hot drinks, as usual, and we could put on a little entertainment, too.'

It's extra work I could do without but it's worth it to see how it's lifting Elizabeth's spirits as she replies.

'I can feel a new tradition beginning, Sienna. Maybe Santa himself could put in an appearance!'

It's like watching a tiny snowball rolling downhill and seeing it grow exponentially before my eyes, but I grin back at her indulgently. 'I'll try my best.'

Grandma sighs, happily. 'Without a doubt you are a shining star.'

Hmm . . . I don't know about that, *mad* is the word that's running through my head right now. As if I don't have enough on my plate already!

'Hi, Oliver. Elizabeth suggested I pop in to see if there's anything I can do.'

It's quite a surprise to see him wearing a pair of old jeans and a thick, navy-blue Aran jumper that looks well loved.

He turns his head, raising an eyebrow. 'I never say no to a little help. Actually, I'm glad you're here, as I wanted to check that you're happy this addition I've built to the stage doesn't extend out too far. I did ask Elizabeth, but she said you're in charge.' He flashes me a silly grin.

Great! It's not exactly little but rather begrudgingly I have to admit that not much thought went into building the original podium. The rectangular raised area simply allows large gatherings to see what's going on. A lot of charity events are held in here throughout the year and it's multi-functional; from auctions to the annual flower shower, it's simply a focal point in the cavernous space.

I stare at the oddly shaped framework he's working on. 'Can you show me how it'll look when it's finished?'

'Sure. I might need a hand butting it up to the edge, as it's a bit unwieldy to move around until I fix the top on.'

'That's not a problem.' I'm always happy to roll up my sleeves.

However, when we start trying to move the carcass, it's a lot heavier than I expected.

'Sorry, it has to be sturdy as it's going to take a lot of weight,' he explains.

The fact that Oliver is apologising is a surprise. I thought he was rather stand-offish when we were in the pub. Is he being overtly friendly because it's in his interests to do so? I wonder.

After a bit of grunting and groaning, we manoeuvre it into place and stand back. Now I understand what he's trying to do.

'Right, I get it.'

He nods his head. 'The main prop is circular and has to be big enough for someone to step inside it. But the other actors need to be able to pass either side of it. I'm creating a wedge-shaped extension to keep it to the minimum. The problem I have is how to attach it to what you have there already, given that it's a temporary fixture. Safety is my biggest concern, with eight people moving around, two of them under the age of ten.'

'Once you've put on the top, won't the weight alone anchor it?'

He rubs his hand along his chin. 'I'll source the heaviest chipboard I can find, but I wouldn't like to take the risk of having it free-standing, to be honest.'

'What if you made it a part of the permanent structure?' I suggest.

He looks surprised. 'Well, that would be easier, obviously.'

'Come with me. I think we have some of the flooring we used on the main stage stored in the stables.' His face immediately lights up. 'I will warn you, though. If Elizabeth, or my grandma, ask you for your comments when we're walking through about which Christmas tree you prefer, it's better to say they're both wonderful.'

He pulls a grimace. 'Thanks for the heads-up, Sienna. It's appreciated!'

If Oliver keeps this up, I think we're going to get on just fine.

It's early evening when there's a knock on my door and I'm shocked to see Daniela standing there with a cool bag in one hand.

'This is a surprise!' I gasp, wondering what's going on.

'I hear that you were working alongside Oliver today. I thought you deserved a little treat,' Daniela muses.

I step back and indicate for her to go through into the kitchen.

'Bribery?'

There's a soft chuckle and she talks as she walks. 'He didn't make the best first impression when we had lunch together at The Sailor's Retreat, did he? The truth is that he was nervous.'

She puts the cool bag down on the table and lifts out a crock pot.

'It's beef in red wine. Just reheat it in the oven for about thirty minutes. It's the least I can do.'

'Nerves . . . hmm. Anyway, he seemed more relaxed today.'

'Oliver was just telling Nigel how helpful you've been, and this is by way of a thank you for jumping in and getting hands-on when it should have been me rolling up my sleeves.'

'It's my job to be helpful. Besides, after getting Elizabeth excited about featuring a live performance, you came to my rescue when my hopes had been dashed.' I give her a rueful smile. 'Do you have time for a glass of wine, or do you have to rush back?'

She's already slipping off her coat. 'No. I left the guys to crack open a beer as the kids are sound asleep, so I'm good for a bit.'

As I grab two glasses and a bottle of wine from the fridge, I talk over my shoulder. 'How did it go last Thursday with the nanny?'

'We spent the entire day playing with the children. Ursula is going to be a godsend; they warmed to her immediately and Pixie has a new best friend. Her aunt lives in one of the Georgian houses up by the cricket green and she's recently moved in with her. She's twenty-eight and gave up her full-time job in tele sales, which was based in Plymouth, to follow her passion. She's doing a BA in photography with the Open University. If it goes well, she's willing to do more than just two days a week.' Daniela is clearly excited about that prospect.

'It sounds like you have a plan in mind.'

'Honestly? I'd love to have my mornings free so I can work on a few projects and spend my afternoons with the kids. If all goes well, I think she'd be up for that.'

'And Nigel is in agreement?'

She grins at me as I pour the wine. 'He simply wants a quiet life and I get that, given how hard he works.'

'But he promised you he won't get pulled away at weekends quite so often?'

She gives me a sober look. 'Promising is one thing, making that happen is another. He's paid to troubleshoot the problems and it's what pays the bills. Having Ursula around will take the pressure off me, and I won't feel so gutted when he does have to drop everything and go.'

Her eyes are shining; she has her sparkle back and it's good to see. 'I'm so pleased for you, Daniela.'

'I know I'll be a better mum if I'm not quite so stressed,' she admits, as I hand her a glass. 'I was at the end of my tether and beginning to take my frustration out on Nigel.'

It's true to say that I had noticed a little tension creeping in between them. I'd assumed it was just tiredness and it would pass in time. 'I should imagine it's hard to go from having a job that fires you up, to being at home all day.'

'Working at The Old Playhouse in Stroud was my dream. I loved directing the productions, but I also love writing plays. Nigel is wonderful, and he understands I'm lost without some sort of creative outlet. But he also needs a wife who can run the household and take care of the family. This way we're both happy. There are no guarantees the plays I write will sell, but who knows? If I don't try, I'll always wonder *what if?* and that's no example to set our children, is it?'

'No,' I state, firmly, 'it isn't. I think that deserves a toast!'

'Here's to a bright future for us all,' she replies as we chink glasses. 'And Oliver was certainly singing your praises when he finished for the day.'

I look at her askance. 'I was just doing my job. Elizabeth said I should give him a hand. To be honest with you, she and Grandma are still sorting out the Christmas decorations and I'd rather say my piece and leave them to it.'

Daniela gives me a knowing smile. 'They're such great friends, but poles apart on some things, aren't they?'

'Tell me about it.' I smile back at her. But there's a question I need to ask. 'You and Oliver get on well. You never mentioned him to me, after I returned to Darlingham.'

Daniela looks at me rather blankly. 'He was just one of the crowd of people I hung around with.'

'But he was in your play.'

'Yes. For an amateur, he's a great actor and I was delighted when he said he'd take on the role. Actually, it cemented our growing friendship. He brought a lot more than just his passion for acting to the table. He brought his design ideas, too.'

'Was there ever anything romantic going on between the two of you?' I venture to ask.

'No! He was fun to be around, that's all.'

I glance at her, and I can see there isn't a hint of hesitation in her eyes.

'He was involved with a classmate, though,' she confides. 'I don't know if you remember Wendy?'

Oh. 'The party girl?'

'Yep. That's the one. Except that Oliver thought he was in

love with her. It kicked off big time. He felt that he made a bit of a fool of himself when he discovered their relationship was an open one.'

My jaw drops. 'Open for her, but not for him?'

'Precisely. He was devastated. I can tell you that it took a lot to get him back on track. She lived close to his parents, although they ended up moving.'

It seems I missed a lot of drama, and I'm not talking about a staged performance. 'That was a bit drastic, wasn't it?'

Daniela sighs. 'Oh, she wasn't the reason. His grandfather had a small farm on the outskirts of Bath. His grandfather's health was failing and his father took early retirement to keep it running. Oliver was going home at weekends, but his head was all over the place. I fear that it reminds him of some of his darkest times now and that's why he dreads going back there. He'd never admit it, of course, so keep this to yourself. He's very stiff-upper lip in that regard, like his father.'

Daniela certainly seems to know an awful lot about Oliver and his family, given that they were just *friends*.

I pull a sad face.

'Oliver loves his life in London,' she continues. 'It was the fresh start he needed and it's where he found success. It was the place to be for an up-and-coming set designer. Now, of course, he prefers working on videos. A lot of what he does involves digital backgrounds and layered screens, not that I really understand much about how green screens and holographs work.'

'It sounds complicated.'

'It is . . . he knows his stuff.'

I look at her, pensively. 'You kept that friendship very quiet,' I tease. I can't recall even Nigel ever mentioning Oliver's name. 'And you remained in regular contact?'

'Not exactly . . . *regular*, but our interests are very similar and we've run ideas past each other from time to time. He was a great contact to have once I got my first job,' she admits.

'I guess that planning your engagement party and then *the* biggest wedding of the year around here, while overseeing the redecoration of that beautiful old house of yours, meant you had your hands full.'

'I don't do things by halves, do I? Having found the man of my dreams, it was all a bit of a whirlwind. But Oliver understands and it's always been *quid pro quo*. I put him in touch with some of my contacts at work and as a set and stage design consultant, he appreciated the leads.'

The question I can't ask but that I am starting to wonder about is how he took the news when Daniela told him she was getting engaged . . . I'm still surprised she was able to talk him into getting involved in the play as a favour. When it comes to Daniela, it seems that he can't say no and, quite frankly, I do find that a little strange.

'It's good of him to come to our rescue,' I reflect, soberly.

'I knew he wouldn't leave me hanging. I know that the city suits him,' she replies. 'It's easy to be anonymous and successful, which he is. His private life is just that – private.'

'Does he have a significant other?'

She gives a dismissive laugh. 'From what I gather, girlfriends come and go. None of them last longer than a few dates. I fear he's a confirmed bachelor because having had his heart broken once, I'm not sure he'll risk it again.'

We lapse into silence. Daniela and I have never kept secrets from each other, but I can't help wondering whether she's simply choosing not to tell me everything.

'Well, thanks for the casserole. And I can't wait to meet Ursula.'

'She's such a sweetheart but my, do Clara and William sit up and pay attention when she talks. I'm actually learning a lot of parenting tips from her. She said her mother wouldn't take any nonsense from her and while she hasn't said it in so many words, I'm sure she thinks I'm a bit of a pushover.'

'You are,' I laugh, good-naturedly.

'I know, but I do try. Ursula has eight siblings, and she says she was a quasi-mum to the four younger ones.'

We sit in silence, sipping our wine while we consider how lucky we are. And yes, I did long for a little sister, or a brother, but eight is incomprehensible.

Wednesday, 1st November

6

The Hard Work Begins

Having spent all day yesterday clearing out the stone shelter opposite the big barn, today I have the estate's head groundsman, Victor, here to help me get it into shape.

'You're hoping to turn this into an outdoor kitchen?' He starts belly-laughing.

'No . . . just a food preparation and covered barbecue area.'

Victor scratches his head and I follow his gaze. Yes, all the piles of rotten wooden pallets have been taken to the tip and I've swept the floor clean, but it looks rough.

'Where do we start?' he asks, looking bemused.

'I'll go and change into my waterproofs ready to jet-wash the flagstones. Could you start brushing off the ceiling and the three walls? It has to be cobweb free.'

He looks at me as if I'm crazy.

'I know . . .' I reply, slightly apologetically. 'I don't like spiders, but they'll get to live another day if you brush them off. Any that are still here when I get back are in for a cold shower they might not survive.'

Victor bursts out laughing once again, as I grin back at him. 'I won't be long.'

He heads off to the storeroom to get the equipment we need, and I make my way over to the boot room in the main house. I hear a car door slam, then a second, and the sound of two men talking. When I saw Elizabeth first thing, she didn't mention she had visitors today. I thought Grandma was going to be here most of the day helping her pack up the boxes of decorations they sorted through to find the feathers and the snowflakes.

When I swing open the back door there's no one around and it doesn't take long to grab the waterproof all-in-one, an extra pair of thick socks and my sturdy wellington boots from my locker. As I stride back towards the shelter, I notice that the barn door is open. I pop my head inside and am surprised to see Oliver and another man carrying a sheet of the spare flooring that was stored in the stables.

'Oh, hi, Sienna. This is my dad, Keith.' A head appears around the side of the massive panel and the man gives me a warm smile. 'I didn't like to knock on the door up at the Hall and disturb Elizabeth, so no one knows we're here. I collected the key from Daniela on my way over. I hope you don't mind that we made a start, as I knew you wouldn't be far off.'

'No, that's fine and it's nice to meet you, Keith. I thought Daniela was giving you a hand today?'

'Me, too. I called at the house and Ursula said she left early and won't be back until mid-afternoon. She has an interview, apparently. I assumed you'd know all about it.'

'It's news to me. Anyway, I'll be working in the courtyard most of this morning. If you need anything, just shout.'

'Will do, thanks! Right, Dad, we need to turn this around and flip it before we lay it on the structure.'

I leave them to it and join Victor.

'Watch out, there's a few big 'uns scampering about. I wouldn't want one of them tripping you up,' he bellows.

I roll my eyes at him. 'It's not funny. It makes my skin crawl thinking about one of them falling down on me.'

'Well, I've brushed that wall on the left, but it'll need a quick flash over with the water to wash off any loose particles. I'll continue working back this way, but I don't think I'll hold you up. It's coming off easy enough.'

I unwind the cable and walk over to the side of the barn

to use one of the outside plugs. As I lift the flap on the box, I catch sight of Oliver and his dad entering the stables. It'll be good to use up some of the offcuts that have been hanging around in there for a few years now. Freddie always said that if you hold on to something long enough, you'll find a use for it one day and he was right.

A while later I spot a movement out of the corner of my eye. Oliver is standing there with his hands thrust into his pockets.

'We're heading down to the pub to grab something to eat, Sienna, and wondered if you wanted to join us? You've had quite a morning, and you must be in need of a warm-up.'

It's true to say that I'm feeling both a little cold and a bit damp from the exertion. Victor looks over at me, his face brightening, and I can tell he's ready for a break.

'Um . . . that would be nice, thanks. If you go on ahead, I'll join you in about twenty minutes?'

'Great.'

'See you in a bit.'

Victor climbs down off the stepladder to rest his broom against the wall.

'He's been about quite a bit lately,' he ponders.

'Yes. Oliver is building an extension to the stage ready for a play that's being performed on Christmas Eve.'

'Oh, I see.' With that, he gives me a funny look.

'What?'

'The missus mentioned it; rumour is that he's an old friend of Daniela's.'

My brow wrinkles as I look at him questioningly. 'Yes. They were at university together. So come on then, what's the word on the street?'

He gives me a bit of a guilty look. 'She overheard someone say that with Nigel often working away from home, he probably isn't happy knowing that his wife is entertaining an old flame.' Victor lowers his voice, conspiratorially. 'To be honest, that annoyed the heck out of me. I don't like to think of a nice couple like that being talked about behind their backs. No good ever comes of this type of silly gossip.'

'Old flame?' I splutter. 'Someone had better put them straight pretty quickly. Oliver's here because he designs sets and backgrounds for videos. Daniela called in a favour as Elizabeth wants to wow her partygoers this year. Putting on a play was my idea, not hers.'

He grimaces. 'Ooh . . . I don't usually get involved. I like to keep my head down, but I'll definitely pass that on to the wife.'

'Well, maybe this is one occasion when you can quote me.' I grin at him.

'Is that an order?' He cocks an eyebrow at me, grinning from ear to ear.

Now it's my turn to belly-laugh. The fact that he chose to mention this to me, is telling. I like Victor, he's a good man.

When I hurry into The Sailor's Retreat, I'm delighted to see that they're all trimmed up and looking very festive. Even better, Oliver got here early enough to snag the table next to the log fire and the heat will be most welcome.

'Well done, you!' I exclaim, as I settle down into the chair he pulls out for me. 'I'm sorry I'm running late but I had to jump into a hot shower to warm up a little. Where's your dad?'

'He sends his apologies, but he had to head back to the farm. One of the generators has stopped working, apparently.'

'Oh, that's a shame. I don't know about you, but I'm starving.'

Oliver's face lights up as he hands me a menu. 'Me, too. I like the sound of the fisherman's pie. Have you tried it?'

'Yes. It has chunks of cod and haddock, and large prawns, with a cheesy potato topping. I think I'll go for that, too.'

He looks up, and almost immediately manages to catch Ruby's attention. Was she keeping an eye out for him? I ponder.

'Are you ready to order now or are you waiting for Daniela?' she checks.

'No, it's just us,' I confirm. I can't help but wonder whether Ruby has heard the rumours, too. If Oliver knew, I think he'd be horrified.

'What can I get you both?' Ruby grins at me before turning her attention to Oliver.

He's a handsome man and it's no wonder she's looking at him all starry-eyed.

'Two fisherman's pies and what are you drinking, Sienna?'

I glance at the empty coffee mug in front of Oliver and the half-full jug of water on the table.

'Oh,' he says, dismissively, 'I just had a thirst on. I'm up for a glass of wine, or a beer. What about you?'

Ruby interjects. 'You could be the first to try our festive hot punch. It's certainly cold enough out there today to warrant it.'

Oliver looks at me and I nod my head.

'Two for the punch as well, then, please. Thanks, Ruby.'

Her eyebrows lift a little and as she looks directly at me there's a teasing glint in her eye. I'm guessing that she's heard the rumours about Daniela and Oliver and is curious as to why I'm the one lunching with him today. I seriously hope I'm not the next in line for the rumour mill.

While we await our drinks, Oliver pours me some water. I will admit that it's hard to believe this is the same man I sat here cautiously observing a mere two weeks ago. That day he was rather edgy and – dare I say it – a little stand-offish. Now he looks comfortable, wearing a grey marl, heavy knit jumper and an old pair of jeans.

'Do you enjoy getting hands-on?' I ask.

The corners of his mouth lift a little. 'It shows, does it? Yes, I miss the old days. I mean, when I was still learning, and a lot of my projects were trial and error. Often done for free, as I worked with a lot of community amateur dramatic groups. Financial support for performances is patchy and, in some instances, non-existent.'

'And now most of your time is spent in front of a PC?'

'Yes.'

Ruby bustles over to us, setting down two tall latte glasses with handles. 'Here you go.'

'Are you allowed to tell us what's in it, or is the recipe a closely guarded secret?' Oliver enquires.

'Um . . . red wine, apple cider, local honey, some orange juice and a mixture of spices.'

'It sounds amazing. Great suggestion, thanks.'

'Well, if the smell is anything to go by, Ruby, we're in for a treat,' I remark, raising my glass in Oliver's direction.

'It's my pleasure; enjoy! Your food will be here shortly, guys.'

We cautiously chink before taking a sip.

'Hmm . . . it's lovely, although it's a generous serving. I'm getting cardamom and cinnamon, for sure,' I enthuse.

'It's not quite as potent as some I've tried,' Oliver replies. 'Adding apple cider instead of brandy, or orange liqueur, is a novel idea. I'll pass that little tip onto my dad. Have you warmed up a little? You looked frozen earlier on.'

'I was. Cold, wet and miserable, but the heat from that fire is bliss.'

'It's not the best day to be jet-washing an open-fronted building,' he points out.

'Tell me about it but it was either that or sweeping the walls and rafters. Victor doesn't bat an eyelid at the size of the spiders, whereas I'd be screeching my head off.'

'I see, and why are you cleaning it up at this time of the year?'

'We're turning it into an outdoor food preparation area for the party. The caterers will rock up with their state-of-the-art roasting kit. It'll take nine hours to cook a whole hog to feed up to a hundred and fifty people. We can get them to spit-roast the turkeys too, for Christmas Day.'

'This party must cost a small fortune.'

'It does but it's in aid of charity. The Blakesleys foot the bill for the evening. The tickets aren't that pricey, considering the buffet is sumptuous and each year the entertainment is different. Because ticket numbers are limited, there's an exclusivity factor.'

'Ah, and that guarantees it raises a lot of cash.'

'Yes, but people come from all walks of life and it's not about those who can afford to pay an exorbitant amount. On the night, guests are free to make a donation, too. Envelopes are sealed and unmarked; I'm always surprised at how generous people are.'

Oliver presses his lips together. 'I see. I think that's a great idea. It certainly embodies the spirit of Christmas, you know . . . it's not about receiving gifts, but the giving.'

Our food arrives and we're both too hungry not to dig straight in. In fact, there are several minutes of silence only masked by the growing background noise.

After several satisfying bites, my stomach is feeling much happier and I'm as warm inside as I am out.

'It was kind of your dad to come and help this morning.'

Oliver rests his knife and fork on the plate, but I notice that he's already demolished a third of the luxury fish pie.

'Mum insisted. She's delighted to have her son home again for an unexpected stay.'

I look at him askance. 'Oh, I assumed you were staying at Daniela's.'

'I . . . um . . . don't want to impose. Daniela has her hands full as it is.' He shifts uneasily in his seat and that's a sure sign there's something he isn't telling me.

'I thought you preferred the delights of London to the rustic vibe of the country?'

'Maybe I'm warming to it. Plus, I can keep my parents happy as well as reducing my travel time.' He gives an awkward little laugh. 'This performance means a lot to Daniela, and I owe her, big time. Besides, I don't cut corners and when I commit to something I give it my all. I want the props to grab the audience's attention; it's a wonderful, if short, Christmas story and it deserves the perfect setting to show it off.' With that, Oliver begins eating again.

'It can't be easy taking time off work at such short notice though.'

'Not for me, being self-employed. I've set myself up in my parents' study. I don't work normal office hours and never have. I often work through the night and catnap during the day when I'm really busy. That's why I'm still single; as my mum points out, no one would put up with my erratic lifestyle. Besides, the drive to Darlingham is less than an hour, and as I'll be back and forth for a bit until everything comes together; it makes sense.'

Or is it quieter without a wailing baby, a tantrummy toddler and . . . just maybe . . . treading warily around Daniela's husband? I contemplate. After a couple of minutes, Oliver finishes eating and pushes his plate away, content to sip his mulled wine.

'Anyway, it feels wrong that you know all about me, but I know nothing at all about you. Other than the fact that you work for your grandmother's best friend, Elizabeth.'

Now he's purposely changing the subject.

I grimace. 'There's not a lot to tell.'

'Oh, don't give me that. I suspect your life is way more interesting than mine.'

'Hardly,' I gasp. 'You must meet some fascinating people in your line of work.'

I finish my meal and settle back in my chair, contentedly.

'It's all video calls these days. When I am required to be onsite for something it's usually sorting out the hitches. If you're imagining me rubbing shoulders with some famous names and having a blast, I usually arrive when everyone is tired, and fed up because something has gone wrong.'

'What sort of problems crop up?'

'Music videos have a lot of working parts on the day, although some elements and special effects are added after the filming is done. But no matter how detailed the designs

I submit are, it's down to the execution. If it's not done right, it can be a bit of a disaster and that's when I get a call and the clock is ticking. It's my job to come up with a quick fix.'

He stares at me, tilting his head to indicate it's my turn.

'What can I say? I was born in a thatched cottage a short walk from here but now I live in a two-bed cottage on the Silverberry estate. I've worked at the Hall for a little over seven years and I love my job.'

Oliver continues staring at me. 'And?'

'That's me in a nutshell. I lead a quiet life.'

'The day Daniela introduced us you mentioned that you went to university in Bristol, too. What were you studying?'

I shift uneasily in my seat. He's got a good memory. 'A BSc in marketing.'

'Ah, that's why our paths never crossed. You didn't hang around with the drama club lot. I would definitely have remembered you if we had ever met! I bet that was interesting.'

'Hmm.' I shrug off his comment, as it's a touchy subject.

Unfortunately, he doesn't take the hint. 'If it's not too personal a question, what brought you back to the village to be a personal assistant at Silverberry Hall, rather than following a career in marketing?'

Oliver has been honest with me, but this is tough.

'I quit after the end of the first year.'

'You did?' He looks shocked. 'I vaguely recall Daniela telling me about one of her room-mates moving out when they were looking for a replacement. So that was you.'

His reaction confirms that she didn't go into details. It was an awful time leading up to my departure, but Daniela always had my back. I was difficult to be around at times and the last thing I needed was getting dragged out to noisy pubs and gatherings, and she understood that.

'I wasn't into socialising much back then. I wasn't enjoying the course and I was worried about my father. He hadn't been well for a little while. He was eventually diagnosed with leukaemia and died eighteen months later. I was angry with life and just about everything else, but most of all I wanted to spend some time with him.'

Well, that's put a damper on a relaxing lunch.

'I'm really sorry to hear that, Sienna. It must have been harrowing for you and your family.'

'It was. And what followed was a very troubled year, during which I tried everything. From waitressing to dog-walking. I don't know how my family and friends put up with me if I'm honest. I should have been supporting them in their grief, not the other way around.'

He sits forward in his seat, leaning in and lowering his voice. 'Look, everyone reacts differently when they lose someone. That's nothing to feel guilty about.' His expression is full of empathy and it's rather touching.

'In hindsight I see that now, but at the time I was a mess. It was Freddie, Elizabeth's late husband, who convinced me they needed a personal assistant and keeping busy did the trick. I turned myself around, but without that encouragement I dread to think what might have happened.'

'So, aside from your year in Bristol, you meant it when you said you've always lived here. That's quite something.'

'Not *here*, as in Darlingham. I was engaged for two years and lived with my partner in a little hamlet the other side of Frampton on Severn. We broke up at the start of the summer.'

He does a double take. 'Oh. Goodness, no wonder you want a quiet life now. That's quite a roller coaster of a journey you've been on.'

'And some,' I reply, sounding rather jaded. 'Liam cheated on me, and I found out.'

Oliver lets out an ironic chuckle. 'How on earth did he think he was going to get away with it? The problem with living in a small community is that it's almost impossible to keep a secret. Honestly, I don't know the guy, but he certainly wasn't deserving of someone like you.'

I've been in receipt of people's sympathy, compassionate hugs and kindness, but for a virtual stranger to say that after a short acquaintance, it really hits home. Oliver is right . . . I didn't deserve Liam's betrayal. I just have to keep reminding myself of that.

7

Teamwork Triumphs

It's late evening and I'm relaxing in front of the fire when my phone kicks into life.

'Sienna, are you sitting down?' Daniela's voice instantly brings a smile to my face. She sounds excited.

'Yes,' I groan, trying to ignore my aching muscles. 'Sorry! I'm exhausted and I've got the mid-week slump; it's been quite a taxing day. Come on then, tell me exactly what made you suddenly take off without saying a thing. Naturally, I'm intrigued.'

'It came out of the blue and you won't believe it; I'm still pinching myself as I keep thinking I must be dreaming! I sent out a few emails to some former contacts in the business. Several people responded to say they'd keep my details and pass them on if an opportunity arises, which is a polite way of saying don't bother me again. After all, my track record ground to a complete halt after I gave up work. However, one old colleague mentioned a new project which he thinks might be of interest to me.'

'Goodness, no wonder you just upped and left.'

'With less than twenty-four hours' notice to meet him for lunch, it was panic stations. If it weren't for Ursula, I couldn't have pulled it off and she agreed to cover until Nigel arrived home last night. I did warn her that sometimes he's called away, so she was ready to stay overnight if necessary.'

I can tell the adrenaline is pumping, so great is her excitement.

'It's to do with the reopening of a grand old stately home; Inglewick Hall in Derbyshire is gearing up to welcome visitors again. The current owners are looking for a script based on the true story of the family who lived there until the nineteen eighties. They intend to film the performance, which will be a part of the official opening ceremony and future visitors will be able to sit and watch it in their small screening room.'

'Oh, Daniela, that's fabulous news!'

'I was shown around and given free rein to take lots of photos. Edward, who is coordinating the event, is also going to send me a mass of files with old photographs and documents. He will also put me in touch with the family's historian. It's a huge task, as I have to wade through it all to piece together how best to tell the history of the house through the generations.'

I'm almost lost for words. 'That's incredible. What a coup!'

'I know! It combines my love of history with my passion for creating a theatrical spectacle. You'll love this bit. I asked him why he was taking a chance on me, when I'm only just tentatively dipping my toes back into the water. Edward told me that he saw the original performance of the short play that we're going to be putting on for Elizabeth's Christmas Eve party. He was on the board of the charity our drama club performed it in aid of, on the night.'

My jaw drops. 'You must share this with Elizabeth tomorrow. She'll be delighted to hear that!'

Daniela clears her throat. 'The thing is . . . I have a bit of a problem.'

'You do?'

'I've agreed with Nigel that Ursula will work five mornings a week from now on, so that I can throw myself into this project. The fee isn't huge but, as you said, it's a coup. It's the work I might get off the back of it that is important. The thing is, I won't be around much to help Oliver.'

My face brightens. 'Oh, that's not a problem. His dad was with him today and I can always step in whenever he requires a second pair of hands. We . . . um . . . ended up having lunch together at the pub.'

'You did?' Her surprise is very evident. 'I feared the two of you got off to a bit of a rocky start.'

'We did. I thought he was rather offhand, to be honest, but I can see now that you were right, I think he was nervous. I was just a tad sceptical because he seemed to bend over backwards to charm Elizabeth. That irked me, as I thought he was merely sucking up to her.'

She starts laughing. 'If he's nervous it means he was trying to impress you. If he's relaxed, as it sounds like he was with Elizabeth, it means he's comfortable being himself.'

'And he wasn't with me that day the three of us had lunch together?'

'I wonder why. It's not like you were judging him, was it?'

I can't suddenly blurt out that I felt he was disappointed it wasn't a cosy lunch for two, can I?

'What exactly did you tell Oliver about me, because you certainly didn't say a lot about this mystery man from your past before we all met up.'

Daniela chuckles. 'I simply told him that you're my bestie from school and that you're single, attractive and intelligent!'

Oh no. 'You didn't!' No wonder he was nervous.

'I knew this little performance for the Christmas Eve party wouldn't get off the ground without his skills and, equally as important, he's perfect in the role of Adam. But after we'd spoken, I . . .' She pauses, ominously. 'He's a great guy and he's sensitive, always was. I thought the two of you might hit it off.' At least she has the grace to sound ever so slightly apologetic.

'Well, I don't know about *hitting it off*, but he was friendlier today.' It wasn't just friendly; we got on really well. However,

I don't want to let her off the hook that easily. Daniela knows how I feel about people matchmaking and I'm no lost cause; I'm just not ready to think about dating again yet.

'Oh, Sienna . . . just give him a chance. He might continue to grow on you.'

I tut. 'Oliver said he owed you *big time*. What exactly did he mean by that?' My heart is thumping in my chest, and I don't know why.

'I told you about Wendy. What I didn't mention was that he started having anxiety attacks shortly after they broke up. I was the person he turned to because no one else was aware of what he was going through. Oliver admitted that he felt foolish and I decided that there was no way I was going to let him fall apart. He's a great guy and he deserved better. We'd spend hours chatting late into the night, and he often ended up crashing on the sofa bed at the house. Gradually, he put himself back together. We were what . . . twenty years old? Egos are fragile at that age, and everyone we mixed with at uni was talking about it. It turned out that the man also happened to be one of the tutors, which is why it became such a big thing.'

'So, when he graduated and headed straight to London and the bright lights, it was to escape?'

'Not really, although there's a lot to be said for bright lights and anonymity when you're heartily sick of being talked about. He slept on a friend's couch until he got on his feet. He had talent, and it was only a matter of time before someone offered him a job.'

'Oh, I see.'

'Oliver has succeeded in building up an impressive portfolio of clients and, usually, he's fine with strangers. He's just a bit of a . . . a loner, let's say.'

'So, it's not that he's allergic to the countryside, he just doesn't like people knowing his business. Village life must feel a little claustrophobic to him.'

'Precisely! Beneath that professional facade Oliver likes to present to the world, he's still a sensitive person. I thought that the two of you might . . . well, that it might develop into something a little more than a casual friendship.'

The woman who dropped out of uni, whose fiancé cheated on her and who ran home to hide in a tiny village as far away from a main road as you can get. I guess Oliver and I do have a thing, or two, in common – like wanting to hide our true selves away. I just didn't have the courage to distance myself from everyone I knew. Oliver and I chose to deal with our problems in two very different ways and I can't help wondering which was the easiest option. People I'm close to are still trying to interfere on my behalf, albeit with the very best of intentions, but some things in life you have to work out for yourself. There are no short cuts.

The door to the study opens and Grandma's head appears. 'Good morning, Sienna. Are you terribly busy on this bright, but chilly, Thursday morning . . . oh, that's a silly question isn't it?' She laughs.

'No, it's fine. You caught me just in time, I'm about to head outside to work on the stone lean-to,' I reply, returning her warm smile. 'Come in and take a seat.'

'I was just wondering how it's going . . . you know, with regard to James.'

My brow furrows: Elizabeth doesn't like to chase me about it, and I suspect that she's asked Grandma to check whether there's any news.

'Look, Grandma, I will be honest and say that I don't think he wants to be found. Richard was the last person he spoke to and that was quite a long time ago. When he tried to call James back a while later, the number was no longer in use.'

She heaves a regretful sigh. 'Ah, I see. So, there's nothing to be done?'

Grandma is clearly disappointed and now I feel like I've failed both her and Elizabeth.

'With the limited information Richard was able to give

me,' I continue, 'I've been doing some online searches and have narrowed it down. Based on the scant information I have, I've mainly focused on larger B&Bs and small hotels within a few miles of Charlestown. He mentioned a headland with amazing sea views, so I've come up with a shortlist.'

'You have?' Her face immediately brightens.

'Yes, but it's taken hours of painstaking research and I'm sure I won't have caught them all. And I might have ruled out a few erroneously because Richard said it sounded like a rather isolated setting. And, of course, some businesses only advertise on their own websites.

'There are literally pages of different holiday accommodation search engines alone. It would be impossible to cover them all, but I have noticed the same properties coming up time and time again. So maybe I haven't missed as many as I imagine. I think it's down to fate now, more than luck, if I do manage to track him down.'

I keep it upbeat with a cautionary note, although it's hard not to disguise an air of pessimism. It's akin to looking for the proverbial needle in a haystack.

'It must seem like an impossibly daunting task, Sienna. What's the next step?'

I hoped it wouldn't come to this. 'I guess I'll have to jump in the car and visit each one. Richard mentioned hearing the name "Ash" being called out that day when James rang him. I can't exactly pick up the phone and ask whether they have someone working there with that name,' I point out. 'However, it's near enough to Mum for it to warrant a long weekend in the area, touring the most promising ones.'

'You won't mention it to her, will you?' Grandma checks, rather hesitantly.

'Of course not. I'll make up an excuse.'

Grandma chuckles. 'You'd better make it a good one. She's very perceptive is your mother.'

'I know. That's why I haven't phoned her yet. She'll be thrilled that I'm finally heading down to see her new home, so

I'm hoping if I have a friend in tow, it will be the perfect excuse to take some time out to do a little undercover investigation.'

'Aww . . . if Elizabeth wasn't so fragile at the moment, I'd offer to come with you.'

'No, Grandma. Mum would then go out of her way to escort us everywhere. And that's the real problem; I need an excuse to show someone around and do a little sightseeing of my own.'

'Ah, yes! If you're taking a few days' holiday with a friend, it's only natural you'd want to go exploring. Daniela might be up for that.'

Hmm . . . I doubt it. 'Given what she's just taken on there's no point in even asking her, but I have a couple of options.'

'It's kind of you to throw yourself into this,' Grandma continues. 'I know it doesn't sit well with you.'

I look at her, solemnly. 'I owe Elizabeth and Freddie so much, it's the least I can do.'

She reaches out to place her hand on my arm. 'I'm proud of you, Sienna. You're made of strong stuff. As Pops would have said, "That's my girl, she never gives up." I can actually hear his voice saying it in my head as I'm talking to you!'

Several hours later, the now pristine outdoor food preparation area is ready for inspection.

'Oh my! This is incredible.' Elizabeth marvels at the sight of the freshly scrubbed walls, beams and floors in the old stone lean-to. 'Are you still thinking of painting, or sealing, the walls?'

I glance across at Victor.

'No, Mrs Blakesley. The stonework soaked up a lot of water during the jet-washing so I think we're best off doing that in the spring. Paint would be likely to flake off, but sealing it is the best option if this isn't a one-off for this year.'

'It's certainly a bonus and I think that's the best way forward by the sound of it, so that would be wonderful, Victor. We'll be guided by you.'

He looks pleased with himself.

'Elizabeth, we originally intended to build a long wooden workbench against the back wall and maybe put a stainless-steel worktop on it. However, Victor says anything permanent will probably rust up during the long winter months, as the shelter is open to the winds and weather.'

She purses her lips. 'Ah . . . yes.'

We stare at each other for a few seconds, acknowledging that Freddie's wish was that next Easter Silverberry Hall would host a big community celebration with an Easter egg hunt and family-orientated games.

'Is there a solution?'

I smile at her. 'There is, but it would cost around twelve hundred pounds, whereas we have a good supply of wood and offcuts that could be used for free. We'd only need to buy the stainless-steel covering but it would deteriorate over time.'

'I'm listening,' she replies, sounding interested.

'You can get stainless-steel workbenches and preparation tables on wheels. It would require maybe a half a dozen of them to give the caterers enough working space. We'd have to store them in the stables when the outdoor food preparation area isn't in use, but it would be easy to bring them across when needed.'

'It's a one-off cost and it makes sense, Sienna. Please go ahead and order them. I love the idea of an outdoor facility and I can see us using it at Easter, and for summer barbecues as well. You've both done well to tackle this project, given how cold it's been, and I thank you for what must have been a damp and dreary task to undertake. But we don't have to worry about rain, sleet or snow now – the chef will be in the dry.'

'And with that hog roasting on the spit, the helpers will be warm, too!' Victor laughs and we both join in.

As I follow Elizabeth back to the house, she does a half-turn to look at me. 'You'll be needing some time off, I hear.' Her smile is a knowing one.

'Yes, a little trip to Cornwall is in order.'

'I know it's not the most convenient time of the year for you, as there's still so much to be organised for the party, but I appreciate it, Sienna. Take as long as you need.'

'It might require two trips to whittle down the list. It's not easy asking strangers questions. If I get what I think is a good lead, I may have to do a follow-up visit to see what else I can glean.'

Elizabeth nods her head in agreement. 'It means so much to me, although I realise it would be foolish to get my hopes up.'

I'm relieved to hear her say that. 'Let me do what I can, and we'll see what happens.'

Her smile is warm. 'Oh . . . yes, I nearly forgot. Daniela phoned first thing to tell me her good news. It presents Oliver with a problem, though.'

I nod my head in acknowledgement.

'I wonder how he feels, now that's he's taking over her role as stage manager? He's not about this morning, which is a shame. I was hoping to have a word with him. Do you think it will put him off?'

Why on earth didn't Daniela mention that when we spoke? I assumed she was simply dropping hints that he'd need help building and painting the props. Unless she's embarrassed, after admitting that she was hoping we'd *hit it off*. I did sort of tell her to back off, didn't I?

I know she has her hands full at the moment and she's so excited to get back to work, but I do think it's a little unfair to expect Oliver to pick up the slack. 'Um . . . I don't know, Elizabeth. I hope not.'

It simply confirms that Oliver just can't say no when it comes to Daniela.

'It would be a real shame if it does. If you think it's asking too much of him, will you let me know?'

This play has become a bit of a buzz word in the village, and it would be embarrassing now if it doesn't go ahead as planned.

'Yes, of course.'

'Good. I'll leave you to it, then, as I suspect you have something pressing to attend to.'

'Oh, yes . . . today I'm off to Brentwood Farm to inspect a pile of old farm carts and see if any of them can be salvaged.'

Elizabeth bursts out laughing. 'Only you could say something like that, and my instincts immediately tell me we're in for a treat! Don't overdo it, will you, my dear? You have a big heart but make some time for yourself. It's such a . . . romantic time of the year.'

Oh no! Not another person who thinks I should start socialising with intent. Intent to find a man!

'I'm happy doing what I do, Elizabeth. And it's a real bonus that I can go and stay with Mum and Greg. They can't wait to show me the house.'

'Now that puts a huge smile on my face. Make sure it's a bit of a holiday as well as . . .' She sighs. 'As well as a massive favour to me.'

'It's not a problem. I'll firm up the arrangements, but weekends work the best for me anyway as it's less disruptive.'

'If you're sure. We can manage here without you for a little while, if necessary, you know.' She gives a tinkling little laugh. 'That's the royal *we*, of course. I'll be pulling in your grandma for support. She won't let me get myself into any trouble and if there's anything you want us to do, or oversee while you're away, you can leave a detailed list. Together we'll make it happen.'

My eyes widen. 'Goodness, the two of you are a force to reckon with and it would be a very brave person who dared to upset your day!'

It's good to see her smiling and hear her laughing. Not many people could survive what she's been through over these last few months. Elizabeth and Grandma hail from a generation with gumption and being around them makes me try harder. And it's high time I got my act together on this trip to Cornwall because I can't keep putting it off forever.

'Am I intruding?'

It's early afternoon when Oliver appears, as I'm sorting through some of the old items stored in one of the horse stalls.

'No, not at all. I'm due up at the farm shortly. I'm hoping to salvage a few items but I wanted to see if there were any little treasures buried among this lot first.'

'What – tins of paint and pieces of old metal and wood?' He grins at me.

'Well, we need a few carts for the courtyard, and they'll probably be shabby. You never know what I might find to brighten them up.'

He rubs his hand along his chin, in thinking mode. 'If you'll give me a hand offloading my dad's van, I'll run you up there in case you find anything. We can bring it straight back.'

'That's a deal!' I reply enthusiastically.

'Great.'

We traipse over to the car park and when he opens the back doors I can see why he needed a large vehicle. The bed of the van is covered in narrow strips of white plastic and to one side, there's a stack of panels. 'None of this is excessively heavy, it's just awkward for one person to manoeuvre,' he explains.

It takes more than a dozen trips to carry everything over to the barn, and never having thought about backdrops and props, I'm curious about what he's building.

'Do you think you'll use all of this?'

'Hmm . . . not all, but I got it for free, so it's better to have more than I need, rather than not enough.'

I slip into the passenger seat, and he fires up the engine.

'Free? I like the sound of that.'

'Yes. The plastic came from a window company; the owner is a mate of my dad's. The panels were left over from a big production at a playhouse that recently shut down.'

Well, it saves on cost so I'm all for that.

Brentwood Farm is just a few minutes' drive away and I indicate that he should take a right turn. 'It's through that gate. I'll just jump out and open it.'

As Oliver pulls into the farmyard, Harry appears from one of the old sheds and I wave to him. 'You've come prepared, I see,' he gives me a thumbs up.

We park up and hurry over to join him. 'Harry, this is Oliver who is designing the set for the play at the Christmas Eve party.'

They shake hands and he leads us back into the shed he was working in. 'I'm sorting out some of the old stuff.'

Oliver gives a little whistle. 'You've certainly got your work cut out for you, Harry.'

'I do. But now I'm taking a back seat, my son has given me my orders.' He breaks out into a huge smile. 'My time is my own, but it's good to have something to do besides helping out with the deliveries. It sounds like you have quite a task on your hands too, Oliver.'

'Yes. And it seems to grow by the day.'

The two men exchange a mirthful look.

'That's life for you. Never a dull moment. Sienna here can attest to that.'

But I'm too busy to reply. My eyes are darting all over the place. 'Ooh!' I gasp.

'I pulled out some stuff that was buried that I thought might be of interest. It's all got to go at some point,' Harry confirms.

'This is like Aladdin's cave!'

'What . . . wonky old carts, dusty wooden wine boxes and weathered pallets?'

I look at him askance. 'Yes, yes and yes! What do you think, Oliver? Will this little lot fit into your van?'

He looks at me and nods his head.

'Let's get to it, then.' Harry's voice echoes around the hollow space. 'It'll save me a few trips to the tip in our old Transit.'

I'm delighted. It feels like Christmas has come early; how sad am I, getting excited over a haul of someone else's junk, but it's made my day.

8

Quid Pro Quo

When we get back to Silverberry Hall, it takes a while to unload the treasure trove and Oliver is equally as enthused as I am about the haul.

'This stuff is much too good to throw away,' he remarks, as we carry one of the carts across the car park. The two metal-framed wheels piled inside of it are rusty, but they aren't buckled.

'I feel the same way. I don't care if I can't get the wheels to go round, but with a bit of tender loving care these are going to look amazing when they're restored.'

It's obvious he has something on his mind because he keeps giving me nervous glances, but I hold my tongue as we tread back and forth. I assume he'll broach whatever it is when he's ready.

With everything safely stowed away in the old stable block, it's a satisfying feeling.

'Do you fancy a coffee?' I ask and his eyes light up.

'Doesn't Elizabeth have a thing on up at the Hall, today? She mentioned something about some sort of tea party?'

'Oh, yes. The lunch club she's a member of are getting together to determine the dates and venues for next year. Hmm . . . I don't really want to get pulled into the preparations. How about we head over to my cottage, instead?' With a bit of luck, because I'm busy, Grandma will take notes when the ladies arrive late afternoon.

'I'm fine with that, if it's not too much trouble.'

We stop to dust ourselves off a little and that sparks an outburst of laughter. 'With old stuff comes dust and debris,' I apologise. However, as Oliver has demonstrated already, he doesn't mind getting his hands dirty. 'But not for long. I have plans for this little lot.'

As we start walking he mutters, 'Hmm,' and I glance at him. 'I was rather hoping to talk you into donating a couple of things, temporarily of course, as props for the play. We can discuss that later.' He gives me a cheeky wink.

I do a running commentary as we walk, pointing out what I think of as things of interest. This time around he's much more amenable than he was on that first little trek from the pub to Silverberry Hall.

It isn't until we're settled down at the scrubbed pine table in my kitchen, that I quiz him.

'You think you can use some of the bits we brought back from the farm?'

He looks very comfortable sitting there, as I carry the two mugs of coffee over.

'I do. Items with wear and tear lend an authenticity that can be difficult to recreate. Because it's a partial set I'm building, every component needs to add something to the overall effect.'

I frown at him. 'Yes, I suppose that's important to take the audience back in time.'

'Less is more sometimes, but if it's all made out of modern materials, which the centrepiece will be, whatever else is on that stage has to add the *feels*. This is the bit where I'll struggle and with Daniela's focus elsewhere—'

'Why? You design sets all the time.'

'On a PC, with sophisticated and versatile software. Other people turn my designs into reality these days.'

He clasps his hands around the mug in front of him, even though it's lovely and warm in here.

'When we get back, perhaps we can put our heads together and see what we can come up with.'

His smile is genuine. 'Thanks, I'd really appreciate that. I don't want to disappoint anyone.'

I can see that.

'I do have another problem. Listening to Daniela talking about this new project of hers, I might need a stand-in for the rehearsals. It sounds quite intense. I know she'll be word perfect on the night, so it's a case of finding someone to read from the script, rather than acting out the part. It's just to get the timing right.'

Oh, my goodness, if he's asking me then it's a firm *no*. 'I can think of someone who might be up for that!' I exclaim.

'Really? That would be a lifesaver.' His smile grows exponentially and I'm pretty sure he's assuming it's me, but that's not something I'd feel comfortable doing, even from the wings. However, Ruby from The Sailor's Retreat has an outgoing personality, plus she might get a kick out of coming to Oliver's rescue.

'This is very cosy,' he continues. 'It's all about the decoration, isn't it, and you have a good eye.' He glances around, appreciative of my little collection of old china plates on the dresser.

'I'm a collector of *things*. I like to mix the new with the old and now I'm free to do what I want. It's a little frustrating as this isn't my forever home, but one day I'll find the perfect place.'

'You balance it well, that eclectic mix. I love that you've painted the mismatched collection of chairs to match the kitchen units. That soft blue adds a sense of tranquillity; it's very homely.'

'And completely different to life in London?' I question.

He gives a dismissive laugh. 'A little. I've had my flat for about four years now. It was newly refurbished when I bought it, and I didn't have to do a thing.'

I bat my eyelashes at him. 'Really? And does it feel like *your* home?'

Oliver pauses, his mug almost to his mouth. 'I'm a train

ride away from my key clients, so it's a great base from which to work. And smart enough to use to hold meetings, as my cleaner keeps it spotless. She won't let me make a mess of the place, even when I'm working.' He shrugs his shoulders before taking a hefty swallow of his coffee. 'It does the job for me, and the views aren't bad.'

I can tell that he's joking, and the views are probably a real cityscape, but that wasn't what I asked. 'It sounds . . .' I cast around for something polite to say '. . . contemporary and shiny.'

'It is. Very.' He takes another sip before diverting the attention back to my situation. 'Would you buy this place, if it were up for sale?'

'It's a part of the estate and it wouldn't make any sense for Elizabeth to sell bits off. Like you, it suits my needs for now. I do love quaint old buildings, though. I can't see myself settling into a newbuild, or anything that modern. This place is cosy. When I shut the front door I can feel the stresses of the day just draining away. I like to spend my winter evenings stretched out on the sofa in front of the log fire and in the summer there's a lovely patio area out the back which overlooks the woods. I often sit outside to read until the light goes.'

'It sounds blissful.'

I can't tell if he's simply being polite, especially given that he obviously prefers living in the midst of the bustle of the city. 'Oakleigh has all the authentic charm of a little cottage, but I doubt there's a straight line to be seen anywhere,' I muse. 'The beams and supports follow the curves of the trees from which they were formed and even the hand-crafted pegs securing them are each unique. That's craftsmanship for you.'

'It's certainly in a nice condition and that rustic look is appealing. Sadly, not all old properties are as well restored, or maintained.'

'On Freddie and Elizabeth's estate they are,' I reply. Then

I realise it's down to Elizabeth now to oversee tasks like that. 'I still get moments when I forget he's no longer here.'

Oliver grimaces. 'It must be hard on everyone. I wish I'd met him; sounds like he was a great guy.'

'He was. The best, in fact.'

'I know your grandma lives on the doorstep. What about the rest of your family? You mentioned that you were born in the village.'

'Mum met someone and moved down to Cornwall in April of this year. I have two aunts but neither of them live locally.'

'That must have been a wrench.'

I stare down into my coffee mug, my thoughts churning. 'It was, but I'm planning a visit very soon.'

'Before Christmas? Aren't things a bit hectic for you at the moment?'

This is awkward. 'Yes. I . . . um . . . can't put it off any longer, though.'

He looks shocked. 'You mean it'll be your first trip since the move?'

'Yes. It's been a difficult time. We talk every couple of days, so she understands.'

Oliver purses his lips. 'I can sympathise with that. It's tough when it comes to handling one's parents' expectations.'

'I feel like I've been a bad daughter and Mum deserves better.'

'But it's not like you have a normal job where you can just switch off, is it? It's obvious that you and your grandma are literally Elizabeth's main source of support while she comes to terms with her loss and keeping everything going.'

His tone is sympathetic but there's a little more to it than that. 'It's just easier if I'm on hand when problems crop up.' That is the truth, but I did escape to spend time with my friend Marissa, recently. I should have gone to Cornwall instead, but it was a little different as it was a rescue mission. I couldn't turn my back on a friend in need and Mum said she understood.

'Don't worry,' I assure him. 'I'll be around most of the time if you need help, and please feel free to call on me.'

'Oh . . . right. Thanks.'

He's so hard to read at times but it's obvious to me that he certainly takes his responsibilities very seriously indeed. In the light of the recent changes going on with Daniela, Elizabeth will expect me to a keep a close eye on him and I will. It's in everyone's interest that the play is a success, so it's a win-win situation for me.

However, I still have the afternoon attractions to arrange to keep the children amused, after Elizabeth decided to bring the carollers on the village green into the courtyard. I'm still mulling that over. But first things first, and that means keeping Oliver happy.

Back in the courtyard, Oliver and I check out the three carts we rescued from Brentwood Farm. 'They all need fixing up, but I'm more than happy to let you have one as a prop.'

'A cart for the stage?' He looks rather perplexed.

'Why not? It has that vintage feel. A little sanding, maybe a coat of paint if you want it to stand out. It's an iconic shape.'

Oliver pauses for thought. 'Actually, that might work rather well. There's a scene where a passer-by stops to chat with a woman selling single roses.'

'There you go, then. A wooden cart loaded with pots of colour – what's more Christmassy than a flower stall?'

He looks at me as if I'm crazy. 'It would cost a fortune to fill it with flowers. We're doing this on the cheap, remember.'

'Silverberry Hall has a greenhouse full of potted plants the gardeners bring on ready to fill gaps if anything dies off, or to plant out when the seasons change. I'm sure they'll be only too happy to lend you some choice specimens for the performance. And the nursery up on the main road usually sells wonderful red poinsettias on the run-up to Christmas. I'll give them a call. I'm sure they'll donate some for free, as Elizabeth sources most of her cut flowers from them.'

Oliver raises his eyebrows. 'Wow! It's not what you know, it's who you know, isn't it? That would be amazing. It would certainly create a great visual, even from a distance.'

'In return,' I warn him, 'I might need a bit of help getting the wheels back on that one.' I point to the saddest of the three, wondering why on earth someone started taking it apart.

'Hey, that's not a problem. I'll clean off all the wheels and check their fixings.'

'Oh, great. I want to sand the wood back a bit to knock off any rough bits. Should I do that first?'

'Yes. Are you going to paint them all?'

'I think it would make them look more vibrant, don't you? I don't know about the one for the stage, though. To be honest I'm not really sure what you're trying to achieve. The bare wood might look better.'

Oliver beckons with his finger. 'Come with me and I'll show you the visuals. I am a bit concerned that Daniela is content to leave it all up to me.'

We make our way back to the barn, and he unlocks the door.

'By necessity, I have to keep it simple as there isn't an awful lot of room. In a theatre, we have things hidden in the wings and backstage, with complicated rigging to support quick scenery changes. This will be a fixed set and the lighting will simply highlight different zones of the stage as the story plays out.'

Oliver grabs his laptop and fires it up. 'Let me find the stage design I put together.'

He's every inch the professional, even though he's doing it for free. He exudes confidence and passion for what he does, and I like that.

Maybe it's a part of the reason why university didn't work out for me. It didn't take long for me to realise I wasn't as confident as most of the other students when it came to pitching my ideas and getting feedback. My heart just wasn't in marketing or selling myself – which is a big part of it.

I've always loved upcycling furniture and making things. As a young teenager I was constantly repainting my bedroom and experimenting with different techniques, including hand-drawn designs. In hindsight, I'd have been much happier studying something like interior design. Dad was a marketing manager and he said it was a diverse career path. He thought it would be an excellent outlet for my creative side, too. I guess you don't know until you try, but it was a total disaster.

'Here we go. This is a visual of what I'm trying to achieve. It mimics what we used the first time around. However, given that I've now been landed with the role of artistic director as well as prop builder, this is just a guide as I'm thinking on my feet.'

I stare at the bare stage and then back at Oliver's clever impression of a street scene from bygone days. 'What's the dark blue?'

'That's the background. It's twilight.'

'And how are you going to achieve that, given what you have is a honey-coloured stone wall?'

'Ah . . . do you remember those panels you helped me carry in? Well, they'll be painted to form a blank canvas. I'm thinking of having a machine that creates the effect of falling snowflakes, trained on the stage. A mate of mine will come and sort that out and is going to lend us some stage lighting. Multiple points of light used at once can create drama and set the tone. He will need to fix the rigging onto the beams overhead.'

The three small spotlights we have in place are hardly going to make a dazzling impression.

'That's not a problem and it sounds like the perfect solution. So, the entire play is set outside?'

'Yep.'

'What's this huge round structure?'

'It's where Daniela will be throughout the entire performance. She'll be inside looking out. It allows her to follow what's happening as it all unfolds around her.'

Hmm. OK.

'My character, Adam, is outside his house shovelling snow. Daniela plays Eloise. The main focus of the story is that Adam and Eloise are talking to each other, but only in their heads. The structure makes it clear they can't hear each other.'

'I think I get it. That accounts for two of the characters and Daniela said there were eight in total, including the two children?'

'Yes. The children are in the centre of the stage, building a snowman. At one point the focus is on them as they're playing. They don't have speaking parts, but there's laughter.'

'Scriptwriters actually do that . . . *character x laughs at this point?*'

'Of course, it adds realism.'

'And building a fake snowman . . . how are you going to pull that off?' I smile.

'Hmm. I'm not sure. The first time around, Daniela had someone build a snowman out of cardboard and covered him in white wadding, the sort that's used in quilting. It looked fine from a distance, and it was the easiest way to get that snowy feel. At one point they added the head, which was hilarious, as they had to pretend it was really heavy and took two of them to lift. Children sometimes overact.'

'I'm not surprised, that's hard to pull off. Does it have to be a snowman they're working on?'

His left eyebrow lifts. 'Why?'

'Well, it's incredibly difficult to make it look convincing.'

He grins at me. 'Correct, but that's my job. Well, my paid job, as a set and design consultant, but I also see it through to the build-out stage, if required. The problem I have is that we're doing this on the cheap.'

'Hmm . . . that doesn't make it easy for you, does it? What if the children were just playing? You know, throwing a few snowballs around every now and again, instead . . .

Wouldn't that give the snowy feel with less work involved? And it would be easier for them.'

He strokes his chin with his right hand. 'Hmm. It would be simpler. As novices, the children will need something to keep them occupied throughout the performance.'

'Couldn't they sit behind a couple of those big old wooden sledges and pretend to be making snowballs, piling them up ready to cart away to bombard their friends?'

I hurry off to climb the steps at the side of the podium and he looks up at me, questioningly.

'Right. Imagine a cart full of greenery and a burst of red colour . . . about here, where you have a street seller on your design, with a basket on the floor next to her.' I indicate, outstretching my arms. 'Your cage is over there on the far side.'

'It's not a cage, it's a ball,' he emphasises.

'You know what I mean. You then have this space to fill if you take the snowman out. If we can get hold of two old-fashioned sledges, the children could be sitting behind them, next to the *ball*, quietly making the snowballs. The audience wouldn't really see that it's cotton wool, or whatever you use, as the sledges would help divert their attention. The children simply take their time piling them up.'

Oliver pauses, casting his eyes over the empty stage while he visualises it. 'It would be less hassle, that's for sure!' He seems impressed.

'What about the other characters?'

'Ah, you've already solved that problem for me with the cart. A part of the dialogue is between the flower seller and a customer. Originally, they were standing off to one side. On the night, when the stage goes dark and the spotlight homes in on them, it'll feel as if the audience is eavesdropping. Another scene is when a man and woman stop to talk to my character as he's clearing the pavement of snow. There's just enough space to divide the stage into three sections: the flower cart on the lefthand side, mid-stage with the children to the front and I'll be standing behind them, then the ball on the right. Hmm . . . that's a good solution.'

I make my way down to join Oliver, who has been tapping away on his laptop the whole time.

'What do you think of this?' he asks, standing back rather proudly.

'Wow! That's exactly what I just described, but better!'

'It's all about illusion.' He beams at me. 'You're pretty good at this.'

'What, creating a false reality, or upcycling?' I laugh.

'Don't knock it. This is going to be quite a spectacle and the idea is to create an enchanting street scene that will captivate the audience. You're a huge part of it now as my assistant set designer.'

I feel a tad embarrassed as our eyes meet and my heart skips a beat. 'I think I'd better grab the sander and start work on those carts.' As I walk away, I call over my shoulder, 'I'll catch you later.'

'Let me know when you're ready for me to fix on that set of wheels and give them all a service.'

'Oh, I will. And I won't forget about the stand-in for the first live rehearsal, it's not a problem.'

It's all in a day's work and, thank goodness, I feel confident reporting back to Elizabeth that Oliver is happy.

9

The Excuse

Late Thursday evening, I call Mum. 'How're you and Greg doing?'

'We're good, my darling daughter. The funny thing is, I was literally sitting here thinking about you. Your grandma was telling me how well the plans for the party are going. That's lovely, but I know it means you're even busier than usual.'

'Yes, and there's still a lot to do. Elizabeth has suggested I take a little break, so I'm thinking of popping down to Cornwall the weekend after next.'

Mum's tinkling laugh echoes down the line. 'Oh, that's amazing news! Greg will be delighted when I tell him. He worries about how much I miss home . . . I mean . . . you and your grandma being able to pop in for a quick cuppa.'

'I know,' I reply, sadly. 'But to be honest, it's been crazy at this end for us all. Grandma is Elizabeth's daily companion now and together we're managing to keep everything ticking over almost like normal.'

Mum makes a worrying 'hmm' sound. 'I guessed as much. Life must be hugely different without Freddie there.'

If it were only that . . . the issues with Elizabeth having a son and now a grandson few people know about, is a heavy burden to carry. Elizabeth and Freddie only became a part of mine and Mum's lives when they moved back from London and settled in the village. Prior to that they were just friends of Grandma and Pop's. They'd all meet up for weekends away at various hotels around the country, usually near a golf course. And they'd plan trips to London to see the latest play, or an art exhibition. Our paths rarely crossed.

I give a little sigh. 'It is. Freddie used to help me, too. He'd come up with the craziest of ideas for the Christmas party and Elizabeth would often seek us out to check what we were up to. Do you remember the year he decided we'd build a tower of champagne glasses as a centrepiece for the buffet? He'd seen it in one of his favourite old black and white films.'

Mum giggles. 'And ended up breaking a lot of Elizabeth's treasured collection of glasses. He was mortified and so was everyone watching!'

'I did tell him at the time that I thought it wasn't the best idea. Although, it did look awesome that night . . . well, until he started pouring the champagne.' Even I manage a little laugh, although it had been a nightmare to clear up.

'Still, I'm glad you're taking a bit of time off. The trouble is, Greg and I are committed to help with running the village's Christmas Fayres. They're being held every Saturday throughout November and December in the local church hall. I'll be flitting between stalls to lend a hand wherever I'm needed, and he'll be setting up the tables. For the rest of the day, he's one of a group of men who will be running the refreshment counter.'

'Oh, that's lovely, but if you don't mind—' I grimace to myself '—I'd, um, rather like to do a bit of sightseeing while I'm there.'

'Perfect. Can you get away early on Friday and I'll cook something special for dinner? There are some wonderful restaurants in the area, though, and I know how much you love fish. I'll see who's free to join us on Saturday night for a meal, shall I? It would be nice to meet up with some of Greg's family. They're down-to-earth people. Both his father and his late grandfather were fisherman, and—'

I stop Mum before she can map out the entire weekend.

'Oh . . . um . . . maybe we can plan that for the next trip? If it's OK with you, I'd like to bring a friend with me. Unless that puts you out?'

'Not at all,' she replies, albeit sounding a tad surprised. 'We have three spare bedrooms. In that case, I'll book somewhere for the four of us on Saturday night and we can walk the cliff path on Sunday, then stop somewhere nice for lunch.'

'That would be awesome. I'm returning a favour, you see. I thought to myself, why not make it a trip to Cornwall so that I can tie it in with a visit to see you both.'

'I know it's been a difficult time for you, my darling. I just hope that's the only reason you haven't made it down here.'

'Of course it is, Mum! I don't want you to think I'm not interested in your new life.' Gosh, that came out sounding a little awkward. 'But Elizabeth has needed my help more than ever. You know what she's like, stiff upper lip and all that. She doesn't want anyone to think she's letting anything slide, but I can't lie, it has been a struggle. It's hard for me to take time off when I know that Elizabeth needs me more than ever.'

I did feel guilty haring off to spend time with my friend Marissa, recently. She and her family moved away from Darlingham just before we started senior school. She was shy, just like me, and the bond I have with her is very different to the bond I have with Daniela. We might not speak as much but in times of need we're always there for each other.

Fortunately, Mum understood when I explained that Marissa had been made redundant. The independent florist's shop she worked for closed down and she was gutted. With overheads rising rapidly, they just couldn't compete. She was, naturally, feeling despondent. Grandma said Mum would be fine about it. My conscience, however, was telling me that I should have made the effort to get down to Cornwall way before now. There's only so long I can use Freddie's passing, coming to terms with the split with Liam and moving into Oakleigh, as an excuse.

'Besides, you won't want to spend every single minute you're here with us, anyway,' Mum laughs. 'It's nice to think you'll have some company and will be able to get out and about with a friend.'

Perfect! Now all I need to do is to give Marissa a call. I'm sure she won't be able to resist the lure of a couple of days near the coast. If she can wangle the Friday afternoon off work, we can take our time driving down.

The call ends on a high, with Mum excited about having house guests. I check the time before I dial. It's getting late, so I'd better make it a quick one.

'Hey, it's only me. How's the job search going?'

Marissa groans. 'I'm still waitressing to pay the rent, but I've applied for four jobs in the past ten days. And . . . wait for it . . . I have an interview on Monday week! It's for another independent florist but working from an indoor market. They supply a lot of floral arrangements for hotels.'

'That's brilliant news, Marissa. I'm so pleased for you, and I'll be keeping my fingers crossed.' In my head I'm already revising the weekend's schedule. 'I'm calling to see if you're free the weekend after next for a trip to Cornwall? We'd be staying at Mum and Greg's place. It would be nice if we could set off the day before, if that works for you.'

She sucks in a deep breath. 'Uh . . . oh . . .'

That's not a good sign. 'You'd be back by Sunday evening, ready for your interview the next day,' I assure her.

'It's not that. I won't be around. I've been invited along to one of these hiking weekends; it's at a posh country hotel in the Lake District.'

My eyebrows shoot up into my fringe. 'That sounds like . . . fun.' And so not something Marissa would normally do.

'It's not exactly my cup of tea, but I've met someone. His name is Tim and I think it's his idea of a romantic weekend away.'

It's hard not to let out a gasp. 'You have?'

'I know what you're going to say. I always rush into things and end up getting disappointed, but this time I think it's different. He's rather shy, which I find endearing, and I honestly believe he couldn't think of any other excuse for the two of us to spend a weekend away together. We'll see how it goes, but he's nice, really nice.'

'Then go for it. Do you even own a pair of hiking boots?'

'No, I don't so I'm borrowing some.' She giggles, but there's a fizz of excitement in her voice. 'I mean, if it becomes a *thing*, then obviously I'll be kitting myself out properly.'

'Well, have a truly wonderful time and I can't wait to hear all about what you get up to.'

'Oh, you will! Maybe Tim has a friend, and we could make up a foursome in the new year?'

We both burst out laughing. 'I'm more the wind in my hair next to the beach sort of girl,' I muse.

'Aww. For all his faults, Liam knew that didn't he?'

'Yes, that was one thing he did get right.'

Argh! Heading down to Cornwall isn't easy for me, and now I have to find someone else to accompany me. A person who won't ask awkward questions when I'm nosing around to glean any information I can about James. Marissa would have been perfect, as she would have just gone along with it. It's back to the drawing board, I guess!

Friday dawns and I'm up and out early. I'm surprised when I see Daniela hurrying towards me as I cross the courtyard on my way to the barn.

'Morning,' I call out. 'Why the long face?' Her frown, together with an enquiring look makes me groan inwardly.

'All work and no play – you know what they say!' She pants, slightly breathless from her exertion. 'It looks like it's the same for you, too.'

'I'm working this weekend, but at the end of next week I'll be spending three days in Cornwall with Mum and Greg.'

'That's great news and well overdue. You are in need of

a break and it's time to accept that Greg is in her life. He's not trying to replace your dad, Sienna, he's just—'

I put up my hand. 'I know. He's turned Mum's life around and given her purpose again. I get it and I do appreciate that.'

'Then why aren't you sporting a huge smile?'

'Oh . . . it's hard to explain.' It's not just about getting pulled into Elizabeth's woes, but staying under the same roof as Greg and Mum in their home is . . . difficult. 'If I go on my own then it's a lot of pressure for the first visit.' I know that's only part of the truth, but my hands are tied.

'I really wish I could say I'll come with you, but we have tickets to take the kids to see Santa on the Saturday up at the canal. It's a thirty-minute narrow-boat ride, a cup of hot chocolate and gingerbread muffins. We get to sing Christmas songs and Santa tells the children a story before handing out a little gift.'

'Aww . . . it sounds lovely. I'm envious.'

Daniela gives a little chuckle. 'It sounds magical, but William doesn't like strange men, so he'll probably start wailing; and Clara will probably ask Santa for a pony. Then I'll have to explain why just asking for something doesn't mean it'll appear on Christmas morning.' She grimaces.

'Yes, but it's memories like that you'll remember forever,' I point out. 'I wonder if I'll ever be in a similar position? It's the sort of thing I can only dream about.'

'Of course you will! When your Mr Right comes along you'll enjoy every single minute of it. I'm not sure I fully appreciated what I had when I met Nigel. Now I look back on it, everything happened so quickly. Maybe too quickly, as I don't think I was ready for what was to come.' Her eyes widen and I'm inclined to agree with her. 'His charm dazzled me, that's for sure. I think I was fixated on the thought of being in love and it's sheer luck he turned out to be a keeper. But even so, I really wish I could be by your side for what could be a bit of an emotional visit.'

'Hey, I didn't mean to put you on a guilt trip.'

'How about asking Marissa, or Lottie?'

'Marissa is otherwise engaged, and Lottie still hasn't forgiven me for chickening out of that blind date.'

Lottie is the office manager at the local vet's surgery, and she was one of our little posse when we were at school. We're friends, and she is fun to be around, but she has a tendency to gossip. I'm convinced that some of the rumours about Xavier are down to her, as she talks about him all the time. I certainly wouldn't want to risk her getting wind of the other reason why I'm heading down to Cornwall.

'You could always ask your grandma to go with you if you think it's going to be awkward.'

Goodness, the last thing I want is for Daniela to start dropping hints to her. 'No. Weekends are tough for Elizabeth. If her family decide to descend upon her, she'll need rescuing. And if they don't, then Grandma is good company for her.'

'Are Elizabeth's brothers behaving themselves? At the funeral I noticed that her eldest brother hardly left her side. At times I could see that he was getting on her nerves. She's a proud woman who hates being fussed over. I thought it was a little . . . undermining.'

'Well, that's Stephen for you, but the youngest one, Matthew, is content to give Elizabeth the space she needs to get used to the new normal.'

Daniela frowns. 'Freddie was active right up until he had that fall, so I'm sure she's feeling his loss in more ways than one. It's obviously had an impact on your job.'

Actually, it was noticeable to Elizabeth, Grandma and me several months before the fall, that Freddie was slowing down. Mentally, as well as physically, and he hated it. Over a protracted period, we began taking as much work off his plate as we could, without eroding his confidence. Grandma too has had an increasing, if informal, role at Silverberry Hall. Between the three of us we keep everything running, but I suspect there will be some significant changes in the not-too-distant future.

My role is more on the financial side now, parties aside, making sure the bills are paid in a timely fashion and keeping the accounts up to date. In a way, it helped to prepare us all for what was to come, but the end for Freddie was so abrupt that it was a huge shock.

I shrug my shoulders. 'Stephen and his wife, Yvonne, would dearly love to move in to *look after Elizabeth*, but as much as she dotes on them all, that isn't her style. She isn't frail and she isn't an invalid; besides, above all Elizabeth values her privacy.'

It's the truth, and the last thing she needs right now is people trying to run her life, no matter how well meaning they are. When she's ready, I'm sure she'll appoint some sort of general manager to take charge of the grounds and general maintenance of the estate. It will probably include overseeing the finances, too. She's dropped a few subtle hints here and there, enough to wake me up to the fact that at some point I'll have another boss to replace Freddie. But it won't be the same.

'I only popped in to say that Oliver mentioned he was looking for some old-fashioned sledges to use as props. I found someone who has two that he can borrow. The barn's all locked up, so I guess he's not here today?'

'Not until lunchtime. He told me that he had a deadline to meet this morning before he can head over.'

She gives me a suggestive smile. 'The pair of you are working well together and having fun, I hope?'

I give her a sobering glance. 'He's pushing hard to finish setting up the stage ready to get the cast together to make sure the layout works.'

'Oh, I see. He didn't mention that. Can you give him the heads up on the sledges and tell him that I've found two local children – not mine, I hasten to add – who are delighted at the prospect of doing a little acting. If it's a trial run, they won't need to be there.'

Daniela certainly knows how to delegate, that's for sure.

I really am beginning to feel like Oliver's assistant. 'And how is your deep dive into the family history of an iconic family going?'

'Don't ask. Nigel has kindly offered to head off with the children and Pixie to his parents' house for the weekend to give me some peace. I'm going to empty out the boxes I brought back from the Manor and sort everything into piles on the sitting room floor.'

'It sounds like fun,' I muse, and she grunts.

'Not. I'll be scouring through old photographs and handwritten letters. If I can home in on a couple of noteworthy events throughout the ages, hopefully I'll find some anecdotal bits that will add some authenticity to my words. I half wonder whether I'm not the first person that Edward asked, but I think I'd rather not know if other people were sensible enough to turn down the job!'

Despite her words, she's buzzing, and this is just the sort of challenge she needs to boost her confidence. 'Anyway, I must get back. My mornings seem to fly by way too fast, but I felt a bit guilty and thought I'd pop in to check that Oliver's coping and it's all good here.'

She's looking for me to confirm that. 'Don't worry. He has it all under control and things are going well.'

A look of relief spreads over her face. 'Brilliant! I knew I was leaving him in good hands. And it's wonderful that the two of you are spending so much time together; it's heartening to see!'

With that she hurries out the door before I get a chance to reply. When she's in matchmaking mode she's not one to give up easily!

10

Feeling Appreciated

As soon as lunch is over I head out to the stables to see if the final coat of white paint I put on the carts is dry. As I'm surveying my handiwork, I hear footsteps and turn to see Oliver grinning at me.

'Wow! You'd never think they were destined for the tip, would you?'

'It's a bit shabby chic, as I didn't want to sand back the wood too much. I wanted the grain to show through. I think they'll look wonderful filled with bags of roasted chestnuts, trays of hot chocolate and mulled wine.'

'And the one with no wheels is mine?'

'It is. Thank you for cleaning off the others for me.'

'Oh, it's the least I could do. They'll take quite a bit of weight, and they wheel pretty easily. It shouldn't take me long to reattach the wheels to the third one.'

'I'm going to stencil some ivy on the two for the courtyard. If you think the one for the stage will look a bit plain, I could add some colourful roses, or maybe paint a name on the side for you.'

'That would be great. As for names, hmm . . . that might take a bit of thinking about.'

'Where is the play set?'

'Christmas Lane.'

Why am I not surprised? 'How about Christmas Lane Barrow? It has an old ring to it.'

His eyes light up. 'Perfect! Thanks, Sienna.'

'Oh, and Daniela dropped by to see you this morning. She managed to track down two vintage sledges you can borrow, and you now have two child actors eager to join the group.'

'The troupe,' he corrects me, smiling.

'And I've spoken to Ruby. She's more than happy to stand in and read some lines if Daniela can't make any of the rehearsals.'

'Ruby from the pub?' Oliver asks. I can't help but notice he looks a little disappointed.

'Yes. She's quite outgoing and I thought it would be the sort of fun thing she'd enjoy doing.' Plus, Ruby instantly took a shine to him, but I can't really say that's why I asked her. I just didn't intend getting press-ganged into it.

'Oh, I see . . . um . . . that's great.'

Hmm. That sounded rather jaded to say the least. Was he really expecting me to jump in and help? It's true to say that it's been nice working alongside each other, but Ruby is more outgoing and I think she'll do a much better job of reading from a script than I would.

'Did you meet your deadline without any hitches?'

A hint of a smile plays around his lips. 'I did and I think taking a break away to come here and get hands-on allowed me to see the wood for the trees, as my mother often says.'

That makes me smile. 'And I thought there wasn't a smidge of the country boy in you!'

'There isn't,' he insists. 'I swear that when I was growing up, visits to my grandfather's farm were my least favourite thing to do. Animals and I don't seem to have any affinity at all. Even the sheep ran at me, threateningly, although Granddad said I was imagining it.'

Oliver slips off his heavy jacket and dons a sleeveless body warmer he keeps on a hook just inside the door. I admire the fact that he's as happy getting hands-on and doing physical work, as he is beavering away on his PC. He certainly has the physique for manual work, with those broad shoulders of his and arms that lift heavy weights with ease. I suppose once this weekend is over I won't be seeing quite so much of him. The majority of the rehearsals are going to be done via video calls.

I kneel down on an old cushion to begin drawing around the outline of the ivy leaves on the first cart.

'Are you nervous about the performance?' I ask, out of sheer curiosity.

'A bit, but I'm playing a character, so it's different. I won't look like me.'

I let out a rather girly giggle. 'You'll be in disguise?'

'No. I'll be wearing a costume. That's part of the fun. I'll have a moustache and a full beard, too. It's not period specific, but it's supposed to look like a scene set in a little hamlet, back in the day when ordinary people didn't have a lot. Albeit my character, Adam, is a solicitor, so he has money.'

Oliver is already threading a bolt through one of the wheels and we lapse into silence. My work requires concentration, and he ends up having to go off and rifle through a box of old bit and pieces in search of some nuts that will do the job.

I'm actually looking forward to helping him get everything ready this weekend. He's already warned me that the ball won't be easy to assemble, and the air might turn a little blue at times. I can't even begin to imagine how he's going to take strips of plastic and make them durable enough for Daniela to stand inside the structure. It's a novel idea creating what in effect will look like a huge Christmas bauble. I can't wait to see Daniela's costume. I wonder if she's an angel? I laugh to myself ever so softly, as I begin colouring the stencilled leaves in a vibrant green. I'm looking forward to doing the finishes touches on the flower cart next. I want everything to look perfect!

Breakfast on a Saturday morning is often leisurely, but today I'm up and out of the cottage early. I grab my backpack and step out into the chilly morning air. Filling my lungs, I can almost taste the woodsmoke from a log fire somewhere close by.

I've always loved the colours of autumn, as nature begins its transition into winter mode. Weekends for me are usually all about brisk walks to clear my head and I look forward to my cosy evenings in front of the fire.

But this year is different. I'm feeling emotionally drained and wondering how *cosy* it will actually feel, sitting there all alone. My life has changed in ways I couldn't even have imagined this time last year, and it's been a protracted period of adjustment. I'm hoping that this year's Christmas party at the Hall will lift my spirits so I can head into a new year with more positivity than I'm feeling right now.

As I cross the car park I spot Grandma up ahead. She's carrying an overnight bag in one hand and has a large box clasped to her chest.

'Morning,' I call out. I quicken my pace to catch up with her. 'Here, let me take that for you.'

She rewards me with a smile. 'Thank you, Sienna, this box is heavier than I thought.'

'Are you staying overnight?'

'Yes. It's time to get all the Christmas cards written and I told Elizabeth I'd give her a hand with hers.'

'Ah, that's lovely. Well, there's a huge pile ready for her to sign on my desk in the study. I've printed off the addresses, so it's a case of sticking on a label and popping the card inside. Everything's all right with her, is it? She seems a bit brighter this week.'

Grandma leans in a little closer, lowering her voice. 'We're joining some old friends for dinner this evening at The Park Lodge Hotel. Elizabeth is using it as an excuse to avoid family descending on her again this weekend.'

'Lovely! I hope you both have a wonderful time. Do you need me to arrange some transport?'

'No, it's all sorted. One of the couples are going to do a

bit of a detour to pick us up. You look full of energy this morning. You'll need it by the sound of things.'

We glance across at the barn, as the reverberation of a hammer rings out around the courtyard.

'Oliver is keen to do a test run of the set with the cast as early as possible. I'm away next weekend and Daniela isn't available, either. So, the bulk of the work has to be completed over the next two days.'

I open the door to the boot room, and Grandma steps through. 'Shall I take your bag upstairs?' I check, but she shakes her head.

'No. Put it in the corner for now. Breakfast is for eight sharp and it's already ten to; I don't want to upset Veronica. Elizabeth wanted us to kick off our weekend in style, so no doubt Veronica will be in a flap. I'll pop into the kitchen first to see if there's anything I can do to help.'

It's wonderful to see Grandma so excited. 'Well, I'd best go and see what Oliver is up to. Have fun!'

'Oh, we will!' she replies, with gusto.

As I hurry past the stable block, I can't help chuckling to myself. With Grandma by her side, I hope that it will boost Elizabeth's confidence. Apart from their regular ladies' lunches, she has declined every invitation she's received since Freddie's passing. It's about time she started to pick up the threads of her once busy social life again.

I'm so deep in thought that as I open the door to the barn, I literally bump into Oliver, who is on his way out.

'Sorry!'

'Sorry!'

We stand there smiling apologetically at each other.

'I wasn't expecting you to appear before at least nine o'clock.' He grins at me.

'Oh, I prefer an early start when there's a lot to be done.'

'I'm the same. It beats lying in bed thinking about it. I'm just going to get a few materials from the stables. I'll only be a couple of minutes.'

Once inside, I keep my jacket on while I light a couple of the heaters towards the top end of the room.

I see that he's already carried some bundles of wood and plastic strips through, and all of the panels, which will make up the screen at the back.

'Oh, some heat . . . well, done!' he exclaims, as he walks towards me carrying a wooden box with some folded dust sheets balanced on top.

'It'll soon warm up. How on earth did you manage to carry that lot in here on your own?'

'I crossed paths with Victor first thing. I was struggling a bit and he very kindly stopped to help. It took no time at all to shift it between the two of us. And while I remember, he said to let him know if you need any additional helpers for the afternoon party on Christmas Eve.' I stare at him blankly. 'For the children's thing?' he prompts.

I slap my hand against my forehead. 'I forgot! Oh, heck. I'm hoping he'll agree to be our Santa Claus on the day. I still have to organise some entertainment.' That's in addition to drafting in help to man the carts with the hot drinks and the mince pies and muffins, of course! But as Elizabeth's family will be staying at the Hall, it should be easy enough to rope them in if I give Elizabeth a list of the help I'll need on the day.

'Sorry to be the deliverer of bad news,' Oliver says, pulling a sad face.

'No, it's fine. I'm glad of the reminder. It is on my list, but I haven't gotten around to checking it this week.'

'It's no wonder,' he replies, frowning. 'And now I feel guilty for commandeering your time this weekend. I'm sure you've plenty of other things to do.'

'I offered and I meant it. Now, what's my first task?'

He stands there with his hands on his hips, while he formulates a plan of action.

'If we lay out the panels, do you mind painting them with a roller?'

'Now that's something I can handle,' I confirm.

'Great. Let's spread out the dust sheets and get you started. If we place the panels on the floor in front of the heaters they'll dry pretty quickly and then you can do the edges afterwards.'

It doesn't take long to get everything sorted and I'm glad that it's an easy task, although it's going to take a while.

From time to time my eyes stray over to the stage, where Oliver is totally engrossed in what he's doing. There's a bit of grunting and groaning, and I think he's struggling. After about an hour, my back is aching a little and I stand to have a good stretch.

'I brought a Thermos flask if you fancy a coffee,' I offer.

He instantly looks up. 'You're an angel. A caffeine hit is exactly what I need right now. This is turning into a nightmare of a job.'

I grab my backpack and saunter over to the wooden steps, then pull out two thermal mugs and empty the entire Thermos into them. 'Here you go.' I join him, as he sits crossed-legged on the stage. He grabs a mug and I lower myself down next to him, extracting the plastic box tucked under my arm. 'I brought some gingerbread men. Help yourself.'

His face brightens. 'Thanks. I'd forgotten what it's like turning a 3D plan into reality,' he remarks, as I put the box in front of him and ease off the lid. 'This will do the trick and kick-start my brain, I'm sure.'

'What's the problem?' I query.

'I'm making the centrepiece for the top of the ball that the plastic strips will slot into. The problem I have is that they're a little too flexible and I don't think it's going to be stable enough, no matter how heavy I make the base. I think I'm going to have to add a central pole, but I fear it will totally spoil the illusion.'

'Ah, it's tough being a perfectionist.'

He gives a dismissive laugh. 'I'm supposed to be a professional!'

'You are. But a professional designer, not a professional handyman,' I point out.

'True.'

'Why will it spoil it?'

'Because a ball doesn't have a central support. The first time we performed this it was made out of narrow metal strips, with a hinged section for access. It was originally used in a circus act, apparently. It was perfect because it was so heavy; it took a bunch of guys to move it.'

'But your version won't work without something to stabilise it?'

'No.'

I sit and ponder for a few moments.

'What if you used a tree?'

Another dismissive laugh. 'A tree?'

I nod my head. 'We have a whole forest of them within walking distance. I'm sure we could find a wind-damaged one sturdy enough to suit your needs and light enough to carry over here. There's are a couple of chainsaws in the stable block.'

Oliver demolishes the second half of his gingerbread man, a pensive look on his face. 'That might work. I mean, it would make for a good background image and it's better than having just a pole anchored to the floor.'

'When we've finished our little break, let's get togged up and see what we can find.'

In truth, I'm feeling pretty pleased with myself for coming up with what I think is quite a clever option. And if it gives me a break from bending over painting, my back will be extremely grateful.

'It's only me,' Ruby calls out, as she steps inside the barn. 'Your food is here. Two steak sandwiches and two cans of beer. Goodness, you have been busy.'

When I rang The Sailor's Retreat to order a takeaway working lunch, Ruby kindly offered to drop it off at the end of her shift. I know she's curious about what we've been doing in the barn and the fact that I'm the one helping Oliver.

She gives him a beaming smile. 'How clever!'

'It doesn't look much now, but when it's finished I think it'll do the trick,' he replies, rather modestly. 'And thank you for offering to step in to read Daniela's lines when we do the first trial run to test out the props.'

Maybe Ruby was a good choice, after all. Any sign of disappointment seems to have totally evaporated.

'It'll be a blast! I bet she's sorry to be missing out on this.' Ruby gives me a sideways glance.

I nod my head. 'Yes. But now that Daniela is working part-time from home, it's too much to juggle.'

'Ah, right. The grapevine doesn't know that yet! I saw Nigel loading up the car this morning on my way in to work and he waved. I thought maybe they were going away for the weekend.'

'The family are, but Daniela is up to her eyes in her new project, so she'll be beavering away at her desk.'

'Poor Daniela, being home alone and working sounds rather dull. Anyway, chef wrapped the sandwiches in foil, so eat them while they're still hot. If you're both here tomorrow and want lunch delivered, let me know mid-morning and I'll drop it over before the rush, around noon. I'm there all day.'

'Thanks, Ruby. Appreciated!'

She hands the large paper bag to Oliver, as she smiles up at him. 'Have fun!'

When the door shuts behind her, he looks at me, puzzled. 'The grapevine? What was all that about?'

'Oh,' I reply, nonchalantly, 'gossip about you and Daniela. People put two and two together and make five.'

He pulls a face. 'I hope Daniela doesn't catch wind of it.'

'We're used to it. Any time a handsome stranger comes into the village it causes a stir.' Ugh. Did I just say handsome?

'Really?'

I can't help but start laughing. 'Don't worry, you'll be old news as soon as they realise they've got it wrong. The fact that I'm here helping you in the barn and not Daniela should scotch that rumour. Our poor locum vet, Xavier, will then be the hot topic once again.'

'Xavier, eh? I can imagine anyone with a name like that attracting attention, but not me.' Thank goodness he finds it funny. 'I'll grab two chairs if you want to unwrap this,' he says, passing the carrier bag to me. But as he walks away, he calls over his shoulder, 'Don't you merit a little gossip, too?'

My chuckle is dismissive. 'No. Having gone through an embarrassingly public break-up I'm allowed a breathing period. You know, as a sign of respect . . . like after a bereavement. People are still in the *feeling sorry* for me mindset.'

'Poor Sienna.'

'Precisely.'

I lean against the steps, taking out the two cans to stand them on the edge of the stage before pulling out the hot sandwiches and a couple of paper napkins.

'Here you go.' Oliver places two chairs side by side, facing down the full length of the barn. 'Oh, we're not having Old Spot beer today.' He sounds a bit miffed.

'I thought you might like to try the Severn Boar. It's mellow, with an interesting fruit flavour, but it does have a bit of a kick to it.'

As I hand him a can and his lunch, he gives me a mirthful smile. 'This I have to try!'

I sit down next to him, placing my can on the floor, as I'm ravenously hungry and my stomach is beginning to make embarrassing rumbling sounds. The instant I open up the well-wrapped parcel, the aroma of caramelised onions and steak fills the air. Seconds later, I'm munching away. It's been a long morning, and this definitely hits the spot.

Oliver cracks the tab on the can and takes a hefty swig. 'Smooth, balanced and I like that touch of lingering fruitiness. Hmm . . . I'd definitely go for this again, even though if I'm drinking beer I prefer it from a keg.'

All thoughts of beer soon disappear once he bites into his sandwich, and he lets out an appreciative groan. 'Now that—' he stabs his finger at it '—is the perfect steak sandwich. You should let me pay for lunch today and tomorrow.'

'No, it's my treat. You're doing Elizabeth – and me – a big favour. Not only are you giving your time for free, but it would have been quite a headache to think of some other form of entertainment. And, like I said, I didn't have anything specific planned for today and tomorrow, so it's not a problem. But I'm away next weekend and I think Daniela is tied up, too, so the timing is perfect.'

'If you're stuck when it comes to organising something for the afternoon of the party – you know, for the kids – there's a guy I recommend to clients who rents out props. He's based in the Cotswolds on an old airfield. He bought up some of the hangars to store his collection. I could run you over there to see if he has anything suitable. I know for a fact he has fairground equipment and, as it's in aid of charity, he might lend you something for free. I put a lot of business his way.'

My eyes widen. 'It would certainly be one less headache for me, but then I'd be in your debt again.'

He gives me a serious look. 'I owe you more than you know, so it's not a problem.'

Just as I'm about to quiz him on that statement, the door opens and Daniela appears.

'Caught you! Why on earth are you eating in here?'

Oliver immediately jumps up, popping the last of his sandwich in his mouth. He strides over to give her an affectionate hug. 'We wanted a quick break. There's a lot still to do.'

'But it's going well, by the look of it. The two vintage wooden sledges have been delivered and I got the driver to drop them off by the stable block. They're well wrapped as they come from a top-end antiques shop in Tetbury. The owner is an old friend of Nigel's and it's from his personal collection. He often uses them as a window display, but this year a stag is going to be the focal point.' She gives a little shudder. 'He is a mighty beast, but I hate stuffed animals.'

'Well, please pass on our grateful thanks and say that we'll take great care of them.'

She rewards Oliver with a warm smile. 'I know you will. And thank you both for covering for me. You know I'm not one to volunteer for something and then pass off some of the work to other people. But this opportunity I have is too good to turn down and while I can't wait to get back on stage—' Her face is glowing and it's obvious she feels she's found herself again. The bit she feared was lost; the spark that adds that little something to her life.

'Hey,' I interrupt, leaning in to wrap an arm around her and give an encouraging squeeze. 'You did the hardest part, writing the play. And I think Oliver might have solved the last of my more pressing problems, one I'd actually overlooked, so there are no complaints from me. Wielding a paintbrush is a small price to pay.'

She grins at me. 'Only a best friend would say that. Once the madness of Christmas and New Year are over, the four of us should get together at the house and I'll put on my hostess hat. I might cheat a bit though, as my cooking isn't quite at chef level.'

'That would be nice,' I reply, but Oliver remains quiet.

'Anyway,' she continues. 'I must get back to work. I wasn't expecting the delivery and they're too heavy to carry down from the house, so I jumped into the passenger seat to show him where to drop them off. Apologies for interrupting your lunch and thank you, guys – you're both going that extra mile for me and I'm so incredibly grateful!'

11

An Offer I Can't Refuse

By three in the afternoon, I hit the point where I'm waiting for the final coat of paint on the background panels to dry and Oliver, too, has ground to a halt. He suggests he give his mate at the airfield a call and saunters off, leaving me to tidy up. About five minutes later, I catch a movement as the door slowly opens and, to my surprise, Harry appears.

'It's only me,' he mutters. 'I heard you was working all weekend. I've brought you a couple of finds I stumbled across that I thought you might be able—' He stops short, staring at the stage. 'What's that?'

'I refer to it as the *orb* because it's shiny and semi-transparent. It's stunning, isn't it?' Admittedly, it's propped up with three temporary supports while the glue holding the top of the structure hardens overnight, but even so, it's impressive.

Harry walks closer and he's clearly impressed. 'Wow – that's big! It'll certainly grab everyone's attention.'

'It had to be large enough to allow a person to walk around the central support.'

'It reminds me of an old-fashioned birdcage.' Harry purses his lips, staring in awe. 'It can't have been easy to construct.'

'It wasn't. First thing tomorrow Oliver will put in the final fixings to stabilise it. The inside will be made to look a little more like a clearing in a forest, ready for the performance.'

Standing eight feet tall, and with the central tree trunk now sprayed white, it'll look enchanting when it's finished.

'Well, you've both done a good job, that's for sure.'

'Oh, it's not down to me,' I inform him. 'My only task has been to wield a paintbrush and roller.'

Harry looks around at the dozen or so panels laid out on dust sheets, and he laughs. 'You like navy blue, do you?'

'Not so much after three coats.' I smile. 'But it's supposed to be the sky on a dark, winter's evening. Tomorrow I get to paint a few soft clouds and add some twinkly stars. How I'm going to get them to look realistic, heaven knows!'

We both chuckle at the pun.

'I don't see how you can do that without real lights. Me friend's son is an electrician; I could ask him to pop in and take a look. All he'd need to do is drill a small hole in the middle of each star, big enough for a tiny bulb on the end of a wire to be slid—'

'What a brilliant idea!' Oliver's voice interrupts us and we turn around to look at him.

'I was just saying what a brilliant job you've done here,' Harry enthuses. 'It's going to be quite a spectacle.'

'It's been a long day and tomorrow won't be much better, but once it's done, it's done. We need to get the cast together for a first run-through to check the layout works, given how narrow the stage is.' I can tell that Oliver is still concerned about the positioning of everything.

Harry utters a 'hmm', no doubt thinking the same thing as me – designing this set wasn't for the faint-hearted.

'I knew you were looking for some old bits and pieces,' Harry continues. 'I found a metal clock and a lantern. Rusty gold, as they say, but a quick polish would add a bit of a lustre.'

I wondered what was in the heavy-looking sacks he was carrying, which he left just inside the door.

We walk over to take a look, as he rolls down the first sack to reveal the clock.

'Oh, Harry. Now you really have outdone yourself!' Oliver looks ecstatic. 'It's finishing touches like this that will really dress the set and bring it to life.'

'The clock will make an interesting display piece on the flower cart,' I agree, enthusiastically and Oliver nods his head in agreement.

'If the lantern is as bold a statement piece as this, I could make a pole so it could be carried around on stage with a battery light inside of it, like a candle,' Oliver replies.

'It might be too heavy for that, but it could be turned into a lamp post,' Harry suggests.

'Well, that should be easy enough to knock up. It's all about proportions when it comes to props and I'm mightily grateful to you, Harry.'

'Waste not, want not.' He grins at us, glancing from me to Oliver. 'And hold off on making a pole for the lamp, Oliver. I'm fairly sure there's something in my scrap pile I can rescue that will do. I'll find some sort of metal base so you can anchor it to the stage. Give me a couple of days to sort it and I'll pop it in to you.'

'I probably won't be around much after tomorrow,' Oliver admits, sounding a tad regretful. 'I'm heading home to London, but I'll be back for the odd day here and there. Aside from the trial run, it'll just be a case of helping a mate get the spotlights sorted at some point and any rehearsals the cast want to do in situ.'

Harry turns to look at me.

'I'm not going anywhere.' I smile. 'I can store it in the stable block ready for Oliver's next visit.' Hearing that he's returning to London so soon is a bit of a disappointment. It's been a great diversion working alongside him; it's the most fun I've had in a long time if I'm being honest with myself.

After we bid Harry goodbye, Oliver checks his watch. 'It's a half-hour drive to Babdown aerodrome, so we'd best make a start. Ron usually shuts up shop at four on a Saturday, but he'll hang around for us.'

'That's very kind of him.'

Oliver winks at me. 'As I said, I put a lot of work his way. He can more or less charge what he likes, because it's getting increasingly harder to find some of the stuff he's managed to get his hands on over the years.'

We gather our things together and make our way to Oliver's car.

'I could drive us, you know,' I offer.

'Yes, but my car is on site and yours isn't.'

'OK, if you're sure.'

'After you've given all those panels three coats of paint?' He reaches out to press the button and the engine kicks into life.

'I've enjoyed doing it.'

'But not as much as you'll enjoy next weekend, I bet.'

I look at him, puzzled, as he eases the car out into the lane.

'The trip to see your mum,' he continues. 'I bet you're looking forward to it.'

Actually, I'm feeling anxious about it and the pause sparks his interest.

'Why the hesitation?' He's genuinely puzzled.

'It's a long story.'

'You've got half an hour . . . it won't take longer than that, surely? I can tell that something's wrong. This is the first time I've seen you looking down in the mouth.'

I'm reluctant to get into this. Oliver is still little more than a stranger to me, even if we do seem to have struck up an easy friendship in a short space of time.

'Look, Sienna, I get it. You're like me; we hate people knowing our business and I'll hazard a guess that our respective experiences have made us hesitant to trust people. But I have a favour to ask you and it means sharing something I'm not comfortable about. If I do confide in you, will you share with me whatever it is that's troubling you?'

'You'll trust me if I trust you?' I joke.

To my utmost surprise he nods his head. He's a genuinely

nice guy and there isn't anything he's said, or done, that indicates he's not being straight with me. Even so, it's a little outside of my comfort zone.

'I don't share other people's secrets, though. And that's a part of the dilemma I find myself in.'

'Then I know I can trust you, so only tell me what you're happy to share.' He sounds prosaic and I wait until he's ready to begin. 'It's likely that I'll be back for a couple of overnight stays, aside from Christmas Eve itself. Daniela keeps insisting that I stay at her place, as it's on the doorstep. She thinks she's doing me a favour, but I need um . . . I'm looking for an excuse to decline her offer, with reluctance obviously as it's kind of her.'

Now I'm confused. 'Why?'

I turn to stare at his side profile, as he swallows hard.

'This isn't easy to admit,' he replies, his voice sombre. 'I feel that Nigel isn't really comfortable having me stay over.'

'What?'

Oliver sighs. 'It's nothing. Just a man thing.'

What on earth does that mean? 'I don't understand. He's such a friendly guy.'

'I know. But he sees . . . no, he *senses* what Daniela doesn't.'

'Which is?'

Oliver makes a soft groaning sound. 'Ugh. Sorry, this is awkward and rather embarrassing.'

'Look, Daniela is my best friend, so maybe you should stop there.'

'It's not her problem, it's mine.' He clears his throat uneasily. 'When we were at uni together and I went to pieces, Daniela assumed it was because the girl everyone thought I was serious about, admitted she was also seeing someone else. Wendy and I only had a few dates, but as classmates and with our parents being neighbours, it must have seemed we were much closer than we were. Wendy was *seeing* a married man and it suited her for people to think there was something more serious going on between us.'

'And you went along with it and ended up getting hurt?'

The way he squirms in his seat makes my stomach turn over.

'Daniela had literally just met Nigel. She talked about him all the time and it was clear from the start they were mad about each other. It wasn't just a passing thing, it got serious very quickly. She . . . um . . . had no idea I had feelings for her, still doesn't. I don't mean now . . . I mean, back then. We were great friends, and I didn't want to lay a guilt trip on her, just because I missed my chance to tell her how I felt. But, yes, for a while there it was like the bottom had fallen out of my world; it was easier to let people think whatever they wanted, as long as no one suspected the truth.'

My jaw drops. 'And Nigel knows that?'

'No,' he stresses, sounding horrified. 'I've never breathed a word about it to anyone, until now. But it's obvious that he isn't comfortable around me and I guess on a deeper level, he wonders whether there was anything going on between Daniela and me, before he came into her life.'

'But there wasn't?'

He gives a sad little laugh. 'No! In hindsight, if anything were going to develop between us it would have happened way before Nigel appeared on the scene.'

'And she never guessed how you felt about her, even afterwards?'

'I had no intention of spoiling her happiness at a time when she was obviously madly in love. She was never like that around me and I realised we'd only ever be friends. But I was devastated for a while, and I let Daniela believe that I went to pieces over Wendy, and not her.'

Oh no, what a mess! 'And that's why you didn't want to get involved in the play, to begin with.'

'Yes. I never met Nigel, and I hoped to keep it that way. But I owe her. Even though she has no idea she trampled on my dreams, her friendship kept me going. Even my parents think Wendy broke my heart and, yes, it was the talk of our little village. If the reason they moved was because of gossip, I might have confessed the truth to them, but they left because Granddad couldn't manage the farm. They were always going to end up there, so it was no hardship.'

'It explained away the unexplainable,' I mutter, softly.

'Yes. And eventually I escaped to London to put it all behind me. I assumed that over time my friendship with Daniela would fade away. It did in a way, as it was just the occasional email, or call, usually something to do with our shared passion for the theatre. She very kindly recommended me to a few of her contacts and I did the odd favour for her. I don't think either of us could deny we had a bond of sorts; she just didn't feel the same way about me as I felt for her, and I'm glad it remains a secret. I only managed to decline an invitation to her wedding, because – thank goodness – I was in France working at the time.'

Poor guy. 'But you ran out of excuses when it came to the play?'

'It means a lot to Daniela and, honestly, I felt it would be like drawing a line under the past for me, once and for all. I'm glad to see how happy she is with Nigel, but I think I've repaid the debt I feel I owe her for what she did for me, without ever knowing the truth. I thought you might understand, given what you've been through this summer. It's about self-preservation, isn't it?'

'So . . . what's the favour you want to ask?'

'I can't use the excuse of sleeping over at my parents for a one-night stay, as she'll be offended. But if someone else in the village was offering me accommodation . . .'

'Me?'

He immediately backtracks. 'Sorry, I don't know what I was—'

'No, no. It's fine. It's not a problem. I have a spare room and you're right; she might think that you were avoiding her if you refuse, and you don't want that. If Nigel isn't happy, then you're doing the right thing.' Oh gosh, this is going from bad to worse, because now that he's bared his soul, how can I not do the same?

'You have no idea what a weight that's lifted.' He lets out a sigh of relief. 'Moving on rather quickly from my embarrassing revelation, you're up next.'

I take a moment to gather my thoughts. 'Like you, I don't find this easy to talk about. There are two reasons why I'm dreading going to Cornwall. The first is that while I want my mum to be happy, the thought of staying in the home she's made with Greg makes it all suddenly feel very real.'

Oliver says nothing, but I can tell by the way he's staring straight ahead that he's listening intently.

'She has a new life, one I've not really been a part of. Oh, they slept at Grandma's house last Christmas Eve as a couple, but that was the first time I'd met Greg face to face. Up to that point, I'd kidded myself that Mum's frequent jaunts to Cornwall leading up to it wouldn't come to anything. Dad hadn't been able to entice her to move to the Lake District, where he hailed from, so I told myself it wouldn't last.' Even to me that now sounds incredibly naive. 'But I was wrong.'

When Oliver starts speaking his voice is soft, and low. 'And now it's time to face the reality that she isn't coming back to Darlingham?'

'Yes.'

Oliver frowns. 'It goes even deeper than that, doesn't it?'

I heave a heavy sigh. 'When Freddie took a turn for the worse and died a couple of weeks after Mum's departure, she wasn't here to help. Grandma was a rock that Elizabeth leant on, and I was the one Grandma confided in at the end of each day. It was quickly followed by my split with Liam less than two months later and I guess at that point I felt that Mum had abandoned us. I know it sounds utterly ridiculous . . .' I tail off, miserably. It's the first time I've really acknowledged that fact.

'No. You're only human, Sienna. The timing was awful,

that's all. It's a real shame, but you can't let that drive a wedge between you and your mum. If she'd come back, even temporarily, what difference would it have made? It must have been heartbreaking for her whenever you spoke and probably took the shine off the happiness of starting over again with Greg.'

I can't even look him in the eye. 'You're right. A part of me knows that, but how am I going to get through this visit? I can't put it off any longer. The only two people I feel comfortable asking to accompany me can't make it.'

Oliver draws in a deep breath. 'I'm free. But you said there were two reasons. I'm guessing the other one is equally as sensitive, as you're clearly worried about it.'

At least he's sympathetic. 'It's a favour for a friend. It's to do with a beneficiary in a will, but the executors haven't been able to track them down.'

Oliver takes his eyes off the road for a brief moment to gaze at me. 'But you think you know where that person is?'

'I have a lead indicating he might have moved to Cornwall many years ago, but it's tenuous.'

'Goodness, Sienna. No wonder next weekend is a huge deal for you. If you're happy to give me an excuse to avoid staying with Daniela and Nigel, I'll be more than happy to help you in any way I can. You tell me what part I have to play, and I'll figure it out. That's what actors do, even amateur ones.' With that, he starts laughing and the mood between us immediately shifts.

Poor Oliver. He lost his first love to a man who makes her so happy, he doesn't want to risk upsetting what they have. As for me, I need an accomplice, and this is an offer I can't refuse.

Monday morning starts off on a good footing.

'A carousel, you say?' Elizabeth repeats and even Grandma stares at me in surprise.

'Yes, and it's being lent to us for free, courtesy of a

company called Backlight Enterprises. They're based in the Cotswolds.'

Elizabeth's hand flies up to her mouth. 'That's wonderful news, Sienna. How on earth did you pull that off?'

'It wasn't down to me, it's Oliver we have to thank, as it's courtesy of a friend of his who rents out props.'

'Well, it's very generous of him. We'll have the collection buckets out for the children's event in the afternoon and hopefully it will really boost this year's donation.' Elizabeth turns to face Grandma. 'Our girl did good!'

I watch as they smile at each other. Oliver isn't ready to reveal the stage to them yet, but I do hope he gives them a sneak preview when the cast get together for their first run-through, as they'll be delighted.

'That's it for news from me,' I confirm. 'This week I'm planning to call everyone in who's involved with the preparations for the afternoon and evening events, to run through where we're at. If there are any hiccups, I want to address them ahead of my weekend away. I'll be leaving on Friday afternoon and won't be back until late on Sunday.'

Elizabeth gives Grandma a pointed look and I wonder what's coming. 'I'm not sure you should go on your own, Sienna.'

'Oh, I'm not. Oliver is coming with me. After all the work he's put in on our behalf, he's delighted at the thought of a couple of days spent exploring the delights of Cornwall. And um . . .'

'It's a good excuse for you to get out and about?' Grandma replies.

'Yes. While we're exploring, I'm sure we'll want to pop into some of the smaller hotels with amazing views of the sea for a cup of coffee, or to rest our legs.' I wink to let them know the secret is safe with me.

Elizabeth puts her hands together in prayer fashion, raising her fingertips to her lips. 'Thank you, Sienna. We've spent a lot of time chatting over the last forty-eight hours, haven't we, Charlotte?'

'We have.' Grandma's expression instantly changes.

Elizabeth continues. 'We came to two conclusions. The first is that if your enquiries don't come to anything, then it's fate sending a message and I must accept that. The other . . .' She beams across at Grandma. 'We've had such a wonderful time that instead of rejecting invitations, in future I'm going to accept them, your grandma too! We're going to start socialising again, I mean, properly. This coming weekend, we're hosting a dinner party here for a large group of friends.'

I look slightly concerned, as I can't imagine Veronica's reaction. She panics when there's a low-key family dinner and all she has to do is reheat what Georgina has prepared.

'Oh, don't worry. We'll be liaising with the caterers to get everything set up in advance. We've hired kitchen and waiting staff to take over when Veronica leaves for the day. And when she arrives early on Sunday morning the kitchen will be spotless.'

It's lovely to see the two of them so animated. 'How exciting!' I exclaim.

'No more excuses, eh, Charlotte?' Elizabeth smiles at Grandma, who inclines her head. 'This Christmas is going to be special for us all, I can just feel it. No more morbid dwelling on past hurts and losses; it's a turning point. It's time to move on and celebrate what I've been blessed with – people who care enough to want to be a part of my life. Freddie would have expected that of me, and I don't intend to let him down.'

It's a thought-provoking moment and Elizabeth excuses herself to meet up with Georgina and begin making arrangements for Saturday night. As the door shuts behind her, Grandma gives me a reassuring smile. Finally, the spark has come alive again in Elizabeth and it's good to see her planning something just for the fun of it.

'That must have been quite a weekend the two of you had,' I reflect, the moment we're alone.

'It was.' Grandma's smile falters.

'What's up?'

She emits a gentle sigh. 'It's been a tough year for us, too. What with your mum moving away, you and Liam parting ways . . .'

I look at Grandma, feeling perturbed. 'I thought this was about Elizabeth's situation – losing Freddie and learning she has a grandson, only to face the fact that he'll never be known to her.'

'Partly. We talked a lot; we laughed, we cried, and we commiserated with each other for what we couldn't fix. Then we realised that next year is uncharted territory, as they say.'

'But Mum is only a phone call away and I'm still here, Grandma.'

There's another sigh. 'I know, but you're young and who knows what exciting things life has planned for you? Change has its ups and downs. I'm so happy that your mum has Greg, and I'm sure before too long you'll find someone to be a part of your life, too. The thing is . . . I'm going to be moving into the Hall permanently.'

My eyes widen. 'You are?'

'We're two lonely old women who've been friends for over seventy years. What we appreciate most these days is company. As you know, Elizabeth's eldest brother has been dropping hints about her finding someone to help her *run things*.'

I make a tutting sound. 'If you ask me, Stephen is overstepping the mark,' I reply, crossly.

'Actually, he touched a bit of a raw nerve. It isn't only your workload that Elizabeth is concerned about.'

'Why on earth is she concerned about me?'

'You're arriving earlier each morning and leaving later most days, Sienna, and it hasn't gone unnoticed. And how often are you here on a Saturday just to "catch up"?'

There's no point arguing with the truth. 'I'm helping to pick up the slack, that's all.'

Grandma makes a tutting sound. 'With you running the office and monitoring the finances so efficiently, Elizabeth looking after the household staff and making sure everything in the house runs smoothly, there's still no one to formally take over Freddie's responsibilities, is there? You'd already taken on everything you could when he started to decline. All you're doing now is firefighting. Am I right?'

It's true. Whenever a problem arises with one of the cottages for instance, or some of the older plumbing in the main house springs a leak, I stop what I'm doing and try my best to get it sorted quickly. But Freddie was very proactive and had a rolling maintenance programme, which has now ground to a halt because there's no one to keep on top of it.

Grandma smiles at me, knowingly. 'I pointed out to Elizabeth that an estate manager might be a useful addition to the team as, essentially, that was Freddie's role. With the tied cottages and the rentals to maintain, and the land management, it's no wonder it's put added pressure on not just you, but poor old Victor, too. Oh, he's very much like you . . . he just gets on with it but it's taking a toll. He's happy managing the gardeners, but he doesn't have the skills to look after the entire estate. Like you, he too is faced with a growing number of problems that aren't his job to tackle. And if it's urgent, it ends up on your desk.'

I can't argue with that. 'But overall, Elizabeth feels confident about the future?' I enquire.

'She admitted that what's missing from her life is companionship at the end of the day; just having someone to talk to who doesn't have an agenda of their own.' I take that to mean interference from Elizabeth's family members. 'And, equally as importantly, waking up each morning with a positive mindset rather than just whiling away the time.'

It's hardly surprising. 'You won't be working for her, as such?'

'No. This is about true friendship. Oh, we'll spend a little time moaning about our aches and pains, and gossiping, but we spark off each other. Elizabeth is keen to open the house up to other people and begin hosting charity dinners again. We're going to have some fun organising that together and doing some good at the same time.'

I'm pleased for them both, of course, but this is the last thing I was expecting. I thought Grandma enjoyed her independence. I know it's different now that Mum isn't able to pop in to see her every day, but River View Cottage has been her home for a long, long time. 'Has . . . um . . . Elizabeth told her family about your plans?'

'Yes. Both of her brothers were rather shocked but were careful how they responded.'

'Really?'

'She's very aware that there's family interest about what will happen to the estate when the time comes. Freddie supported a lot of charities, so I think there's an assumption that there will be a long list of beneficiaries. But, obviously, Elizabeth has four nephews and nieces that both she and Freddie doted on. I'm betting that there's an expectation they will inherit something, too.'

It feels wrong sitting here discussing this topic. 'Well, whatever . . . hopefully that's a long way off.'

'Ah, but it leads me rather nicely into my next piece of news, my dear. I want to pass the deeds to my cottage to you.'

My jaw drops. 'Grandma! What if . . . I mean . . . why don't you rent it out and if you ever want to move back in at any time in the future, then it'll be there for you.'

'I've talked this through with your mum. At my time of life, it's not about making money, it's about enjoying each day as it comes and not having the burden of looking after bricks and mortar. And it will give me immense pleasure to know that you have something you own, here in the village. It'll set my mind at rest. Now, I have a list as long as my arm of things to do. I haven't felt this excited in a long time; it's enlivening, so don't rain on my parade with "ifs" and "buts" – it's time for action.'

12

It's Been a Crazy Week

Considering the explosive start to the week, by Friday afternoon I'm feeling a tad more reflective. Elizabeth and Grandma have made some progress with their proposed plans, but as I've not been actively involved, I'm not sure what exactly they've been up to.

I'm hoping that Grandma will rethink the idea a little and decide the sensible thing to do is to stay at the Hall weekends only. It makes a lot more sense to me. River View Cottage is only a short walk away and it's where she and Pops welcomed Mum into the world. It's her sanctuary and so it should be.

There are so many 'what ifs' at the moment in the light of Freddie's passing. What if Elizabeth gives in to her brother, Stephen, and appoints him as estate manager? He'd love that and I'd bet good money it wouldn't take him long to insist he and his wife should live on site. Or maybe James will suddenly loom up out of nowhere, and who knows what changes would follow?

As I finish packing my suitcase, I keep an ear out for passing cars. I'm actually grateful that Oliver offered to drive us down to Cornwall. However, I'm feeling jittery. It's not just nerves about sleeping under Mum and Greg's roof for the first time, or even the search to find James. No. Everything around me feels like it's in flux again and it's unsettling.

When there's a sharp rap on the front door, I glance out the window but I can't see Oliver's car. Hurrying downstairs,

I ease the front door open to see Daniela standing there smiling at me.

'I'm so glad I caught you! I wasn't sure what time you were leaving.'

She steps inside and follows me through into the kitchen.

Glancing up at the clock, I notice that it's almost four. 'Oliver said he'd be here by four thirty at the latest. He's driving down from London.'

'It's a shame he couldn't get away a bit earlier. I'm aware that work has been causing him a few problems, lately.' Her eyes flit around the kitchen and she looks a little edgy. 'Anyway, I . . . um . . . thought I'd pop in just to say have a great time and do give your Mum and Greg my best regards.'

'I will. Do you have time for a quick coffee?' I indicate for her to take a seat.

'Just for a few minutes, as I ought to get back. Nigel finished early and he's looking after the kids. Clara is unbearably excited about having tickets for Santa's first canal boat ride of the season, tomorrow. Honestly, you'd think it was Christmas Eve and I should have known better. Now, every morning will be a countdown to the big day!'

My face lights up at the thought. 'It's all about the kids. I didn't realise the rides started this early.'

'It's the way the holidays fall this year. They run it for six consecutive Saturdays and the final Saturday before Christmas is the festive market, which is on the twenty-third this year.'

She's still avoiding eye contact with me. 'At least with Christmas Eve falling on a Sunday, more people are off work and able to enjoy it. Are you sure about that coffee?'

Now she's fiddling with the placemat in the centre of the table, her fingers sliding it to the right a little, so that it's square on.

'Daniela, what's up?'

'I think I might have upset Oliver. Maybe I've asked too much of him, but he's gone quiet on me.'

'What makes you think that?' A little chill begins to creep down my spine.

'A couple of the cast members messaged me, asking whether I'll be there next Saturday afternoon for the first run-through to test the set. I've assured everyone that of course I'll be there. I sent out a round robin email yesterday afternoon inviting everyone back to the house for dinner afterwards, but Oliver hasn't responded and—'

Thinking on my feet, I immediately interrupt her. 'I think he assumed you couldn't take part because the weekend is family time for you. I know he has a tight deadline to meet today, so he probably hasn't been checking his emails quite as frequently as usual. Ruby has swapped shifts to make herself available.'

'Oh, right; it's my fault, then, for not confirming the date with him. I don't think it'll be necessary to pull our two youngest actors into the run-through, so it'll be handy having Ruby there as she can be their stand-in. It'll allow me to determine where exactly we'll want to position them. It's very good of her.'

'She told me she's looking forward to it.'

'When he didn't respond to the group email, I wondered whether he felt I was muscling in on his arrangements. He's gone the extra mile to get everything ready and I don't want him to think I'm not terribly grateful.'

'I'm sure he'd say if he wasn't happy about something,' I assure her.

She looks relieved. 'I'm glad that Oliver is accompanying you to Cornwall. It'll make it easier . . . you know, the visit won't be quite so intense having someone else there.'

'That's what I'm hoping,' I admit. 'Are your little troupe all staying overnight?'

'Yes. I've offered the use of my two spare bedrooms, and I've booked some rooms at the pub. They said they'd toss a coin on the day to decide who sleeps where.'

'Oh . . . um . . . I don't know if Oliver mentioned it, but

I've insisted that whenever he's in Darlingham I put him up. All I've done is a little painting and aside from the time he's put into getting everything ready for the play, he's also organised a fairground ride at the Hall for free on Christmas Eve afternoon. And now he's going to help take the pressure off me this weekend. Honestly, I owe him big time.' She stares at me for a moment. 'What?'

'Is he the first man you've had under your roof since you moved into Oakleigh?'

I roll my eyes. 'The first *friend*,' I emphasise. 'If Marissa, had been free to go with me, he'd be all yours.'

'All mine?' she questions, laughing. 'He never was mine, Sienna. But after you returned to Darlingham he was the person I turned to, and likewise I was there for him.' She eases herself up off the chair. 'When he stayed with us I think he found the kids a bit noisy, but I think your offer would have been hard for him to refuse, kids or no kids.' She smiles. 'Besides, it makes me happy to think of you having some male company.'

There she goes again. 'The only company I need at the moment is someone to get me through this weekend!'

Daniela steps forward to give me a hug. 'Don't fret. The first trip was always going to be hard on you. I do feel guilty for not stepping up, but Oliver is a knight in shining armour. I know you'll be in good hands. Anyway, I'd best get back to the bedlam.'

I can see by her expression that she feels she's let me down. 'Hey, I'll be fine. Now go and rescue Nigel; and have a wonderful trip on the Santa Express cruise.'

We stroll through to the hallway, and she does a half-turn to look at me. 'I'm going to give Santa a list of my own. Item number one is a Christmas miracle, that the performance is as good as the set that Oliver has built. Everyone is talking about it, and if anything goes wrong, I'll never forgive myself.'

Daniela is really anxious, and I don't think I realised how

important it is for her morale. Especially given how awful the timing is, now that she's taken on a huge task that could kick-start her career again. 'The stage is looking awesome, and everything will be simply fine. Oliver knows what he's doing.'

'And you helped to get it to this point, Sienna. I won't forget that, my dear friend.'

For the last couple of minutes all Oliver has done is apologise, after we ended up setting off an hour later than planned.

'You can't control the traffic, or this dreadful rain,' I interject. 'And, besides, there's a reason I'm not too concerned.'

'There is?'

'Yes. It means I can text Mum and tell her we'll stop for something to eat on the way.'

Oliver frowns, as he checks left, then right before pulling out on to the main road. 'Won't she be disappointed?'

My throat is dry, and I give a little cough to clear it. 'I want her to be happy, I really do,' I state, firmly. 'But this is hard for me.'

The silence is awkward, but where do I start to explain how I'm feeling right now?

'Your mum sold the family house to set up home with Greg. That must have been a wrench for you all, including your grandma.'

'It was and I felt bad about it. Mum didn't want to sell up, but renting would have meant a whole host of strangers coming and going. That was too much for her to bear. I know she would have loved for me and Liam to move in. She even offered it to us rent free, but he said it's too out on a limb and would have added another twenty-plus minutes to his daily commute. It was a huge blow for me, because Mum wanted to give us a chance and money was never a driving factor for her. Maybe it was the final straw that made me realise Liam wasn't the one. She was prepared to forgo having a comfortable nest egg, for my happiness.'

'That's quite something, Sienna.' He glances at me for a second or two, before refocusing on the road ahead.

'In hindsight, I think I already knew that something wasn't right, but I'd convinced myself that Liam and I were just going through a bit of a stale patch.'

Oliver shrugs his shoulders. 'You weren't to know what was going to happen a few months down the line.'

'Logic doesn't really come into this. Our family home is gone forever because of me.'

We're queuing at traffic lights, and he turns to face me. 'That's a crazy way to look at it! Have you ever stopped to consider that it might have been better for your mum to make a clean break? A house is only bricks and mortar, after all. The memories remain forever.'

I tilt my head back, letting a weary sigh escape from my lips. 'I get it. My problem is that with Grandma adamant she's going to move into Silverberry Hall to be Elizabeth's permanent companion, it feels like nothing is ever going to be the same again.'

'Ah . . . more change and upheaval. It's obvious Elizabeth is desperate for company, and I think the same might apply to your grandma. The two of them have been best friends forever, haven't they?'

'Through thick and thin, and even when they were living miles apart,' I concede. 'But Grandma's cottage is all my family has left of the past and I'm not ready to take it on.'

'Nothing stays the same forever, Sienna. If your mum still lived here, would you have turned down Oakleigh and simply gone back home to live?'

I find myself chewing my bottom lip as I give it some thought.

'No. I'm used to my independence and that's why I didn't take up Grandma's offer to stay with her.' Even if I had moved back in with Mum, it wouldn't have been enough to stop her feeling lonely. 'Greg has given her a new outlook on life.'

How can I even begin to explain the tangle of emotions I'm dealing with right now?

'I was shocked when my parents ended up moving to the farm to look after my granddad. It was his lifestyle choice, not theirs. Then I realised that it held a lot of wonderful memories for my father. He spent most of his career in banking but when he returned to his roots, he was a different person. If I'd spent the best part of thirty years cooped up in an office, maybe I'd feel as he did at the time. My mother loves it. Every single one of their chickens has a name and I have a sneaking suspicion that the sheep do, too!'

We both give a little laugh.

'But it's not your thing?'

'Definitely not . . .' He grimaces. 'I don't mind a brisk walk in the countryside, but farming holds no interest for me and, fortunately, my parents both accept that. They don't understand the electronic world in which I work, and why should they, but they don't judge me for it. They know that I won't be following in their footsteps but they're happy knowing that I love what I do.'

'Isn't that a little . . . sad?'

'Why should it be? I'm sure the farm will end up in the hands of someone who has the right skills to keep it going and probably expand the operation. As I said, life doesn't stand still – for anyone, or anything.'

Am I desperately trying to cling on to the past out of some sort of misplaced sense of loyalty? 'I miss my dad and I miss the old days.' There, I've said it.

'That's only natural,' Oliver replies, his voice full of empathy. 'I miss my granddad. He was funny, straight-talking and didn't suffer fools gladly. How I wish I'd turned out more like him; he made me feel special in my own way. He said some people were meant to work with their hands and others with their brain. He said I was one of the latter, and it was a blessing. But I doubt he'd be happy about where I've ended up.'

That's quite a telling statement to make. 'Why on earth would you think that?'

'The honest answer is that I've had more pleasure getting the stage ready for this play, than I have about anything else I've worked on recently. In fact, the project I'm involved with now isn't a flashy set for a music video, but the backdrop for an exciting new play we hope will end up in the West End.'

'Really? That's awesome news, Oliver.'

He sounds pleased.

'There isn't as much money in it, but I'm doing a heck of a lot more socialising. Anyway, it's going to be at least an hour, or two, before we're likely to find a place to eat. Talk me through my role in this visit.'

I reach for my backpack and pull out two energy bars, tearing off the end of one and passing it to him. 'I simply said that you're an old friend of Daniela's. Mum already knows, from Grandma, that we've been working together in the barn getting the props ready for the play. I explained that it's been a while since you visited Cornwall and we're going to do a bit of exploring.'

'Old?' He laughs.

'You know what I mean. I wasn't looking forward to kicking off the visit with us all sitting around the table this evening, sharing a meal and facing the usual questions. Arriving later will cut that short and it would be impolite for them not to ask what you do. I'm sure they'll be fascinated, so don't miss anything out.'

I wait a few moments while Oliver finishes eating. 'Oh, so you're using me to take the pressure off you! I get it; it's like that for me whenever I visit my parents. They want to know everything I've been doing but it's always more of the same. I often feel that in some ways I'm a bit of a let-down to them.'

'I'm sure you're not! I'm grateful that you understand, though. Tomorrow won't be too bad. There's a Christmas Fayre being held in the local church hall and both Mum and Greg are committed to being there all day. Aside from breakfast, as long as we pop into town to say a brief hello, the rest of the time will be ours until we meet up in the evening. Mum has booked a table for us all for Saturday evening; by then, hopefully, it'll just be general chatter about where we've been and what they've done.'

'OK. Do you have an itinerary planned?' Oliver questions.

'That's where the other reason for my trip takes over.'

'This search for a *friend* of a friend?' he asks, his brow wrinkling.

'Yes.'

'You're not going to tell me what's really going on, are you?'

'I can't.' My tone is apologetic.

'Fair enough. I understand. What's Greg like?'

I smile to myself. 'He's a nice man, kind. He loves my mum, and he loves boats and fishing. Unfortunately, that means the conversation between us so far has been rather limited.'

'Boats? Right up until my teen years, we'd often take weekend trips down to Cornwall. My dad's boss had this huge house and a thirty-two-foot, open wheelhouse boat. We'd take a little ride along the coast doing a bit of fishing, in between anchoring up and heading inland to go for some long walks.'

Is this an omen? I seriously doubt either my first or second choice of companion for this weekend could have boasted about that.

'The plan is that we arrive late enough to have a hot drink together before we turn in for the night. There'll be just enough time to let Mum and Greg get acquainted with you and for me to bring them up to date on some of the latest goings on in Darlingham.' Then tomorrow morning, after breakfast, the detective work begins.

Hopefully, on the way there tonight we'll stumble across a nice little pub, or inn, where Oliver and I can enjoy a leisurely meal. I want to tell him about Daniela's visit, as he needs to reassure her everything is fine. She has no idea he cares enough to make sure he doesn't upset Nigel. I can't help wondering whether it's Oliver's imagination though, as Nigel isn't the jealous sort. And, as far as I can see, he has no reason at all to feel that way. Daniela only has eyes for her adorable husband.

Mum swings open the front door to Anchor House and her face instantly lights up. 'At last! Come in, come in.' She steps back, turning her head to call over her shoulder, 'Greg, get the kettle on.'

'Sorry, we're later than expected – there was a huge flood and nothing could get through.'

She shakes her head, sadly. 'Oh dear! We guessed as much. The rain has been torrential at times. Did you manage to find somewhere to stop and grab something to eat? If not I can rustle up something hot for you.'

Greg appears and we're all crammed into the narrow hallway. 'Don't stand around in a huddle, come on through to the sitting room.'

As we filter inside, the warmth is very welcome. We follow Greg into a wonderfully cosy room which has a roaring log fire.

Mum throws her arms around me, hugging me so tightly it makes me catch my breath. 'Oh, it's so good to see you, my darling daughter!'

'Same here. Sorry it's taken so long. Anyway – this is Oliver, Oliver Townsend.'

'I'm Helen and this is Greg; it's lovely to meet you!' Mum beams at him.

They all shake hands and Greg looks at me rather nervously. It's the first time I've seen him in person since last Christmas. He approaches and I smile as I accept his hug.

'Right,' he says, rubbing his hands together. 'Let me take your coats and come and sit by the fire to warm up. Are we going for hot drinks, or a nightcap?' he asks.

'Both would be very welcome after that drive!' Oliver smiles, gratefully.

'That was one convoluted detour,' I explain. 'At one point we were driving through single-track lanes and ended up drawing to a complete halt. There was a stream of cars coming towards us but we were heading up a long queue that stretched way back. It was a total impasse, until a farmer heard the honking car horns and opened up the gate to his farmyard. We were like the proverbial Pied Piper leading a convoy off road to clear the lane.'

'We'd heard on the news that some parts of Devon had serious flooding when a river burst its banks,' Mum remarks. 'I've been worried sick, so it's a huge relief now that you're here. Greg, you pour the drinks and I'll make the coffee.'

Greg heads off to hang up our coats as Oliver and I take a seat on the sofa facing the fire. After what turned out to be quite a stressful journey, we both look a little haggard.

'You certainly kept your calm, Oliver, which was more than I can claim.'

He gives a chuckle. 'I did notice at one point you had your eyes closed.'

'Oh, yes . . . when that van came towards us and forced you to mount a bank. Seriously, I thought we'd get stuck and end up stranded overnight!'

'Some people like to bully their way through, and it was obvious he wasn't going to back down.' Oliver sighs, sinking back into the sofa and stretching his legs out in front of him.

I take a moment to gaze around the room. It's homely, comfortable and, with waxed floorboards and rugs, practical.

'Are you all right?' Oliver straightens, leaning in and keeping his voice low.

'Yes. I'm fine. It's just different . . . not quite what I was expecting.'

Greg's voice announces his arrival as he re-enters the room. 'Right, I have just the drink to warm you up from the inside out, as my granddad used to say.'

Oliver glances at me rather apprehensively. I think he was expecting a beer.

'Helen tells me that the two of you have been working together preparing for a play at Elizabeth's Christmas Eve party?'

'I've been doing a bit of painting: nothing complicated, just background panels. Oliver designed the set and is making the props. He's also one of the two lead characters.'

Greg seems genuinely interested and engages Oliver in conversation while I glance around, surreptitiously. It's a strange feeling being here, as I feel like a visitor . . . but he's family now.

Mum enters with a tray. 'Greg, can you grab the footstool for me, please?'

He hurries over to drag it into place in front of the sofa and then draws two wing-backed chairs closer.

'There you go. I made it black so help yourself to milk and sugar,' Mum says, laying the tray down in front of us.

Seconds later Greg carries over two glasses. 'Same for you, my dear?'

Mum nods her head. 'Please.'

It's an interesting-looking drink served in a small tumbler with a thin slice of lemon floating on the top. Oliver and I wait until we're all seated, and Greg raises his glass. 'To rod and line, may they never part company!'

Mum giggles like a schoolgirl. 'Greg! These two aren't interested in fishing,' she berates him. 'Here's to a wonderful Christmas and New Year!'

We all take a sip and, to my surprise – and Oliver's too, judging by the look on his face – it's very palatable.

'Now this is very pleasant indeed,' I comment. 'What is it?'

Greg raises his eyebrows. 'You can't guess?'

I pause for a moment, taking another sip. 'Mmm . . . gingery and something fruity . . . cranberries?'

'Close enough,' he confirms. 'It's home-made sloe gin with ginger ale and a dash of lemon.'

Bless him, Oliver is quick to respond. 'Well, it's a real winter warmer.' At which, a little smile plays around his lips. 'And, as a lad who acquired his own rod and reel at a young age, I think that was a perfect toast!'

Mum looks directly at me, smiling. 'Maybe we missed out, Sienna, what do you think?'

I give her a horrified look. 'Taking a hook out of a fish's mouth? I think not . . .' To which everyone begins to laugh.

The ice is broken, and we spend a very pleasant hour during which Oliver seems content to explain what he does in more detail, and I give an update on the plans for the big party. But it isn't long before tiredness threatens to overwhelm me. It must be obvious to Mum because she stands and begins loading up the tray. I grab a couple of the glasses that won't fit onto it and follow her through to the kitchen.

To my surprise, she immediately puts the tray down on the island in the centre of the rather charming kitchen and shuts the door behind us.

'I . . . um . . . made up two rooms for you and Oliver. Is that all right? You said he was Daniela's friend?' Her voice is low.

'Yes. Sorry, I should have been more specific. It's just a fun weekend away and he was at a loose end. Oliver has taken time off work to transform the stage in the barn and it's good of him, as he's self-employed. He used to spend a lot of time here in the summer with his parents many years ago.'

She breathes a huge sigh of relief. 'I see.' But there's a little lift in her voice. 'It's just that the two of you seem very comfortable together.'

'Oh, working side by side recently has formed a bit of a bond. Daniela is panicking, as she literally dumped everything into his lap. But he's back in London now, and after this weekend, our paths probably won't cross again until the party.' That's not strictly true, but I don't want to mislead Mum into thinking there's anything going on between us.

'I see. Well, he's a nice young man and I won't feel so guilty now about Greg and me being tied up most of tomorrow. If you get a chance to pop in and see us, great, but if you're sightseeing and having fun, don't worry about it. I've booked a table at our favourite restaurant in Charlestown tomorrow night for seven thirty.'

Suddenly, I'm feeling emotional, and I throw my arms around her shoulders. 'I'm glad you've settled in so well here, Mum. I really am. But I do miss you.'

When she replies, her breathing is a little uneven. 'Me, too, Sienna, me too!'

13

Few and Far Between

'This is the fifth place we've visited since nine this morning. I've drunk all the tea, coffee and bottled water I can take, Sienna, unless I can grab something to eat. And I don't mean a slice of cake.'

The novelty of driving around working through the list of B&Bs and small hotels, in elevated locations and with wide-ranging sea views, is tiring. They're all within a reasonably short drive of Charlestown, but the enthusiasm is already beginning to wear off. We started at the furthest point away, a place near to Polruan, which was about a forty-minute drive and are now working our way back towards the other side of Charlestown.

It's almost twelve thirty and Oliver is right. 'I know it's been a pain, but we're whittling them down.'

'Look, I don't really understand what this is all about, but wouldn't it have been simpler to pick up the phone and just ask a few questions?'

'It's not quite as easy as that. It's . . . um . . . not the sort of information people give out.'

'Can you at least tell me what questions you ask when you saunter off to find the powder room, leaving me alone at a table nursing my drink?'

It seems that my attempts at being discreet aren't really paying off. 'The truth is that I don't have a lot to go on.'

'What *do* you have?'

Will it hurt if I tell him? He doesn't know the whole story. 'Just a Christian name and the fact that the owners, a mother and son, bought a small hotel, or B&B, in this area about twenty-odd years ago.'

'That's all?' He sounds astounded and a little disbelieving.

'Well . . . aside from the fact that it's set in an elevated position, rather out of the way and has awesome views. We're down to the last two, though. One's at Gorran Haven and the other near to Mevagissey Bay. Take your pick.'

'Which do you think is the most promising, bearing in mind that Mevagissey is probably the closest.'

I lean forward and enter the postcode for Gorran Haven into the satnav. 'If your stomach can wait another twenty-three minutes,' I chuckle, 'I know this one has a restaurant. I think the other one only serves food to people staying overnight, but it does have a bar, so it would be a pint and a packet of crisps.'

'Gorran Haven, it is then,' he confirms. ''Cos I'm starving!'

The hotel isn't quite as isolated as I was expecting from the photos I saw online, but it stands alone on a raised peninsula overlooking the beach. The village is nestled in the background as we pass the church, then take a right turn and follow the road that leads into the car park of Rock House Hotel.

'You look a little surprised,' Olivers says, glancing at me as we park up.

'I didn't think it would be so close to other properties, but it has the views, all right.'

'And some.'

It feels good to stretch our legs, but my stomach is starting to rumble. 'Shall we head straight inside to see if we can get a table?'

'Definitely.'

We make our way to the reception and the smells from the restaurant, which is off to the right, make my mouth salivate.

'Hi,' Oliver greets the receptionist behind the desk.

'Oh, sorry . . . I was deep in thought there. I think I might have broken the computer,' she laughs. 'How can I help?'

'We're exploring the area and wondered whether we could grab something to eat?'

'Have you booked?'

'No, like I said, we were just driving around.' Oliver gives her one of his special smiles and she blushes.

'For some reason I can't get up the seating plan; it's my first week here,' she explains, her eyes not wavering from Oliver's face. 'Give me a minute and I'll check with our restaurant manager. Is it just the two of you?'

'Yes,' I reply.

'Perfect!' With that she hurries away, while Oliver and I look around.

'I'd say this was the original building, wouldn't you?' he remarks.

'Probably, looking at the thickness of those windowsills. But they've done a decent job on the modern extension, although beneath the exterior render I bet there's some stunning stonework.'

'Yeah . . . but it must take a battering being so exposed. I guess it's easier to repaint it every few years to keep it looking fresh, rather than having to repoint the brickwork further down the line.'

'Sorry to keep you waiting,' the young woman calls out. 'If you'd like to come this way, they're just setting up a table for you.'

'Ah, that's wonderful, thanks!' Oliver pipes up. 'With views like that, we just had to try our luck!'

'Well—' she smiles at him, engagingly '—we hate to turn anyone away.'

'How many rooms do you have?' he enquires. I glance at him, amused that he's playing detective.

'Twenty in total. Originally there were only eight, I'm told, before the new addition was added by the current owners, Mr and Mrs Parker.'

She leads us up to a set of double doors, holding one open as we pass through. 'Well, they've done a lovely job of it. We must come back and stay sometime soon, Sienna, for a weekend break.'

The woman's eyes light up. 'I'll grab you a brochure and bring it over to you in a moment. I'll hand you over to Sarah, the restaurant manager.'

By the time we take our seats, the receptionist is back with a handful of leaflets which she hands to Oliver, who duly thanks her.

As she walks away, I lean in a little, lowering my voice. 'You have a fan, there. Thanks for kicking off the questions.'

'Did it help?'

'Well, it rules her out as a source of information if she's only been here a week and the surname Parker doesn't mean anything to me.'

He pulls a sad face. 'Sorry. I thought I was helping.'

'Oh, you were . . . you are.'

Sarah reappears with a glass of white wine for me and half a pint of local beer for Oliver. This time he leaves it to me.

'Thank you. What a beautiful spot.'

'It is, isn't it?'

'You must love coming to work. There's something about the sea that's so relaxing. We were just saying that we must come back very soon. Do all the rooms have sea views?'

'Yes, and some have dual aspect views. Ask for room number six or eleven.' She gives me a conspiratorial smile.

'How long have you worked here?'

'Ever since the new owners took over about nine years ago. It was a smaller operation back then. The expansion plans took about eighteen months to complete.'

'Ah, that explains it then, Oliver.' She looks at me askance but so does my trainee investigator. 'An old friend of mine from university moved to the area a long time ago with his mother. The last I heard they were running a small hotel looking out over the beach. I can't remember the name of the place, but I think this might be the spot.'

'If the name Freeman rings a bell, you might just have found the right place,' she exclaims. 'It was a mother and her son who ran it.'

My stomach is all a flutter, and it isn't hunger. 'Did you know them?'

'No. That was before my time, I'm afraid.' She glances around, conscious that other customers are waiting for her to clear their tables, ready for dessert and coffee. 'Anyway, can I take your orders?'

Oliver can see that I'm busy thinking and he gallantly steps in. He orders two of the specials off the fish board. Immediately Sarah is out of earshot he looks at me in earnest. 'Does that name ring a bell?'

'No, but the fact it was a mother and her son, does.'

'That's a start. I'm just . . .' He draws to a halt.

'What?'

'I know I shouldn't question you, but why don't you know this person's surname?'

He pours us both a glass of water from the jug on the table.

'Because when they moved they wanted to disappear, so the likelihood is that they changed their names.'

Oliver puts down the jug to stare at me.

'People actually do that?'

'If there's a reason to start afresh, yes, apparently.'

'Forgive me for asking this, but you're doing this for a *friend* – you're not trying to track down someone from your past, are you?'

I gasp. 'No! I've nothing to hide.'

'Are you doing it for Elizabeth?'

My expression freezes. 'Why do you think that?'

'Because it's obvious your mum doesn't know what you're doing, so it's not family business. And you'd do anything for your boss because she's like extended family to you.'

Inwardly, I groan.

'You can trust me to be discreet, Sienna. Really you can. You're the only person with whom I've shared the fact that I had feelings for Daniela. Well, until Nigel appeared in her life and swept her off her feet. It was a huge deal for me to admit to that, even though in hindsight I can see that it wouldn't have worked out between us, even if she had felt a little spark of attraction. We were only destined to be friends and I hope I haven't alienated Nigel in any way because if I have, it might make her suspicious and—'

I put up my hand to stop him right there. 'It's fine. She popped in to see me before I left, and your name cropped up. When you didn't respond to an email she sent out to the cast, she was worried that she might have upset you in some way. I said you'd been busy but you do need to get back to her. I also took the opportunity to tell her that I felt I owed you – several times over – which is why I've offered to put you up whenever you're in Darlingham. She thinks you might find the house a little noisy with the kids, that's all.' I don't add that she was delighted to think I'd finally have a man sleeping at Oakleigh, even though it does make me smile.

He lifts his glass to his mouth, then pauses for a second. 'Thanks for having my back. I'd be truly mortified if—'

'Two baked sea bass with lemon butter sauce, capers and lattice potatoes,' Sarah gushes, as she lays the plates down in front of us. 'Enjoy!'

Oliver and I stare at each other for a second. 'I understand,' I reply, softly. 'Let's eat.'

It's time to relax, unwind a little and gaze out at the stunning view. The sun has put in an appearance, and while the breeze is bitingly cold, the sea is a sight to behold, as the soft peaks shimmer with an enchanting golden hue.

'I'm not happy about you paying for lunch, Sienna,' Oliver complains, as we step out onto the terrace that runs along one entire side of Rock House Hotel.

'I told you, it's courtesy of Elizabeth, she insisted.'

'Well, it's kind of her but she doesn't owe me anything.'

'She does, actually. The play is an important part of the Christmas Eve celebrations and you've managed to snag us a wonderful fairground ride for the kids in the afternoon, for free. Freddie would have been over the moon about that.'

'Did he miss the buzz of city life after he and Elizabeth made the move?'

I pause for a moment to consider that question. 'I guess he did in a way and maybe that's why he was always up for throwing a big party. The more people he could include, the merrier. When he first retired, he was deluged with invitations to attend medical conventions as a guest speaker. He certainly knew how to capture an audience's attention and his sense of humour had an air of flamboyancy to it.'

'That must have been a little dull for Elizabeth,' Oliver points out.

'Oh,' I laugh, dismissively. 'She rarely accompanied him. At that time the Hall was undergoing major renovations and the builders worked six days a week, sometimes seven. I think he often accepted invitations simply to take a break away from it. Elizabeth was in her element but he found the noise and the disruption an annoyance.'

Oliver chuckles. 'Well, between them they ended up with a beautiful home and a long and happy marriage. You can't knock that.'

We saunter over to the waist-high perimeter wall to stare out over the water. Something tells me this is where James and his mother, Briony, settled. It would have been perfect for them and manageable without the new extension.

Living on the edge of a small village community in a quiet and rural backwater would have given them a sense of privacy and time to integrate with the community when they were ready. Over the years I have no doubt that the place itself has grown and attracted more tourists, but it seems likely that after her death, James would have decided to move on yet again. And who could blame him? I wonder whether he's married. He'd be in his early thirties now, by my reckoning.

'You're deep in thought.' Oliver steps closer. 'Is this the end of the trail? The man you're looking for could be anywhere and you've run out of leads.'

I sigh. 'I know. It would be nice to think that he's happy, wherever he ended up. Through no fault of his own, he was distant from his wider family and that must have felt rather isolating at times. Especially when they began their new life here.'

The sound of a chainsaw kicking into life makes us both spin around. Curious, Oliver walks over to the far side of the terrace. It isn't until I realise he's chatting to someone over the wall that I drag myself away from gazing at the lustrous and mesmerising swell of the waves.

'. . . a lot of work for you.' Oliver turns, hearing my footsteps. 'Sorry, Sienna, I got distracted. Are you ready to go?'

I nod my head as I peer over the wall and see an older man looking up at Oliver.

'Hi,' I call out. 'You're going a great job.'

'But I'm out of petrol,' the man laughs. 'Sod's Law, isn't it?'

He's perched rather precariously, as it's quite a slope. The grassy bank leads down to a sudden drop, beyond which is a collection of sharp rocks and deep water.

The man pulls himself up to stand on a flat, shallow ledge while he untethers himself. His head and chest are now visible and we watch as he wraps the line – which is anchored to a metal hook embedded in the top of the wall – around his arm several times. Oliver leans over, extending his hand to grab the chainsaw from him.

'Appreciated. You appeared at just the right time.'

Oliver lays the heavy bit of kit on the floor and then immediately extends his hand to help the man clamber up onto the wall. 'That's quite a perilous job. You need a good head for heights, that's for sure!'

'It's easy to miss your footing, but I'm a dab hand at it now.' He stops to catch his breath. 'It's just that the wind is blowing up, so it's time to quit before I make a mistake. I should have waited until Monday when my assistant was around, but we were worried if the branch toppled off the edge it might hit a passing boat, given the wide overhang. Some people sail very close to the cliffs, looking for caves.'

Oliver nods his head. 'Best to be safe than sorry.'

The man swings his legs over the wall, while he detaches the rope from a harness around his waist and begins rolling it up.

'Anyway, thanks again. Right place, right time!' The man sticks out his hand and the two men shake.

'I'm Oliver and this is Sienna.'

'I'm Martin. Are you staying at the hotel?'

'Sadly, no,' I reply. 'My mum lives a couple of miles from Charlestown, and we've been exploring. We've just had an amazing lunch in the restaurant, though.'

He stands, heaving the large coil of rope over his shoulder, and bends to grab the chainsaw in the other.

'I'll carry that.' Oliver steps forward to take it from him.

'That's kind of you.' The man turns to lean back over the wall, heaving a backpack up and slinging it over his other shoulder. 'My van's in the car park.'

'I'm assuming you're a local?' Oliver engages him in conversation as I follow on behind them.

'Yes. Born and bred in the area, that's me. I do general maintenance. Mainly outside work.'

'Sienna here thinks she knows the people who sold this place to the current owners,' Oliver continues, and the man turns around to look at me.

'Is that so? Mrs Freeman was a lovely woman. Everyone thought highly of her.'

Well done, Oliver. 'I didn't know her personally, but her son was a friend of a friend.'

'Oh, Ashley! He was one of those lads who wanted to have a go at everything,' he laughs. 'He was like my sidekick every time his mother called me in to do a job.'

My mouth goes dry. 'It must have been a wrench to leave this place.'

'It was but it wasn't the same after his mum passed.'

'Yes, I'd heard about that, but my friend said they lost touch. Do you know where he is now?'

'Him and his partner run a gift shop in Charlestown – Driftwood, you might know it? It's in that stone building they call The Old Fisherman's Store.'

I can't believe what I'm hearing, and I must look as dazed as I feel.

'What a coincidence, we're headed that way next, so we'll pop in and say "hi",' Oliver replies, being on the ball. 'Where do you want this?' He indicates to the chainsaw.

'I'll open up the back of the van. I don't keep anything on site these days. The Parkers are good clients, but with Mrs Freeman and her son, they needed more of a hand . . . you know, what with her being a widow. She was kind enough to let me use that old shed over there to house a lot of my stuff, as most of my jobs are in this area. It's different now, of course, and I have a lock-up garage in town.'

All credit to Briony. Hearing Martin acknowledge that it must have been a struggle for her at first, rings true. It's easy to see why James was eager to learn, to ease the load for his mother. According to Briony's cousin, James . . . I mean, Ash, was about eleven, or twelve, when they moved here. He was too young to have many life skills, but I'm sure he learnt a lot from Martin.

'Here, Sienna.' Oliver holds out his hand. 'Take the keys and I'll join you in a bit.'

I leave the two men to walk over to Martin's van, hardly daring to believe that in the next hour, or two, I could be face to face with Elizabeth's grandson.

* * *

The Old Fisherman's Store is home to three separate businesses, each having its own floor. Driftwood, advertised as *nature's gifts*, is at the top of two rather steep flights of stairs but the views it commands out over the harbour at Charlestown are incredible. Gazing out at the tall ships moored up, all battened down to withstand the winter storms, would normally be enough to inspire my imagination. But today it isn't wistful images of sailors milling around, saying goodbye to loved ones before they boarded their boats, that fill my head. I'm standing here psyching myself up, wondering whether or not I should march up to the desk in the far corner and ask the attractive young woman if Ash Freeman is in the building.

To my surprise, Oliver grabs my hand and I turn to look at him.

'Are you sure you want to do this?'

I nod my head, unable to speak until I clear my throat and lean into him, my voice low. 'I'm going to wander around taking a few snaps of the displays with my phone. I'll find something that's a one-off and when I hand it to you, can you walk over to the desk and ask if they have another one like it?'

From the constant clatter and general noises that intermittently fill the air, it's obvious that someone, possibly several people, could be working away in the back rooms behind the desk.

'Okaaay . . . but why?'

'If a man appears, I want to take a photo of him, discreetly, of course. Then I'll come over and pay for the item.'

'What if it's an old guy, or the woman says they only have what's on show?'

'Then, I leave with a gift for Grandma. Ash might not be here today, but I note that they open Sundays, we could pop in again tomorrow.'

I slowly slip my hand out of his, our fingertips touching

for a few brief seconds as we disconnect, and I search in my bag for my phone. 'Goodness,' I reply, raising my voice a little, 'Grandma would adore this place!'

Oliver looks a tad surprised, before he twigs what I'm doing. 'That means we're going to be here a while,' he groans. 'Let's split up, darling, and shout if you see anything you think will be perfect for her.'

Hearing our chatter, the young woman's eyes follow Oliver, and not me, as I mingle among the half a dozen other people browsing. Luckily, I'm not the only one taking the odd snap here and there. It's not solely items made out of driftwood, but skilfully hand-carved gifts and beautiful salad bowls turned on a lathe. There are also a lot of beautifully crafted silver boxes, a range of jewellery with semi-precious stones and handmade candles. It's a delightful place to shop, but I need to find a solitary item and Oliver is already glancing over at me, impatiently.

'Oliver,' I call out. 'Come and take a look at this!'

He strolls over to me nonchalantly, looking slightly bored as if shopping isn't his thing. I find it hard not to smirk as he doesn't turn a hair, instantly morphing into some imaginary role. 'Already? That's unusual for you,' he chuckles.

Having taken a photo of it, I place my phone down on the display unit while I gingerly pick up the piece. It's a gorgeous length of knotted driftwood, into which holes have been drilled and four tea lights sit in the recesses. 'It's perfect, but when Mum sees it she'll want one for the centre of her dining table, too.'

Oliver takes it from me. 'I'll find out if they have another in stock.' His smile is playful as he turns on his heels and heads for the sales desk. I continue to browse, taking a few more random photos of items that catch my eye.

I'm straining my ears, but I can't hear what he's saying to the woman as they're too far away. The sound of a buzzer kicking into life attracts my attention and I slowly make my way towards Oliver. Suddenly, a man appears in the doorway and just like that I get the shot, slip the phone into my bag and step up the pace.

'Ash, I think this is the last one, isn't it?' the woman behind the counter checks.

My goodness, my heart is literally pounding in my chest, and I can feel the heat rising up from my neck.

'Yep, 'fraid so,' he confirms.

While I'm gathering my wits about me, Oliver turns to face me. 'Do you want to look for something else for your mum, darling?' I'm standing here blinking at him, not sure quite what to do, or say. 'Or give this to her and look for something else for your grandma?'

'Oh . . . right, um . . .'

'Look, if you can give me a couple of days,' Ash interrupts, 'I have some more driftwood drying out. I can make something up for you. Each one is a unique shape, obviously. What size did you want? The same as this one, or smaller . . . larger?'

It's hard to take in Ash's words. I'm seeing his grandfather's hazel-green eyes staring back at me; the same flecks of gold that lit up Freddie's eyes like a starburst, make my heart skip a beat.

'Oh, that's kind of you. We're heading home tomorrow, but my mother lives close by and can collect it herself. If you can make one that's a little bigger so it accommodates five tea lights, that would be perfect,' I enthuse. But it's not over a custom gift, it's the realisation that the search is probably over. It shouldn't take the solicitors long to follow the trail that led me here.

'Hey, no problem. We like unique and bespoke, don't we, Jasmine?' They exchange fleeting smiles.

I watch the young woman carefully wrap the gift in pale blue tissue paper and notice she's wearing a beautiful white gold engagement ring. She slides the package into a smart brown carrier bag with string handles, sporting the shop's logo.

'We open seven days a week, ten till four,' she informs us.

'Perhaps give Ash until Thursday to get it ready?' She glances at him for confirmation, and he nods his head, giving us a parting smile before disappearing back into the workshop.

As I make the payment with my credit card I'm still in a daze, so Oliver grabs the bag, thanks the young woman and catches my free hand to steer me towards the exit.

Once we're out on the small landing, he immediately turns to look at me.

'You think it's him, don't you? Did you get your shot?'

'Yes, and yes.' And I'm reeling. My heart is still pounding so fiercely in my chest that my legs feel a little unsteady and Oliver tightens his grip on my hand. I'm so very grateful for his support as we make our way back out into the fresh air.

The impossible has happened, but I'm not sure exactly what to do next. It feels wrong to just walk away and yet that's the remit I was given. But I'm feeling conflicted and I don't really know why.

14

A Huge Dilemma

We're back in the heart of Charlestown this evening, sitting opposite my mum and Greg at The Lobster Pot. Ironically, this amazing restaurant is only a short distance from The Old Fisherman's Store.

'I'm so glad you had time to call in to the Christmas Fayre.' Mum smiles proudly at me, then Oliver. 'It's being held every Saturday up until the big day and is a little boost for a number of cottage industries around here.'

As we shopped, I noticed her flitting around, standing in for several of the one-man-band stallholders so they could take a break.

Greg reaches out to grab Mum's hand. 'It's going to be even more successful this year now that you're running it, Helen.'

'You are?' I had no idea, I thought she was just helping out.

'Yes,' Greg replies before Mum can utter a word. 'The lady who used to organise it retired after last year's event, saying it was too much for her. To be honest, nothing had changed for years, and it was usually the same old thing. You know, a raffle just inside the door, home-made cakes, a flower stall, second-hand books, a tombola, some hand-knitted items . . .' He pats Mum's hand lovingly, before withdrawing it.

'Well, it took me by surprise,' I remark. 'There was a fabulous selection of handmade items.' Both Oliver and I walked away with a carrier bag full of some delightful festive gifts. They were more reasonably priced than you'd find in the shops, obviously, because the overheads are lower.

Mum's eyes sparkle. 'It seems there used to be a bit of a ... pecking order when it came to allocating spaces. I decided to shake it up a bit and now it's first come, first served.'

Greg bursts out laughing. 'And you reminded them all that the second-hand stuff is fine for summer events, but at this time of the year people are looking for inspiring items to wrap up and place under the tree.'

'Was I that blunt?' Mum questions, a look of anxiety flashing over her face.

'No. Of course not,' he instantly reassures her, his eyes twinkling.

Even a stranger can see that he's head over heels in love with my mum.

'You were diplomatic, but to the point. It's one of the things I admired about you when we first met.'

Mum's cheeks begin to colour up. 'I'm not usually a clumsy person and bumping into you was a total accident.' She gives a light-hearted little laugh. 'After making you spill most of your drink down the front of your shirt, I wasn't about to let *you* buy *me* a drink.'

'Ah, but the second time our paths crossed, you did.'

Oh, how I wish the ground would open up and swallow me!

Oliver looks on amused, while I say the first thing that comes into my head. 'That's Mum, all right. But the whole of Darlingham misses her organisational skills.'

It sounds awkward but I wasn't prepared for this. The strong connection between them is so obvious it's almost embarrassing to watch. But if I had any doubts about Greg's intentions, they've certainly evaporated. It's just a lot to handle right now. I make eye contact with Oliver, hoping he'll take it as a hint and change the subject.

'It's been a fun day,' he chimes in on cue. 'I particularly loved the old skittle alley. I haven't played since my granddad was alive. Unfortunately, his local pub was turned into a wine bar a couple of years after he died, and they ripped it out.'

'Oh, we have it all here! Skittles, darts, and in the summer even French *boules*. It's a lot more fun than lawn bowling, as I swear it's more about luck than anything else,' Greg chortles.

'That's because you're not very good at it,' Mum quips, and he pretends to be crestfallen.

I sit back, only half listening to the banter but it's good to see. Mum said that I *shouldn't have*, when I asked if she could collect the little gift I'd ordered for her from Driftwood as a thank you for this weekend. She said she was simply delighted that I was happy to come and spend time with her and Greg. A part of me did feel a tinge of guilt for the other reason behind the gift, but I know she'll love the centrepiece for her table.

Coincidentally, it turns out to be one of Mum's favourite places to shop and the silver leaf-shaped earrings she gave me last Christmas came from there. Mum told me that Jasmine makes the jewellery and the silver boxes herself, so together she and Ash make the perfect team.

I'm so glad I didn't say anything to him, although I sorely wanted to. He came across as such a genuine and friendly guy, but where would I begin a conversation like that? Besides, that's not what Elizabeth asked me to do.

Oliver, Greg and Mum have slipped into a lively conversation about fishing. Much like me, it's not exactly Mum's idea of fun, but the guys insist it's not about the catch, it's simply a wonderful way to relax. Greg goes on to suggest that Oliver might like to join him and his friends on their first boat trip next year and I'm genuinely surprised.

'And how about you, Sienna?' Greg immediately turns his attention to me.

'Oh, I'm not sure I have my sea legs, unless the water is so calm there isn't a ripple.' I laugh it off.

'You'll come, won't you, Helen?' Greg turns to look at Mum.

'Hmm . . . I think maybe I'll pass this time. I'm sure Oliver will enjoy a day out with you and your buddies while Sienna and I find something else to do.'

Did Mum put Greg up to this? I wonder. What on earth is Oliver going to think? I thought I made it very clear to her that we aren't a couple. Now there's this expectation that if he's going to pay a visit, we'll be together.

'That sounds like a plan to me,' Greg, replies, with gusto. 'I think we should raise a toast to seal the deal!'

I grudgingly join in, trying not to look as uncomfortable as I feel.

'Oh, we should also toast Grandma, as she's about to make the big move to Silverberry Hall,' Mum adds as our glasses chink. 'And Sienna moving into the cottage where I was born, of course. At last, my darling, you'll be putting down some permanent roots!'

Oliver glances at me for a brief moment before plastering on a genial smile. Greg goes on to say something about it being *all change*, but my thoughts are whirling. It's time to speak up, albeit that this really isn't the best time to be discussing family stuff. 'It's not definite, Mum.'

'That's not what I was told,' she insists.

'Well . . . I'm not sure it's wise for Grandma to give up her independence and move into Silverberry Hall permanently. Wouldn't she be better off just spending the weekends there to keep Elizabeth company and help host whatever do's they have in mind?'

Mum's expression is one of genuine surprise. 'Elizabeth needs a companion, and in return, your grandma will be guaranteed a comfortable home, worry free, for the rest of her life.'

'But what if anything changes—'

'No one goes on forever, but this is an estate we're talking about, Sienna. If you're fearing the worst . . . there are a number of options if that should happen. Even the cottages are well maintained, and you can guarantee that Elizabeth will make provision for her old friend.'

It's what Mum doesn't know about the other things going on in Elizabeth's life that worries me. 'Yes, but—'

'Sienna, your grandma rang me yesterday afternoon to talk about what she's going to do with her furniture. There are only a few pieces she intends to take with her. She said most of the furniture is too old-fashioned for you and asked if there was anything in particular I'd like. As far as she's concerned, the decision has been made.'

Greg and Oliver exchange awkward glances.

'I still think it would be a good idea to have a . . . a trial run for a few months and see how it goes.'

'Inheriting your grandparents' beautiful cottage and making it yours would make her happy, my darling. Just accept that with good grace.'

Greg clears his throat. 'Maybe Sienna has a point, Helen. It's a big decision for your mother to make and it all seems a little rushed,' Greg points out.

'I think that moving in with her recently widowed friend of over seventy years, when they're both on their own, is a sensible idea. It's worse for Elizabeth as she's saddled with that big old house, but even my mother admits that living on your own isn't easy the older you get. They're perfectly capable of deciding for themselves what will make them happy and that's companionship.'

Ooh, I think Greg regrets getting involved now and he takes a hefty slug from his wine glass. Oliver, too, is looking a bit hot and bothered.

'I check on Grandma every single day, Mum, and I can be there in minutes if she needs anything at all. I love River View Cottage, of course I do, not least because it's full of wonderful memories, but the timing isn't right.' Mum's face pales and I feel I need to justify myself. 'Can't it wait a while until Elizabeth is back to her old self?'

'Oh, I see.' Her voice softens. 'When someone loses a lifetime partner, nothing is ever the same again, my darling. I know Elizabeth hasn't found it easy, but are you saying that she's starting to go downhill?'

This is going from bad to worse. Oliver has seen for himself that Elizabeth and Grandma are strong women who have a lot of life left in them, and I can't lie, but I also can't mention Elizabeth's grandson. It's a complication that could have ramifications, but we won't know for sure for a while yet.

'No, no . . . I agree that she would benefit from having a constant companion for the time being, to help lift her spirits. However, that might not always be the case.'

'Well, it's what they're set on doing.' Mum presses her lips together, ostensibly putting an end to the conversation.

I'm left feeling exasperated and it's time to throw a spanner in the works, as it's the best I can come up with. 'I don't mean to sound ungrateful, but I'm not ready to take on a four-bed cottage when there is only me. And what if Elizabeth allows Stephen to talk his way into getting hands-on at Silverberry Hall? We've never got on and if he takes on the role of estate manager, I don't think I could stand working in the same office with him. In my opinion, he's no replacement for Freddie, that's for sure.'

Mum gasps. 'You'd consider changing jobs?'

'All I'm trying to point out is that I don't know what my future holds.'

Fortunately, the waitress arrives with our starters, and once we're eating, Oliver ever so politely changes the subject and gets Greg talking about the boat repair business.

I can't let Grandma give up her cottage when I have no idea what Elizabeth's reaction will be when I tell her I've found her grandson. I know she said she didn't want to get involved, but did she really mean that?

What a mess I've gotten myself into this weekend. Still, I don't think Oliver will be in such a hurry to take up Greg's offer now after sitting through that little ordeal. He's not the only one who values their privacy, and I can't even imagine what he thinks of my family, other than they don't hold back – even in front of new acquaintances. Poor him!

When we get back to Anchor House it's almost midnight, and Mum and Greg look weary, so they say goodnight. The conversation ruined the ambience of the evening, and we all feel awkward about it. It's a bit of a relief to have Oliver to myself, because I couldn't let him go to bed without some sort of explanation about my behaviour this evening.

It's obvious he can sense how upset I am and he hangs back.

'Is it too late to suggest I make us a coffee?' I offer.

He shakes his head. 'I sleep like a log no matter what. I'll make it if you point me in the right direction.'

While he's waiting for the kettle to boil, I sit myself down at the kitchen table, nervously fiddling with a pile of handmade wooden coasters and wondering whether they came from Driftwood.

As soon as Oliver is seated next to me, I turn to look at him. 'I'm so sorry about this evening. Mum always says what she thinks, a bit like Grandma.'

He gives a little shrug. 'Hey, I understand. I've had an enjoyable day and sorted most of my Christmas shopping in one fell swoop. Not that I buy a lot of presents, admittedly. Most of my friends usually get an expensive bottle of wine in a bottle bag,' he muses.

'I'm glad Mum has managed to join in and become a real part of the community so quickly. But it's true to say that our village isn't quite the same without her presence.'

'You're all going through a period of change, and when that affects three generations, it's not going to be easy on any of you.'

Wise words, indeed. I stare down into the coffee mug in front of me. 'It's what I can't say that could upset things. That's why I'm so desperate to have Mum on my side to encourage Grandma to keep her options open. Just for a little while.'

Oliver sits back in his chair, drumming his fingertips lightly on the table. 'You don't have to explain anything to me, Sienna. I'm just passing through and grateful to return a favour when you've been so generous with your time. I hope you don't mind me saying this, but this thing with Ash, will it affect your mum, or your grandma, the most?'

'A firm no, to the first and a *maybe* to the second, but only indirectly.'

'Ah.' He shifts in his seat. I can tell that while he's not comfortable asking me questions, he's only trying to be helpful. 'So, your mum isn't in the picture?'

'No and she may never be. That's one of the problems at the moment, always trying to be one step ahead in my thinking in case I let something slip that I shouldn't.'

'Fortunately, the worst-case scenario rarely happens.'

'You're saying that I should think positively and assume the solution will be straightforward?'

'Why not? It's less stressful for a start. Besides, Elizabeth and your grandma, Charlotte, are ladies with spirit. They're going to be in their element, and they'll take care of each other no matter what.'

I take a sip of coffee, disparate thoughts filling my head.

Oliver's eyes meet mine. 'It's not just that, is it?'

'I know Grandma means well, but, for starters, I've never owned a house before and been responsible for maintaining it.' I take another sip of coffee, trying to explain why I'm feeling so conflicted. 'As I said, the truth is that I don't know what the future holds for me.'

He frowns. 'Because Elizabeth isn't getting any younger?'

'Not exactly . . .'

'OK. Now you've lost me.' He lowers his voice, although the walls in this house are a good two-foot thick. 'I'll throw this out there and you can tell me to mind my own business if you like. I know Elizabeth has brothers, nieces and nephews, but has she asked you to track down Ash because now that Freddie has passed, she's revising her will? Lots of families have secrets that remain buried, but if ever a wrong is going to be put right, a will is a convenient time to do that.'

In fairness, it's a logical enough conclusion to make, given what happened today. Maybe he's imagining the offspring of a love child, or – something closer to the truth – a relative who was cut off. However, if Oliver hadn't accompanied me, I probably wouldn't have stopped to talk to Martin at Rock House Hotel and I might never have found Ash.

'I feel I owe you some sort of explanation, but it's complicated and probably not quite what you're imagining. But, yes, a wrong was done a long time ago, but when people change their name it usually means they don't want to be found.'

'It's tricky when someone simply wants to make amends for the past, I should imagine. And you're the go-between?'

'No. I merely hand over the contact details and my job is done. There's a third party involved.'

He shakes his head at me, sceptically. 'But now you're conflicted about something, and you feel guilty. Could it upset things between Elizabeth and your grandma in some way?'

Oliver is very perceptive in piecing things together. 'Possibly.'

He pauses, takes a long swig of his coffee and sits there cradling the mug in his hands. 'You're a good person, Sienna. Do what feels right. It sounds to me that, whether you like it or not, there's going to be fallout. But who, in your opinion, is the innocent party in all this?'

I answer almost without thinking. 'Ash.'

'Then do right by him, and your conscience is clear.'

I'm not even sure that's possible, given that Elizabeth is also an innocent party, but I appreciate Oliver's candour and empathy. And it directs his thoughts away from this being a family matter; Ash could simply be a distant relative who was wronged.

'Thanks. I just feel like I'm being pulled in all directions at the same time. And now I've upset Mum, because she has no idea why I'm trying to persuade Grandma she doesn't have to effect the changes overnight.'

'It's not an easy topic of conversation for either of you. Maybe . . .' His words tail off.

'Maybe what?'

'What if this isn't so much about your grandma, as it is about you? My parents are the same. I'm happy as I am, but they keep dropping hints about me settling down.' He starts laughing. 'I live in a nice apartment in London overlooking the city. I have a job I love doing, but I'll never be Mr Nine-to-Five. One day they'll come to understand that I like my life just the way it is, but, somehow, I don't think the same is true for you.'

'No, maybe you're right. The truth is that I'm heartily sick of change. I just want life to quietly tick over for a while so I can fathom out what I want,' I reply, stifling a yawn. I stand, grab the mugs and walk over to put them in the dishwasher. Oliver stands, hovering in the background.

'I've learnt that some problems fix themselves over time. But when it comes to this particular issue that you're grappling with, I'm guessing you see it as more of a moral dilemma. That means you feel you could influence the outcome, but you don't know that for sure. Secrets lie buried for a reason, because some wounds never heal. With the best will in the world, not everything is fixable.'

I step forward, thinking he's about to turn and head upstairs, but he doesn't move and now we're less than a foot apart. He stares down into my eyes and then, without any warning, he stoops to plant a kiss on my cheek.

'Sleep well, Sienna. Tomorrow is another day.'

I find myself having to catch my breath, but he's already opening the door into the hallway, and I follow a few steps behind. As Oliver draws to a halt outside of his allocated bedroom, he half turns to smile at me, mouthing, 'Goodnight.'

I'm left, standing here as he quietly closes the door behind him. Oliver has a way of looking at things and summing them up quite succinctly and dispassionately. How I wish I could just sit back and simply let life unfold, as he does. Sadly, I'm not like that. I have this strong desire to fix things I think are broken, and there's where the real problem lies.

It doesn't only influence my dealings with the people I love, but the way I live my own life. I wanted to put down roots with Liam. I longed to follow in the footsteps of Grandma and my mum, finding someone who would make my life complete. And whenever I see Daniela, even when she's sleep-deprived, stressed because Nigel is working away and feeling she's lost any sense of self, I'd dearly love to have what she has.

Liam cheated on me because . . . because maybe I wasn't enough. It left me feeling rejected, miserable and alone. The last thing I can cope with now, when I'm finally beginning to pick myself up, is even more upheaval.

I find myself sighing. Drinking coffee this late was a huge mistake. My mind isn't ready to switch off and it won't, not until I've decided what exactly I'm going to say to Elizabeth on Monday morning. My head is saying keep it simple, give her exactly what she asked for, and no more. But my heart is saying that if Elizabeth and Ash could just meet up . . . who knows what might happen?

15

Damage Limitation

'Morning, Georgina. How was your weekend?'

'Lovely, thank you. I managed to get tickets for the Santa Christmas Cruise, and I had a wonderful afternoon with my daughter and the grandkids, up at the canal at Frampton on Severn. We bumped into Nigel and Daniela; what a lovely little family they are but, oh my, do they have their hands full. Pixie kept straining on her lead and almost pulled poor little Clara over. And William spent the entire time we were chatting trying to escape from his pushchair. How was Cornwall?'

She pours me a large mug of coffee and I smile, gratefully. 'We had a wonderful time, but this morning I'm feeling shattered. Yesterday, we did a two-hour ramble along the cliff path and back, and a walk along the beach, before enjoying a traditional Sunday roast at Mum and Greg's local pub. My calf muscles are aching like crazy this morning. Is Elizabeth, or Grandma, up and about yet?'

'No. Veronica left me a note to say all the bedrooms were occupied on Saturday night but there are only two for breakfast and they won't be down until nine. I guess the party weekend went well.'

'Oh, I didn't realise they had plans for yesterday, too. Gosh, they've got more stamina than me!' I laugh.

'You know what they're like when Elizabeth and your grandma get together to let their hair down. Still, the kitchen was spick and span when I arrived first thing. If I'd known it was going to be a full house, I'd have got my ladies in early this morning to make a start stripping the beds.'

Even so, her expression tells me that she's not complaining. 'It's not been an easy time for anyone, has it?'

Georgina lets out a poignant sigh. 'Elizabeth used to brief me every morning straight after breakfast. That hasn't happened since Freddie passed. Admittedly, with very little happening here by way of entertaining, there hasn't been much going on during the week for me to organise. Whenever I get the chance I do ask her if she's expecting company at the weekend. She'll often look at me rather vacantly and mutter something about not being sure. So, I simply order a little extra, just in case, because I know she doesn't like to waste food and neither do I. However, several times I've arrived on a Monday morning to find the fridge almost empty and it's obvious they descended en masse.'

'And probably unannounced,' I add, tetchily. I know it's been annoying Elizabeth. She's too polite to turn family away and tell them what she really needs is a little recovery time, alone. 'It's not your fault, Georgina. You've been doing your best during a difficult period.'

'Yes, but I'm worried her brothers might feel I'm not doing my job properly.'

'Well, what they think doesn't really matter. Everything has been in limbo and we've all been treading carefully around Elizabeth, out of respect. If Freddie were still here they wouldn't be inviting themselves over unannounced.' It makes me fume!

'I'm not complaining, Sienna . . . I just wanted you to be aware. Your grandma had a quiet word with me and she's assured me I'll be in the loop from now on. But you know what Elizabeth's family are like, the changes will no doubt cause a bit of a stir. When it comes to weekend events, your grandma and I are going to put our heads together to get everything organised well in advance.'

'That's great news, Georgina. It should definitely help to get things back on track.'

'I hate bothering Elizabeth when it's obvious that her thoughts are elsewhere. Often, she raises a smile, but she wears it like a protective coat.'

The look we exchange is empathetic.

'I know. I get that too, but maybe things are finally about to change for the better.'

'Yes, well . . . let's hope the family back off a little, eh?'

I raise my eyebrows to the heavens, thinking that'll be a miracle in itself and Georgina gives a little laugh. I hope it sends out a clear message to them all that they can't simply regard Silverberry Hall as their personal home-away-from-home just because Freddie is no longer here.

'Right, if anyone asks, I'll be in the study and I probably won't surface until lunchtime.'

'I doubt you'll get any interruptions. The partygoers will need time to recover,' she giggles, as I head off to start my working day.

I grab the carrier bag I'd left in the boot room, eager to get started. To my surprise, when I sit down at my desk there's a small piece of paper tucked under the edge of the keyboard. I unfold it to see it's a note from Grandma.

Morning! When you get here, text me and I'll be straight down. We had two very late nights, but you know me. No doubt I'll be up with the lark and lying on the bed reading. x

As my fingers tap away, I wonder what this is about. I hope Mum hasn't spoken to her about the little exchange we had on Saturday night at the restaurant. By comparison, yesterday was much more relaxed and the two of us got to wander off together and chat a little more openly. I apologised to her for overreacting, but she said there was no need. Mum said that she regretted not being there for me after the split with Liam, and that it was only natural that I needed time to think about my future.

In the car on the journey back to Darlingham, Oliver seemed to think it wasn't quite as awful an exchange as I'd perceived it to be. He said it was simply a frank discussion, but my recollection was that there was a distinct edge to Mum's tone. I felt she wasn't really listening to what I had to say, and to my embarrassment, in standing my ground I succeeded in making both Greg and Oliver feel uncomfortable.

When I switch on the PC I immediately begin trawling through my emails. I'm delighted to see one from Ron, at Backlight Enterprises, confirming that the carousel will be delivered the afternoon before Christmas Eve. He'll arrange for it to be collected on Boxing Day morning, as it has to be taken to a film set in Somerset. I thank him and give him my mobile number, suggesting that he give me a call when he sets off so I can get people to move their cars ahead of his arrival.

There's a tap on the door and Grandma appears. 'It's only me!' She hurries over and sinks down into the seat alongside the desk. 'Well? How did it go?'

I take my hands off the keyboard, surprised to hear the excitement in her voice. 'Fine. Mum's really settling into the community there and—'

'Oh, I know she's fine, but what about the other little matter?'

I grab my phone, get up the photo I took of James and hold it out to her. 'I think I might have found him.'

Her jaw gapes as she stares down at it. She passes the phone back to me, putting a finger in the air. 'Give me a moment!' And off she scurries.

Please, please don't fetch Elizabeth down here, Grandma, that inner voice pipes up. But I needn't worry, as she returns with one of the photos Elizabeth keeps on top of the piano in the main sitting room. She places it on the desk beside the phone and we both stare down in amazement.

'He has Freddie's eyes!' she half whispers.

'I thought the same thing. And his chin, too. Are there any photos of Peter?'

'Not on display, but I know Elizabeth has a special album she keeps in her bedroom next to her bed. Oh, Sienna! Tell me all about it.'

I explain that it was more by chance, and down to Oliver striking up a conversation with someone working in the garden, rather than my detective skills, that tracked him down. 'As soon as I saw him, despite the fact he goes under another name, I knew it was James.'

'But he's not James Stuart-Adams anymore?'

'No. He's Ashley Freeman, Ash for short, and he lives with a young woman named Jasmine. Together they run a shop in the heart of Charlestown.'

'As in *Free Man*?' Grandma gasps in disbelief.

'Gosh, the irony of that went right over my head!' I muse. I hand her the carrier bag tucked beneath my desk. 'I brought this back for you. Ash is a carpenter and he made this in his workshop.'

Grandma unwraps it, setting it down on the desk as if it's not simply a lump of driftwood, because we both know that it's so much more than that. 'It's beautiful. What are you going to tell Elizabeth?' she asks, a little breathlessly.

'I don't know. He's a nice guy, hard-working and oblivious to why I was there.'

Grandma closes her eyes for a second. 'I was worried you might have inadvertently let something slip, but that's not what Elizabeth wants.'

'I know, but our paths only crossed fleetingly and he had no reason to suspect I wasn't just another customer.'

'It's a lovely gift, Sienna, and I appreciate the thought but I would love it if you gave this to Elizabeth as a *memento* of your trip, without telling her what the connection is. It seems only right.'

'Aww . . . that's a lovely thought, Grandma. I have what

she needs to pass on to the Italian solicitors – the name he now goes by, a contact address and even a telephone number, so I know she'll be happy.'

'The solicitors won't ring him. It'll all be handled via correspondence, but you did well.'

Obviously, Grandma thinks my job is done. 'Do you think it's best not to show Elizabeth the photo I took, or tell her what I discovered?'

'Only if she presses you. She doesn't want to cause James any upset whatsoever but there's also an element of self-preservation to it. Contacting him directly would be an emotional nightmare at a time when she's still extremely fragile.'

'It doesn't feel right, Grandma. I can see Freddie in him,' I appeal to her. 'He might resemble his father too, but I guess Elizabeth will never really know for sure, will she?'

Grandma suddenly looks rather agitated, lifting her hand to her mouth and pressing a finger to her lips. I'm no expert at body language, but it's as if she's willing herself not to answer my question. Seconds pass and her eyes tell me she's in two minds about what to say.

'It's simply too painful for her to comprehend, Sienna. It was cruel of Peter to keep James's existence a secret for all these years.'

'I understand that, but once things calm down, isn't there a chance she might change her mind and reach out to her grandson? Unless she has her doubts that Peter is James's father, of course.'

Grandma's brow furrows. 'Peter wouldn't have included him in his will if he wasn't one hundred per cent sure James was his son.'

'You think there's some other reason Elizabeth is holding back?'

Grandma lowers her hand, letting it fall haplessly into her lap. 'Perhaps, but I can't be sure of that. What son doesn't row with his father as he's growing up and asserting his independence? The young Peter wasn't a bad lad, although he was feisty. I didn't really get to see much of him as he grew into adulthood. However, I'm led to believe that the final row was something entirely different.'

'How?'

I can see that she's torn, probably feeling that I deserve to know whatever she's privy to, while feeling it's no one's business but Elizabeth's.

'The truth is that I don't know.'

'But you were in regular contact back then?'

'Yes, of course! I do remember being shocked when Elizabeth eventually confided in me – several months down the line – that Peter still hadn't been in touch. Whenever we met up, if anyone mentioned Peter's name Freddie immediately changed the subject. Before long, everyone got the message that it wasn't a topic of conversation but, as far as I'm aware, no one really knows what caused Peter to disappear from their lives.'

I feel my whole body sag. 'Elizabeth must have been distraught.'

'Much later, she wept when she eventually shared how she'd tried to get Freddie to calm down and listen to what their son had to say on that fateful day. She said that they were shouting at each other across the room and she watched, horrified and unable to do anything about it. When Peter stormed out, she begged Freddie to go after him but he was so angry he turned his back on her. Can you imagine that?'

'It must have been a truly awful thing to witness,' I mutter, feeling the hopelessness of the situation.

'Afterwards, Elizabeth said that Freddie bitterly regretted losing his temper and the harsh words he uttered that day. His son left the house believing that his father would always look on him as a failure. The damage had been done and I think they all knew there was no going back.'

My jaw drops, as I sit here in disbelief at what I'm hearing. A *failure?* 'That doesn't sound like Freddie at all.'

'Unbelievable, isn't it? I got the drift that Peter was in some sort of financial trouble and it was serious. If what Richard told you is true, suddenly, ten years later he's made enough money for him to hand over a considerable sum to Briony, just like that? It doesn't make any sense.'

'Oh . . . I see what you mean. He was starting from scratch with nothing and that can't have been easy, especially as at some point he got married.'

'I'm sure he would only have handed over a lump sum of money if he had proof that James was his.'

'A DNA test, maybe, or perhaps a photograph of the baby, so that Peter could see for himself the family resemblance before destroying it?' I ponder.

'Who knows? It's a poignant ending to a sorry tale. In one way, it's closure for Elizabeth after all these years of wondering whether one day her son would simply turn up at the Hall.'

However, I can't help wondering whether Elizabeth has good reason to feel it could do more harm than good by reaching out to James. What if he asks awkward questions that she isn't prepared to answer, because the truth is too painful to acknowledge?

'I wonder whether, as the years went on, not being a part of his son's life lay heavily on Peter's conscience,' Grandma continues. 'The dear boy thought he was doing some good by including James in his will. However, in making that gesture, it's triggered a search and that has had an impact on both his wife and his mother. And what about James? It's his birthright, but how will he feel about being tracked down and having the past raked up again when the solicitors make contact?'

And that's my fault.

'Oh, Grandma. It breaks my heart to think that he doesn't know how much Elizabeth would love the chance to welcome him into her life if . . .'

'If they choose to focus only on the future and ignore

the past? He's bound to be curious.' She sighs. 'Even so, it's terribly, terribly sad. I can't even begin to imagine how different my life would have been without you in it, Sienna. All those precious memories are dear to my heart. You're my little ray of sunshine and you always put a smile on my face. You've had your fair share of battles and setbacks, but I really do think your life is about to blossom. I'm proud of the woman you've become.' A solitary tear tracks down Grandma's cheek and I jump up out of my chair to stoop and wrap my arms around her.

'Aww. I feel blessed having two strong women as an example to help pick me up every time I fall. And you're right, each little battle has taught me something . . . hopefully,' I quip.

'A couple of weeks ago, Elizabeth admitted to me that she can't take any more sadness. That's a large part of the reason why I'm moving into the Hall. The weekend was so light-hearted and fun. We laughed, we had a jolly time among caring friends, who'd backed away because they wanted to give Elizabeth her space; but I know exactly what she's going through. Freddie's passing, your mum moving to Cornwall and you breaking off your engagement have all thrown me into . . .'

I straighten and she stands, grasping one of my hands in hers.

'It was as if everything in my life was falling apart,' Grandma admits. 'We knew we had to turn it around and accept that with change comes new, exciting opportunities. But, as far as Elizabeth is concerned, she's going to change her will to include James, in addition to various bequests to her nephews and nieces. It will give them all a nest egg. But more importantly, James won't feel obliged to keep this place going, they will all simply benefit from it and continue on with their lives.'

'But—'

'No *buts*, Sienna. This is what Elizabeth wants. Just give

her the details you have, so that she can forward them on to the Italian solicitors and include Ashley Freeman in her will. Then let her and James get on with the rest of their lives in peace.'

Grandma hugs me fiercely, as if she senses that I'm struggling to accept this is absolutely the right thing to do.

'There are only so many times a person our age can recover from having their heart torn apart. I think it's time Elizabeth put herself first for a change. That means waking up each morning with a smile on her face. And spending time with friends she knows will gladly donate to her favourite charities if plied with gourmet food, fine wines and music! I think she's earned that, don't you? And I intend to be her companion throughout. When I lost Pops, I had you and your mum to keep me going. But it was Elizabeth and Freddie who made sure I didn't have time on my hands to dwell; that was what saved me from myself. I'm simply repaying that kindness.'

We both swipe away our tears and do what we always do. Push our shoulders back, hold our heads high and get ready to make the best of the day ahead.

'OK, Grandma. I hear what you're saying.'

'Thank you, darling. I truly believe it's what Freddie would have wanted.'

And who am I to argue with that? Sadly, the one thing no one can change is the past.

'I've been waiting for a call, or at the very least a text. How did your trip to Cornwall go?' Daniela's clearly a little miffed at me.

'Sorry. It was lovely, if tiring,' I apologise. 'And today was full on; it was one problem after another.' I was going to say an emotional day, but Daniela would have been eager to know why.

'And did you and Oliver get to enjoy some quality time alone together?' The inflection in her tone is one of amusement.

'No, it wasn't like that. We ended up sitting around a table at a wonderful restaurant on Saturday evening while Mum and I had a bit of a heated discussion, and it was highly embarrassing. Fortunately, Sunday was much more relaxed. We all went for a long walk before lunch and then bid them goodbye early afternoon. Mum and I managed to have a quiet chat while we did the cliff walk and we both admitted things had gotten a little out of hand the night before. It's to do with Grandma moving into Silverberry Hall.'

'Really? What a brilliant idea!' Daniela enthuses.

'What, Grandma moving out of River View Cottage permanently and handing it over to me? I'm not ready for that sort of responsibility.'

'Nonsense!' she insists. 'You sort out all the bill paying and wages at the Hall; taking on a four-bed cottage would be a doddle by comparison.'

'It's . . . um . . . the upkeep and the maintenance bit that worries me. I don't want to take on that sort of challenge right now. I'm happy with things the way they are for the time being.'

There's a momentary hesitation before she replies. 'I can't think of a better way of spending your savings than giving the place a refresh. I know that splitting up with Liam hit you hard, but this is a perfect opportunity to get out of the slump you've been in since you moved back to the village.'

'I'm in a slump, am I?' I challenge her.

'Please don't take this the wrong way, because I only want what's best for you. It's like you're standing still. You let one day follow another and what . . . almost six months on from the split and you're still not dating, or even trying to expand your horizons. Marissa managed to drag you away from Darlingham for a whole weekend, but aside from that you spend the majority of your working days in the company of two elderly ladies. It's time to rejoin the world and start considering your future.'

Talk about tough love. If it were anyone else saying this

other than Daniela, I'd brush it off, even though she's right. Elizabeth didn't even look at the details I tried to hand her when I said I thought I'd found James. She simply broke into a wistful smile, then asked me to email everything to the Italian contact and to her own solicitor, Mr Berridge. Grandma was right, she's not going to risk reaching out to her grandson. She did ask me if he seemed happy and I told her that he has a good life in Cornwall.

In fairness, I can see where her thought processes have taken her. No one will hold it against him if he feels nothing but contempt for his father's family, given what happened.

'I'll get there, Daniela, but now is not that time.' And no one's going to wave a magic wand so that a grandmother can be united with a grandson she's never met. Life is a process and in between the high points, the harsh lessons take a while to sink in.

'Honestly, I don't know what's going on with you at the moment. Most of the time you seem distracted. I hoped that spending a little time with your mum and Greg would finally help you to see that change can be good. Instead, you sound down. However, I'm really glad that Oliver's been around because his presence has definitely perked you up a bit. I'm hoping this is just the start of the new you and you'll come bouncing back.'

It's nothing to do with Oliver. Daniela doesn't know that she was his first love, maybe his only love, so she couldn't be further from the mark. He and I have become friends, which is why Mum thought there might be something more going on between us, but I'm no substitute for my talented friend. She's intelligent, ambitious and fascinating, whereas I'm more of a plodder, a bookkeeper and an organiser. How could I ever compete . . . even if I were tempted?

'I don't know about that, but I was so grateful he was there to get me through the weekend. Mum felt I was being ungrateful when I said I didn't think it was a great idea for Grandma to move into the Hall permanently. It was one of those conversations where she didn't actually say the *one day everything I own, too, will be yours* speech, but it was on the tip of her tongue. I just think things are moving too fast and I don't want Grandma to have any regrets.'

'Gosh, poor you. No one likes talking about that stuff, do they? But she has a point. Every time you walk past your old family home you get prickly about the changes the new people are making. You don't want to see strangers in River View Cottage too, do you?'

'No, that's the last thing I want. But this came out of nowhere.'

'See it as a blessing, Sienna. Think how exciting it will be putting your stamp on the place. Your grandma will be there encouraging you to look at paint charts and you can upcycle some of the furniture. See it as a bonding thing, something that will give her a great deal of pleasure to witness. Let's face it, she spends most of her time at the Hall now anyway, since Freddie passed. And together she and Elizabeth bolster each other's spirits; it keeps them young.'

'Not you, too! I had to listen to all that from Mum,' I moan. 'It's time to change the subject. How was your weekend?'

'Fabulous! Clara and William were enthralled by Santa, although Pixie wasn't too impressed. The bonus was that Nigel's parents offered to have the kids overnight at their place. Undisturbed date nights are few and far between at the moment, so it was heavenly.'

She does sound all loved up, like she was in the early days before she found herself going to bed before Nigel, because she couldn't keep her eyes open.

'And you deserve it!'

'Well, after immersing myself in the history of Inglewick Hall, and stumbling across some rather intriguing family secrets that are best left buried, I was ready for some light-hearted fun. But I have the bare bones now and a firm idea of how I'm going to shape it into an interesting retelling of the history of the property.'

'You do sound like you've cracked it.'

'It's a turning point, as now I just have to write the script. Anyway, will you be joining us on Saturday for the run-through?'

'Sadly, no. Veronica will be on hand to give you the key as I'm not in at all this weekend.'

'Don't forget that I'm having a bit of a jolly afterwards back at my place, if you're free to join us then.'

'I'll have to pass on that too, I'm afraid.'

'Aww . . . that's a shame. They're a noisy bunch and it might be a late one, so I have no idea what Nigel will make of it. Fortunately, my parents have offered to have the children for the entire weekend. It will make life easier, and I'll be getting caterers in. Although my other half loves donning his chef's apron and he makes a good beef bourguignon, they'll all deserve a sumptuous three-course meal after what I'm going to put them through,' she laughs.

'Right. So, bed and breakfast at Oakleigh for Oliver this weekend then.' I smile to myself.

'What fun!' she replies, suggestively.

'What? I'm simply looking forward to having some company to brighten my Sunday morning, now that Grandma is staying at the Hall.'

'Of course, it's all change for your weekend routine, too. Are you sure you won't join us Saturday evening for dinner? I'm sure Oliver will be disappointed by your absence. After all, we wouldn't be ready to test out the stage if you hadn't stepped up to help.'

'It's kind of you to offer, but I have my afternoon and evening all planned out. I've downloaded an entire series I've been wanting to watch for ages, and I fully intend to lounge around eating ice cream and snacking.'

'Really? That sounds a bit lonely.'

'Believe me, I'm looking forward to it. It's going to be a busy week at the Hall, and I probably won't be good for much by then. At least if my eyelids droop, I won't risk offending anyone,' I chuckle. 'I'll simply rewind whatever I'm watching and pick up at the point where I drifted off. I'll give Oliver a key and he can let himself in, as I'll probably be sound asleep by ten o'clock.'

Daniela makes a tutting sound. 'I know you're shouldering a lot more than usual in the run-up to the party, but please pace yourself or you'll fall prey to the winter lurgy. And get your head around moving into River View Cottage. Once my project is out of the way, I'll be around to lend a hand. We can go shopping for furniture, bedding and curtains. You know me, I love to shop!'

'I do, but I think I'm going to take it slowly. Who knows, Grandma might have a change of heart in the meantime.'

'Hmm, don't bank on it. Anyway, I must go. Nigel is cooking dinner, and my stomach is rumbling. Just take care of *you* and stop worrying about your grandma; she's perfectly capable of steering her own future.'

Now that's something I can't dispute. Grandma knows exactly what she wants, whereas I feel like a work in progress, stretching out endlessly with no hint of any milestones on the path ahead.

16

There's No Going Back

Less than half an hour later, I find myself smiling when I see Oliver's name come up on my phone. 'Thanks for your text yesterday and sorry for going dark on you. I've had one hell of a Monday, including the dreaded black screen on my PC that prompted a dash to get a replacement. Anyway, you were right. I totally missed the email from Daniela, but I got straight onto it as soon as everything was up and working again. We're all set for Saturday's test run. And you're sure it's all right if I stay at your place overnight?'

'Of course.'

He lets out a sigh of relief. 'Thanks. With two of the cast members staying at Daniela's, as long as one of them isn't me I think Nigel will be happy.' His attempt at a dismissive laugh doesn't quite work.

'It's not a problem. It's payback for coming to my rescue and it sets the precedent for any future nights you stay over in Darlingham. I'll leave a front door key with Daniela just in case you go straight to the barn. I gather afterwards there's a bit of a party and she said it could be a late one.'

'You're not joining us?' Daniela was right. Oliver seems to have assumed I'd be there.

'No. I'm having a self-imposed duvet day, binge watching a series I've recorded and just relaxing. It'll be good to have some company for breakfast on Sunday morning, though.'

'You do sound tired. The weekend was draining for you emotionally, wasn't it?'

There's no point even trying to deny it. 'And some. But now it's behind me, if I can just stagger through the rest of this week without any mishaps, I'll be OK.'

He gives a rumbling little laugh. 'A day chilling out is probably exactly what you need. And how are Charlotte and Elizabeth doing?'

'They're making my head buzz just listening to the number of evening *get-togethers* they intend to host. It'll be like the good old days again, after a prolonged period of not much happening. I suggested that drinks and canapés are easier to organise than full-blown dinner parties and they seem to be taking the idea on board.'

'Does it involve extra work for you?'

'Not really, mainly just more invoices to pay. They're handling all the arrangements between themselves. Veronica liaises with the caterers when they're on site and will ensure they have everything they need before she leaves each Friday.'

Oliver tuts. 'You can't tell me it's not adding to your workload in one way or another. You're the one who keeps all the working parts moving; it's not easy being a problem-solver and doing that in a diplomatic way.'

'I don't mind,' I reply, cheerfully. 'Besides, Silverberry Hall is a place made for entertaining and Elizabeth is tiring of only having family members around her. Her brothers mean well, but she's a lady used to fun social gatherings and letting her hair down, not constantly being reminded she isn't getting any younger and should be taking it easy. That's not her style.'

'I'm glad to hear she's finding her feet again. The first time I met her, she confided in me that grief will suck the life out of you if you let it. She told me that she misses the old version of herself. The key, apparently, is to keep your mind busy and your feet active. To which I said, "Just like you," and she laughed. I take it that your grandma is still intent on a permanent move?'

'She is.'

'And what about you?'

I sigh. 'I told Grandma that I have my hands full right now and she said she understood.'

'It's a reprieve, then.'

'For now, but she's still pushing forward.'

'If you ever need a listening ear, Sienna, I'm only a phone call away. If I don't get to see you earlier in the day on Saturday, I'll be quiet when I let myself in. And I'm cooking breakfast on Sunday morning – deal?'

'Deal.'

Oliver clears his throat. 'Good. And that other matter from the weekend. Did you manage to get it sorted?'

'Yes. I did exactly what I was asked to do and left it at that.'

'That's probably for the best. By the way, I sent your mum and Greg a bouquet of flowers and a box of chocolates yesterday, as a thank you for putting me up. It was a fun weekend.'

'Fun?' I burst out laughing.

'It's not often I get to chat to anyone about fishing, that's for sure. Anyway, if we don't speak before, I'll see you at the weekend. Take care, Sienna.'

Do you know that feeling? The one where you awaken feeling refreshed after dropping into bed the previous night so exhausted that you're convinced you won't be able to sleep? Well, that's me on this bright and frosty Saturday morning.

Lately, it's felt as if life has been constantly throwing me curve balls and the minute I bat one away, the next one is incoming. After a really productive week – where I managed to catch up on a backlog of paperwork – and with a leisurely weekend ahead of me, I'm beginning to feel a bit more like my old self. I'm not sure it's the same one Daniela was referring to as, quite frankly, I don't think she exists anymore. I'm evolving . . . albeit ever so slowly.

A brisk walk before breakfast helps to clear my mind and it occurs to me that, in some respects, Elizabeth might be feeling the same way. The old me had plans to settle down and I thought my future was all mapped out. Starting afresh is daunting and it's the same for her. But people don't always understand that having gone through a major event in our lives, how can it ever be the same again? It changes us. Elizabeth is learning to live her life without Freddie next to her and I have some big decisions to make about my future, because, at the moment, I'm treading water.

I spend a while perched on a lichen-covered rock, just gazing out over the estuary. The problem is that I don't have a plan for the future. The harder I think, the more my brain begins to hurt. I tilt my head back, staring up at a line of small, fluffy white clouds as they aimlessly drift by.

'Daydreaming?' A voice interrupts my concentration. 'That's not like you!'

'Hello, Harry. How're you doing?'

'Good, ta. I've just finished doing my rounds in the village and I like a bit of a walk before I head back to the farm for the second run. I see your grandma and Elizabeth have upped the order again this weekend. Seems like things are getting back into some sort of routine at the Hall again.'

'Yes, and with the arrangements for the Christmas party in full flow, it's livened things up a little.'

'It's about time. Life's for the living and it's a lot shorter than we think.'

I shuffle over, patting the rock to indicate for him to join me. 'Sad, but true. This view never disappoints. No matter what the weather, it always takes my breath away.'

'I see there's comings and goings up at the barn, too. I bumped into Oliver, and he told me that they're doing a run-through of the play. I thought you were involved in it?'

I shake my head. 'No, I just lent a hand painting a few things, that's all. The carts cleaned up really well.'

'And I thought they were only fit for the bonfire,' he chuckles. 'Anyway . . . how are you doing these days?'

Harry has known me all my life and a casual 'I'm fine' won't do. 'Confused and heartily fed up with change.'

He grins at me. 'Can't say I'm surprised; it's been one heck of a year for you. But you're a survivor. You'll figure it out.'

'I do hope that's the case, but at the moment I'm struggling. I can't make a plan when I don't know what I want.' Sometimes the truth is scary but it's good to admit that.

'You're getting a bit of pressure, are you?'

I give a little groan. 'Hmm . . . not really. I just don't like people worrying about me. Besides, it's high time I stopped feeling sorry for myself.'

Harry does a belly laugh. '*You*, feeling sorry for yourself when you're busy running yourself ragged to keep everyone else around you ticking over?'

'Well, it's more the *why me* syndrome, I suppose. As in, how did I manage to mess up again?'

'Did you? Stuff happens. Things go wrong. People move out of your life and new ones come in. You left Darlingham and then you came back. Then you left again, I know it was only a few miles away . . . but now here you are. The trick is to suss out what makes you happy.'

Harry's the sort of man who doesn't suffer fools gladly and he has the height, and the muscle, to make someone think twice about upsetting him. Even so, he has a gentle nature.

'It's as simple as that?' I question, trying hard not to sound dubious.

'I'm speaking from experience. The wife wanted me to retire early, which I did and six months later I was back working on the farm. Oh, she was right. With our son now running things the pressure is off me, but pottering around the house decorating and trimming the hedges was never going to keep me occupied.'

He smiles and I nod my head in agreement. 'Every single thing you do is appreciated, Harry. I know that.'

'Hmm . . . it is. I like helping out with the early-morning deliveries and pottering around clearing the accumulation of junk in the old barns. It keeps me out of mischief for a few hours every day and the wife is glad to get me out of the house.' He chuckles to himself.

I take a slow breath in and hold it for a few seconds before letting it go. 'I've lived here most of my life but now that Mum is down in Cornwall it all feels different.'

'Like something is missing, I should imagine.'

'Precisely!'

'But you seem happy enough doing what you do, and Elizabeth couldn't manage without you, neither could your grandma.'

It's funny, Oliver was sort of saying the same thing. 'Feeling needed is all I have at the moment, Harry. But am I settling for the easiest option because I'm scared to take a risk and see what else life has to offer?'

'From what I've seen, you aren't scared of anything, Sienna. You rise to every challenge that comes your way, and you'll have a go at anything. Not a lot of people can say that.'

He glances at his watch.

'I'd best get back. I'm hoping to take two van-loads to the tip this morning before I finish. I'm glad I bumped into you, though. It's not often we get to chat about real stuff.'

'It's the same for me.'

Harry stands, taking one last look out across the fields behind us. 'Some people are born adventurers, others are homebodies, as my old mother used to refer to herself. She was a hard-working woman and my father worshipped her. She ran the house, the family and the finances, and he always said she was the kingpin of our family. Don't underestimate your skills, my dear, just because they come easy to you. Big cities don't suit everyone, and that's the truth. And I'll, uh, give you a shout if I stumble on any more old treasures I think might be of interest to you.'

'Thanks, Harry. And for the pep talk. Enjoy the rest of your day!'

After an invigorating walk, I decide it's time to turn my attention to cleaning and making the cottage sparkle. It doesn't take long to dust and vacuum from top to bottom and double-check there are enough towels in the guest shower room.

However, it does set me thinking that it would be nice to have a bit more space to spread out. I'd love a separate study with a desk and a centrally heated utility room, rather than a chilly old stone outhouse, to accommodate my washing machine and clothes dryer.

By the time I end up settling down on the sofa with a tray of goodies, I can't wait to immerse myself in a series about a young vet from Bristol, who moves to a small practice in Lancashire. Several hours later, I've laughed, cried, gasped out loud and found myself wondering why on earth I don't have a furry companion of my own. Some of the stories are heartwarming, others heartbreaking and even though it's fiction, it's easy to suss out that a lot of this is based on anecdotal information.

When the phone goes, I reluctantly press pause on the remote, until I see that it's Oliver calling. 'Hi, how's it going?'

'Good. I've had to reposition the cart so there's more room centre stage. Ruby has been amazing as a stand-in for the two children and it's obvious they're going to need a bit more space to move around in. The ball works great and using that tree as a central support means it's really stable. I'm just calling about the lamp post . . . I don't suppose Harry has mentioned it?'

'Oh, my goodness, I'm so sorry. It's in the stable block. He wrapped it up in old sacks as he ended up spraying it black and he was worried the paint might chip.'

'Good man!'

'It's rather heavy and it took two of them to carry it across the car park. Victor should be around, and he won't mind giving you a hand. I'll text you his number.'

'Thanks, and sorry for disturbing you. How is your marathon TV day going?'

'I haven't laughed so much in ages, although it's been a bit sad in places, so I had to grab the tissues. And now I'm desperate to get a dog.'

'A dog?' Oliver repeats, laughing.

'I'll explain when I see you; there's a chance I could still be up.'

'It sounds like you're having fun. I'll see you later.'

It's just after nine o'clock when a sharp tap on the door knocker makes me jump. I know I said I'd be up, but Oliver could still have let himself in, I reflect, as I stride into the hallway. But when I swing open the door, it's Liam I see standing there, looking very ill at ease.

'Sienna. How . . . um . . . how are you?' I freeze, unable to move or speak. 'I'm sorry. I know it's late, but I was passing, and I thought I'd drop by.' He shuffles from foot to foot, awkwardly.

'I . . . I see.'

'Can I come in for a moment?'

I'm blocking his way, but I don't feel inclined to take a step backwards. 'You aren't passing, Liam. Unless you're going for a stroll in the dark.'

He hangs his head, avoiding eye contact. 'We need to talk.'

'No, we don't,' I reply, emphatically. A slight shiver begins to run through me as the chilly night air drifts inside, but I don't move an inch.

'I've come to my senses. It's you I love; I always did but things got a bit—' He casts around for the right word.

'What's the word you're looking for . . . stale? Boring? We're done, Liam. You made your choice, and it wasn't me.

And instead of telling me, you left it to someone else to break the news. There's no going back from that sort of hurt.'

'But now I see it for what it was, just a stupid fling and it's over. Please don't shut—'

'Sienna, is everything all right?' Oliver's voice looms up in the darkness and Liam's jaw drops, as he turns to face my visitor.

'Yes, Oliver. Liam is just going.'

The two men stare at each other for a few moments and Oliver doesn't flinch, giving Liam no option other than to mutter a brief, 'Goodnight' and walk away. I immediately stand back and Oliver, with his overnight bag in one hand, follows me inside.

Once I hear the door slam shut, I slump against the wall, my legs trembling. 'I don't believe that just happened!' I exclaim, sounding a little breathless.

'So, that was your ex.'

'Yes. I can't believe he had the audacity to turn up unannounced like that. I'm livid. Sorry, my nerves are in tatters, and I'd better sit down before my legs give out.'

What a situation for Oliver to walk into.

'Go and collapse on the sofa and I'll make us both a hot drink. I've had quite an evening of it myself.'

'Thanks. I'll have a chamomile tea, you'll find them in the cupboard above the kettle,' I reply, feeling like the worst host ever but I need a few moments to compose myself.

'Sensible choice; I think I'll join you.' He grins back at me.

By the time Oliver places the mugs down on the coffee table in front of me, I'm feeling a lot calmer.

'Your timing was impeccable,' I giggle. 'You have no idea how grateful I am, because I wasn't expecting you this early.'

'No. I bowed out apologetically, saying I was shattered after a heavy week. Does Liam turn up on your doorstep often?'

I can tell from his expression there's more to his little story, but he's looking at me expectantly.

'I've had no personal contact with him at all since the day I packed my bags and walked out – only a string of text messages he started sending me after the new love of his life dumped him. I chose not to respond and ended up blocking him. Oh . . . I bet I look awful, too!' My hand instinctively goes up to my hair, which is piled on top my head in a messy updo, fastened with a scrunchy. Wearing a pair of leggings with a baggy old jumper thrown over the top, I'm not exactly dressed to receive visitors, or to face a confrontation.

'You look cosy and warm. Besides, you're entitled to lounge around in your own home,' Oliver insists.

'Yes, but wouldn't it have been fun if I'd been all dressed up?' I muse. 'Anyway, I'm not falling for it. Liam's fickle; he had his chance, and he blew it. Why would I trust him again?'

Oliver shakes his head. 'When something is over you just know, don't you?'

I look at him askance. Is he talking about me, or him?

'Yes, you do. And I'm glad he turned up like that, out of the blue. My first thought was, why are you bothering me after all this time? Seeing him again unexpectedly there was nothing there . . . no moment of hesitation and no regrets.' Actually, it's a relief. I knew it was highly likely that at some point in the future our paths might cross again, but I had no idea how I'd react. And now I know for sure.

Oliver sits opposite me in the armchair I inherited from Mum's old house, cradling his mug.

'You look a bit dazed,' I comment.

'It shows, does it?'

'I'd be lying if I didn't say yes.'

'Daniela was tense during dinner. I think she and Nigel had words in the kitchen just before we sat down to eat. There was an edginess between them I've not seen before. Unfortunately, I was sitting opposite him, so I tried my best to avoid any eye contact. Maybe we were all a bit too hyped up, you know what I mean? It was like a class reunion. We'd had a good day, so we were all on a high and he wasn't.'

'Hmm. Maybe he felt a little left out?' I suggest.

'Perhaps, but it was Daniela's reaction that got me. She was subdued and kept glancing at him nervously.' Oliver sounds troubled.

'Couples have their off days,' I reassure him. 'Nigel has a stressful job and with Daniela now working part-time, it's a period of adjustment for them both.'

'Whatever it is, he's not happy about something.'

Nigel was so keen for Daniela to carve out some time to expand her horizons; does this mean he's already backtracking on that decision?

It's time to talk about something a little happier. 'How was the rehearsal?'

'Great. And the lamp post is simply perfect. Everyone was impressed with the set.'

'Of course they were, it's amazing. When's the next rehearsal?'

'Mostly we'll run through the script via video calls. In the run-up to the performance we'll have the full cast on site for a day of tech and dress rehearsals.'

'It's beginning to feel very real now, isn't it?'

'It sure is. The wardrobe lady came in. Ruby took the seamstress around to Mrs Jessop's to sort out the children.'

'Oh, so it's more or less all set up now?'

'Yes. I managed to get the lamp post in situ and make a couple of adjustments to the positioning of the cart and the two sledges. Everyone seems happy. Now we just need to learn the words all over again.' He rolls his eyes.

'You can't remember them?'

'Bits, but it's been a long, long time. And you know Daniela, she gave us all a revised version as she's been tinkering with it. She's such a perfectionist, but that's who she is.'

We lapse into silence. He'll never forget his first love; as for me, I'll never forgive mine for taking something I thought was special and trashing it.

'Did you just groan?' Oliver asks, staring at me.

'Sorry. I wasn't aware . . . I was just thinking.'

'In which case, it can't have been good,' he jests, lightly.

'Actually, it was good. Seeing Liam and realising there is no going back for me is liberating.'

Oliver stares across at me and I realise I'm smiling as if I've just scratched off a winning lottery ticket. Grandma and Mum have the courage to make major changes in their lives and I do, too. Unless Grandma changes her mind, River View Cottage here I come! And, before I forget, there's something I must ask Oliver, but I have to wait for the right moment to pose the question. Perhaps I'll leave it until tomorrow morning.

17

Two Wrongs Don't Make a Right

'Is Oliver still there?' Daniela asks, the moment I put the phone to my ear.

'No. We were up early. He made a wonderful breakfast for us both and set off home about half an hour ago, why?'

'Thank goodness! Nigel just stormed out of the house and he's on his way to confront Oliver. There was nothing I could do to stop him.'

'What happened?'

'He thinks there's something going on between Oliver and me. Oh, Sienna, I don't know what to do. It's crazy, because it's all in his head and I've told him that, but he won't listen.'

'Don't worry, when Nigel gets here, I'll calm him down.'

'You don't think . . . I mean you believe me, don't you?' She sniffles.

'Of course I do. And I've spent enough time with Oliver to know he genuinely wants the best for you.'

'We were close, but we were only ever friends, I promise you. His heart was broken, and I know that you, of all people, can empath—'

A load rapping on the door makes me end the call abruptly and I rush to the door.

'Nigel,' I act, surprised. 'Come in.'

'I don't want to interrupt but . . .' He falters and maybe he's rethinking his strategy.

'Come on through to the kitchen. I was in the process of making a cup of coffee. Will you join me?'

'Um . . . are you on your own?' He obviously wasn't expecting that but why would Oliver hang around?

'Yes. Oliver had to rush off. He's working on a new project; he's such a workaholic.'

Nigel immediately relaxes his shoulders as he turns to shut the front door behind him. 'Yeah, that sort of comes across. Do you know him well?'

He follows me into the kitchen, and I indicate for him to take a seat while I make us a drink.

'I didn't before he came to build the set ready for Elizabeth's Christmas Eve party.'

It's the first time I've seen Nigel looking so nervous. He interlaces his fingers, as he stares around the kitchen. 'He's a clever guy, by the sound of it.'

'He is.' I turn my head a little to talk over my shoulder. 'He likes fishing, too! He was a real hit with Greg when we visited.'

'Greg? Oh . . . your mum's new partner?' Instantly, his voice changes.

'Mmm. It was the first time I'd been to Anchor House.'

'How's she doing?'

'Fine. It's just different, you know?'

'Yeah, I can appreciate that. But the visit, uh, went well?'

'It did. Mum's talking about us heading down there again soon, just for one night. Some sort of party Greg and his friends have every year in the run-up to Christmas.'

'Us . . . as in you and Oliver?'

I carry two mugs across to the table. 'Yes. Anyway, it sounded like yesterday went well. We're all excited about the performance.'

Judging by the slightly confused look on Nigel's face, I'm guessing that wasn't what he was expecting to hear. 'Daniela's nervous, of course, but they seemed happy with the run-through. I stayed well clear of it, of course. It was a late one though. Daniela is doing brunch before they all head for home. I just . . . um . . . popped in to see whether Oliver wanted to join them, I mean, us. I should have called, really.'

Now Nigel is feeling awkward. If Oliver was still in love with Daniela, they've had plenty of opportunities to meet up in private. Coming to Darlingham only goes to prove that what he told me is true; he feels he owes Daniela a debt of gratitude. He certainly wouldn't have gone haring off to Cornwall with me on a jaunt, even as payback, if he were setting his sights on her.

'I should imagine they're quite a vibrant bunch of characters,' I laugh. 'I admire anyone who has the courage to stand up on stage and perform in front of an audience of strangers. It's the last thing in the world I'd consider doing.'

He gives a little chuckle. 'Me, too. They talk over each other all the time and it's like having several conversations going on at once. Honestly, last night it did my head in, but please don't repeat that. Having a quiet coffee here with you like this is bliss.'

'Take your time and enjoy it. I'm sure they can keep themselves entertained.'

'And some,' he groans. 'Daniela seems different around them and it threw me a little to see her so carefree and joking around. It made me wonder why she chose me in the first place. I mean, she was popular and had guys falling all over her.'

I look at him, my eyes widening. 'Because you're the one, Nigel. And she realised that from the start.'

'Hmm, I like to think so, but . . .' He turns to stare at me, rather intensely. 'Family life is wonderful but it has its highs and its lows. I fear that Daniela bears the brunt of it and I know there are times when she finds it all a little overwhelming. I try to ease the load when I'm there and make sure she has some alone time to unwind. But the way she's thrown herself back into work and now with this play, it makes me wonder whether she resents me for what I've taken away from her.'

My eyes widen. 'Taken away from her? You have two utterly amazing children and yes, they're exhausting at times, but the moment I step inside your home they put an instant smile on my face.'

'They do, don't they?' He grins at me. 'Even when I get home from a long and stressful day at work they instantly turn my mood around. Everything I do is for my family.'

'Believe me, Daniela understands and appreciates that. She's simply enjoying having a little time to do something that makes her feel there's still more to her than simply being a wife and a mother.'

'You think I'm being paranoid?'

Oh, Nigel! Oliver isn't a threat, well . . . not in the way you fear. He cares too much for Daniela to rob her of her happiness. You're her soul mate and that's obvious to everyone around you. It's in the secret glances you both steal, thinking no one notices, and the way your eyes seek each other out across a crowded room. It's a match made in heaven.

'It's added a touch of excitement to her normal routine and, in her enthusiasm, she's overcommitted herself, but Oliver and I are helping to address that. It's about self-worth, that's all. She's checking that she still has what it takes to function in the big wide world and make a difference. Personally, I think she'll soon settle down and find the happy medium, because family comes first for her, too.'

'You're a good friend, Sienna.'

'I like to think I am to both of you,' I reply, with sincerity.

'You're heading down to Cornwall again so soon? That's wonderful news!' Grandma makes no attempt to hide her surprise when, on Monday morning, I tell her about the last-minute plans for the coming weekend.

'Greg and a group of friends all meet up at his cousin's restaurant for a meal just before Christmas. It's Mum's first time being a part of it and, reading between the lines, I think she's a bit nervous about going. She asked if I'd like to join them. It's all couples and she suggested that if Oliver was free he might like to come along, too. I didn't like to say no and, to be fair, when I asked Oliver about it over breakfast yesterday morning, he was delighted.'

'Well, I'm sure your mum will appreciate having you there and Oliver is such good company. It's not awkward for you, is it? I mean, the two of you seem to get on really well.'

'Oh, we do. He's easy-going and reliable; that's exactly what I need right now.'

'Daniela has a lot on her plate at the moment, doesn't she?'

'Yes, and I don't want to put her on a guilt trip about my problems, so it's kind of him to accompany me. I was just a bit surprised Mum felt she needed—'

'A little support?'

'Mmm. I guess you could say that.'

'Don't we all need that, at times?' Grandma points out, raising an eyebrow.

'I guess we do.' I go on to tell her about Liam's surprise visit and her reaction is one of relief when I tell her that as far as I'm concerned that's all in the past now.

As she gets up to leave, there's a sharp tap on the door and it slowly swings open.

'Hello . . . Oh, hi, Charlotte. I won't disturb you, I just wanted to leave something with Sienna.'

'It's lovely to see you, Ruby,' Grandma replies. 'Elizabeth and I were only saying the other day that we must pop into The Sailor's Retreat one lunchtime. It's been too long.'

'It has,' Ruby agrees, flashing me a smile. 'Let me know when you're coming, and I'll reserve the table by the fire for you.'

'I will. Anyway, I have a number of phone calls to make, so I'll leave you to it.'

Ruby has an A4 envelope in her hand which she passes

to me, as Grandma makes her way out. 'I wasn't sure when Oliver is here next, and I forgot to give this back to him on Saturday. It's a copy of the script he marked up for me.'

'Don't hover, take a seat. I heard it all went well. Did you enjoy yourself?'

Her smile grows exponentially. 'It was amazing and a lot more technical than I was expecting. I thought you'd be there for the meal afterwards at Daniela's as you've been a big part of it, too.'

I wave my hand in the air dismissively. 'Oh, painting a few panels wasn't arduous. Oliver did all the real work. I bet it's a bit of a raucous affair when they all get together.'

'It was. But it was also a laugh and they made me feel very welcome. So much so, that after a chat with Oliver he's encouraged me to join one of the local amateur dramatic clubs. Even if it's just helping out, I'd love to get involved. He asked if I could make myself available to look after the two children who'll be a part of the performance on the day and be there during the rehearsals beforehand.'

'How exciting!'

'Yes. I was delighted, although I thought maybe he should have asked you first?' She poses it as a question.

'Oh, no . . . I've no aspirations to get involved in the play, at all. Besides, on the night I'll be on duty making sure the party goes as smoothly as possible.'

She looks relieved. 'I didn't want you to think I was . . . I mean, what's the story with Oliver?'

'What do you mean?'

'I know he's a friend of Daniela's from her university days, but Nigel was noticeably distant with him at the dinner party. It was obvious to everyone. There's nothing . . . I mean, Oliver and Daniela aren't old flames, are they?'

I swallow hard before managing to laugh it off. 'No, of course not! The troupe were all studying the same course, that's all. It must be difficult for Nigel, as he doesn't really know any of them.'

'Ah, that explains it, then. You and Oliver seem to work well together.' Now she's fishing.

'We've been helping each other out,' I explain, trying to make it sound quite matter of fact.

'I see. Great. Oh, I nearly forgot . . . guess who Xavier took out to dinner the other night?' Her eyes light up.

'Surprise me. I have no idea whatsoever.'

'Only Lottie, and she tried to keep it quiet, but I know one of the waitresses up at The Brass Mill.' I was half expecting her to say something about my trip to Cornwall with Oliver, but obviously that isn't common knowledge, thank goodness. This, at least, is a distraction, but poor Lottie is about to have all eyes turned on her.

'Are you sure it was a date, and he wasn't just thanking her for her help, as she literally keeps that veterinary practice running.'

'We'll soon find out for sure one way or the other. They've held the interviews for the permanent position and the partners are about to announce the name of the successful applicant.'

I'm surprised to hear Ruby gossiping about Lottie and I simply shrug my shoulders, not wanting to get pulled in.

'Right, I'm in early this morning to help do some prep in the kitchen.' She stands, glancing around the study, her eyes settling on the empty desk in front of the window. 'You must really miss Freddie.'

I sigh. 'I do. We laughed a lot; you know what he was like. Always joking and light-hearted whenever I needed cheering up and quiet when I was head down concentrating. Sometimes I glance up and imagine him sitting there and it's a comfort.'

Her face puckers up. 'Aww. Once Christmas is out of the way, you must join me, Lottie and whoever else we can draft in, for one of our fun-seeking girls' nights out. It's about time you started socialising properly again. Maybe we'll head into Stroud to broaden our horizons,' she giggles, to which I shake my head.

'As you say, maybe.'

'Hmm . . . I'll take that, it's better than a firm no. Having a new face with us on one of our little excursions might attract a little more attention.'

'For whom?' I groan.

She gives another girly giggle, walking over to the door and turning to give a little wave as she leaves.

All in all, I think I got off quite lightly there. But Xavier and Lottie . . . now that's a real surprise. It wasn't that long ago she was trying to get me to make up a blind date foursome and I assume it went ahead as a twosome. Which means he was yet another *thanks, but no thanks*.

Elizabeth, Grandma and I spend all afternoon wrapping presents for the children's party. Sourcing the gifts was hard enough. We settled for a range of storybooks, hardback notebooks with novelty pens, a mesh ball that lights up and stays airborne so it can be thrown from person to person, and several different superhero jigsaw puzzles.

'This is making me feel so festive,' Elizabeth declares, happily.

'Hmm . . . let's see if that's still the case by the time we've filled those sacks,' Grandma retorts, raising an eyebrow.

'Someone is going to have to make sure Santa hands out the appropriate gift each time.' I jump into the conversation.

'Good point,' Elizabeth replies. 'I'm sure I could talk one of my nieces into doing it, unless you fancy stepping in, Charlotte. We'll have a full house, with plenty of helping hands.'

'You're going to make them work for their supper,' Grandma muses and I try not to look surprised. She really is beginning to stand her ground.

'Well, they've all backed off a little thanks to your presence. On the whole, they mean well, but there's also a concern that I'll have a head fit and leave everything to an animal sanctuary, or to protect . . . bees, or something.'

'Lucky bees,' Grandma laughs. 'Anyway, it's entirely up to you.'

'Yes, but people think that as you get older you're more likely to get talked into things, or your mind goes and you're susceptible to flights of fancy.'

'You . . . flights of fancy?' I guffaw. 'Honestly, Elizabeth, if that happens, I'd be the first to point it out and—'

'We're the three musketeers, aren't we?' Grandma interjects. 'We look out for each other and we're relying upon you, Sienna, to step in and be the voice of reason if the two of us get out hand.'

They're both laughing, but why do I feel there's a hint of seriousness to this?

'And in the same spirit,' Elizabeth continues, 'we're delighted Oliver is accompanying you to Cornwall again.'

I gasp. They've been gossiping about me. 'Really?' Is that the royal *we*? I ponder, thinking these two ladies are a force to be reckoned with.

'Now, come on, Sienna,' Grandma teases. 'You know we both want you to be happy and settled.'

'I am, thank you very much. And Oliver is just a friend.' Seriously, this is getting embarrassing now.

'Yes, and it's a good start. When you move into River View Cottage you'll need a . . . handyman,' Grandma insists.

They glance in my direction all bright-eyed and positive, unable to comprehend why I'm feeling uncomfortable about this conversation.

'I'm perfectly capable of organising what I need without leaning on a . . . friend,' I state, firmly.

'There you go, Elizabeth,' Grandma replies with relish, 'I said she was coming around to the idea.'

'Why do I feel like I've been set up? This wasn't a ploy of Mum's—'

'Hello?' Victor's voice stops us short. It's unusual for him to come up to the house.

'Come in, we're just wrapping gifts ready for Santa's arrival,' Elizabeth calls out.

'Georgina said it was OK to come through.' Even so, Victor looks apologetic. 'I spotted a man wandering around the car park, and when I started walking over to him, he ran off. If he was looking for directions he wouldn't have fled. I fear he might have been an opportunist, scoping out the building.'

Elizabeth sighs. 'We haven't had any break-ins in the area for a long while, so this is concerning.'

'It's the time of year when thieves are about because the pickings are good. But it's more about the shock factor and I'd hate for any of you ladies to be confronted by a stranger up to no good.'

Suddenly, the mood in the room changes.

'Thank you for the heads-up, Victor. Is there anything else you suggest we do other than be extra vigilant?'

He fiddles nervously with the woolly hat he's holding in his hands. 'First and last thing I do each day is to check all the outbuildings are secure. But maybe you and any visitors should make sure vehicles aren't left unlocked, even if it's just to pop back inside to grab something. And, at night, double-check that the ground-floor windows and external doors are locked.'

Elizabeth sighs. 'We're a little off the beaten track, being at the end of a single-track lane off the High Street. Hopefully, strangers will be easy to spot. It's a sad state of affairs, but I can't thank you enough for being so on the ball, Victor.'

'My pleasure and I'll ensure my presence in the car park and around the main buildings is a little more obvious for a while. Anyway, I'd best leave you to it. You're doing a wonderful job there!' Victor smiles, as he surveys the mountain of gifts we still have to wrap and the solitary sack that is pleasingly full.

'It's all in a good cause,' Grandma replies. He acknowledges that with a tilt of his head and a broad smile.

'Do you have time for a hot drink before you go?' I ask, as I stand and follow Victor out into the hallway. As soon as the door is closed, I lean in, to whisper. 'Did you recognise this man, at all?'

'No,' he replies, keeping his voice low. I can tell he's concerned. 'I don't think he's a local because even though he was panicking to get away from me, when he got to the gate he hesitated as he wasn't sure whether to head left or right.'

'I . . . um . . . there's a chance it might not be someone looking to steal something. My ex-fiancé unexpectedly turned up on my doorstep on Saturday night and I refused to talk to him. I hope he got the message that he wasn't welcome but if he didn't, this is where he'd come to find me.'

'Sorry to hear that, Sienna, but it's private property so he's taking a risk.'

'I know but I wouldn't rule it out. He's tall, with dark hair . . .'

Victor purses his lips. 'The guy was too far away for me to really get a good look. He was wearing a navy-blue padded jacket. What made him stand out was that he had his hood pulled up, even though he was wearing a baseball cap. It looked like he was trying to obscure his face as much as possible.'

'If it is Liam, he doesn't mean any harm, he just wasn't expecting me to turn him away.'

Victor looks uneasy. 'That's as maybe, but if someone is skulking around, they know they're not welcome, so just watch yourself, Sienna.'

'I'd . . . um . . . appreciate it if we could keep this little incident at the cottage just between us? Grandma is aware, but she won't pass it on to Elizabeth. I don't want anyone worrying unduly and it could be paranoia on my part to even think it might be him.'

'Of course, I understand but call me if you have any problems – any time of the day, or night, whether it's here or at Oakleigh. You promise?'

'I promise and thank you, Victor, it's appreciated.'

Liam was wrong to put me on the spot like that and if he's the mystery man he'd better watch out, as I have no doubt at all that Victor won't put up with any nonsense.

18

Things That Were Left Unsaid

It feels good to be heading back down to Cornwall on a gloriously sunny Saturday morning. This time around I'm feeling a lot more relaxed about the visit itself, even though it's been a trying week.

'And you still don't know for sure whether this mystery man was Liam, hoping to bump into you at the Hall?' Oliver questions, after I tell him what happened on Monday.

'No. The second time this mystery person was spotted was when Georgina went out to put some vegetable peelings on the compost heap next to the kitchen garden. The guy didn't hear her approaching and she said he was equally as shocked as she was. She shouted at him, saying he was trespassing, and he turned tail and ran. It's a shame that she's never met Liam and neither has Victor, but the description they gave really sounded like it might be him.'

'Without proof, there's not a lot you can do.'

I shrug my shoulders. 'Well, if it continues that might be possible. Victor suggested Elizabeth should consider having some security cameras installed. She's horrified at the thought and I feel guilty it's come to that. I should just go and confront Liam, let him say what he needs to say and hope that's the end of it.'

'I'm not sure it would be a clever idea to meet up with him alone, Sienna. I'm more than happy to drive you to meet him and wait around just in case you need some backup.'

I try to contain a smile. 'That's kind of you to offer, but he's just angry with himself, not me.'

'Yeah, well . . . it's better to be safe than sorry. Anger can turn ugly when you least expect it.'

Gosh, that sounded personal. 'It can?'

'Trust me. I know you think Nigel has an even temper but everyone has their breaking point. The signs might be subtle, but they're there.'

And what about Oliver? He was certainly quick to action when he saw me barring Liam access to Oakleigh. Now I'm curious about what exactly happened at the dinner party to make him leave early. Did Nigel say something to upset him and he was already riled up when he arrived?

'That's out of character for him. Like most people, I guess if he'd had too much to drink . . .'

'Yeah, the age-old excuse.' Oliver isn't buying it. 'Anyway, let's move on. How are your festive preparations going?'

Talking about the master plan for getting the lights put up in and around Silverberry Hall, hits home to Oliver what a massive task it is. It takes a small team of guys to get everything prepped in advance of what I call *decoration day* and a lot of organisation to pull it off. We put up three large fir trees in the actual house itself and a twenty-six-footer graces the front lawn. Then there are the lights that run the length of the stable block and continue on past the barn to our new outdoor food preparation area. This year Elizabeth wants the whole of the courtyard to look colourful.

'Oh, I have an envelope from Ruby in my bag. Remind me to give it to you. It's the script you lent her last weekend.'

'She could have kept it as a souvenir,' he chuckles. 'Daniela has just issued what she assures us is the definitive version. Honestly, you'd think we were going straight from Silverberry Hall to perform at Covent Garden. But we're all on a high about it. I know Elizabeth and your grandma are going to be delighted on the night.'

'It's exciting and the closer it gets to the big day, the more

I'm feeling it's finally coming together. Let's hope there's nothing I've forgotten and there are no last-minute panics.'

'It's no mean feat to organise, that's for sure.'

'It's not just that. Elizabeth doesn't count the cost because it's in aid of her favourite charities, but I do, on her behalf. Thankfully, local companies reach out to offer freebies – like some of the presents we wrapped for the children the other day. And the use of the two cherry pickers when it comes to putting up the lights in and around the grounds. I make sure we recognise their generosity in the official Christmas Eve at Silverberry Hall programme.'

'There's a printed programme?'

'Yes. This year, the printing company I work with have linked up with the local schools. They held a children's painting competition, and twelve winners have had their artwork used to create a calendar. The resulting profits, together with the ticket sales for the main party, should make it a bumper one. Everyone who offers services at cost – including our printers – feature in the programme, as well as those who donate goods for free.'

'And all of this is down to you.'

'No!' I reply, emphatically. 'Elizabeth, Grandma *and* me. We're a team.'

'And a formidable one, at that!'

This time, when Mum flings open the door of Anchor House, I don't feel apprehensive. The first time around I hadn't appreciated that I wasn't the only nervous one; in hindsight, Mum, and Greg, were a little anxious too.

What helps is that Oliver just seems to fit in with ease. When Greg says he has something to show him outside in his workshop, the two of them head off like old friends, nattering away.

'Greg's been working on this boat, restoring it for a customer and he wants to show it off,' Mum laughs. 'You look well and happy. Thanks for coming down again so soon.'

'I'm good and everything is ticking over nicely back in Darlingham, as the Christmas plans are now well under way. So, why wouldn't I come?'

I put my overnight bag down next to Oliver's and follow her into the kitchen.

'Coffee, tea or hot chocolate and marshmallows?'

'Ooh . . . it has to be hot chocolate,' I reply, as I lean against the countertop. 'And how are the two of you doing?'

'We're fine. Greg has been busy, despite the fact that it's the quiet season, so that bodes well.'

'And you?'

Mum pauses for a second, the kettle halfway to the tap. 'I'm much happier than I was a couple of weeks ago.'

I catch my breath. 'My first visit didn't unsettle you, did it?'

'Yes, and no. Greg says it's time I let go of the guilt.'

'Guilt?' I question, my voice wavering a little.

'There are so many things that got glossed over in the weeks leading up to my move here. Things that normally you and I would have talked through in detail.'

'Hey, it was a hectic time. And my head was somewhere else, you know that.'

'I do. But when I came here it didn't just . . .' Mum clears her throat, taking a few moments before continuing. 'It didn't just turn my life upside down, but yours and your grandma's, too.' She finishes filling the kettle and I wait anxiously until she turns back around, glancing in my direction. 'You both encouraged me to take a risk, but I know how hard that was for you in particular. To have you here with us for this meal tonight means a lot to me. It means you've forgiven me.'

The gas burner beneath the kettle sparks into life and she steps away. I move closer, wrapping my arms around her affectionately. 'There's nothing to forgive, Mum. I'm the one who should feel guilty for not being more supportive. I'd retreated into my shell because I knew things weren't right between me and Liam. I was so caught up in my own troubles that I wasn't there for you at a time when you needed me.'

We hug each other with a fierceness that tells me this is long overdue.

'That's not true, you helped whenever you could. The timing was awful, and it just seemed that almost as soon as I got here—' Her voice sounds full of regret.

'Nothing that happened after you left was because of you, Mum. Freddie . . . Liam . . . my return to the village and now Grandma's plans—'

'I know, but I should have been there . . .' Her words trail off and I stand back so we have eye contact.

'It wouldn't have made a difference, would it? It takes time to adjust to life-altering events and come to terms with the changes. I was mad at myself for messing up my life and, believe me, I wouldn't have been good company. Finally, I'm beginning to see a glimmer of light at the end of the tunnel. And you and Greg needed some time alone to start your new life together. That's only natural.

'What I loved when I first walked into Anchor Cottage, was that everywhere I looked I could see the little touches you'd added to make it feel like home. And, clearly, Greg appreciates it.'

Mum sniffs, squaring her shoulders and giving me a watery smile. 'Home from home, my darling. And you're always welcome here.'

'Now, why aren't you helping at the fayre in the church hall today?'

'Because my daughter and her friend are here, naturally.'

As I pull out a chair to sit down at the table, I cast her a disapproving glance. 'I don't think you should get off that lightly. How about we ask the guys to drop us off in town and we can both lend a hand for a few hours. What do you think?'

Mum's face brightens. 'You don't mind?'

'Not at all. I still haven't finished my Christmas shopping and if I can slope off for half an hour, I'd like to pop into Driftwood and pick up another of these.' I reach out to run my fingers over the wooden tea-light holder I ordered that Mum picked up from the shop. I can't tell her that Grandma insisted I give the one I took back for her to Elizabeth, but I could tell it caught Grandma's eye, too.

'What I love about it is the simplicity of the design and how tactile it is. Sometimes I pick a few sprigs of holly or cut a twig or two of eucalyptus and just lay it either side. No one can resist reaching out to feel the smoothness of the grain.'

'I wonder how long it floated around in the sea before a swell washed it inland, awaiting an eagle-eyed beachcomber.'

'Well, hopefully Ash will have more on display, certainly after the storms we had last week. All manner of things turn up and he told me that once he reclaimed a small tree. It took two of them to carry it back to his workshop. Here you go. I'll let you add the marshmallows yourself.'

'Thanks, Mum. It's just like old times.' Home from home indeed, and I couldn't be happier for her.

Lending a hand providing cover for some of the stallholders to have a comfort break is fun. Everyone is in a festive mood and the Charlestown village hall is full of eager shoppers.

Mid-afternoon, Mum sidles up to me. 'I think I can manage if you want to take a wander around the shops. There's only another hour and a half to go and I think the main rush is probably over.'

'OK. Is there anything I can get you?'

Mum beams at me. 'I haven't even drawn up my Christmas present list yet but if you see anything that takes your fancy, ask Jasmine to put it to one side and tell her I'll pop in on Monday to pay for it.'

'Mum!'

'Go on . . . take a stroll, it will do you good. And head down to the cove afterwards. On a day like this, as long as you're wrapped up well, it's heavenly.'

She dismisses me with a laugh and a wave of her hand.

Once outside, I take a few deep breaths of sea air and it's invigorating. I can almost taste the salt on my tongue, and I listen to the raucous calls of the seagulls circling overhead as I pick up the pace.

There are two beaches at Charlestown, which is a short walk from the church hall. It sits at the top of the hill leading down to the main hub. The part sand, part cobble swathes of beach sit either side of the harbour. One is accessed by steps from the harbour wall and the other via a slipway.

I walk with purpose, determined to find a suitable decoration for Grandma and then while away half an hour just gazing out over the sea. I think I deserve a little quiet time and I don't feel at all guilty that Greg and Oliver are off doing their own thing. Fishermen love sitting around telling tales of the one that got away, and as someone who has never fished, it all sounds a bit dreary to me.

There's a constant stream of people coming and going. With several eateries close together, there's something for everyone, and when I climb the stairs to Driftwood, I'm surprised how busy it is. In the background, Christmas music is playing, but it's low level and atmospheric, as opposed to some of the more raucous compilations. Being on the top floor has its advantages with the view, but the two long flights of stairs are a bit of a drag.

However, the shop is warm, cosy, colourful and inviting. Jasmine and a younger woman are busy serving and I'm glad that there's no sign of Ash as I begin to nosey around. Perhaps I should look for something slightly different for Grandma. It doesn't take long for an item to catch my eye and I find myself immediately breaking into a smile, knowing that she'll love it.

It's another driftwood item, but it stands about twelve inches high and it's a clever use of what I should imagine was originally a large knot on a tree trunk. Weathered until it's silvery-smooth, it's been hollowed out to hold two attractive cranberry-coloured shot-size glasses. They could be used for tea lights, or to hold small items of jewellery, or even a little potpourri.

I wait in line to pay, and when it's my turn to step forward, Jasmine smiles at me with her eyes. 'Back again, I see.'

'I couldn't resist. The driftwood pieces make such a lovely gift. My mum was thrilled with hers.'

'I didn't realise you were Helen's daughter. My parents are long-time friends of Greg's. They make such a lovely couple, and your mum has settled in really quickly.'

Jasmine wraps the awkwardly shaped item with ease, covering it in bubble wrap before placing it into the stout paper carrier bag.

'Yes, thankfully. I think having been born in and growing up as part of a small community makes it easier to understand life outside of a town, or a city. People need to know they can rely upon each other in an emergency, don't they?'

'They sure do. I live about a twenty-minute drive away in a row of houses set in a bit of a dip. Every winter without fail what we call the hollow in the middle of the lane gets flooded and we need to get the sandbags out. Everyone mucks in. There you go. That should survive your journey home intact.'

'Thank you. I doubt I'll be back again this side of Christmas, so have a lovely one.'

'You, too!'

19

An Awkward Confrontation

Five minutes after stepping back out onto the street, I'm strolling downhill towards the harbour, happily swinging my beautifully wrapped parcel in one hand and feeling relaxed.

'Excuse me!' I hear a voice somewhere behind me, but it isn't until a hand touches my arm that I realise someone is trying to get my attention.

I turn, and to my dismay it's Ash.

'Sorry, I wasn't ignoring you. Did I forget something?'

'No. No. Um . . .' He casts his eyes around nervously, but no one's really taking any notice of us.

'Can you spare me five minutes?'

I give him a questioning smile. 'Is this a customer survey?'

'Uh, no . . . this is about . . . do you mind if we find somewhere quiet to sit and chat?'

A lump rises in my throat. 'Look, I'm just visiting, and I need to—'

'I know who you are,' he retorts, cutting me dead. 'A friend rang to tell me that a couple were up at Rock House Hotel asking questions about the previous owners. Coincidentally, it was the same day that you called into the shop that first time, but I had no reason to think it was you. I do now.'

My stomach begins to churn as I glance at him momentarily. When I don't make any attempt to move, he continues.

'I took a trip to Silverberry Hall in Darlingham, and I saw you not once, but twice. Do you work there?'

I nod my head. 'Maybe we should find somewhere a bit more private,' I agree, albeit with an air of reluctance.

Ash indicates to our right. People are milling around, some with dogs on leads, and as we make our way down the sloping concrete run leading onto the smaller of the two beaches, neither of us says a word.

The pebbles crunch beneath my walking boots as I step off the ramp, giving way slightly with each step I take. I focus on avoiding knotted clumps of shiny black seaweed that look slippery. At one end there's a low concrete section and we make way over to it. It's a good enough seat, and far enough away from the main hub to guarantee that we won't be overheard.

'On a day like this the sea is glorious.' He's nervous and trying to disguise it by making polite conversation. 'It's a bit choppy but when the sky is this blue, even though the water is freezing, it always looks inviting.'

'You obviously enjoy living here,' I reply, wishing he'd just get straight to the point.

'I do. My life changed completely when we moved to Cornwall.'

The silence is awkward. I gaze around, fascinated by the foamy tide as it creeps up the beach. There's a whooshing noise as the waves break, followed by a loud clattering sound of the pebbles when the water ebbs away, sucking them almost dry. He's waiting for me to say something and there's no point pretending I don't know at least a little bit about his life.

'It can't have been easy leaving everyone behind.'

He turns to look at me. 'I missed my friends at school, but it was always just Mum and me, really. We rarely had contact with family and when we did, we often received a frosty welcome. Mum never got on with her dad.'

'That's sad, for her and for you . . . I mean, not having an easy relationship with your grandparents.'

'Hmm . . . it was all I knew, and I was on Mum's side. No one had the right to tell her how to live her life. My grandparents were only worried about what people thought about their daughter being abandoned by the father of her child. I once overhead her dad ask whether she even knew who he was. I was too young to rush in and defend her, but if I'd been older I'd have lashed out at him for making her cry. It was easier after we came here. People didn't ask questions, they just assumed she was a widow, and they were respectful.'

'Changing names . . . why bother, when her family had no idea where you were anyway?'

Ash stares off into the distance, a fleeting smile playing around his lips as, no doubt, a distant memory replays inside his head. 'And yet you managed to find me. Can I talk frankly, as I have a favour to ask.'

I nod my head, wondering where this is leading.

'Good. Mum said a fresh start required a new name, something that wouldn't constantly remind us of the past. She said that in life you get to choose your friends but not your family, and it was good riddance to the lot of them!'

'That must have felt liberating for her.'

'It was. She kept saying, "Your dad won't forget us," and, as it turned out, he didn't. The move changed everything. We soon got to know the locals and then when the holiday season hit, well . . . I was old enough to lend a hand after school and at weekends. It was fun and she was so happy running the hotel – happier than I'd ever seen her before.'

He stares down at his boot, scraping it over the pebbles while deep in thought.

'You said you have a favour to ask?'

'Yes. I couldn't get up the courage to go and knock on the door of Silverberry Hall. I tried . . . twice. I stayed one night in a B&B a few miles away, but after the second attempt I headed back home. When I saw you, I knew it was the right place, but it wasn't what I was expecting.'

'What led you to Darlingham?'

'Curiosity, when, out of the blue, I received a letter about my late father's will. I decided to jump online and do a bit of digging. I was lurking outside the Hall and when I spotted you walking across the car park I knew then that someone had sent you here to look for me.' He laughs, dismissively. 'I'm just a guy leading an ordinary life and it was too much of a coincidence to put it down to chance.'

'I wasn't spying on you, please don't think that. My grandfather knew your maternal grandfather; they were members of the same golf club, as was my employer's late husband. I was simply asked to make a few discreet enquiries, that's all.'

Trying to appear calm isn't easy as my stomach is doing somersaults. What if he starts quizzing me about Elizabeth and Freddie?

'But you succeeded where a professional investigator failed.' He seems to find that thought rather amusing.

'The intention was well meant, I can assure you. It's all in the hands of an Italian solicitor; they simply needed an address.'

Ash leans back, gazing out to sea, where a large tanker slowly edges its way across the horizon.

'Yes. I had a heads-up a while ago, when my maternal grandmother told me about the guy they employed to trace me. I get it, they have to exhaust all avenues, but I'd already made it clear to her that I didn't want my details given out to anyone. At least she honoured that.'

'You're in touch with her?' I let out an involuntary gasp. 'I was led to believe that your family didn't know where you were.'

'It's not common knowledge. My grandfather isn't aware of it. He and Mum hadn't spoken properly in years. The thing is, he's always been a bit of a bully and Mum wasn't one to just toe the line for the sake of a quiet life. When she died, I wrote to them, but I didn't give any contact details.

Then I had a change of heart. I found their number on Mum's phone, and I rang them a few days later. I thought they might want to attend the funeral. He wouldn't come. My grandmother sobbed down the phone, but she didn't come either. To be honest, I think Mum would have preferred it that way. But I figured I owed it to them, to at least give them the option.'

'*You* owed it to *them*?'

He shrugs his shoulders. 'Some people think death is final, and if that's what they believe, I didn't want that on my conscience. My grandmother and I talk occasionally, but she respects my privacy. We don't have a lot in common.'

How can he talk about this without any trace of emotion? I'm feeling tearful just listening to him because it's so terribly sad.

'You don't understand, do you?' he asks, his eyes searching mine.

'I'm trying to, but—'

'Look . . . my father's hands were tied when he found out my mother was expecting a baby. He'd not long arrived in Italy, having made himself an outcast to his family.'

My jaw literally drops. 'You know the full story?'

'I do and I'm guessing that you do, too.'

That throws me into a bit of a spin. 'No . . . um . . . only a little because of the task I was given. I wasn't sure—'

'Ah, you had to be talked into it. Well, that says a lot about you.' He pauses, looking at me quizzically.

'Oh, sorry! I'm Sienna . . . Sienna Sanderson.'

I stick out my hand and we shake.

'I like that you're loyal to your employer, but you don't blindly do as you're told.'

I feel myself recoiling. Is he goading me? 'I'm sorry, this really is none of my business. No one, aside from the Italian solicitors, will bother you precisely because of your right to privacy in this matter.'

His expression changes and he frowns. 'I get it. You thought you were doing me a favour, right? And the person who sent you thought the same thing.'

He has Freddie's posture; his back is straight, and he holds his head high, but instead of dark brown hair, it's a lighter colouring, sandier, and a mass of curls that seem to have a life of their own.

'Well . . . yes. If I left someone a gift in *my* will I'd expect the people closest to me to honour my wishes out of respect, not just because of the legal aspect.' He can see I'm growing anxious about this conversation. 'You're in touch with the right people now, so it's entirely up to you what you do next.'

'You think I'm ungrateful, don't you? But money isn't everything.'

This is exasperating. 'No. It's not for me to have an opinion about this at all.'

'But we both know that your employer has an opinion.'

If he wants to play games, I have a few questions of my own. 'Why go all the way to Darlingham without getting the answers you seek?'

He turns to face me, raising his eyebrows. 'I don't need, or want, answers. I was just being nosey, I suppose. I was told that my father's family lived in London, so I didn't understand the connection to the Cotswolds at first. He wrote me a letter, which my mother gave to me when I was sixteen years old.'

My pulse is racing, and my eyes are constantly drawn back to his face as he stares off into the distance.

'You do know that his family had no idea you even existed until now? It's not their fault—'

He gives a dismissive chuckle. 'Ah . . . *what if* or . . . *if only* . . . but I've come to the conclusion that it's all irrelevant now.'

Suddenly, a chilling thought strikes me. Does Ash blame Freddie and Elizabeth for what happened? Does he feel that by making contact, it would be disloyal to his father's memory? That's some messed-up thinking and I'm dismayed, because it seems his mind is already made up.

'You have every right to be curious about your roots, you know,' I encourage.

He draws in a deep and meaningful breath. 'As I stood looking up at the Hall I thought to myself why rake up the past now? Who does it benefit? Certainly not the people living there. I can't imagine it's the sort of thing they want made public after all these years, is it?'

This is agonising. It's sounds to me that he isn't even aware that Freddie is no longer with us.

'It benefits *you*,' I state firmly.

'I am who I am, and knowing more about my father's parents isn't going to change anything. As Mum said, at least we get to choose our friends. I'm surrounded by some very loyal and kind people, who've been there for me through some tough times. I've never felt there's anything missing from my life, so why get myself into something I might end up regretting?'

My breath catches in my throat. 'Ash, why are you telling me this?'

'Because there's no one else I can talk to. I realised that knocking on the door of Silverberry Hall was a bad idea almost as soon as I arrived in Darlingham. I have no sense of connection to the people there, or the place.'

'And you're serious . . . you really want it to remain that way?' I ask, my voice wavering as I think of Elizabeth.

'I think it's the best way to handle it.'

'But you don't have to prove who you are . . . you do know that? Peter's widow accepts that you exist. You're a beneficiary and it doesn't come with any strings attached.'

'Let's not pretend it's as clear cut as that. I don't want the complication that comes with having to manage other people's expectations. It's better to quash them and move on. Like father, like son.'

'But you couldn't bring yourself to do it face to face at Silverberry Hall?'

'No, I couldn't. Then, when I glanced out of my workshop just now and I saw you, I knew it was the perfect solution.'

I stare at him aghast. 'I can't be your messenger.'

'Why not? I could argue that it's your fault I'm in this position.' He doesn't sound angry, just a little put out.

'If you'd met Elizabeth Blakesley, you'd know why.'

He shakes his head. 'None of it is my doing and it's not right that I should be pressured into explaining my actions.'

'I was asked to find you precisely because this is about protecting your privacy. It's not about your father's family, believe me. But now we've talked, I'll be honest with you – I think you're making a huge mistake for all the wrong reasons. The past is just that. But can you imagine the emotional impact of knowing you exist? You're . . . their flesh and blood.'

He stands, looking down at me with a pinched expression on his face. 'And I should feel guilty about it because . . . why? I don't owe them anything. That's a "no" then to delivering my message, which I thought was a kinder way of saying, "Thanks, but no thanks."'

I ease myself upright. 'Kinder, how?'

'They can all go back to pretending I don't exist and none of this ever happened. I have a house and I run my own business. As far as I'm concerned, my parents already left me a legacy, so my mind is made up. I don't intend to get drawn into a past that is best left buried.'

'Well, the decision is yours. I'm sorry, really sorry for the part I played in this, and I wish you well for the future, I really do.'

As he trudges away, I feel gutted. For him, and for Elizabeth. What is surprising, given the situation, is how calm he is about it. There's no anger and no recriminations. He's had a happy life and that was down to the strength and determination of his mother. His father supported them in the only way he could, and without interfering. A part of me can't help but wonder whether there were times when he wished it could have been different.

The real tragedy is that I truly believe Freddie would have found a way to resolve whatever issues Peter was struggling with, if they'd just been able to sit down and talk calmly. I know that, because I knew Freddie and you can only judge a person by their actions. And, yes, he was a practical, law-abiding man in every way, but he was also compassionate. He treated me with respect, despite the mistakes I'd made which got me into a mess. He gave me a chance, an opportunity to feel good about myself again, when I was at an all-time low. Sadly, Peter taking flight didn't give Freddie the opportunity to admit he'd overreacted. And even worse, it robbed Elizabeth – them all, really – of so much more.

What is heartbreaking is that if Ash met Elizabeth, he'd be left in no doubt at all about how proud she'd be to acknowledge him. She doesn't care about the past, either. It's today and tomorrow that count. None of us knows how many years we have left on this earth, but whatever time Elizabeth has would be joyously happy with a grandson in her life.

The Line and Sinker Bistro is quite a surprise. When Greg, Oliver, Mum and I bustle through the smart glass doors in an alleyway off Charlestown Road, my first thought was that it was a quaint little place. I had no idea how far back the narrow-looking building stretched, or that we'd be eating in a new glass addition to the rear. It looks out onto a small, but colourful courtyard.

'This is a real gem of a place,' I remark to Oliver, as he helps me off with my coat.

He grins at me. 'It was worth dressing up for.'

I chuckle to myself, as he disappears to hang up our coats. I did have a bit of a *what to wear* crisis earlier on and got him to check out the two outfits I'd brought with me. It's cold, so leggings were a must, but I'd brought a soft blue jumper to match my eyes and a cerise, mid-thigh-length figure-hugging top with large black flower heads that I wasn't sure was really me. He said the cerise was the hands-down winner and I could tell from his face that he meant it.

The table is set for twenty people and we're the first to arrive. I hover, looking at the artwork display on the walls, as Mum and Greg are deep in conversation with one of the waiters.

By the time Oliver returns, they're seated, and he pulls out a chair for me next to Greg. I find myself biting my lip; maybe I should have sat down next to Mum, so Oliver could chat with Greg but it's too late now.

Oliver slides onto the chair next to me and leans in while my thoughts are still churning. 'It's nice to look out over the courtyard, isn't it? Do you know any of the people who are coming?'

'No. They're all long-time friends of Greg's,' I reply, keeping my voice low. 'That's why Mum was a bit nervous, you know, it being the first time they've all got together. I guess it's a tradition and now she's a part of it.'

Greg turns to me. 'What's your preference, Sienna? And Oliver, wine or beer? They have a few on tap.'

We both plump for red wine, as it's just easier if we all have the same thing, but before the waiter returns a steady stream of people join us and the introductions begin. To my utmost surprise, Jasmine is among them, and she gives me a friendly wave across the table. She's with her parents and a younger man, named Eric.

'Welcome, folks! Here's tonight's menu and the specials are at the bottom.' The waiter passes the menus around. 'We'll just sort everyone's drinks and give you a few minutes to make your selection.'

The noise of the chatter around the table seems to fill the

glass extension, which is very much like a garden room. I lean into Greg. 'This is a wonderful restaurant. Do you always come here for the big meet-up?'

'Yes. It's owned by my cousin, Cole, and his wife.' As the introductions were a little haphazard, Greg goes on to talk me through who's who around the table. When he comes to Eric, I ask if he's Jasmine's brother.

'No, they're a couple. They got engaged a few months ago.'

I turn to look at him, puzzled. 'I thought she was Ash's partner.'

This comes as quite a shock. It was nice to think that at least Ash had someone special in his life.

He seems surprised. 'No. Ash owns the store and Jasmine serves there three days a week in return for being able to display her jewellery. She has a website and sells stuff online, too. He was seeing a lady named Cali, but she hasn't been around for a while.'

Jasmine's father catches Greg's attention now that everyone has a drink and Greg proposes a toast. 'To friends, old and new, gathered around the table. I hope everyone has an amazing Christmas and New Year. Here's to us all!'

A chorus of response fills the air. Mum had no need to worry; she's deep in conversation with the woman next to her, leaving me to touch glasses with Greg. 'Thanks for coming, Sienna. It means a lot and not just to your mum. Are you looking forward to the party on Christmas Eve, or will you be glad to get it over and done with?' He gives a little laugh.

'Honestly? A bit of both, but I put on a brave face until it's in full swing, as it's only then I can relax.'

'Well, here's to a successful evening in Darlingham.' We chink glasses. 'Your mum and I can't wait. Last year I felt a bit out on a limb if you know what I mean. Like your mum feared she'd feel this evening, but it's just a group of people having a bit of fun. And it's the same for the party. If anything goes wrong it's not the end of the world and everyone appreciates all the arduous work that goes into it.'

Aww. That's exactly the sort of pep talk my dad would have given me if he'd been sitting in that chair. A little kindness goes a long way and I'm touched.

20

Wondering Why . . .

After a windswept Sunday morning walk along the cliff path, followed by a wonderful roast lunch sitting next to a roaring log fire, the journey back to Darlingham is a reflective one.

My attempts at being jovial come out sounding half-hearted. I try to mask a sense of disappointment in myself, as some of the things that Ash said to me keep invading my thoughts. Oliver probes a little, but when I'm not forthcoming he backs off, and I get him talking about his new project.

'This job started out well, but a sudden change of management means that new ideas are being thrown at me daily. There's no point tinkering with what I have, so I've told them straight that they need to redefine the brief. Effectively, everything is on hold and the plan is to have a few round-table sessions to thrash it out. It's not an ideal situation, because in good faith I've done a lot of work based on the original specification. I fear most of it will be scrapped.'

'That's a tough situation to find yourself in.'

'You can say that again,' he sighs. 'There's no way I'll be able to charge them for every hour I've worked; if I do, I doubt they'll use me again, even though it's their dithering about that has wasted a lot of time.'

I'm happy to sit back and listen, as he explains that it's all about managing people's expectations. It isn't easy when the team he's working with has diverse points of view and it's already caused one major shake-up. I can understand that all right, and just how easy it is to compromise for all the wrong reasons.

I allowed myself to be swayed by Grandma and Elizabeth when I should have stood my ground. Now, the part I played in finding Ash seems to have sunk any chance of Elizabeth and her grandson ever meeting up.

In my head I imagined a man in his prime, angry about the way he and his mother had been treated. While money can't heal old wounds, the fantasy was that it would all come good in the end. He'd realise his father had deep regrets about the past. Ash would be touched to know that he wasn't forgotten. I thought . . . no, I assumed, that he would be curious about his father's parents and his roots. He'd seek out Elizabeth and discover that she's simply a mother grieving the loss of her estranged son and stunned, but also overjoyed, to discover she has a grandson.

Oliver's voice interrupts my inner dialogue. 'Hey, you're frowning. I didn't mean to bore you with my problems.'

'Sorry. It's not that, I just have a bit of a headache coming on.'

'If you reach behind you, you'll find a six-pack of water bottles. Help yourself. We're probably a little dehydrated after last night. Red wine usually does that to me.'

I reach back and grab two, cracking the lid on one and placing it in the console between us. 'There you go.'

'Thanks. I had a text from Daniela. She's suggesting we do a full rehearsal on Saturday the ninth of December,' he continues. 'I'm not sure if she's expecting me to liaise with you on that, regarding access to the barn.'

'No, she hasn't mentioned it, but I'll put it on the calendar, and I'll be around if you need anything.' I down a third of my bottle of water in one go, hoping it'll help to clear my head.

'Last night went well,' Oliver reflects. 'It was nice that you got an opportunity to have a long chat with Greg.'

'Yes, thanks for seating me next to him.'

He glances at me momentarily. 'When I saw you loitering,

I guessed you had a bit of a dilemma going on. I meant well and I'm glad it turned out to be the right thing to do.'

That phrase 'I meant well' seems to rattle around inside my head, taunting me. How I wish I hadn't got involved with the search for James.

Well, reality is a harsh wake-up call. Ash is happy with his life and Elizabeth is left to cope with a sense of loss for something she never had. From the little Elizabeth told me it was obvious that she'd tried to be a peacemaker between her husband and her son. Now she's left to mourn not just the loss of Freddie, but what could have been if the two men in her life had listened to her.

'I wish you'd tell me what's wrong.' The words are spoken softly, almost as if Oliver doesn't want to upset me but he can't stop himself reaching out. 'I thought you'd be going home on a high.'

It's hard because I can't tell him why I'm feeling so down. 'Oh, I'm just tired and you're right, the water is helping a little already.'

'It was nice that you and your mum got a chance to talk to Jasmine from Driftwood when you went to grab the coats. Did I see you exchanging phone numbers?'

'Yes,' I reply, brightly. I think it's time to inject a little humour. 'With all the chatter about the first fishing trip of the year she suggested Mum and I might want to join the alternative club.'

He guffaws. 'What's the alternative?'

'Jasmine said that us non-fisher folk get to laze around at a spa,' I muse. 'Mum was over the moon when she said that.'

'We're not going to be able to get out of it, are we?'

He's right; the assumption is that we'll both head down to take part in their fun weekend adventure.

'No, it seems not! Still, Greg's mates are hilarious, and I'm sure you'll enjoy the trip. As for me, well, I'm always up for a bit of pampering and Mum thinks it will be a great bonding experience all round.' I shrug my shoulders. 'The decision was sort of made for me, anyway.'

'You should have checked out the boat that Greg's working on, ready to put her back into the water: she's a beauty. It's similar to the vessel Jasmine's dad owns, apparently, and he's going to be our skipper on the day. Greg said it'll probably be some time in February, as when winter turns into spring, many species of fish head away to spawn. Most of the commercially run tours happen in June, July and August when the seas warm up.'

I hope by then it won't feel awkward between Oliver and me, as that seems an awfully long time away. I shake my head at him, amused by the awe in his voice. 'After that glorious meal last night, I will say that I'm very appreciative of freshly caught fish,' I admit. 'But I have no desire whatsoever to swap sides and jump aboard a fishing boat.'

'I'll probably throw anything I catch back into the water,' he replies.

'I'm surprised, because I thought that was the whole point of the excursion.'

'Not for casual anglers. I get a thrill out of just being on the waves, although I rarely get a chance these days. You see things from a unique perspective, and it sort of shakes up your world a little. You know, doing something out of the ordinary can be thrilling and scary at the same time, depending on how high the waves are. And the difference between having your feet on solid ground, as opposed to being at the mercy of the sea, is humbling. I have a lot of respect for fishermen.'

There's a question that's been on the tip of my tongue and now is as good a time as any to ask it. 'Me, too. Um . . . I haven't seen much of Daniela this last week. I think she had another trip to Inglewick Hall.'

I feel mean checking but after Nigel's visit I need to make sure. After all, Liam managed to play me for a fool, and I had no idea I was being lied to.

'Yes, she did mention that when we spoke. It sounds like

she has it all under control, although how she manages to juggle everything, I have no idea.'

The relief is incredible. There's no way there is anything going on between the two of them; Oliver is like an open book.

'I know. Are there plans for another dinner party after the first full rehearsal?'

He shakes his head. 'Not as far as I know. We had a video call run-through on Thursday night with the updated script, but I don't think anyone is word perfect yet. I'm certainly not, but aside from Daniela, I have the most lines.'

Hmm. If that means more video calls between the two of them, that might not sit well with Nigel. 'But as she wrote the play, aren't the words all in her head?' I muse.

'Pretty much, but it's getting the timing right between the two of us for the longer duologues. Most of the other dialogue is snappy back and forth between the other characters, where they reflect on the past, revealing the backstory. It's also important to pause every now and again to give the audience a few seconds to allow what's happening to sink in.'

'Oh, I see. It sounds complicated.'

'You should come along and see for yourself.'

'No. That would spoil it for me on the night,' I profess. 'Anyway, I'm assuming you'll be staying at mine?'

'Only if it's convenient. If you have plans, then I'll head home. Rehearsals should finish by five o'clock at the latest, as I gather that Daniela and Nigel have a party to attend in the evening.'

'It's not a problem if you want to stay. It would be a long day for you with the drive back. Maybe I should book us a table at The Sailor's Retreat for dinner. What do you think?'

'Only if it's my treat. I still feel bad that Greg insisted on paying for our meals last night.'

'He just appreciated us being there. Mum did, too, but I think she would have been fine, even if we hadn't been there.'

'I agree. Maybe she wanted you to go so you'd feel a part

of her new life. It's a bit like my parents. Every now and again I have to pay them a visit like a dutiful son, even though farming isn't my thing. Now if it were a fish farm with lakes full of trout, I'd be spending every single weekend there.'

'Fish farming?' I gulp. 'I don't even want to think about that!'

He gives a dismissive laugh. 'Unfortunately, I'll be up and out early tomorrow morning. I received a text earlier on to confirm that the meeting I'm attending on Monday morning has been brought forward. It starts at eight thirty sharp now, so I'll tiptoe around to avoid waking you. I can stop and grab coffee at one of the service stations.'

'That's not a problem. Besides, this is twice now you've driven down to Cornwall and back, Oliver. You should at least let me go halves on the fuel.'

'No way!' he replies, adamantly. 'Yet again, I've had a great weekend, thanks to you. Your mum and Greg are wonderful hosts and it's been fun.'

It seems we've progressed beyond it being about paying each other back for favours. But where exactly does that leave us? As if he can hear my thoughts, Oliver suddenly turns to glance at me, his eyes lighting up.

'You should come up to London one weekend and stay at my flat. I could show you the sights.'

Butterflies immediately begin to fill my stomach as, for one brief second, our eyes meet before he turns his attention back to the road ahead.

'Maybe when things calm down a little,' I propose. For some reason, his suggestion has sent me into a bit of a panic. 'Life's a bit crazy right now, but that would be nice.'

Nice? Oh dear. That's not a very inspiring word to describe his offer, is it? I berate myself. That inner voice whispers in my ear. *Could Oliver turn into more than just a friend?* The answer to that is I simply don't know. My thoughts are in turmoil. If I was wondering whether I'm ready to think about having a relationship with someone again, I guess that tells me what I need to know. I'm not quite there yet but hopefully I will be, one day soon, because I really like Oliver and who knows what the future might hold?

'This is such a treat for a Monday evening; just the peace and quiet is like music to my ears!' Daniela laughs as she eases herself back on the sofa, a glass of white wine in one hand.

'We haven't had a real chat for ages, have we?' I reply, feeling a tad guilty for enticing her away from Nigel for an hour, or two, with wine and nibbles.

'No and it's about time we caught up properly. It doesn't hurt Nigel to occasionally sort bedtime on his own. At one time, he was spending more time away than he was at home, so it reminds him of what I've had to cope with.'

'I'm glad he took your concerns on board.'

She wriggles back contentedly, nestling into the cushions, and follows me by slipping off her shoes and putting her feet up on the coffee table.

'He had no choice; I laid down the law. We've always been straight with each other, and I think that's important, don't you?' She frowns and I realise it's a serious question.

'How would I know? I didn't get past the fiancée stage.' I grin at her, then roll my eyes. 'Maybe that was the reason why. We avoided talking about the proverbial elephant in the room.'

'Which was?' I can see she's curious.

'This is going to sound awful . . . in hindsight, boredom, I suppose. At the time I thought of it as comfortable companionship; I assumed that was what marked the move from that instant physical attraction into a more lasting relationship.'

'Good grief, Sienna! A relationship should never be boring. The point of arguments is that it's wonderful making up afterwards because it reminds you why you're together.'

'Which is? I guess what I'm really asking is how do you know if you've found the one?'

Daniela looks at me, studying my face. 'You're asking me for advice now and I'm no expert. I was hooked from the moment I first saw Nigel across the dance floor. Maybe it's different for every couple.'

'No, I think you're right in what you said. When two people stop talking it's a sign of trouble. Look at my parents, and my grandparents come to that, their marriages survived some very different and strong points of view. And look at Freddie and Elizabeth. Gosh, they had some blazing rows and there was even a bit of door slamming at times.'

We both chuckle.

'That's because beneath it all is always that undercurrent of passion. You know you can't live without that person, even when they're so annoying it makes you want to scream. A couple of hours later, it's like the row never happened and you fall in love with them all over again.'

'You softie, you!' I exclaim.

'What? Nigel is infuriating at times, and you know it. But it takes one to know one!'

I almost choke on the sip of wine I've just taken. 'Yes, I do know that. But I thought Liam was the one. How do I know I won't make a mistake like that again?'

'Is this about Oliver?' Her eyes widen.

'No. Maybe. Oh . . . I'm not sure.' I'm not avoiding the question; I simply don't know the answer.

'When I walked in on the two of you, heads together working out the plan for the stage, I thought you made a lovely couple. You obviously get on really well when you're alone together, as you wouldn't have taken him down to Cornwall if that weren't the case. So, what's the problem?'

'Hmm. It's . . . difficult. Greg and Mum seem to assume we're more than friends but are keeping it low-key. The invite to the party last Saturday was extended to us both and there's a weekend thing in February being planned. And now Oliver is talking about inviting me to stay at his place to go sightseeing.'

Daniela can hardly contain her excitement. 'But that's great, isn't it?'

'Yes, I suppose it is.' She's right. 'I'm probably just being overly cautious. You know, once bitten, twice shy and all that.'

'Oh, my gosh . . . the thought of my two best friends in the whole wide world getting together is amazing! And I know you'll be in safe hands, because Oliver isn't just a gentleman, he's a gentle man, too. He has a big heart.'

Yes, one that you broke without even knowing it, my lovely friend. Besides, Oliver and I haven't even kissed, aside from on the cheek. There have been moments when we've come close to it at the cottage, but he senses a hesitancy in me. Am I holding back because knowing that Daniela was his first – and only – love, by the sound of it, I worry that I'd never be exciting enough for him?

'You won't say anything, will you?' I press her.

'Of course I won't! I'm well aware that this is a huge deal for you, and you'll want to take things slowly.'

'Thanks for understanding. I've told Mum, and Grandma, several times over that we're just good friends, but I know they're both hoping it will develop into something more.'

'He's not the sort of man to rush into anything, Sienna, so take your time. Let it all happen naturally and you'll be just fine.'

Oliver is tall, dark, handsome, intelligent and fun to be around, but there's an interesting undercurrent that Daniela once described as a Mr Darcy trait. The serious side of him is very serious indeed and it's enigmatic. He can't see it, but other women can, and it's compellingly attractive – but is that enough of a basis for me to throw caution to the wind and begin opening up my heart again?

The following morning, when Elizabeth and I get together to go through the monthly household accounts, she seems a little preoccupied. There are no surprises, and everything is ticking over quite nicely, but she's obviously troubled about something.

'I think that about wraps up November, unless you have any specific questions?'

'No. As usual, you're doing a marvellous job of keeping on top of everything, Sienna.'

'I have a printout of what we've spent so far with regard to the party and a pretty firm forecast for the total spend once all the invoices come in.'

Elizabeth merely glances at the bottom line on the sheet. 'It's good to see we're on target and will be within budget. It's going to be the party of all parties.' She stares off into the distance for a few seconds. Maybe this is one of her off days – times when a haunting sadness threatens to overwhelm her, and I've learnt not to react to it. After all, words are just words when what she's missing is the presence of the love of her life.

'Can I get you a cup of tea, or coffee?' I check, wondering if she'd appreciate being alone in the study to reflect. It was Freddie's favourite haunt, and he spent a lot of time in here.

'No,' she replies, snapping back into normal mode with surprising alacrity. 'My brother, Stephen, is pressuring me to allow him to do a thank-you speech at the party.' Her expression is steely. 'I told him, firmly and very politely, that no one can replace Freddie. He was an accomplished after-dinner speaker, a wonderful raconteur of jokes and a joy to listen to. Stephen will turn it into a long dedication to Freddie, followed by a list of thank-you messages, when we have the official magazine to do that. Do you think that people will be put out if we break tradition and dispense with the customary speech? I'd rather like your grandma to express our thanks to the cast once the play is finished and announce that the buffet is open. And that's it.'

I pause to reflect, coming to the conclusion that she's right. No one can replace Freddie. 'It's exactly the right thing to do, Elizabeth. Everyone knows it's in Freddie's honour and we'll all be thinking of him on the night.'

She gives me a watery smile. 'My sentiment to a T! The last thing we want is people going home feeling tearful, isn't it? I love the photograph of my darling husband that's on the flyleaf of the programme. And his favourite quote in Latin – *memento vivere*, remember to live. If my brother spent more time attending to his own life, rather than trying to meddle in mine, we wouldn't be having cross words.'

My goodness! Elizabeth rarely expresses her annoyance, but her fuse has certainly been lit.

I'm about to say, *I'm sure he means well*, and, thankfully, I manage to stop myself in time because it's not true. That term 'lording it' really does apply to Stephen if he's given a chance. He rarely acknowledges any of the staff; we're just there to do our jobs, and while he's more than happy to bark orders at us when Elizabeth is out of earshot, no one takes him seriously.

People work at Silverberry Hall because we're like one big family and now that Elizabeth is on her own, it's about making sure things run smoothly. To my knowledge, the only person who has ever been handed a lukewarm cup of coffee is Stephen, and Georgina did it with a sickly sweet smile on her face. I'm not a mean person, but it's a day I remember with a sense of mischief and satisfaction. No one points to her, calling her over with an impatient wave of the hand and a flippant, 'You, there!' when they want something.

I bet Freddie is up there laughing right now. But Elizabeth is no pushover and if Stephen doesn't back off soon, sparks will fly!

Saturday, 9th December

21

An Exhausting Day All Round

'How is it looking up at the Hall?' Grandma asks, as she continues to place some clothes in the garment carrier boxes.

'Chaotic,' I reply, truthfully. 'Daniela's troupe will all have arrived by now. They'll be using the toilets at the far end of the barn as changing rooms.'

'I think we're better off here today, out of *everyone's* way.' She pulls a grimace and I'm in total agreement.

'Why is it that every time there's a family birthday, they all descend on Elizabeth?'

Grandma smiles as she gathers another armful of clothes. 'Because she's a natural-born host, and after all this time, it's a given. Still, at least it's only a light breakfast and a few hours in the games room before the minibus arrives to take them off to the hotel for Yvonne's celebratory birthday lunch.'

Yvonne is Stephen's wife and Elizabeth gets on well with her. If only Stephen wasn't so overbearing, but in his family what he says goes. His son and his daughter have, thankfully, grown up to be a little more relaxed, like their mother. But all of Elizabeth's nephews and nieces are frequent visitors, simply because she loves them to bits and has always made them feel welcome.

'I gather Stephen's son's wife is expecting a baby in the spring.'

'Yes, and Yvonne, in particular, is so excited. It's their first grandchild and she finally gets to be a grandma.'

Elizabeth's other brother, Matthew, has two grandchildren already, so I guess it was just a waiting game.

'Is there a reason you chose to absent yourself from the Hall today? I mean . . . we could have finished packing up this little lot any day of the week.'

She half turns to smile at me. 'Oh, I was invited, Stephen is careful not to upset Elizabeth by snubbing her in any way, but they've had words about me moving in as her companion.'

'Ah, I see.'

I guess it was only a matter of time until Grandma found out what was simmering away in the background.

'I thought it was best to bow out graciously on this occasion, as the argument is still quite raw. Like every family upset, it will resolve itself in time. Elizabeth won't take any nonsense and she certainly doesn't intend to let Stephen meddle in—'

There's a rap on the front door and I hurry over to the window to see who it is. 'Oh, it's Ruby. She's probably on her way to the barn, as she's the official prompt if anyone forgets their words. She's also looking after Mrs Jessop's two grandchildren, who have non-speaking parts.'

'Oh, how wonderful! That'll be the main topic of conversation for Mrs Jessop's customers this morning as they buy their stamps and send their parcels.'

I hurry downstairs, swinging open the door with a bright and breezy, 'Morning!'

'Daniela said you'd be at your grandma's. I'm just off to collect the kids so I can't stop. She wanted me to check in with you to ask if it's all right if we keep the cordon up all day? Just for the section of the car park you designated for the wardrobe lady's and the lighting technician's vans? They might both need to go and collect items and they don't want to get in the way of Elizabeth's other visitors.'

'Yes, of course. That's not a problem. How's it going?'

'They're sorting the costumes first and Oliver is just undergoing his transformation. He looks really good with a beard,' she laughs.

'Is everything all right with you? You're not in trouble at the pub for taking today off?'

'I'm good, really good and no, because Ben owes me. I'm always swapping shifts for other people. I . . . um . . . bumped into Liam the other day when I was shopping in Stroud. He told me he did something stupid and asked me to tell you that he realises it's too late. He said your message was loud and clear. Has he . . . um . . . been bothering you?'

I lean against the door jamb, letting out a sigh. 'Liam just needed to hear me say it's over and there is no going back. It was a shock, when he turned up on my doorstep unannounced.'

'Well, you look perky enough today. Oh . . . did you hear the news about the new vet who's starting on the first of February?'

'Is it anyone we know?' I grin at her, expectantly.

'No, it's a total stranger and Lottie has given in her notice.'

My jaw drops. 'Why? She's a great office manager and I thought it was her dream job.'

'Well, the dream has changed. Xavier is off to a practice in Norfolk and she's going with him. They'll be throwing an engagement party before they leave.'

We gawp at each other. 'It must be something in the air,' I chuckle. 'I had a text from my old friend Marissa inviting me to her engagement party in January.'

'There's hope for us yet!' Ruby exclaims. 'I must go. The kids will be eager to try on their costumes and practise the snowball fight. Oh, and Daniela asked if you could add my name to the attendees list on the night, as I'm now officially one of the team.'

'Of course. I'm glad you mentioned that actually, as we're pretty close to our limit on numbers. I've been meaning to warn Elizabeth and Grandma, as they've already added a few new names, but I think we have to draw the line now.'

'Great, thanks for that, Sienna. I must admit that I'm

thrilled to be a part of it. It's so exciting. Anyway, we must have a proper catch-up real soon.'

'Definitely!'

'Don't keep me in suspense any longer, were there any problems?'

Oliver is sitting opposite me in The Sailor's Retreat, and he looks shattered.

'Not bad for the first dress rehearsal and proper run-through. The lighting took a bit of adjusting to get it right, but we got there in the end. And the twinkly lights in the panels you painted look just like stars from the front of house.'

'How were the kids?'

He stops to take a hefty swig of his pint of Old Spot, and I wait as he savours it. 'I really needed that. They were amazing and had us all in fits of laughter. Ruby was brilliant organising them. In between people popping off to see the seamstress to adjust a few things, she did numerous run-throughs with them.'

'I didn't think they had speaking parts?'

'Well, they didn't but orchestrating a snowball fight without some sort of dialogue didn't work. Now they have a few "You missed" and "Got you! Ha! Ha!" and that sort of thing. We're assuming we can have access earlier in the day on Christmas Eve to do a couple more rehearsals?'

'Of course. It'll be free until noon without interruption. After that there'll be a couple of deliveries with people traipsing back and forth. I'll also be organising the helpers to get the buffet tables in situ, put out the floral arrangements and generally get things ready for the caterers. We'll trim up the inside of the barn the day before, so that's one less job to do. Obviously, the courtyard will be crazy from two o'clock until five and it'll be noisy. I'll put a "Staff Only" sign on the barn door in case anyone is tempted to wander off limits, but it'll be unlocked in case you need access.'

He smirks at me. 'Why am I not surprised to hear that you've literally thought of everything?'

'That's exactly what Elizabeth pays me to do, but it will be a relief when it's over. I just want everything to go smoothly as I'd hate to disappoint her.'

'It will and I seriously doubt you could ever do that. You'd do anything to make her happy . . . and you've certainly gone that extra mile for her.'

Ruby appears with our food.

'The local lamb looks amazing, thanks, Ruby!' He glances up at her and they exchange beaming smiles. 'You did great, today. Everyone appreciated your input.'

'Aww, thanks, Oliver. It was fun. Enjoy your meal!'

However, I find myself staring at Oliver, surprised that he was referring to our first trip to Cornwall. But we're both starving and eager to tuck in. It isn't long before I can feel his eyes on me.

'Greg texted me today with two potential dates for the fishing trip. He's canvassing all the guys to see which one works best.'

'I'm not sure who arranges the spa day, but Mum hasn't mentioned it to me.'

'You're still up for going, then.'

Sitting back to sip my glass of buttery Chardonnay, I nod my head. 'If I'm free, it's a yes.'

'I can accommodate either date, but I'm not sure I should go if you don't.'

'Why?'

'I don't want to impose on your family, it doesn't seem right.'

'You're Greg's friend now, as well as mine,' I point out.

He beams at me. 'I guess I am.'

We continue eating and it isn't until we're leisurely sipping our coffees that he looks at me pointedly.

'This other thing you went down to Cornwall to sort out. Is that all settled now?'

'I think so.' It's a strange thing to ask, out of the blue like that.

'That's good. I just thought I'd mention it in case there were developments, and you needed a listening ear.'

Goodness, it's like Oliver can read my thoughts. I was sitting here thinking of Ash.

'You know when you get talked into doing something, but deep down you have this misgiving? Well, I think it's all sorted now, but in hindsight I think it was wrong for me to get involved.'

His forehead puckers up. 'And you feel guilty?'

'Regretful is probably a better way to describe it. I think the outcome might have been different if I'd refused. Oh, maybe not now, but at some point in the near future. The problem is that I made the decision based on the information at hand, so I was going in sort of blind.'

'And it's what you didn't know that might have led to a different result?'

'Possibly, but it's too late now.' I feel a yawn coming on and I do my best to stifle it. 'Sorry. It's been a long day.'

'And a physically and emotionally draining one for you, I should imagine. How's River View Cottage looking?'

I pull a sad face. 'It wasn't too bad when our local *man with a van* and his mate finished loading up, ready to deliver the boxes and a few of Grandma's treasured pieces to Silverberry Hall tomorrow. But after one of the local charities called to take away some of the furniture Grandma hopes will go to good homes, it looked bare. There isn't much left now.'

'I bet it was a poignant moment for you both.'

'In one way, yes. We talked a lot about the past and we did laugh at times, but it was tinged with sadness.'

'The place is ready for a fresh start,' Oliver replies, cheerily.

'Yes, I suppose it is.'

He glances at me, frowning. 'You don't feel excited about making it yours?'

I shrug my shoulders. 'I thought . . . I thought it would still feel the same, even without the old things in it. When we shut the door, Grandma turned the key and handed it to me, and I hesitated. She pressed it into my hand, saying that it would take a little while to sort out the paperwork and she was meeting up with her solicitor in the new year. I just felt . . . numb.' To my horror, I feel a tear trickle down my cheek.

'Come on. Finish your coffee while I go up to the bar to pay and we'll head back to Oakleigh. I think we both need more than a single espresso before we retire, don't you?'

I force myself to smile through watery eyes. 'Definitely. And thanks, Oliver.'

'For what?'

'For understanding.'

If anything were going to happen between us, tonight is not that time. Yet again, it's as if life is conspiring against us. Or slowing things down, because every time there's an opportunity to test our feelings, something puts a damper on it. Maybe patience is a virtue, or maybe we simply aren't ready.

It was a night I spent tossing and turning, slipping in and out of a dream that at times felt like a nightmare. All I could think about was Elizabeth and Ash, but Freddie also put in an appearance, and it all felt very real. At one point, I walked into the dining room at the Hall and the three of them were having breakfast together. Freddie looked up at me with the biggest of smiles and said, 'Our grandson, James, is here. Pour yourself a coffee and join us!'

I awaken with a start, unable to get back to sleep. After a long while I end up grabbing my phone, with the intention of diverting my mind by looking at some interior design ideas for River View Cottage. But when it kicks into life I notice there's a text from Daniela. Worryingly, it was sent about an hour ago.

I'm playing night nurse, walking up and down to soothe a poorly baby with a bad cough. How was your meal with Oliver at the pub? 😊

Aww . . . she must be shattered after the day she's had. She's a great mum but doesn't she have anything else to think about?

Fine. Poor you, and poor little William. Sending him a hug! x

The moment I press send I groan to myself. I hope she has the volume turned off if her phone's still at hand. Less than a minute later, there's a ping.

What are u doing checking your phone in the early hours?

My fingers get tapping.

I can't sleep.

Her response is almost instant.

You're not in bed with Oliver?

Ugh. Why didn't I leave it until the morning to send a reply?

No! It's too soon.

Don't give me that. If you wait until you're ready, you'll never take that leap.

I'm not falling into that trap, so I ignore Daniela's comment.

How's William?

We're on the sofa and he's asleep with his head nestled against my chest. I can't lie him down as he just starts coughing again. No sleep for me so I'm surfing the net!

I'm free tomorrow once Oliver leaves. I'll pop round for a couple of hours so you can get your head down if you like. Nigel will have his hands full with Clara.

You're the best friend ever, do u know that? And just a tip . . . serving a man coffee in bed is the perfect start to the day. Then have breakfast . . . afterwards.

Enough! I'll see you mid-morning. 😂

When I do, eventually, drift back to sleep, I'm standing on the ramp that leads down to the pebbled beach at Charlestown. I'm looking across at two people sitting on the low concrete wall, chatting. As I get closer, I realise it's me and Ash. I can't hear what's being said. I begin to run across the pebbles and the masses of seaweed, but I keep slipping. A sense of overwhelming panic starts to consume me. If only I could stop them talking, everything will be OK, but they keep getting further and further away . . .

'Sienna, you sound a little out of breath.'

'Hi, Mum, I'm on my way to Daniela's house to look after William for a couple of hours. He has a bad cough, and she was up with him most of the night. She rang the helpline and they said it's probably croup. Her mum is taking over later. She told Daniela to turn the shower on full and to sit in the bathroom with the door shut. I didn't even know that was a thing.'

'Yes, it's an old wives' tale but it works. It helps to open up the airways. Anyway, I won't keep you long. I'm going to text you two dates in February for this get-together. You know . . . the fishing trip and the spa visit. Let me know your first and second preference and I'll report back.' She gives a little laugh. 'I think Greg texted Oliver yesterday, but he hasn't responded yet. Jasmine's mum only got in touch with me this morning.

'There are a couple of potential parties coming up after Christmas, but hopefully they won't clash.'

'Ah, I hope not. Still, we'll be seeing you and Oliver on Christmas Eve, anyway. I assume he's staying overnight at your place?'

'Yes, that's the plan.'

'Is everything good between the two of you?' she asks, trying to sound nonchalant and I know she's hoping that we're growing closer by the day.

'I guess so. Oliver suggested I visit his place in London sometime in the new year.'

'That's a good sign, but you sound hesitant. Liam's visit hasn't given you second thoughts, has it?'

'No. I just need to get the party and Christmas out of the way before I can start making plans, that's all.'

'Well, that's understandable, my darling. It's OK to take time out to catch your breath and get your head sorted; don't say yes to anything if you're not up to it.'

Is Mum referring to the fishing/spa trip, or Oliver's invitation? I wonder. 'I won't. Anyway, I'm at Daniela's front gate now. Have a relaxing rest of the day and give my regards to Greg. Love you!'

'We love and miss you, too.'

Has Mum done that before and I just haven't noticed? Or was the slight emphasis on the word 'we' a reminder that Greg is now a part of our family? As with my feelings for Oliver, it's early days; you don't just wake up one morning and feel comfortable using the word 'love'. Or at least, I don't – whether that's the significant other in Mum's life, or someone I'm becoming increasingly comfortable sharing my innermost thoughts with.

Oh well, I tell myself firmly as I hurry along the path to ring the doorbell, a couple of hours of cuddles with William will probably sort me out. He's such a cutie and he beams whenever I sing him nursery rhymes. Mind you, I can only do that when no one else is within earshot, as singing isn't one of my natural-born gifts. But hey, children don't care about a song being pitch perfect, do they? It's the love and attention they appreciate, and I have a lot of that to give.

22

It's Time to Try to Turn the Tide

By Monday lunchtime it feels like all hell has let loose and I call Mum to let her in on today's developments.

'Elizabeth asked me to call you; we have a bit of problem.'

'You do?'

'It's about you and Greg staying at Hawthorn Mews on the estate at Christmas. Elizabeth would have called you herself, but she's in her room, resting.'

'She's all right . . . is she?' Mum's tone is one of concern.

This is awkward. 'Yes, she's just overdone it a little, that's all. Too much excitement,' I quip.

'It was good of Elizabeth to offer us an alternative now that your grandma's cottage is all but empty. If it's not convenient, though, I could give Harry up at the farm a call. They might have a room free.'

'No, Hawthorn Mews is empty, awaiting the family who are taking occupation in mid-January, but how do you feel about one of Elizabeth's nieces and her husband staying there too?'

'That's not a problem, at all,' she replies, happily. 'Christmas is all about sharing! And with your grandma settled in at the Hall, they'll be pressed for space this year I should imagine.'

That's precisely the problem. Two of the bedrooms at Silverberry Hall have now been turned into a suite for

Grandma. Builders will be putting in a connecting door between her bedroom, and what is now her personal sitting room, early next year. With only three spare bedrooms now, this year things are going to be a little different.

'Yes, they're one bedroom short, but it appears that Stephen assumed it would be Grandma who would move out over the Christmas period, to accommodate them all as *per tradition*, and Elizabeth is understandably incensed.'

'The cheek of the man!' Mum sounds flabbergasted.

'Yes. Please don't repeat this to Grandma, as she isn't aware that Stephen had a full-blown meltdown over it. Georgina witnessed the whole thing when she was serving them mid-morning coffee in the orangery. Stephen said something about family should come first and Elizabeth walked out of the room. Georgina only mentioned it, because she thought someone should go to check on Elizabeth, hence this phone call.'

'It's unbelievable. The woman can do exactly as she pleases in her own home.'

'Yes, but that's not how Stephen sees it. At least offering alternative accommodation within the grounds should solve the problem. Admittedly, Elizabeth's other brother – Matthew – and his wife live the closest, so it would be less inconvenient for them if they didn't stay this year; but it means a lot to Elizabeth to have them under her roof at Christmas. They never invite themselves to stay at random times, as Stephen does, and their offspring are happy to travel back and forth for the festivities, so they're no trouble at all.'

'Yes, but Elizabeth couldn't possibly put them out in order to accommodate one of Stephen's children. I mean, all of her nephews and nieces are grown-ups, for goodness' sake, and she can't be seen to favour one brother over another!'

'Precisely. The point is that things are going to be different moving forward and they all have to accept that.'

'She's newly widowed and they're fools if they didn't expect the old normal to change.'

'My sentiments entirely! They usually return home on Boxing Day morning, after the leisurely family brunch. If we can't sort this to everyone's satisfaction quickly, the atmosphere this year is going to be unbearable and Grandma is going to be in the midst of it, too! But Elizabeth wants to send out a very clear message. In future, stays at the Hall will be by invitation only and I have a feeling she intends to tone it down next Christmas.'

'I did wonder. It seemed a little strange to ramp it up this year, even though I know she's doing it to honour Freddie. But it's a lot of pressure, especially when people take advantage.' Mum tuts. 'Greg and I will go along with whatever works best, no matter what. We're on countdown now and don't worry, there'll be so many people there that the odd grump in the gathering won't even register.'

Well, I can only hope that Mum is right, because Stephen likes the sound of his own voice. He might convince himself that he's simply trying to protect his sister, but what he sees as *help* is beginning to look suspiciously like *bullying*.

I spend most of the evening on the sofa wrestling with my conscience, until I eventually get up the courage to contact Jasmine and ask for Ash's mobile number. She doesn't hesitate, no doubt thinking that I want to place a bespoke order.

It's not for me to meddle in Elizabeth's family affairs, but it's becoming increasingly clear that Stephen is trying to undermine her confidence. When Elizabeth is on her own she's an easy target and I find it deplorable that he's starting to make her second-guess herself.

We all know there will be changes, but it's entirely up to Elizabeth what those changes will be and when she chooses to implement them. For now, things are ticking over and that's enough for her.

The only reason Elizabeth is in this precarious position is because she feels she can't openly acknowledge her grandson. I understand why, but Stephen is a man on a mission.

I happened to walk past the orangery this morning and the door into the hallway was open. I was horrified when I heard his booming voice say *he could take all her worries away*. It stopped me in my tracks and I froze, unable to move in case I made a noise. He went on to say it would guarantee the long-term future of the Hall.

My heart was thumping in my chest. His proposal was that he and his wife move in and manage everything, leaving Elizabeth and Grandma to focus on hosting charity events and parties. I had to put my hand over my mouth, as I almost groaned out loud.

It's no secret that Elizabeth intends to leave something to all of her nephews and nieces, but what happens to Silverberry Hall? It's Stephen who has his eye on the big prize. In return for running the estate and ensuring its future, everything she and Freddie have worked for would continue to stay *in the family*. If I hear that man say 'in the family' one more time I won't be held responsible for my actions.

She's vulnerable and he's playing on that, but if Ash came forward everything would change in an instant. Elizabeth would have a reason to reconsider her options. At the moment, it's hard enough for her to get her life back on an even keel and cope with family squabbles, let alone think about filling the hole that Freddie left. But what can I do on a practical level?

I dial the number.

'Hello?'

'Ash . . . it's Sienna Sanderson. I hope you don't mind but I got your number from Jasmine. Sorry it's late . . . I um . . . wondered if you could spare me a few minutes?'

'OK . . . should I be concerned?'

Oh gosh, he thinks I'm delivering some sort of bad news.

'No, um . . . but after our chat down at the beach it's only just occurred to me that you might not be aware that your grandfather, Freddie, passed away earlier this year.'

He sucks in a deep breath and the line goes quiet. 'So my grandmother lives there all on her own?'

At least his tone is empathetic.

'No, not entirely. She has a live-in housekeeper and my grandmother, whom she's known since they were at school together, has recently moved in as her companion.'

He breathes out heavily. 'Losing my father, too, must have hit her very hard indeed and I'm sorry to hear that.'

I don't know why, but my heart leaps in my chest. He's listening and he isn't being dismissive. Despite the fact that he said he doesn't owe anyone anything, he's still able to be compassionate.

'It's fair to say that she's struggling to come to terms with what is an enormous loss.'

'Look, I don't know why you're telling me this now. It's not as if I can be of any help.'

If only I knew what to say. He's Elizabeth's flesh and blood and I have one chance to get this right.

'Your grandparents never got over the loss of their son. And now to discover she has a grandson, only to be hit with the realisation that he's lost to her, too . . . well—'

'Did she ask you to ring me?' His tone changes and there's an edginess to his voice that wasn't there before.

'No. This is all my doing. I'm sure you can imagine how hard it is for your grandmother to soldier on. She's not getting any younger and . . .'

I pause, trying to figure out where to take this next.

'When we talked, you said there were *no strings attached* and I'm still not sure where this thing with the solicitors is going. Besides, no one lives in a huge place like Silverberry Hall unless they have a large family and a lot of friends around them, do they?'

I'm losing him.

'I know how it looks, but Elizabeth is a woman who has endured so much heartbreak that I fear she's growing tired of fighting.'

'Fighting?'

Argh. Maybe I could have chosen a better word. Or maybe not.

'It's inevitable that the loss of Freddie will mean changes at the Hall, but she's emotional and vulnerable. Yes, she's surrounded by people, but you're not just *people*, are you? I truly believe that this wonderful woman feels you are all she has left. And I know that sounds like I'm . . . I don't know, applying pressure, but I'm simply stating the truth. It's not something you'll hear from anyone else, and least of all Elizabeth, unless you seek her out.'

'You don't hold back, do you, Sienna?'

He doesn't sound angry and I don't know why, but I do feel that he's been taking on board every single word I've said. There's no hint of dismissal, or annoyance in his tone.

'Elizabeth lives for today; she knows she can't change the past. But all she can do is fill the future with hosting charitable functions and pretending she's bearing up, when she isn't. You see, because you don't know her, you have no idea how special she is. She would love you unreservedly for who you are, not simply because she regrets what happened in the past.'

'You must really care a lot about her to risk sharing that with me, but . . .' He sighs and I sit here trying to calm my erratic heartbeat. 'As lovely as she sounds, our lives are poles apart.'

My stomach begins to churn. 'I understand, but will you at least sleep on it? Give it some thought and if you want to talk at any time, just give me a call.'

'OK, I'll think about it; that's the best I can do, I'm afraid. I'll be honest with you; this is all way outside of my comfort zone and it's unsettling. I've lived my life sort of expecting people to let me down, it takes the sting out of it when they do. I'm not sure I'd know how to act, if you can understand that.' He gives a dismissive little laugh, but for some reason it gives me a glimmer of hope. 'You make it sound easy. Maybe it is, I don't know. Anyway, thanks – I can tell that was difficult for you.'

'It was. But I can assure you that you'd simply have to be yourself, Ash; that would be more than enough.'

'Right. Thanks. I'll uh . . . give it some thought.'

When the line goes dead I can only hope I've done no harm, but at least I tried.

23

A Step Too Far

It's been one of the worst weeks of my entire life. As the days passed, with still no contact from Ash, it became increasingly hard to look Elizabeth in the eye without blurting out what I'd done. You can't change someone's mind for them, can you? What was I thinking? And then, late Friday evening the impossible happened. My phone pinged and it was a text from the man himself.

Sorry to be a pain as I know it's late. Are you working tomorrow?

My heart skips a beat. I did intend to spend a couple of hours in the morning clearing some paperwork but there's nothing there that can't wait.

No, why?

It's a big ask, but would you be willing to meet me somewhere halfway, so we can talk in private? It's all been going around and around inside my head and there's no one else I can talk to.

Yes! All is not lost. Well, not yet anyway. I feel like punching the air but instead my fingers get clicking.

That's not a problem. You'll have to suggest a place as I can't think of anywhere off the top of my head.

Great, appreciated. I'll send you a link to a little place I know your side of Taunton. It'll probably take you about an hour and a half to get there. Is that OK?

Perfect. What time?

Say around eleven?

See you there.

Thanks. It's just been a tough week.

Goodness, tell me about it! Well, I guess I shouldn't get my hopes up, but the thought of meeting up with Ash tomorrow sends a little thrill coursing through me. How ridiculous is that? But one thing I do know for sure, is that tonight I'll sleep well for the first time since we spoke on Monday.

I make my way inside the very charming inn known as Little Hollows. Considering that it's a bit off the beaten track, quite a few of the tables are occupied. I hear my name being called and Ash jumps to his feet, waving me over as if we're old friends. He's chosen a quiet corner table.

As we greet each other, I notice there's a pallor to his face that surprises me.

'Thank you for coming, Sienna, I really appreciate it.'

'That phone call I made . . . I didn't mean to unsettle you.'

He indicates for me to take a seat as a waitress approaches.

'Can I get you something to drink?' She smiles at me and I glance at the coffee cup in front of Ash.

'A cappuccino would be lovely, thanks.'

'Make that two,' Ash pipes up.

She picks up his cup, hurrying away.

The seconds tick by and he glances at me nervously. 'I guess it did, a little. However, that day I waylaid you in Charlestown was unfair of me and I've been on a bit of a guilt trip ever since.'

'Why? I was the one who caused—'

'Let me stop you there. If I'd been in your shoes, thinking I was being helpful, I'd probably have done the same thing.'

I find myself anxiously chewing my lower lip. 'Really? I'll be honest with you and say that I didn't really understand what caused the rift between Freddie and your father in the first place. I had some reservations about getting involved.'

The waitress returns, and in the silent moment that ensues, when my eyes meet Ash's what I see makes my heart constrict.

The moment she's out of earshot he shifts uneasily in his seat. 'It was wrong of me to ask you to deliver a message on my behalf, it was the coward's way out and I'm sorry I put you on the spot like that.'

'Oh . . . please don't apologise to me.'

A little smile plays around the edges of his lips. 'OK, let's say we're even, shall we? We were both in the dark about a few things when we spoke.'

I can feel the colour rising in my cheeks, as I'm not normally that direct when it comes to talking to a stranger. 'When you said your mind was made up about not making contact, I just felt there were things you should know. Elizabeth is a good person – Freddie was, too – and I refuse to believe that their son was any different, despite what happened.'

Ash looks surprised by my words so I decide to continue.

'We all have problems – some we make for ourselves; others are created by the people around us. I know, because I've been there myself, but it was Freddie and Elizabeth who helped to pick me back up.'

I lift the coffee cup to my mouth, waiting to hear what he has to say. Ash's eyes don't stray from my face and my heart starts to hammer away in my chest when he starts talking.

'What struck me was your reaction to some of the things I said. It was obvious you didn't want to get pulled in any further and yet you stuck your neck out. In hindsight, it dawned on me that you had nothing at all to gain, so why bother? Why would you do that for a stranger? The only answer I could come up with is that you truly believed what you were saying.'

My hand trembles a little as I set the cup back down on the saucer. 'You were right when you said that you don't owe anyone anything, Ash. But two wrongs don't make a right. Your grandmother is a wonderful lady who is grieving the loss of not only her husband, but her son. And, in a way, now, the loss of you, too.'

Ash places his elbows on the table, clasping his hands together as he leans his chin on them while staring directly at me. 'You make a compelling case, Sienna, but I fear if you knew the whole story you might feel a little differently. And I'm looking at this from my grandmother's point of view, here.'

'Then tell me what you know. We didn't drive all this way just to apologise to each other, did we?'

He gives me another of his ever-so-slightly cool and enigmatic smiles.

'The irony of the situation is that you're the only person I can talk to. No one in my life now knows anything at all about my past. Our life began in earnest the day Mum and I arrived in Cornwall. I wanted us to meet up because what you said made me stop and think that maybe, just maybe, I was being a little rash. Something deep down inside is warning me that it was stubbornness that got my father into trouble. I don't want history repeating itself.'

'I am, and you don't?' I reply, a sense of hope flooding through me.

'I told you . . . he wrote me a letter and that was my *real* legacy from him.'

Peter bared his soul to his son to make sure he didn't

make the same mistakes. That tells me he had a heart, and a loving one.

After our leisurely coffee, the inn started serving food at noon. It was obvious that this little get-together was going to take a while and over lunch it seemed only fair to let Ash quiz me about my past. If he were about to trust me with his own life story, how could I not do the same . . . warts and all? I didn't leave anything out, even when his eyes grew dark when I told him about Liam having cheated on me. I laughed it off, saying that some things happen for a reason, but my instincts told me that he understood it was just my way of dealing with it.

By the time our dessert arrived, it was his turn.

'Freddie and Elizabeth's parents had bequeathed money to them and they decided to put a chunk of it into a trust fund for my father, who was in his early teens at the time. Freddie administered it and my father received a lump sum at the age of eighteen. When he turned twenty-one, he was added to the trust as a signatory.'

'Oh . . . so money wasn't a problem, then?' Now I'm confused.

Ash shakes his head. 'Oh, it was a problem, all right! My father admitted that despite a rather stern warning, he ventured into business with someone his parents had reason to believe was a bit of a shady character. It wasn't until the guy suddenly disappeared that Peter admitted he'd put every penny he had into what turned out to be a fictious business opportunity. Even worse, he'd borrowed heavily to increase his investment in the belief that it would all come good and he'd prove them wrong.'

I draw in a sharp breath. 'He lost everything?'

'Everything he could get his hands on at that point, but it still wasn't enough to clear his debts. He was desperate and he was also ashamed of the way he'd blatantly refused to listen to the warning he'd been given.'

'That must have been tough for him to admit,' I remark.

'He said he wanted me to know he brought his woes on himself.'

Wow! That's quite an admission to make to a son he'd never met. Ash was right, Peter's legacy wasn't just the money for the new start, it was a life lesson he'd learnt the hard way.

Ash pushes away his plate, collapsing back against his chair as I nibble away absentmindedly at the cheesecake in front of me.

'But you've lost me . . . if he was left with nothing, how could he afford—'

His eyes flicker over my face as he sits there frowning. 'That's what the argument was about. Withdrawals from the trust fund required two signatures, so in effect the money was untouchable, but my father was demanding access to it. Freddie didn't want his son wasting his grandparents' hard-earned money, so he agreed to pay off the debts out of his own pocket. He made it clear his son would have to prove he'd learnt his lesson before he would let him touch another penny of the fund.'

'I see. No wonder there was ill feeling between them.'

Ash's frown deepens. 'It also caused a major upset between his parents, too. His mother felt that he'd been through enough to have learnt his lesson but Freddie seemed to sense that he wasn't telling them the whole story. And that's what angered him.'

'What a horrible situation to find themselves in. I can understand Freddie not wanting his parents' legacy to be . . . misspent, but a part of it came from Elizabeth's family, so she should have had a say in it.'

He tuts. 'Well, the awful truth is that my father lied about the full extent of his debts and what Freddie ended up paying off was only a part of it. A few days later, my father forged Freddie's signature and emptied the entire fund.'

My hand flies up to my face but it's too late, and I let out a gasp. 'And that's how he managed to finance his new life and, eventually, provide for you and your mum.'

'As you say, eventually. He left the UK owing nothing, as he didn't want to bring that disgrace on his family, but it didn't leave him with much. In the process of doing what he thought was the right thing, he only succeeded in breaking their hearts. They had no idea about the full extent of his losses and, as far as I know, still don't.'

I'm reeling. 'But . . . it was only money, no one died!'

Ash's eyes widen. 'My father committed an act of fraud. He not only lied about his financial problems but he stole from his parents when they were only trying to protect him from himself. That day I stood outside Silverberry Hall, I realised how broken my father must have been to know how badly he'd let them down. He fled because he was ashamed of the mess he'd gotten himself into, but they thought he left because he was greedy and had no conscience.'

My heart is hammering away inside my chest. To an honourable man like Freddie, who set the bar high when it came to standards and morals, it must have felt like the ultimate betrayal. And yet, I also feel sorrow for Peter, so desperate he felt he had no other option left.

'Did your mother know the full story at the time?'

'Not all of it. Their relationship had already ground to a halt as my father had become unreliable, turning up at her flat at odd hours and then having no contact for days at a time. She ended up telling him she'd had enough. It was only a few days later that he rang her to say how sorry he was that he'd messed everything up. He'd been drinking and ended up telling her that he'd done something very wrong and that his family would never forgive him, so he was heading to Italy.'

'Ah . . . they weren't together at that point, then.'

'No. His erratic behaviour had become too much for her to cope with. She was worried about him but when she tried to call him back, the number she had was no longer in use. A short time later, out of the blue, he rang her in a bit of a panic. He'd heard from an old friend that his parents were desperately trying to track him down and he made her promise if they approached her, she'd say she had no idea where he was. He said it was for the best. He gave her a contact address in case she heard anything. He told her he would be changing his number again in order to cut all ties with everyone in the UK.'

'That must have been harrowing to hear and worrying, too.'

'Yes, because a part of her longed to turn back the clock. He was a different person before his life fell apart and that was the man she always loved, right up to the very end.'

It's too sad to comprehend. 'That's why she wrote to him when she found out she was expecting you, and despite the risk, he kept the letter.'

'Yes.'

'What was his reaction?' I find myself unwittingly holding my breath. This is edge of the seat stuff. I push my plate away, my appetite having evaporated a while ago.

'He asked her to join him but . . . how can I put this? His life was in flux and they'd only known each other for a little over six months, two of which were while he was acting totally out of character. She had no idea whether their relationship would last the course, or the pressures of having a baby. There were no guarantees and for her it would have been a huge risk. While her family weren't very supportive, the friends she had around her were.'

The eye contact between us is rather tense and I can see how painful it is for him to acknowledge, but in a way strangely cathartic I should imagine, to get off his chest. It's just sad that the only person he's happy to do that with is a virtual stranger, but someone he can trust because he knows I won't utter a word of it to anyone else. 'Was your father disappointed?'

'Mum said that he was a man who simply didn't want to make yet another mistake. She felt he was saying all the right things, but maybe it was a bit of a relief when she declined his offer. He wasn't really in a position to settle down, was he? He'd recently invested in a small business and it probably took every penny he had left. But he promised her that when he was financially stable, he'd make sure my mother and I were comfortable.'

'Which he did, eventually,' I murmur, 'and that's when you made the move.'

Ash inclines his head. 'He honoured her wish that from there after they'd have no further contact. It was the fresh start my mum deserved. As for my father's will . . . that wasn't a part of the agreement.'

'The agreement?' I almost wince. 'That sounds so cold-hearted.'

'Was it? My father had disgraced himself and he didn't want my mum, or me, to be tainted by that. If she'd found out sooner that I was on the way, before he'd left the country, maybe things would have been different. Who knows?'

'Different, how?'

'My father made some poor decisions. Sadly, his own father didn't understand how desperate he was to prove he'd learnt his lesson, but his options were limited and that changed everything going forward.'

'It must have been tough for your mother managing all on her own in those early years.'

'We got by. She wasn't looking for him to support us on a daily basis, if that's what you think. But she accepted his help when it came, because she said it was my due, that it was my inheritance.'

'How does that differ from what he's bequeathed you in his will? Doesn't it mean anything, the fact that he never forgot you?'

Ash sighs, lowering his chin to his chest and for the first time what I'm sensing is raw emotion. 'He wasn't a bad man; he was wronged. But his father only saw things in black and white; he broke the law, and if he did it once, would he be capable of doing it again? As it turns out, he used that inheritance wisely; he built up a successful holiday rental business. He took care of his wife and the people he loved. The people that he'd had no choice but to leave behind.'

'You and your mum.'

'Exactly.'

'Oh, Ash. If only Elizabeth could read that letter—'

'It would heal her broken heart? The thing is, Sienna, isn't it best to let the past go? I wouldn't fit into her life. How would she introduce me? I live simply and I'm happy. As I said that day we sat together looking out over the sea, isn't it kinder this way? I don't know exactly how old she is, but she deserves a quiet life. That's my gift to her.'

When we eventually part, he gives me a genuinely grateful hug and it makes me feel tearful. It's as if he knows we'll never meet again and this is his way of saying goodbye. And yet I feel I know him better than I do many people I've known for almost a lifetime. Parting makes my heart ache and I'm at a total loss to explain how truly devastated I feel. And it's not just for Elizabeth, because for whatever reason Ash has touched my heart. But it's more than that. He's stirred up something deep down inside of me, something I've never felt before. Is it merely a level of compassion, that's so deep it's almost scary? The answer to that is I simply don't know and I'm not sure how I feel about it.

24

All the Feels of Christmas Past

It's eight o'clock on Christmas Eve morning and it's all about to kick off. Oliver has dropped his bags off at Oakleigh, and we stand side by side, as his eyes wander around the barn, taking it all in.

'This is amazing, Sienna, truly amazing. It even smells like Christmas!'

'Well,' I laugh, 'there's a forest of cuttings in here, with just about everything colourful or fragrant that nature gives us for free.'

'How long did it take?'

'Two full days. Elizabeth, Grandma and I organise a large team of helpers. It's a huge task, to turn sacks of fresh greenery into garlands and we all have to roll up our sleeves and get stuck in. Several of the farmers around here donate van-loads of holly, ivy, mistletoe and small branches from a variety of firs, even eucalyptus trees. The beams are too high up to reach, even with the portable scaffolding tower, so they're hung from the walls in swags and it's extremely time-consuming.'

'I bet!'

'It's great fun, though, because so many people lend a hand. It's a real community effort. As a thank you, they were treated to high tea here in the barn yesterday afternoon, after it was finished.'

I can honestly say that the last week and a bit have been a blur. Not least because the tension between Elizabeth and

Stephen has put a damper on things. Stephen's daughter and her husband are delighted to be staying at Hawthorn Mews, as the bedroom has an en suite. That's a real plus for someone who is expecting a baby, avoiding the traipse along a draughty hallway late at night. However, Stephen is fuming, as he sees it as a snub. In his eyes, Grandma isn't family, she's merely a companion – an unpaid member of staff living there for free. Fortunately, Grandma has no idea that's what the argument is about and Elizabeth intends to keep it that way.

And, after getting my hopes up that Ash and I might continue our conversation, despite the fact we parted with a hug that felt like a goodbye, his silence has shattered any illusion I have of a miracle happening. Having to let go of that hasn't been easy, but in hindsight, it was all wishful thinking on my part and I'm totally gutted.

'It's good to see that the carousel arrived safely,' Oliver says, brightly.

'Yes. Stephen's son-in-law is going to be in charge of it. Your friend, Ron, did some training on it with him yesterday. He and his wife are a nice couple, they're staying at Hawthorn Mews here on the estate, with Mum and Greg.'

'That worked out well, then. When are your parents arriving?' The moment Oliver finishes speaking his eyes widen at his faux pas. 'Sorry . . . I meant your mum and Greg.'

'It's fine, it's just a slip of the tongue.'

Now he feels awkward. 'Um . . . The cast will be here at nine o'clock sharp. We won't be in your way, will we?'

'No. Elizabeth, Grandma and I have given everyone involved, including family, a list of tasks. There will be a fair bit going on outside in the courtyard once breakfast at the Hall is over, but no one should require access to the barn until after noon. A couple of deliveries are due between twelve and one o'clock.'

'Perfect.'

'Everyone was saying yesterday how wonderful the stage looks. Honestly, this is going to be *the* highlight of the party, Oliver.'

He smiles, then leans in to give me a hug.

'What was that for?' I ask when he releases me.

'You're a good person, Sienna. Some people make a lot of noise to get themselves noticed; others are natural, shining stars, and they serve as an inspiration to the rest of us. And then there are the quiet ones, like you, who make things happen; life's journey is a little smoother because of them and they truly are a blessing.'

Daniela is a shining star, I know that, and I wouldn't have it any other way.

'And which one are you?'

'Oh,' he states, emphatically. 'There's a fourth category.'

'Which is?' I muse, as our eyes meet.

'People waiting to find out who they are and why they're here.'

I stare at him for a moment, frowning. My goodness . . . that's exactly the problem I'm wrestling with right now. Is it a coincidence Oliver feels exactly the same way . . . or is it fate?

'Sienna!'

I turn, to see Harry standing in the doorway. 'I have the grill for roasting the chestnuts. Where do you want it?'

'Thanks! I'll be with you now, Harry.' I turn to look at Oliver. 'I guess we'll catch up a bit later. Good luck this morning, I hope the rehearsals go well.'

Oliver holds up one hand, crossing his fingers. 'Hopefully, there won't be any last-minute hitches, or mental blocks as the nerves kick in.'

'Think positively . . . or is it *break a leg*?' I retort and he grins at me before I turn and head outside.

Today the sky is gloriously blue and once the sun warms up a bit to melt the hoar frost, the weather couldn't be more perfect. People can bundle up to keep warm, but rain or sleet would have been a disaster.

Gazing around, it's truly wonderful to see the stark outline of the trees and shrubs covered in hair-like crystals as if it's been snowing. The air is crisp and sweet: it's good to be alive!

* * *

At two o'clock sharp, the afternoon festivities begin, and families start streaming into the courtyard. Everyone is wearing thick coats, gaily coloured scarves and gloves. But the sun delivered, and the sky is still an almost perfect shade of azure blue.

A queue is already forming for the carousel and the excitement reflected on the children's faces, as they take in the colourful displays all around them, is heartening. It's been challenging, but the reward is plain to see.

I pop my head into the newly painted hut, to check on Santa. 'Are you ready?'

'Ho! Ho! Ho! Ready and waiting, my fine young elf! I'm just warming my hands on the heater.'

Victor's deeper than usual tone makes me laugh. 'You look awesome, Santa. Here, let me straighten . . .' I glance over my shoulder as I walk towards him, checking no little ones have wandered inside. 'This wig is a little off centre,' I whisper, as I sort him out.

He does look the part, sitting on a recycled chair we found in one of the horse stalls. Inside, the old hut has been turned into a spectacular grotto, with baubles hanging from the ceiling and several wreaths of fresh greenery to brighten the white-painted walls. The plush new seat matches the scarlet red of his outfit, and when he laughs, his padded stomach jiggles. 'There you go, you're all set.'

'I'm here,' Grandma's voice calls out. 'Sorry for the delay. The florists just delivered the flowers for the buffet tables, and I couldn't find the key to the outhouse. My, don't you two look a picture!'

I jiggle my head so that the bell on the end of my green elf's hat jingles and both Santa and Grandma break out into a smile.

'And what a grand Mother Christmas you make!' Victor retorts. Grandma's cheeks begin to colour as she flutters her eyelashes at him, doing a twirl.

I will admit that since she moved into Silverberry Hall,

Grandma too has benefited from Georgina's healthy-eating kick. More vegetables, fewer sugary snacks and crisps is now becoming a way of life and maybe we all need to get with the programme – including me.

'The sacks are labelled with the various age groups,' I confirm. 'Right, we have some eager customers lining up outside, so I'll leave you both to it.'

As I exit swiftly, I start humming to myself, *Jingle bells, jingle bells . . .* it's time to get this party started.

I'm delighted when Mum suddenly appears at my side, having taken a break from helping out at the roasted chestnut and waffle stall.

'Hey, how're you doing?'

Her cheeks are flushed, and her eyes keep darting around as she waves to old friends. 'Business has been brisk, and I've finally got the hang of turning out a good waffle without any air bubbles in it,' she declares with gusto. 'Look at Elizabeth, she's in her element!'

Most of the younger children around here know her well, as she often pops into several of the local schools to help with their reading sessions. She's the most wonderful storyteller and has a knack of enthralling her audience as she draws them into a fictional world. They all want to say hello and she makes time for each and every one of them.

'A lot of her smiles lately have been plastered on, but it's good to see her face shining with happiness.'

'It certainly is and, hopefully, this will help heal her heart a little. Anyway, you look toasty, although I thought you might be a little chilly in that outfit.'

'No, I have two layers of thermal underwear on beneath my snazzy attire,' I divulge with an elfish grin.

Grandma appears at the door of the grotto, shepherding two small boys back to their waiting parents. The little girl at the head of the queue alongside me eagerly holds out her ticket. 'I'm next!'

I lean forward to take it from her. 'You are, and Santa's waiting for you.'

She must be about five years of age and she stares back at me for a moment, wrinkling her brow. 'I want to check he knows where to find the key tonight, as we don't have a chimney,' she replies, with all seriousness.

'Ah! That's quite an important message to deliver, so you'd better hurry inside.'

As I straighten, Mum and I exchange soulful smiles. I can't think of a better way to spend Christmas Eve afternoon, than being reminded of my own childhood. It was a time when I thought that almost anything was possible, because there was no limit to my imagination.

Grandma reappears to take her inside and Mum and I stand back a little.

'Are you and Greg all settled into Hawthorn Mews?'

'Yes, it's absolutely lovely! We weren't expecting it to be all trimmed up.'

'Grandma and Elizabeth did it yesterday. They wanted to make you feel at home.'

'Ah, well, we certainly do. Stephen's daughter and her husband are a nice couple. They're both eagerly counting down the weeks until the baby arrives and it'll be Yvonne and Stephen's first grandchild.'

We both instinctively glance across at Elizabeth's other brother, Matthew, who, together with his youngest daughter, is dispensing hot chocolate, coffee, tea and free mince pies from one of the decorated carts. The courtyard has a nostalgic look to it, and this really does feel like a bygone Christmas experience.

'Yes,' I reflect. 'Matthew's grandchildren are both school age now, so Yvonne and Stephen have been waiting rather impatiently.' I pull a long face, as nature's course is in natural timing and that can be frustrating.

Stephen's the sort of man who expects his family to expand and continue on, and he's made that very well known.

Elizabeth has said on several occasions that putting undue pressure on a young couple by constantly bringing up the subject of having children doesn't help.

Mum lowers her voice as she begins speaking. 'People always covet what they don't have and maybe once the baby is here, Stephen's relationship with his younger brother will be a little easier.'

What she avoided saying, is that jealousy is a destructive thing because it creates barriers where there shouldn't be any. But on a day like this, as I stand next to my mum, with the carollers singing in the background, the hubbub of a multitude of voices laughing, children screeching as they enjoy the ride . . . none of that matters, it's all about creating some wonderful memories to look back on.

When I walk into the kitchen at Oakleigh, having spent a leisurely hour soaking in a bubble bath and then getting ready, Oliver stops what he's doing, and we simply stare at each other.

'My goodness, a beard and moustache really suit you!' I gape at him, in his costume. He's wearing a tailored black suit: the jacket is a longer cut, as they used to wear long ago. And he's wearing what I think they refer to as a neckerchief; it's burgundy with tiny black dots on it. 'You really look the part of a gentleman from the olden days.'

'That's the general idea. And you – wow! I thought you were keeping your elf costume on, it was rather becoming,' he jokes.

'I think a cocktail dress is more appropriate for this evening, don't you?'

'Well, you look stunning and that colour really suits you. I like what you've done to your hair.'

I did go the extra mile this year. It took me ages to find this dress and the rich burgundy colour of the sleek, fitting contour matches Oliver's necktie. With my mass of curly dark hair in a French twist, fastened with two substantial diamanté hair clips to keep it in check, it adds that touch of glamour.

'It was worth the trouble, as long as it stays put. Right, we'd best get off. Are you nervous?'

He holds out one of his hands, palm down, and I can see a slight tremble. 'Daniela always said that if we aren't nervous, we won't give our best performance. I hope she's right!'

The courtyard looks amazing. Everything is bathed in the light from thousands of tiny white bulbs and together with the colourful carousel, the carts dispensing hot toddies, and the carollers in their Victorian costumes singing their hearts out, it's like a scene from an old-fashioned Christmas card.

The smell of the hog roast in the outside facility makes my stomach rumble and I realise I've hardly eaten a thing today. At least the buffet will open as soon as the play finishes. People can't dance the night away on an empty stomach.

'Everyone is going to think you and I are two of the singers who've wandered off,' Oliver chuckles.

'Hey, I'm loving this black velvet cape and hood.' I do feel the part, but he might have a point. However, when Oliver escorts me into the barn it's already buzzing, and the atmosphere is simply enchanting. The rich colours of the ladies' gowns and the suave-looking gentlemen are a sight to behold.

'We don't look out of place, at all.' Oliver's mouth gapes. He releases my arm so I can slip off my cape. 'And that's saying something, considering I'm wearing a false beard. These people certainly enjoy dressing up!'

'It's all a part of the fun,' I half-whisper, although no one can hear us. We continue to cast our eyes around the vast space, taking it all in.

'There's Elizabeth.' I nudge his arm. 'Oh, and Grandma! Don't they both look amazing?' And svelte.

Elizabeth is wearing an elegant, long-sleeved full-length black dress with a silver thread running through it; it sparkles a little as she moves. Grandma is wearing a calf-length, purple-coloured cocktail dress with a slightly fluted hem. They're both busy circulating, greeting new arrivals and directing them to the drinks tables.

'Well, this is quite a spectacle to behold.'

I do a half-turn. 'And look at that stage. Even without any lighting on it, it's a wonderful, old-fashioned backdrop.'

Oliver and I make our way closer to it. As we pass small groups of people standing around chatting, we hear several references to Freddie, and I force myself not to get maudlin.

It's time to focus on the dazzling evening we have ahead of us.

'You're right,' he replies, softly, 'it certainly does the job.'

The street scene awaits the actors to bring it to life. From the grand-looking lamp post to the over-flowing flower cart, the vintage sledges and the small heaps of snow that lie all around, it's enthralling. But in pride of place is the globe. It looks quite stark; a huge white ball, with the white-painted tree in the centre, it is a real statement piece.

'And the panels look good, too,' I muse, unable to hide a self-satisfied little smirk.

'You did a great job. The evening sky with the softest hint of clouds will be brought to life when the twinkly stars are lit. Are you happy?'

'Ecstatic. It's everything I hoped it would be and I know that Elizabeth will feel this is a fitting tribute to Freddie's love of Christmas. It feels weird though.'

'In what way?'

'I don't know. I can't really put it into words.' It feels like an ending and my eyes begin to smart because I know it's not. This tradition will continue as long as Elizabeth resides at Silverberry Hall, even if it won't be quite on this scale ever again.

Oliver clears his throat. 'The fact that people miss Freddie so much is the mark of a very special man indeed.'

I glance at him, and my lower lip begins to wobble. 'He was and the world is a sadder place without Freddie in it, but he'll never be forgotten.'

25

A Magical Evening

Oh, my goodness! You could almost hear a pin drop as everyone waits with bated breath for the play to begin. The stage is in darkness still, and as the lights in the barn are lowered, the shadowy forms of the actors move almost silently into place. In the wings, I spot Ruby and I bet she's nervous. Her eyes will be firmly on the script in case anyone forgets their lines.

We borrowed forty chairs from the village hall, for people who couldn't face standing for the thirty-five-minute performance but there are still half a dozen seats free. Everyone else is standing behind the two rows of seating, seemingly content and all appear to have a clear line of sight.

Suddenly, a switch is flicked, and snow starts falling on the stage. It's obviously a projector, but it really sets the scene and it's such a clever idea.

Seconds later, a spotlight bathes the globe and Daniela, wearing a long, full-skirted dress with a woollen shawl pulled around her shoulders, in light.

'I'm here, my love, I'm here. Can't you see me?' she calls out, as a second spotlight shines on Oliver, playing the character of Adam. He's standing beneath the lamp post, checking his pocket watch and he doesn't seem to be able to hear her, even though she's only a few yards away.

Daniela turns to gaze at the two children, knelt down making snowballs. 'Oh, my darlings, my little darlings . . .

the fun of throwing snowballs! Your hands will be cold. Why didn't your father get you to wear your gloves?' The woman is clearly growing distressed.

By the time we get to the part where we realise that Oliver is playing the part of a widower and that the woman inside the snow globe – the mother of the children – is his deceased wife, there's a sharp intake of breath from many of the people in the audience. She's not real, she's a ghost. The tender way she watches her children playing in the snow, pulls on the heartstrings.

It's a poignant moment, as two women standing at the Christmas Lane Barrow, talk about Daniela's character, Eloise, and how awful it is for her husband and children now that she's gone. At one point, another man and woman stand together looking over at Adam. He throws a snowball at his children, laughing to himself as he returns to clearing the path with a shovel. Their concern is that he isn't coping with running his business, the house and the children. The woman says it's time Adam moved on and found someone new to be by his side, but the man simply shakes his head. 'He feels it would be betraying Eloise; she was the love of his life.'

Now, as I look around, lots of the audience seem to be either blinking quite rapidly, or actually brushing a tear off their cheeks. Daniela and Oliver portray the agony of a woman encouraging her husband to let go of the past and start living again. The representation of her being trapped in a snow globe is so clever. It's obvious she isn't really there and yet she is.

It isn't until the final moments, when Adam stops to talk to a young woman buying flowers at the barrow, that it becomes clear why Eloise is at pains to talk to her husband. The mood shifts because a miracle is about to happen. She's setting him free to love again.

The lights go out and when they come back on, Eloise is gone. All that remains in the ball is the stark white tree, and little peaks of snow lying at the bottom of the globe. Eloise is free to follow her journey into the afterlife knowing that she's leaving Adam in good hands: the hands of a woman she knows will love him and her children.

The applause is tremendous, and it goes on and on as each of the cast take a bow. The children were amazing, frolicking, laughing and throwing carefully timed, fake white snowballs back and forth across the two old-fashioned sledges, on cue. Everyone seated stands and calls of 'Well done' and 'Bravo!' echo around the barn.

Elizabeth and Grandma make a beeline for me, their tearful smiles a joy to behold. It was everything they'd hoped for, and more.

'Oh, Sienna! Wasn't that simply marvellous?' Elizabeth croaks. 'What a perfect, and uplifting, ending.'

'I know. It wasn't at all what I was expecting. And they were all word-perfect!'

'We have some bouquets to give all of the performers. Can you join me and your grandma on stage?'

'Oh, of course. Who's fetching them?'

'Stephen offered but maybe you can give him a hand?'

I hurry off to find him as they make their way to the side of the stage. All around, small groups of people, their faces animated, discuss the twists and turns of a Christmas story filled with love, sadness and new beginnings.

Oliver makes his way over to the edge of the stage to help Elizabeth up the deep steps and, with an armful of flowers, I link arms with Grandma. Centre stage, Oliver's friend and his assistant are fiddling with a hand-held microphone. Elizabeth indicates for Grandma to take it just as Stephen appears at her side, clutching the remainder of the flowers.

'Can you hear me?' Grandma checks, but it's obviously not live. One of the guys takes it from her and taps the top. There's a sudden loud popping sound, so at least it's working. He hands it back, and as Stephen passes the first of several bouquets to Elizabeth, Grandma thanks each of the troupe for the magnificent performance.

The two children get the longest round of applause and shout-outs. Considering they are only six and eight years old, respectively, they were amazing and Mrs Jessop and her husband, who is rarely seen out and about, look overwhelmed with pride.

Now it's time for Grandma to announce that the buffet is open both inside and outside the barn. 'Without further—' But the microphone stops working and only the people at the very front can hear her voice.

Suddenly, Stephen steps forward literally grabbing the wireless bit of kit from her hand. He fiddles with a switch on the side, thinking maybe Grandma touched it without realising it would turn it off. Then he holds it up to his mouth.

Elizabeth turns to look at me, her eyes blazing.

'What a wonderful . . .' He tails off when he realises it's still not working. But, to Elizabeth's horror, and my dismay, he simply lowers it and raises his baritone voice, loud enough to be heard. 'In honour of—'

Elizabeth hurries off stage, Grandma in hot pursuit. I sprint forward, grabbing the microphone from Stephen's hand. Then I get ready to raise my voice.

'Sorry!' I bellow, as loud as I can. 'Slight technical hitch everyone,' I apologise, my voice barrelling out of me at a level I didn't know I could reach. 'The buffet is now open, please enjoy!'

If looks could kill . . . Stephen will never forgive me, but it's Elizabeth I'm concerned about.

'Stephen was totally out of order, Sienna.'

I'm sitting next to Elizabeth in the study, having encouraged Grandma to go back to the party to check that no one else feels it necessary to seek out Elizabeth to see what's going on.

'I felt bad shutting Stephen down like that, but when I saw the look on your face I just sprang into—'

'He didn't like it when I said there'd be no speeches this

year and that I'd asked your grandma to thank the cast and announce that the buffet was open. When I made it clear that I didn't want him meddling in my affairs, he said I was losing my grip. He said some awful things about the changes I've made recently. Unforgivable things and that's why I had to storm off, or . . . risk saying something that would forever come between us. I've had my fill of family rifts and arguments but there's only so much I can take!'

'He doesn't approve of Grandma moving into the Hall to become your companion and assistant, even though the two of you have been lifelong friends?'

'That's about the sum of it.'

She looks agitated, twisting her hands in her lap. 'Do you think I'm acting out of character, Sienna? Do I need to see a doctor to check that I'm still mentally . . . capable?'

'No,' I blurt out, horrified that Stephen should have sown seeds of doubt in her head. 'There's nothing wrong with you, Elizabeth, other than you're missing Freddie. That's a huge, life-changing loss to come to terms with for anyone, at any age. Stephen should be sensitive enough to understand that, and he owes you an apology for his appalling behaviour.'

My words seem to make her rally a little. 'It wasn't his place to step into Freddie's shoes, but I know that's what he's wanted all along. No one can do that.' The exasperation in her tone saddens me.

'And you were right to speak your mind. Freddie was the life and soul of the party, and you were always the person beavering away in the background. Tonight, you and Grandma did a splendid job of greeting everyone, circulating, making introductions to ensure no one felt they were on their own. In your low-key way, you've done Freddie proud. No one can take that away from you and now they get to eat, drink, dance and be merry.'

Elizabeth wipes her eyes. 'But you're the one who pulls everything together, my dear, and it's been that way since the day you first came to work at the Hall. You turn ideas into reality. And that play . . . what a superb cast, the audience was spellbound. There wasn't a dry eye in the house, as they say.' She smiles, staring into the distance. 'Freddie and I always thought of you as the granddaughter we would have loved to have had. Tonight, you stepped in at the right time, and if you hadn't, I might have said something I would have lived to regret. Even though Stephen has overstepped the mark, he's still my flesh and blood. That means something to me. So, thank you, from the bottom of my heart.'

I reach out to grab her hand, giving it a reassuring squeeze. 'It was always going to be a difficult and emotional couple of days, Elizabeth. So far, so good, and everyone is having an amazing time. Honestly, the only person who was put out by that little incident is Stephen. I don't think anyone else really noticed there was a problem aside from an equipment failure.'

'It's kind of you to seek me out to put my mind at rest. As you know, I'm not usually one to let my emotions get the better of me.' She looks downcast and apologetic, which is crazy. She's holding up really well, all things considered.

'The truth is that I can't seem to make sense of my life at the moment. Without Freddie, it's a constant battle and if weren't for your grandma, who has kept me grounded . . .' Elizabeth lapses into silence.

After a few moments I sit back in my chair, giving a little sigh. 'It's strange you should say that. Grandma told me that when Pops died, she kept going because of me and Mum. I guess it's a sense of duty, really. I mean . . . you can't let the people you love down, can you, when they're grieving too? But she went on to say that it was you and Freddie who made sure she didn't have time on her hands to dwell. She said it saved her from herself and that thought stuck with me. There is no giving up, is there?'

Elizabeth stares down at her hands. 'That's the very point at which I find myself now. Each day is a new trial but also, I'm coming to realise, a new adventure. Your grandma found her way through her grief to comfort you and your mum and look at her now – she's full of life and raring to go.'

'I know. And she was glad to shut the door on River View Cottage that last time, before she handed over the keys to me. At first, I couldn't understand why she was so happy to turn her back on it, but I believe I do now. It's easier to hang on to the past because it's what we know, but nothing wipes out the memories and there are new ones to make.'

Elizabeth lets out a determined sigh. 'Don't worry, I'll get there – if only because I have some wonderful friends who'll give me a nudge if I take a step in the wrong direction.'

At last, there's a spark of hope in her voice again and a hint of a twinkle in her eye. 'We'd best get back to the party before Stephen thinks he has the better of me. He always had a bit of a chip on his shoulder when we were growing up. I'm the eldest and that never sat well with him for some reason. Probably because I never listened to anything he said, and I don't intend to start now. We might be siblings, but we're two very different personalities.'

Elizabeth stands, ready to freshen up her makeup, while I make my way back to the party. As soon as I step inside the barn, it's obvious that Oliver has been keeping an eye out for me, and when he sees me, he indicates with his hand that I should stay where I am. He disappears from sight and a minute or two later reappears next to me, carrying a glass of champagne in each hand.

'You look like you could do with this.'

'You're a lifesaver. Did I make a fool of myself just now?'

'Not at all. I think you saved the day. Is Elizabeth all right?'

'Yes, she's just taking a moment to calm herself down. Um . . .' I nod my head in the direction of the dance floor at the other end of the barn.

'You want to dance?' he asks, and I shake my head at him.

'No, Ruby is hovering, and she looks a bit lost for company. I'll take your glass; you go rescue her. Go on, I'll be fine.'

With that, I down half of a glass of champagne in one

go. And boy, does it hit the spot, even though the gassy bubbles seem to be making my nose fizz. I pour what's left into the other glass and place the almost empty one on a small side table.

As I look up, I see a fraught-looking Nigel striding towards me, and I wonder what on earth is wrong, as he inclines his head, indicating for me to follow him. We make our way to the far end of the barn, to stand in the shadows at the side of the stage.

'Be straight with me, Sienna. I know you're Daniela's best mate and you're very loyal, but I need to know what's going on.'

'What do you mean?'

'You led me to believe that you and Oliver were seeing each other and now he's up there . . .' Nigel points to the dance floor '. . . dancing with Ruby and looking very cosy together. It doesn't make any sense. He's here because of my wife, isn't he? Have you been helping to cover that up?'

I look at him aghast. 'No, I never said that Oliver and I were together. If it weren't for the play, our paths would probably never have crossed. We've become friends, as you well know. But he's only here because of the play and why wouldn't Daniela have contacted him to be a part of it?'

'Hmm . . . it's also a good excuse to reconnect in a more meaningful way.'

He sounds choked up and I wonder just how much he's had to drink.

'Do you really think I'd endorse something like that? And it's even worse if you think Daniela is capable of doing that to you. It's madness on your part.'

He runs his hand through his hair, a desperate look on his face, but it's the sadness in his eyes that is devastating to see. 'She's hiding something from me, and I don't know what it is. It's like she's not been herself lately. At first, I thought it was getting back into work mode, but did the two of them . . . did they have an affair when they were in Bristol?'

An involuntary gasp makes Nigel stare at me, his scrutiny intensifying as if he's challenging me.

'And all these little trips to Inglewick Hall,' he continues. 'How can I be sure it's just work and she's not meeting up with him in secret?'

I shake my head in disbelief. 'You need to have this conversation with your wife, Nigel, not me. You're not going to believe anything I say, or Oliver, for that matter. And, yes, he and Ruby do seem to be having a wonderful time, but surely that's a good thing? If you were here to impress a woman, slow dancing with someone else isn't exactly a clever idea, is it?'

Now he looks confused because Oliver and Ruby do look very cosy together indeed!

'Would you tell me if you suspected Daniela and Oliver were more than just good friends? Be honest, please, because I feel like my life is falling apart around me.'

'If I believed that were the case, I'd have challenged Daniela about it because there's no way I'd be a willing party to a cover-up. You seem to be forgetting that Liam cheated on me, and I know how much it hurts when you discover the truth from a third party.'

That seems to stop him in his tracks.

'I like to think that you regard me as your friend, too, Nigel. I mean . . . I'm godmother to your children! What I will say is that Daniela is loyal to you and she's not capable of doing something like that. But don't take it from me, you need to ask her outright. Whether you believe her is between the two of you, but jealousy is a reaction to a perceived threat. Why are you feeling so . . .'

'Vulnerable?' He almost barks at me and I take a step back.

He panics, reaching out to place his hand on my arm. 'It's just that if I lost her I don't know what I'd do.'

'Talk to her, Nigel. Tell her just that and listen to what she has to say before your fears alienate her. How would you feel if it were the other way around and you were innocent?

If you really love her, tell her that and explain why you're feeling like you do and maybe, just maybe, you can work this out.'

'Sorry, I'm so sorry. I don't know what I was thinking . . .' He looks miserable.

'Don't wait; talk to her now. And I think you're right about Oliver and Ruby; by the look of it, they seem to be getting on very well. You see, Oliver is an easy man to be friends with because he doesn't play games. But when there's a spark between two people, well . . . you only have to look at them to see that's the case.'

Nigel's eyes follow mine and I can see him visibly relax. He leans in to kiss my cheek. 'Thank you. Good friends don't judge us when we mess up, do they?'

'No.' I smile at him. 'They don't.'

As he goes in search of Daniela, I continue to glance over at Oliver and Ruby. Their faces are animated as they dance around each other now, without a care in the world. That's the look I want on my face when I realise I've finally met *the one*. They may not acknowledge it yet, but it's plain to see.

Looking back, that day Daniela and I had lunch with Oliver at The Sailor's Retreat, I clearly remember the way Ruby looked at him. For a brief second she faltered, before her eyes lit up. He'd literally taken her breath away.

How I wish now that I'd paid more attention. As my uneasy acquaintance with Oliver developed into what I hope will be an enduring friendship, did Ruby avoid him because of me? Did Oliver avoid her because he was confused? Did I hold back because deep down inside my instincts knew that we weren't destined to be more than simply good friends?

Wow. When something is meant to be, it seems there's no avoiding it, even when it takes a while to understand what's happening. Maybe everything does happen for a reason. Is that why Oliver and I . . . why we never did find that perfect moment alone together?

26

Do Dreams Really Come True?

Oliver and I stand, gazing out over the orchard and zipping up our coats as it's numbingly cold. Even though it was forecast, and I heard the lane being gritted in the early hours of the morning, having four inches of snow overnight was a bit of a surprise to wake up to.

'If we'd had this yesterday it would have spoiled all our plans, wouldn't it?' I remark.

'You can say that again. But doesn't it take your breath away? A coating of snow turns the ordinary into the magical, and it allows us to see everything through a different lens.'

'It does. But if Freddie were here he'd already have had everyone outside for a snowball fight,' I laugh and then heave a big sigh. 'After the excitement of last night's party, Elizabeth is really struggling today. The realisation that Christmas is never, ever going to be the same again has suddenly hit her full force and it's heartbreaking.'

'I had noticed. She's been very subdued. The trouble is, Silverberry Hall was made for entertaining, wasn't it? What she really needed today, was a quiet little gathering. Just a couple of people who understand what she's going through.'

'Yep. Instead, everyone descends on her because she can't say no. It certainly brings the place to life and it's what drew Freddie and Elizabeth here. But now he's no longer at her side, the future is going to be different and I'm worried about what's to come. She's locked into a life that isn't easy to change. For her, or for the people whose expectations she has to contend with.'

Oliver grimaces. 'That's a big burden to carry, isn't it?'

'I'm afraid so.'

'It's certainly been a Christmas Day I'll always remember. Both chaotic and fun, but for a grieving widow . . . well, I don't know how she's managed to get through it. There were a lot of chefs in the kitchen today, but they all pulled together. Is it always like that?'

'Pretty much. If I'd realised . . . I'd . . . I'm sure Elizabeth would have invited Ruby along.'

Oliver looks at me rather sheepishly. 'She's working at the pub. I'm meeting up with her a bit later. Something happened between us yesterday and it shook us up a bit.'

'I did notice,' I reply, softly. 'I'm pleased for you both, Oliver.'

'When it hits you – out of the blue – that's when you know it's the real thing. It's rather exciting and scary at the same time, to be honest. How are you doing after all the drama?'

He turns his head to look at me and I can see how much he cares.

'It was touch and go for a moment here and there, but it ended on a high.'

'Honestly, from a guest's point of view it was a massive success. Heck, look what ended up happening to me!' He roars with laughter. 'But seriously, you managed to diffuse that little incident with Stephen, very adroitly. I think it was lost on most people that he'd tried to take control of the microphone.'

'I don't know about *adroitly*, but did you notice that he had a piece of paper in his hand? He had a speech all planned out, despite the fact that Elizabeth had made it clear that Grandma would simply commend our star performers for the marvellous play, thank everyone for coming and formally announce that the buffet was open.'

'I've never seen Elizabeth looking so angry, but it was the

expression on your face when he interrupted your grandma that was a classic. Honestly, the last thing he expected was the way you yanked the microphone out of his hand before he could even figure out how to turn the thing on.'

'If I'd been further away, I might have done a flying tackle!' I admit.

'Hmm . . . I don't doubt that. So, why did you want to come out to grab some fresh air? Your mum flashed me a look of surprise and I gave her a nod to let her know it's all OK. I'm right, aren't I?'

'Yes and no. Ugh . . .' I groan, pulling my hood even tighter around my head as the chill courses through me. 'I've done something really stupid. Something I might live to regret.'

'You? No, I don't believe it. You're just a little shaken up after the events of yesterday.'

'I'm being serious here. It's the reason why I suggested you go on ahead to the Hall for breakfast and tell everyone I'd join them a bit later. I didn't want Elizabeth to delay things because of me.' The air is cold on my teeth as I draw in a deep breath before continuing. 'I had a missed call from Ash early this morning and I couldn't just ignore it.'

The look on Oliver's face as his head whips around to look at me again is one of shock. 'He rang you on Christmas morning? Why?'

When I explain about the day I was shopping in Charlestown when Ash sought me out to talk, I can almost see the pieces slotting together in Oliver's head.

'That's why you were upset on the journey back. He decided he didn't want anything to do with Elizabeth?'

'Yes. However, I told him he was wrong, and that he was in danger of making a huge mistake. We've spoken several times since actually, but this morning he was emotional.'

'It must have been quite a long and difficult conversation for you. By the time you joined us everyone had finished eating. I was tempted to come and find you, but everything you do is for a reason and I knew whatever it was, it was important.'

'Thank you for understanding. I couldn't have eaten anything after that, anyway.'

'So why did you make the call, if you feel so uneasy about it now? Is it wise to get pulled into this even further? You did what you were asked. Can't you leave it at that?'

'There's something about Ash and his situation that just touched my heart. Do you think it's wrong of me, because it's none of my business, even though it feels like it is?'

Oliver isn't the sort of person to answer a question like that blithely and I watch as he mulls it over. 'No, if you felt that strongly about whatever it was you had to say, then you just needed to get it off your chest.'

I let out a huge sigh. 'Thank you. I trust your judgement implicitly. He asked for my advice and I answered truthfully. It means a lot to hear you say that, as there isn't anyone else I can have this conversation with. Not Daniela, Grandma or even Mum.'

'I'll always be here to listen if you need me, Sienna. I told you things about my life I've never shared with anyone else. And you know that I'll always talk frankly. Now, put it to the back of your mind and let's head back inside. Nothing will change things between us, will it? I mean, it won't be awkward that we're just friends?'

'No, of course not! I hope that date in February is in your calendar because I have no intention of going on my own. Maybe Ruby would like to join us, too.'

He's unable to hold back his smile. 'Really?'

'Yep. Although she might surprise you. I think she'll be up for the fishing, more so than the spa.'

Oliver shakes his head at me. 'She's going to change my life completely, isn't she?'

'She most certainly is!'

Timing, as they say, is everything. It's late afternoon and who doesn't need a long walk after a hearty Christmas dinner? With stomachs full, everyone disappears ready to congregate in the car park, eager to make the most of the winter wonderland. I manage to catch Elizabeth as she's just about to go upstairs and steer her into the study.

'I . . . um . . . I have a surprise present for you,' I half-whisper as we step inside.

Elizabeth narrows her eyes, frowning. 'What have I done to warrant two Christmas presents?' She laughs, as we both take a seat.

'This one's a bit different, it doesn't come wrapped in paper and a bow.'

Her eyes widen. 'Oh, my . . . is it one of the puppies from the farm?' She breaks out into a huge smile. 'Your grandma and I have been talking about getting a dog. All that walking will be good for us.'

'No.' I shake my head, as my pulse begins to race. 'Your grandson is here, and he'd like to talk to you. He arrived about half an hour ago and he's sitting outside in his car with the engine running. The drive here was quite an ordeal.'

Her hands instantly fly up to her face as she sits there staring blankly at me, blinking. 'James?' she gasps.

I nod my head and she appears to be holding her breath. A few seconds later, she expels it noisily, as the enormity of what's about to happen sinks in.

'He hasn't used that name in a long time, Elizabeth,' I remind her, gently. 'It's Ash now – short for Ashley – remember?'

She presses her hands together, curling her fingers into a ball and I watch as her knuckles start turning white. 'Ash. Yes. Ash. But what do I say to him?'

'His visit wasn't planned but the fact that he texted me to say he was here, well . . . I took that as a good sign. He was at a Christmas party with longtime friends, but he drove here just to see you. He said that he realised today would be tough on you and he wanted to reach out and reassure you that he's fine, just fine.'

She gives a shaky sigh and a little laugh catches in her throat, as she beams from ear to ear. 'Oh my goodness, what a thoughtful young man.' She swallows hard and it's painful to witness. I know what a struggle today has been for her and oh, if only we could turn back the clock!

'Ash has a good heart, Elizabeth, he really does.'

She smiles, and despite her tears, her eyes start to light up. 'It was both a joy and a sorrow to discover that Peter had left us a wonderful gift. I just didn't dare to hope this day would ever come and yet the impossible has happened.'

We sit in silence, as we both swipe at our cheeks. I watch Elizabeth take a few slow and calming breaths.

'I'll have a quick check that everyone is gone and then I'll bring him inside to leave the two of you to talk. You'll have an hour at least, without any interruptions whatsoever. I've told him that he can't possibly drive back to Cornwall this evening, so he's going to stay overnight at my place on the pull-out sofa.'

'Thank you for everything you've done, Sienna. This wouldn't have happened if it weren't for you and I feel so blessed to have you in my life, my dear. And Freddie would thank you, too, if only he were here.'

'Aww . . . but I think at some point Ash would have sought you out, Elizabeth. When you hear what he has to say, I'm sure you'll be proud of both your son and your grandson.'

I hurry away, conscious that Ash probably has the car heater on full while he agonises over whether he did the right thing jumping in the car and driving here, or not. But in my experience, if you go with your heart, then you'll never find yourself wondering *what if*. And I meant it when I said that Ash has a good heart. He said that my words gave him the courage to take a risk and he told me I was his Christmas angel. That made me smile to myself.

As soon as he spots me, he opens the car door and eases himself out of the seat. Ash is so nervous that even from here I can see the pallor on his face as he zips up his coat. I indicate with my hand for him to come inside and he clicks his key fob, then strides forward.

'Is she alone? So many people streamed out of the house, and they were all chatting and laughing, eager to enjoy walking in the snow. I really don't want to spoil—'

'You aren't spoiling anything, Ash. Elizabeth is about to get the best Christmas present anyone has ever given her! Trust me; it's an emotional day for her and this might be exactly what she needs to help her to get through it.'

He reaches out to grab my hand, and as he looks into my eyes, I find myself catching my breath. To my utmost amazement his reaction mirrors mine. In that split second something happens between us, but Elizabeth is waiting. Today is about two people meeting up for the first time and putting right a wrong that neither of them were a party to.

'Thank you, Sienna. Somehow you seem to understand the feelings I've kept buried for so long. Your phone call changed everything.'

He's still holding my hand and we both give a nervous little laugh as he reluctantly releases it.

'Every single day of our lives is the chance to have a new beginning, and this is yours, Ash. I'll show you where to find your grandmother.'

'When we're done, you'll still be here . . . I mean, at the Hall?'

I feel as if something inside of me has suddenly been lit. It's like a fire . . . a warm feeling that makes me feel weak at the knees and I know I'm grinning at him like a mad fool. 'Of course, I will . . . I'm not going anywhere, I promise.'

One year later, to the day

Meadowfield Farm, Greenacres,
near Charleston, Cornwall

27

The End of One Chapter,
the Beginning of Another . . .

It's Christmas Day and, as usual, it's accompanied by the sort of chaos that ensues whenever a group of people get together.

'Charlotte, have you seen the large casserole dishes? I'm sure we unpacked them.' Elizabeth is opening and closing kitchen cupboard doors as she works her way around her wonderful new farmhouse kitchen.

'They're here somewhere but where exactly is the question. Shall I pop back to mine, as I know where I can put my hands on two sizeable dishes.'

Grandma is busy scooping balls of chestnut, apricot and sage stuffing onto a baking tray, while Mum is whisking up a large bowl of Yorkshire pudding mix.

'If you tell me where to look, I'll fetch them, Grandma,' I offer.

Elizabeth shuts the last door and turns to look at me, smiling. 'I give up! And we seem to be missing some gravy boats, as well.'

'Some?' Grandma quizzes.

'Oh,' Elizabeth chuckles, 'what am I thinking? Another one will suffice.'

I untie my apron and grab my coat to pop next door. I didn't realise I'd left my phone in my pocket, and when it begins to buzz I fumble around for it.

'Hello?'

'Sienna! Merry Christmas! How's it going at your end?' Daniela raises her voice to compete with the cacophony of sound in the background.

My little chat with Nigel at last year's Christmas Eve party made him stop and think about why Daniela was suddenly trying to reinvent herself. Then it dawned on him that it wasn't for Oliver's benefit and he had no reason at all to be jealous. It had been a while since he'd told Daniela that she was still the love of his life. She wasn't simply a wife and a mother, but she was still the only woman in the world he wanted to be with. And supporting her dream to reawaken her creative side was the way in which he could demonstrate his love for her.

She's still totally in the dark about being Oliver's first love, but that doesn't matter anymore. He's with Ruby now and she's about to join him permanently in London.

'Merry Christmas to you and the family. It's all good here. We're still finding our way around Elizabeth's kitchen, but another hour and we'll be sitting down to christen the handmade stripped pine table. How about you? I bet the kids had you up early.'

'Just before five o'clock, but Clara didn't even fall asleep until gone eleven last night because she was so excited. They'll both conk out early and will probably have a nap once we've eaten. I have a film for us all to watch after dinner, and they're bound to drift off. Hopefully for an hour, so Nigel and I can have a break. Aside from that, it's all change at Silverberry Hall, but then we knew that was coming, didn't we?'

I swing open the gate to Grandma's cottage and make my way up the stepping stone path. There's snow in the air and I stand under the canopy above the front door while I slip off my glove and fumble in my pocket for the key. 'I had heard on the grapevine. Ruby rang to tell me her news about moving to London and she mentioned that Stephen has started a new tradition. No more fund-raisers at the Hall.'

'No, instead he's having a family party on New Year's Eve. It's the end of an era. How's Elizabeth doing?'

Stephen is no Freddie. Oh, he'll entertain to show off his new home, but he certainly doesn't have a charitable side to his nature – especially when it comes to money – unless it benefits him personally, in one way or another.

'Good, really good. You wouldn't believe the change in her. The move to Cornwall really was the turning point in letting go of the burdens of the past. She told me it was freeing and instead of carrying around a multitude of worries, life here is simpler.'

'Oh, that's so good to hear.'

'Word is that there have been a lot of staff changes at the Hall.'

'Sadly, most of them have moved on – only Veronica and two of the gardeners remain, mainly because they live in the village and it's convenient. Stephen isn't an easy man to work for, is he?' Daniela points out. 'So, this year it's just Elizabeth, Charlotte, your mum, Greg and, uh . . . you and Ash!'

'Yes,' I sigh, contentedly. 'Elizabeth keeps forgetting that we're not catering for a huge party of people and we're going to have way too much food. But she's in her element.' I turn the key in the lock and swing open the front door to Cherry Tree Cottage.

'That's so good to hear, my lovely friend, even though I miss being able to pop in and see you more than you can imagine. I can't wait to catch up with you all in January. Will you and Ash be in your new place by then?'

I wander through to the kitchen, leaning against the wooden countertop and gazing out over Grandma's pretty little garden and the fields beyond. The snowflakes are falling much faster now and it's starting to look really pretty.

'No. There's still a fair bit of work to be done and the builders shut down for two weeks over Christmas and New Year. Still, it's starting to take shape and is already looking less like two little holiday cottages and more like a family home.'

Daniela chuckles. 'Honestly, buying up a cluster of holiday rentals and turning them back into permanent homes is no mean feat. You do know that you're all living the dream, don't you?'

'What, looking out onto rolling countryside, or being a stone's throw from a beautiful beach?' I muse.

'Both!'

'It's not so very different from Darlingham. We've swapped a river walk for a stroll along the beach, but we still get woken by sheep bleating away in the fields. No cockerels though, I'm glad to say.'

'And no regrets?'

'None whatsoever. Grandma loves her cosy, two-bed cottage and it only took a lick of paint, some new furniture and a few soft furnishings to make it hers.'

'And Elizabeth is adjusting to downsizing?'

'Yes and her new life really suits her. For starters, everything is a lot more manageable and aside from her cleaner, Alice, she and Grandma spend a lot of time cooking and stocking up the freezer. In the spring I suspect most of their time will be spent pottering in the garden. They're having fun.'

'It sounds idyllic,' Daniela sighs, dreamily.

'Meadow Farmhouse is so pretty, with its thatched roof and traditional cottage garden. Once Ash and I are living on the doorstep, if Elizabeth or Grandma need anything, life is going to be so much easier for us all. Ash is a real handyman, but in the meantime we're only a fifteen-minute drive away, and Mum and Greg are just two miles down the road.'

'How's Bartie coping?'

Elizabeth got her puppy; Harry took the last one of the litter down to Silverberry Hall, knowing full well he'd find him a new home.

'He's grown beyond belief! And he, together with Grandma's little Westie, keep them both on the go. Honestly, there's never a dull moment when Bartie and Archie are around!'

'It's funny how things have turned out, isn't it?' Daniela muses. 'If your mum hadn't moved to Cornwall, you might never have met Ash. Anyway, have a fabulous day and we'll speak soon. We're all sending our love!'

As the line disconnects, a flutter in my chest is tinged with guilt. No one, other than myself and Grandma, is aware that Ash is Elizabeth's grandson and they're both adamant that's the way it should stay.

To say that Daniela was shocked when at the start of the year I took a trip down to Cornwall and returned to Darlingham *smitten*, as she referred to my emotional state at the time, is an understatement. Daniela knows me so well, but having fallen in love with Nigel at first sight, she never questioned how quickly, or how hard, I fell in love with Ash. She was simply thrilled to see how happy I was.

It didn't happen quite as quickly as she assumed, of course. The first time I saw Ash at Driftwood, I thought it was the resemblance to Freddie that threatened to overwhelm me. Those mesmerising eyes, the way he carried himself . . . it was a shock. But when you start dreaming of someone you hardly know, it's a sign that deep down inside there's something else going on, even if you can't explain it.

If I hadn't dreamt of Ash, I wouldn't have ended up calling him to let him know that Elizabeth was struggling. The fact that he came to her rescue demonstrated what sort of man he is. Kind, selfless and loving. The sort of man who puts other people first. And it was then that I knew he was special. Very special, because he turned out to be *the one* for me.

And now, here we are, a year later, and the seemingly impossible has truly happened. It's been a whirlwind, but what I've discovered is that change isn't unsettling if you simply view it differently. It's all about perspective. We were two lost souls, thrown together under difficult circumstances, who gravitated towards each other as if it were always meant to be.

I grab a shopping bag from the drawer for the two large serving plates that have graced many a festive table over the years and go in search of the gravy boat. Little vignettes of the past year flash through my mind and a sense of wonderment floods through me.

'Hello?' a voice calls out and seconds later Ash walks into the room. 'There you are! You've been gone for ages. Everyone was getting worried. Have you seen how thick that snow is getting?'

'Yes, isn't it lovely? Daniela called and we had a bit of a chat.'

'Ah . . .' He sidles up to me, leaning in to kiss my cheek and I recoil a little as his nose is cold. 'Sorry. The temperature is dropping and it's going to freeze by the look of it. We might end up getting snowed in if it continues.'

'Elizabeth would love that,' I reply, my eyes gleaming because she would.

'I know.' He stares at me for a few seconds as if savouring the moment, before leaning forward to kiss me softly on the lips. It's as if everything around us starts to spin and a little shiver of excitement begins to creep down my spine.

'I can't wait until you open your present tomorrow morning,' he whispers, slightly breathlessly. 'It took me a long time to make it.' His face is aglow with excitement.

'All I ever wanted for Christmas,' I breathe, shakily, 'is the man of my dreams! And here you are . . .'

'Here *we* are! Every morning when I open my eyes and see you lying next to me, I still can't believe how lucky I am to have found you, Sienna. When I lost Mum it felt like a part of me had died, too. I thought that she was the only person who would every really understand me because of everything that had happened. Well, the me I couldn't acknowledge and the things I kept hidden deep down inside.'

My heart constricts in my chest. 'I think I sensed that the first time we met,' I admit.

'I didn't dare to believe that you'd leave Darlingham to

come and live with me and I couldn't believe it when you said yes.'

'Ash! I moved to Charlestown because I wanted to be with you. I realised that it's not where you live that matters, it's *who* you're with. If you're happy, then your loved ones will support you no matter what.'

The truth is that I didn't even have to stop and think about it. Moving into Ash's tiny two-up, two-down old fisherman's cottage, with its bijou bathroom extension at the rear, instinctively felt like the right thing to do. Suddenly, nothing else mattered. Of course, Mum and Greg were delighted, knowing I'd be living close by, but it was Grandma and Elizabeth who, a couple of weeks later, shocked us all.

Ash leans back against the countertop as I place the crockery in the plastic bag.

'It's certainly been an unusual journey, hasn't it?' He smirks, as we make our way out into the hallway.

'You can say that again! When Mum and Greg insisted on throwing a little engagement party for us, none of us were expecting what was about to happen.'

He gives a throaty laugh. 'When you told me that Elizabeth and Charlotte were a formidable team, I had no idea how true that was.'

We stop for a second to glance at each other, as our smiles grow exponentially. 'When they said they were considering a little project of their own, moving to Cornwall was the last thing that sprang to mind.'

'Coming here with the estate agent to look around Meadowfield Farm the following day, blew my mind,' Ash admits.

'Mine, too. Given that the holiday business had gone bust, I thought Elizabeth was about to make a huge mistake and the look I gave Grandma that day when she was backing her up . . . well, I couldn't believe what I was hearing.'

Ash nods his head. 'I remember the shocked hush that

descended over everyone that day. Even Greg couldn't muster a joke to break the silence.'

That memory makes me chuckle. 'It was awkward, until we got back to Mum and Greg's place and we all sat around the table to discuss it. It wasn't some half-cobbled-together plan, but a way of realising all of our dreams in one fell swoop.'

'You were hesitant about selling your grandma's cottage in Darlingham, though, weren't you?' He opens the front door and I turn to look at him as we draw level.

'Yes. When I came to live with you, Grandma and I had agreed to rent it out, as I still saw it as her safety net. But finding a buyer meant that Grandma could buy Cherry Tree Cottage from Elizabeth—'

Ash cuts in. 'And when Elizabeth told us that the two semi-detached holiday lets, and the barn, would be our wedding present it all seemed too good to be true!'

The smile we exchange says it all. If you're going to dream, dream big.

As Ash pulls the door shut behind us, I remain under cover sheltering from what is now turning into a blizzard. 'How ironic that it was my father who brought us together, Sienna,' he states, his words tinged with sadness.

'He did, didn't he?' I agree, grinning back at him. To my delight, what I see reflected on my fiancé's face is a sense of well-being. Accepting that destiny had a hand in everything that has happened, as painful as the respective paths we travelled to get here have been, is mind-blowing. The various twists and turns were sometimes hard to bear.

'And now it's down to us to live our best lives, together, working side by side to make it happen.'

Once our new home is ready, the barn alongside it, which was once a farm shop, will soon complete the first stage of the dream. We still don't have a name for the new business, but I'll be spending my days upcycling furniture, while Ash continues to create wonderful new pieces out of nature's cast-offs. Jasmine will be joining us, too, as after making what I swear is the most perfect engagement ring for me, we couldn't leave her behind.

And, at some point in the not-too-distant future, hopefully we'll be blessed with a family.

'Life doesn't get any better than this, does it?' I ask, my heart skipping a beat.

Ash takes the shopping bag from me and we clasp hands as we start to trudge along the path, which now has several inches of snow covering it. I look up to see the curls of smoke from the two chimneys in Meadow Farmhouse hanging like silver-grey ribbons in the sky. With the festive lights peeking out through the windows this is just a taste of what's to come as we all work to bring the former farm back to life.

'Our first real Christmas together!' Ash declares, sounding ridiculously happy. 'And this time next year we'll be married and living here, too.'

He's buzzing with excitement and when I compare it to just twelve months ago, with everything that has happened, it truly is a miracle. It just goes to prove that life can be full of surprises and that's why giving up is never an option.

In order to find a silver lining, there has to be a cloud. Inside my cloud, was Ash and now it truly is a case of the best is yet to come!

Acknowledgements

Special thanks go to editorial director, Martina Arzu. It's a real pleasure working with you – you are an inspiration!

A virtual hug to the wonderful editorial team on this project and sincere thanks to the amazing cover designer. I also want to acknowledge the network of people who beaver away behind the scenes to promote and generally spread the word about my newest release.

Not forgetting the other incredible driving forces behind the Embla team because *our lives are built on stories, and each book does matter*! It's a thrill to be a part of it.

Grateful thanks also go to my wonderful agent, Sara Keane, for her sterling advice, support and all those long phone calls spent putting the world to rights. It's been an amazing journey since the day we first met, and your friendship means so much to me.

To my wonderful husband, Lawrence – always there for me and the other half of Team Lucy – you truly are my rock!

There are so many family members and long-term friends who understand that my passion to write is all-consuming. They forgive me for the long silences, and when we next catch up, it's as if I haven't been absent at all.

The amazing kindness of my lovely author friends, readers and reviewers is truly humbling. You continue to delight, amaze and astound me with your generosity and support.

Without your kindness in spreading the word about my latest release and your wonderful reviews to entice people to click and download, I wouldn't be able to indulge myself in my guilty pleasure – writing.

Wishing everyone peace, love and happiness.

Lucy x

About the Author

Lucy Coleman always knew that one day she would write, but first life took her on a wonderful journey of self discovery for which she is very grateful.

Family life and two very diverse careers later she now spends most days glued to a keyboard, which she refers to as her personal quality time.

'It's only when you know who you are that you truly understand what makes you happy! Writing about love, life, and relationships – set in wonderful locations – makes me leap out of bed every morning!'

About Embla Books

Embla Books is a digital-first publisher of standout commercial adult fiction. Passionate about storytelling, the team at Embla publish books that will make you 'laugh, love, look over your shoulder and lose sleep'. Launched by Bonnier Books UK in 2021, the imprint is named after the first woman from the creation myth in Norse mythology, who was carved by the gods from a tree trunk found on the seashore – an image of the kind of creative work and crafting that writers do, and a symbol of how stories shape our lives.

Find out about some of our other books and stay in touch:

X, Facebook, Instagram: @emblabooks
Newsletter: https://bit.ly/emblanewsletter

Printed in Great Britain
by Amazon

49435776R00192